JOSHILYN JACKSON is the *New York Times* and *USA Today* bestselling author of nine other novels, including *Never Have I Ever* and *gods in Alabama*. Her books have been translated into more than a dozen languages. A former actor, Jackson is also an award-winning audiobook narrator. She lives in Decatur, Georgia, with her family.

Website: JoshilynJackson.com
Facebook: facebook.com/JoshilynJackson
Twitter: @JoshilynJackson
Instagram: @joshilyn_jackson

MOTHER MAY I

JOSHILYN JACKSON

R A V E N BOOKS

LONDON · OXFORD · NEW YORK · NEW DELHI · SYDNEY

RAVEN BOOKS
Bloomsbury Publishing Plc
50 Bedford Square, London, WC1B 3DP, UK
29 Earlsfort Terrace, Dublin 2, Ireland

BLOOMSBURY, RAVEN BOOKS and the Raven Books logo are trademarks of
Bloomsbury Publishing Plc

First published in 2021 in the United States by HarperCollins
First published in Great Britain 2021
This edition published in 2022

A catalogue record for this book is available from the British Library

ISBN: TPB: 978-1-5266-3385-9; PB: 978-1-5266-3387-3;
eBook: 978-1-5266-3388-0; ePDF: 978-1-5266-3691-1

2 4 6 8 10 9 7 5 3 1

Printed and bound in Great Britain by CPI Group (UK) Ltd, Croydon CR0 4YY

To find out more about our authors and books visit www.bloomsbury.com
and sign up for our newsletters

For Caryn Karmatz Rudy

PART I

MOTHERS

1

I WOKE UP to see a witch peering in my bedroom window.

She was little more than a dark shape with a predator's hungry eyes, razor-wire skinny but somehow female, staring in through the partly open drapes. Sunrise lit up the thin, silvery hair that straggled out from under her hat. I should have leaped up screaming. I should have run at her with any weapon I could find.

Instead I thought, *I hope she's not standing on my basil plants*, hazy and unworried. Even half asleep, I knew that there was no such thing as witches. I'd long forgotten the most important thing the theatre had ever taught me—that the human body can hold two truths at once. Even truths that seem to rule each other out: There's no such things as witches, true. And I was looking at one.

I didn't understand she might be a real person until our eyes met. Hers widened in surprise. She lurched sideways and was gone, leaving me with the impression of a craggy old-lady face with a sour, turned-down mouth.

I bolted upright, heart rate jacking, letting out a strangled sound that wasn't quite a scream. Too soft to disturb the kids, but it woke up my husband.

"Bree?" Trey's voice was thick with sleep.

"I thought I saw someone. Looking through the window at us."

That got his eyes open.

"A person? In the backyard?" He was already climbing out of bed.

There was a careless six-inch gap between the edges of the drapes. Even as he pushed one all the way aside, my rational brain was catching up, trying to dismiss it.

I said, "It was a witch. I mean, I thought I saw a witch. So . . . grain of salt."

Trey was peering out, forehead pressed against the glass, but that turned him back to me, a smile starting. "Big pointy hat?"

The memory was dream-soaked, but when he said it, my brain made it so, snapping my hazy mental picture into focus. Not a cardigan. A tatty robe. Not a knit cap. A pointy witch hat. It made the whole thing ridiculous. Of course there was no witch in our backyard, staring in with hungry, haunted eyes.

"I think so," I admitted. "Her mouth was sunken in, and she was all in black."

I must have been dreaming, I decided. I was prone to postpartum nightmares, though not usually about anything so concrete as witches. My bad dreams after each of the girls had been almost Victorian, all footsteps and fog.

"The gate is closed and locked. Unless your witch looked spry enough to bounce over an eight-foot privacy fence . . ."

That made me laugh, though it was more of a relieved puff of air. "Nope."

Trey let go of the drapes. "Want me to go outside and check?"

"Do I want you to sashay around the backyard in your boxers looking for a witch?" I asked. "No. No, I do not."

He grinned, and I smiled back, even though the animal at the base of my brain was saying that yes, actually, I did want him to He-Man out there and stomp the perimeter, preferably with a golf club cocked up over his shoulder. It was a primal thing, physical and irrational.

There was no witch, obviously, and even if I had seen someone, a flesh-and-blood little old lady was the least threatening type of person on the planet. Only in stories did crones offer poisoned fruit to princesses or snatch up tasty children. But I couldn't think of an innocent reason for anyone to watch us as we slept. And her flat, greedy gaze! Not confused or blank, like someone's sweet lost granny. Her hunger was the clearest thing in my memory.

Trey read my doubt. "Seriously. I'll grab some pants and go check. Just to put your mind at ease."

I shook my head. I'd been raised on Grimms' fairy tales by a mother who saw the world as something huge and wild— carnivorous. Her world was full of witches. She'd have already called the cops by now, or even snatched one of Trey's hunting rifles out of the gun safe and loaded it. She'd be in the backyard already, making the world safer by accidentally shooting our neighbor's nice old Labradoodle. Or worse, shooting our nice old neighbor.

I wasn't like her. I didn't want to be like her, so I pushed away that small, wise voice in my head that kept insisting, *You saw something. You saw someone.*

I told my husband, "No. Come back to bed."

Trey tumbled in, and I rolled toward him, running my hand under his T-shirt to feel his heartbeat. It was slow and steady, same as always. Wearing a shirt to bed was new, though. Trey had turned fifty this year. He'd always been built thick, but now he had a bit of a belly, and his chest hair was going gray.

"I hate this stupid shirt," I told him. I wanted the comfort of tucking in close to his bare skin, wrapping my arms around the warm, strong bulk of him.

He pulled me closer. Close enough for me to know he wasn't thinking about witches. "I could ditch the shirt. We are up early."

I glanced back at the clock. "The alarm goes off in twenty minutes. You think you can make it worth my while?" I said it flirty, like a challenge, cocking my eyebrow at him.

His teeth flashed in the dimness. "I can damn sure try."

He kissed my neck, my shoulder. To my surprise I felt a twinge of something good starting. My sex drive had flatlined in my third trimester. I'd assumed it would resurrect in a few months, when Robert started solid food. That's how it had worked after the girls. But here was our familiar magic, already sparking up between us.

Maybe it was the dream. That witch had genuinely spooked me, dumping a ton of adrenaline into my blood. As my husband kissed me, my body arched into him, electric, as if to say, *We could all die! Quick, make more people!* It apparently hadn't gotten the memo about Trey's vasectomy. I kissed him back, serious about it.

"Yeah?" Trey said, surprised.

"Yeah," I said, but I couldn't stop thinking about the window. Of course there was not a witch in the yard. Or anyone. But I added, "Close the drapes all the way and you're on, mister."

He hurried to yank them shut while I started peeling my nightgown off over my head.

That, of course, was the exact moment a soft gurgle came through the baby monitor.

We both froze, our eyes meeting.

"Oh, Bumper, no!" Trey said.

"Oh, *Robert*, no," I corrected automatically. I wasn't going to bend on this. When I was pregnant, we'd all called him Bumper, as in "the bumper crop." That had been cute back when it meant my swelling belly. Trey, who'd grown up in Buckhead with Scooters and Biffs and Muffys, still thought it was cute.

The sound faded. We waited, holding our breath. It could go either way. After ten silent seconds, I lifted a victory fist and Trey started toward me.

Robert started babbling then. He was awake and pleased about it, but if I didn't go get him, he'd start fussing.

"So close!"

"Rain check for tonight?" I asked, pulling my nightgown back on.

Trey shook his head, rueful. "I wish. I fly to Chicago today."

"Ugh, that's right. I must have repressed it." I got up.

He'd be there through the weekend and most of next week, too, thanks to Spencer Shaw. Spence was less than a bosom friend but more than just his partner at the law firm. Their mothers were cousins, so they'd gone to the same schools from the time they were three, even pledging the same frat at UVA. They hadn't gone their separate ways until law school.

Spence had opted out of this Chicago trip because tonight was the firm's annual Spring Gala, and he wasn't one to miss a party. He loved himself a top-shelf open bar and pretty women in cocktail dresses.

Trey wanted me to go to the gala, too. To represent. But I always felt a little out of place at firm events without him. I'd said I would, unless Robert had a cranky afternoon. I had a strong premonition that he would.

"Spence is having a rough time, Bree," Trey said.

Spence was in the middle of an ugly divorce, his second. My husband would carry him through it, just as he'd carried him during his first ugly divorce.

"So are you. You're working crazy hours," I said, shrugging into my robe. "Mostly because of Spence."

"No. It's this client." He and Spence were working with a large Atlanta-based company that was absorbing a family-owned chain of grocery stores. "This is not a marriage of equals we're officiating." He leaned close, as if telling me a dirty little secret. "Our groom is a cannibal."

I let it go. Trey was an equity partner, but Spencer's name was third on the firm's letterhead. His father's name had been first before he died. Also, Robert's babble was getting whiny around the edges.

"I'll plan us a date for next weekend. Dinner, wine, kissing," I promised, then went next door into the nursery.

This room used to be my office, before Robert surprised us. Now the heather-gray walls were covered over in giraffe wallpaper and my desk nook had a changing table in it.

I didn't mind. I didn't need an office now; I'd rolled off the boards of the Alliance Theatre and a statewide literacy nonprofit, promising to roll back on in a year or so. The girls had taught me how brief Robert's babyhood would be. I didn't want to miss it. I'd blinked, and here he was, already ten weeks old.

I bitched about Trey's job sometimes, but I was lucky. When I was growing up, my mom worked full-time as a 911 operator plus waitressed on the weekends to make ends meet. I might not love Trey's long hours, the travel, or the social obligations, but Trey's career meant I got to watch Anna-Claire's voice lessons and rehearsals, go to Peyton's quiz-bowl and robotics meets, and still have time and money to support causes I loved.

I bent over the crib, and Robert kicked his chunky legs, happy to see me. He cooed as I lifted him, trusting that a fresh diaper and a warm bottle were next. I inhaled the crazy perfume of his head. Nothing on earth smelled as delicious as new baby, and this version was particular to him. Not just the scent of baby. This baby. My baby.

I took him to the changing table, and he gave me the goofy grin he'd invented just last week, toothless and so charming. He was easy. A good sleeper, a good eater. Anna-Claire had been trickier, lovely as long as everything went her way but instantly enraged by dirty diapers and late breakfasts. She was so mercurial and demanding that I'd planned a three-year gap before the next one, but she was barely Robert's age when the stick turned blue. Peyton had been born anxious, and she never slept. Even when I was pregnant, my little insomniac kicked and spun inside me all night long.

"You are my sugar baby," I told Robert, tucking his fat potato feet back into his pajamas and refastening the snaps. "You're going to be a nightmare as a toddler to make up for it, aren't you?"

I toted Robert down the hall to the kitchen to warm his bottle, then sat in the great room, holding him close while he pulled greedily at it. By the time he'd taken his five ounces, the sound of squabbling girls was drifting down the stairs. I kept an ear cocked as I marched Robert up and down, trying to thump a second burp out of him. He had one, I knew it, and he'd be colicky if I didn't coax it out. I hoped the fussing upstairs would resolve on its own. Often it did. But late last year Peyton had gotten her period. She'd instantly synced up with Anna-Claire, and right now we were heading into danger week.

"Mo-om!" Peyton hollered in two aggrieved syllables. "She took my . . ." I missed the last word.

I toted Robert to the bottom of the stairs, jouncing and patting as I walked.

"Anna-Claire," I called up.

She poked her face over the banister. She was sleep-rumpled, her masses of dark hair a tumbled mess, and still beautiful enough to take my breath away.

"You always take her side!"

She had a point. I did tend to take Peyton's side. But life had taken Anna-Claire's. She was built like me, tall and slim, and where I was pretty, she was gorgeous. She had my even features, but her true violet eyes tilted like kitten eyes, and her lips had a natural upturn, as if she were holding a delightful secret in her mouth, readying to speak or swallow it. She'd also come with a whopping scoop of Trey's confidence and extroverted charm.

She'd never had an awkward phase, while Peyton was slap in the middle of hers. Right now puppy fat clung to her middle, and her skin had gone a little crazy. She was as cute as a button, with her dad's round face and snub nose, but when she was next to her sister, people overlooked her.

Peyton joined her sister at the banister. "I haven't even gotten to wear it yet!"

"Give it back," I told Anna-Claire, mild but serious, still thumping at Robert.

"Fine. It's in my middle drawer," Anna-Claire told her sister, then gave me the eye roll she'd perfected in third grade. "It's too big for me anyway."

That was straight-up bitchy, but I let it slide with a warning look because Peyton was already off to go get the whatever-it-was. The fight had been derailed.

I felt a sense of relief that was larger than the moment warranted, as if I'd stepped in and diverted a tempest. I shook my head. It was that awful dream. It still felt like a portentous one. The witch's gaze had been so avid. I felt more than I thought, *Something bad is coming for us.*

I shook the little voice warning of doom away. My mother owned it. The voice in her own head must be a stentor. My father by all reports had been a piece of work. I'd never met him, and I was grateful, considering. He was the reason she wouldn't get on an elevator with any man. Not alone. She kept a loaded handgun in a safe by her bed and was always gifting me pepper sprays and safety whistles. I had never once wondered where Peyton came by her anxiety, but I didn't live like that. I refused to see the world that way. And I wasn't going to borrow trouble when I was facing a week of single-parenting two hormone-crazed middle-school girls and a baby.

Anna-Claire stomped down the stairs to the first landing and cocked her hip at me. "Remember you're a snack mom for rehearsal this afternoon."

"I know." Robert let out that last, sneaky burp. It was a whopper.

"Don't bring bananas," Anna-Claire said. "Cara's dad always brings those gross generic fruit-snack things, so you need to bring something edible."

I kept my smile in place, but it went a little stiff when I heard that Marshall Chase was the other "snack mom." They really called it that, as if male parents were incapable of passing out raisin boxes and bottled waters. To be fair, he was the only dad I'd ever seen do it. Marshall was tall and lanky and attractive; the other moms made jokes about *him* being the snack, but a couple of months back, when *Grease, Junior* was cast, Anna-Claire got the alto lead. His own daughter got Marty. It was a good part with a solo, but it wasn't

Rizzo. I hadn't ever thought of Marshall as the stage-parent type, but there was no denying that the balmy air between us had gone cool.

I hated it; Marshall and I had both grown up way out in Hurd County, Georgia. His wife, Betsy, had lived across the street from me. She'd been my best friend since before I had concrete memory. She and Marshall dated for most of high school, but they'd broken up when Betsy and I moved into Atlanta to attend Georgia State. Betsy had always been wilder than me, bolder, both more reckless and more fun. By the end of freshman year, she lost her scholarship, and she wasn't even sorry. She went home, got a job, got back with Marshall. They'd gone through the police academy together and gotten married.

Our lives had forked, but Betsy and I had stayed close. We'd been each other's maids of honor, and we'd been pregnant together; Cara was born a month before Anna-Claire. I'd always liked Marshall, though in that best-friend's-husband way that rendered him more Ken doll than man.

When Betsy died in the line of duty, five years back, he'd wanted to move to a safer job, for Cara's sake. Trey had hired him as an investigator. The firm had been thrilled to get him. Marshall was excellent; he'd been one of the youngest cops ever to make detective in Atlanta.

Last year Cara's public school lost its arts funding. No more chorus or drama club, and Cara was distraught. Trey put in a word at St. Alban's, and they'd offered her a scholarship. I'd hoped she and Anna-Claire would bond, like a mini me-and-Betsy, because Anna-Claire was also hip-deep into musical theatre and choir. Instead they were competitors, always up for the same parts and solos.

I couldn't make them love each other, but I could threaten my too-pretty, too-popular daughter with phoneless exile and unending extra chores if she did one single thing to make Cara feel picked on or unwelcome. Cara had quickly found her own friend set, and her grades were excellent, so I considered the transfer a success. For her.

I'd hoped it would finally give me a real friend at the school. I had more in common with Marshall than with any of the other snack moms. At thirty-eight we were a decade younger than the remaining first wives and a decade older than the stepmothers. Most of these women had grown up with ponies and summers in Provence, while Marshall and I had had secondhand bikes and vacation Bible school.

Instead he'd gotten cooler and cooler, until I worried that my daughter was stealth-hazing his. I'd snuck around, eavesdropping at rehearsals, only to find them working well together. Friendly if not friends.

Even so, Marshall got ever more polite, gravely asking me how my day was going in the same professional, cool tone he used on the pampered Gen Two baby-wives of some of the other lawyers at the firm, like the one divorcing Spence right now.

I hadn't hired a full-time nanny and made a career out of yoga class and blowouts. I hadn't gotten into an affair and busted up Trey's first marriage either. He and Maura split up amicably a year before we met, mostly because he wanted children and she didn't. Marshall knew all this. He knew me, knew my family.

It bothered me, and I guess it showed, because Anna-Claire caught my stiffness and added, sly, "You should bring those organic Bunny Fruit Snacks. So Mr. Chase knows not to perpetrate that crap." My eldest had a nose for drama, even when she was offstage.

I shook my head. "All fruit snacks are just tarted-up candy."

"Ho snack!" Anna-Claire said, laughing, "I should tell Cara that you said her dad brought a ho snack. The cheap kind!"

"If you do, rest assured I'll be bringing nothing but bananas for the rest of the year." She made a face. "Now, scoot. Car pool comes in twenty minutes."

"I'm mostly ready." She came all the way down to pet her

brother's head, peeping up at me. "Aw, you look sleepy. Want me to take Bumper so you can get a shower?"

"Robert," I corrected, but I was smiling. Typical Anna-Claire. She'd torment her sister, push boundaries with me, then instaflip to thoughtful. Moments like these I knew she could grow into a lovely, kindhearted woman, as long as Trey and I kept the parenting tight. She was so beautiful that kids and adults alike catered to her in ways that weren't good for her. It was hard to find the balance between pushing back on that while still being a hundred percent on her side. "You're sweet, but I got it. Thank you."

I kissed her and went to check Trey's packing. He was so color-blind that left to himself he could end up looking like a Mardi Gras float. I narrowly averted a green/blue disaster, then got him out the door. The girls' ride showed up soon after, and I fell into my day.

Just errands and emails, but I was operating on New Baby Time. Even the simplest things took four times longer than normal. The final bell was ringing as I pulled in to the parking lot by the new Performing Arts Center at St. Alban's. Hordes of kids began streaming out of the buildings. I hurried as fast as I could while lugging Robert in his infant carrier, his diaper bag, and a reusable grocery bag full of snacks.

The PAC had a long, narrow greenroom between the chorus's practice room and the orchestra's, furnished in a hodgepodge of donated chairs and sofas. The whole back wall was windows, facing the parking lot. I saw Marshall already in there and broke into a trot. He was dressed for work in a blue suit that was older than Anna-Claire. I remembered Betsy buying it. It hung awkwardly on his long frame.

By the time I got inside, he'd already set up the table and was laying out fruit snacks and Capri Sun pouches for a steady stream of chattering kids.

"I'm here, sorry!" It came out chirpy and overbright.

"No problem." He didn't look up.

I set Robert's carrier on a nearby sofa and started putting out milk boxes and Ziploc snack bags of baby carrots with hummus cups.

Marshall looked at my offering, his eyebrows lifting. "Does every bag have the exact same number of carrots?"

They did, actually. Ten. I felt a blush beginning, but I was saved from answering by Cara's entrance. She looked so much like her mother that it hurt my heart every time.

"Hey, Sugar Peep," Marshall said.

She shot him a mortified glare at the nickname and then said, "Hey, Auntie Bree," overly loud and bright.

I said, "Break a leg today, kiddo," and handed her a milk box.

She hurried out, and I gave Marshall a commiserating look. "Both my girls are in that same stage. Sweet to me at home, but in public I'm poison."

He smiled, unworried. "I hear that in high school they stop pretending that they budded off of Rihanna and will admit to actually having parents."

Just then Anna-Claire bounded through the door in full sunshine mode, her friend Greer in tow. She released Greer to hurl her arms around me. "Mom! Hummus! If you'd gotten pita chips, it would almost be a worthy snack!"

"Oh, yeah. I see how it is for you." Marshall sounded good-humored, but not like Marshall. I couldn't explain it, but I'd known him long enough to feel the difference.

Greer ignored the snacks. "Hi, Ms. Cabbat! Did you bring the baby?" As soon as she said it, she saw the car seat and dropped down to her knees in front of Robert. He was awake and beginning to make hungry noises. "Hi, Bumper! Oh, I love his feet! He's so little. I can't stand it!" She pinched his toes, distracting him, making him gurgle.

"We call him Robert," I said.

"That's right, Bumper, we call you Robert," Anna-Claire said, grabbing snacks and then hauling Greer to her feet. They went galloping out in a swirl of plaid uniform skirts.

I turned back to Marshall to say something about adolescent mood swings, but what I saw over his shoulder froze my body, inside and out. It was a blotch of slow-moving darkness on the other side of the big wall of windows. It stopped my words, my very breath. It was *her*. The witch, from my dream. The one I'd seen peering in my window this morning. She was in the parking lot. Right beside my SUV.

2

SHE WAS NOT a witch, of course. Just a little old lady in a baggy black dress and cardigan. She lurched past my car, hurrying across the lot with a limping, pained gait. She did have a hat on, a dark knit cap that came to a sort of peak, but it was not tall or excessively pointy.

"Bree?" Marshall said, concerned. I wasn't sure what my face was doing.

I pushed past him, running to the windows.

He joined me. "Are you okay?"

"I'm fine." I didn't sound fine, even though this woman was the least threatening thing that I had ever seen. She was ancient, and toting an earth-conscious reusable grocery bag much like mine, for God's sake.

But she did resemble my dream witch. Especially her hair, striped gunmetal gray and silver, the thin locks straggling out from under her hat.

I wondered if I should call the headmaster, or even the police, just to get a report on the record. In case the witch hadn't been a dream but a thing my subconscious had made out of this actual woman. In case she really had been lurking in my backyard.

It seemed ridiculous, though. I knew what they would think

of me, a mom with a new baby, overanxious and sleep-deprived. I could perfectly imagine their amused glances if I called them to report seeing a little old lady, maybe twice. It would be worse if I was truthful and mentioned the dream I'd had earlier. *A witch, you say?* They would be polite, but only because we lived in Decatur; we had high property taxes and our own police force. Money bought manners, and Trey made a lot of it. Otherwise I knew how it would go.

I knew because when I was growing up, my mother called the police on the regular. She lived convinced that my father might come back, even after he'd gone to prison. Even after he was dead. She'd hear him creeping around under the house or on the roof at night. And yes, she often thought she saw a figure peering in our windows.

I knew most of our regular beat cops by name. Officer McKenzie would at least shine his light into the crawl space, but his flat gaze and long, slow exhales made it clear he thought my mom was crazy. Officer Loblis was more blunt about it. *There are people in actual trouble. And here I am. With you. Again.* Officer Dobson was the worst, looming over us, anger palpable in the lines of his big body. Once I heard him mutter, *I ought to give you something to be scared about, lady,* as he left. He was only a little less frightening than the imagined man she'd called about.

When I got pregnant with Peyton so soon after Anna-Claire, my mom let us buy her a condo near us. I'd long wanted to evacuate her from the leaky two-bedroom ranch where I'd grown up, but she wouldn't move until she believed she was doing it for me. It *was* wonderful having her close when I had a newborn and a one-year-old, but the best part of the condo was the on-site security. All guests had to sign in and out, and only residents had key cards that would activate the elevators. Mom hadn't called the cops once since she moved in, and yet, as I considered calling them myself, the mingled shame and fear from childhood were churning in me. I'd never learned my born-wealthy husband's ease. In his mind the police worked for him, cruising our neighborhood to keep us safe. Whenever I saw them passing through or parked on our corner, I was swamped with the irrational, anxious feeling that I'd done a crime so secret that even I didn't realize it.

Maybe I should tell Marshall? For all his recent coolness, I still trusted him. If he took my witch sightings seriously, it would be permission for me to as well.

"Did you see that woman?" I asked. She was already out of sight.

"The meemaw?"

"Did she look like a . . . ?" I couldn't bring myself to say the word "witch." Marshall didn't have time for this nonsense any more than the actual police would. "No, it's stupid. Never mind." He was concerned, though, leaning toward me like the old friend that he was. It felt like an opening to fix whatever this breach was, and surely that mattered more than a bad dream. I touched his arm. "Do you have to go straight back to work, or can you stay and watch rehearsal with me?"

He blinked and stepped back. I could almost feel a wall of cool air whoosh back between us. "They let you do that?" There was a slight emphasis on the "you," as if he thought I'd finagled some rare privilege.

"Any parent with a kid in the show can," I assured him. I wasn't sure if this was technically true, but a lot of moms did it. "If we sit up in the balcony, Ms. Taft won't even notice."

Marshall's eyebrows came together. "There's a balcony?"

"Yes. You haven't gone in to see the performance space?" The new PAC had been open for only eight weeks. *Grease, Junior* would be the first middle-school show on the big stage. "It seats five hundred."

"Practically Broadway. That'll be fun for the kids," Marshall said. "And I bet Anna-Claire will be front and center every show."

It sounded like a compliment, but Marshall knew that Trey's family had paid for a good bit of the construction. Trey and his sister were both alumni, and our nieces attended high school here.

Was Marshall implying that the Cabbats were buying roles for Anna-Claire?

I felt my cheeks go pink, indignant. Marshall had been at work during auditions, but I'd watched. After Anna-Claire sang "There Are Worse Things I Could Do," I'd heard a mom behind me whisper to her friend, "Wow. Guess we know who'll be Rizzo."

I'd agreed. I was biased, sure, but I'd also majored in Theatre. I'd had lead parts in a ton of shows, starting in middle school myself. I still loved theatre, and Trey got the whole family season tickets to the Fox and the Alliance for my birthday every year. I'd taken the girls up to New York for Broadway weekends ever since they were old enough to sit through a show. I'd done and seen enough to know that my talented daughter had beaten out every other kid, including his, that day. By a mile.

I stopped myself before I said any of this to Marshall, though. Anna-Claire had polished her audition for weeks with her vocal coach, Mr. Reggie, who'd been on Broadway himself. He cost a hundred and fifty bucks an hour.

Cara was as naturally gifted as my kid, but her talent was raw. Early in college I'd lost parts to girls who'd grown up with money for drama camp, acting classes, vocal training. I remembered being eighteen years old and already feeling so behind.

So I only said, "Well, I'm going to watch," and picked up Robert's carrier seat. He made a *pah* noise. "Almost suppertime," I promised him.

To my surprise, Marshall asked, "So where are the stairs?"

I was still smarting, but I gave him the warmest smile I could. "This way."

In the balcony Peyton was already sitting in the back row, reading. I set Robert's carrier down beside her. If he started squalling, I wanted a straight shot out into the stairwell, so we wouldn't disturb rehearsal.

I'd brought his bottle in a warming sleeve, and as I got it out, Peyton asked, "Can I feed Bumper?"

"Robert. Sure." I peeled him out of his chair and settled him in her arms.

Marshall had made his way to the middle of the balcony's front row. I went down to join him, but I sat on the end, still smarting from his insinuation.

The performance was a week away, so they were running full scenes. They were in the park now, and Anna-Claire was singing "Look at Me, I'm Sandra Dee." It was cute, though in this junior version there was no mention of drinking, smoking, or swearing, much less sex. Instead Rizzo mocked Sandy for her good grades and being a "square."

As Anna-Claire vamped across the stage, I realized the bit about not "coming across" had survived the edits. I don't think Ms. Taft, who was in her twenties, knew it was sexual. And neither did our new young headmaster apparently, because he had approved the script. St. Alban's was Episcopalian, quite liberal for a church-run school—but not that liberal.

I shot an amused smile at Marshall, but he was watching Cara dance with the other Pink Ladies.

Peyton came up and joined me. I glanced back at Robert's carrier seat, still by the back row.

"Asleep?" I asked quietly.

"Dead to the world."

"Did he burp?"

"Twice, Mom." Peyton gave me her mild version of her elder sister's eye roll. "I know how to do Bumper."

"Robert."

"She really is talented," Marshall said in a gruff whisper. He was looking at Anna-Claire now, his face impassive.

If this was an apology, I'd take it. "Cara is, too. Her big number is in the sleepover scene. She kills it."

The director called the kids in for a huddle. I glanced back over my shoulder. The car seat sat sideways to me, so all I saw was

Robert's feet in their puppy socks, but this was his biggest nap of the day. I could probably click the carrier into the car and drive home before he woke up.

I told Marshall, "I'm going to clean up the greenroom." I knew from experience the kids would have stuffed fruit-snack wrappers all down in the couch cushions.

He was already rising. "I got it."

"You did the setup," I reminded him.

"Stay. That table's heavy." He turned toward the other aisle so he wouldn't have to climb over my knees.

"Want to help?" I asked Peyton. No response until I put my hand in between her face and the page. "Hey. You coming down?"

"I'm going to read here until it's really time to go. A-C takes forever to peel herself off Greer."

"Anna-Claire," I corrected. Honestly, "A-C" was as bad as "Bumper." "Your sister is not a cooling system."

"She kinda is." Peyton shrugged, jealousy and admiration at war in her expression. "Greer says Anna-Claire makes any room she's in feel cool. Now everyone calls her that."

I glanced after Marshall, already disappearing into the stairwell on the other side. If I didn't hurry, he'd clean up alone. More proof that I was a spoiled second wifey. Still, my middle child needed a moment.

"I think you're cool," I told her.

She snorted. "You're my mom. The fact that you think I'm cool means I'm for sure a dork."

"Well, cool is overrated. And sometimes it's code for a little bit mean. But you? You're smart. A good student. Super cute. Best of all, you have a kind heart."

She shrugged it off, disappearing into her book again, but I could see her fighting a smile.

"Good talk," I said to no one. But it had been.

Peyton went back to reading. Ten seconds later I could have set a bomb off beside her and she wouldn't have heard it. I used to read like that when I was young. Before I was a mother. Now nothing took me that far from reality.

Except maybe watching my children perform. Ms. Taft had decided to run the Sandra Dee song one more time. It was time to clean up, but Marshall had told me I could stay. Anna-Claire came center and began, and the whole world fell away again. It was the same when I was at a robotics match and Peyton was at the controls. At ten weeks all Robert had to do was show his brand-new toothless smile to put me into a trance.

When she finished, I stood and gave her huge, silent thumbs-up, then patted Peyton's oblivious knee. When I turned to go, I didn't see Robert's car seat.

But that wasn't possible. It had been right there.

I hurried up the aisle, caught in a chilly disbelief. Maybe the seat was behind the chairs? But who had moved it? No one else had been up here. I tried to remember the last time I'd looked back to check on him. Not long. I didn't think. But I'd been talking to Peyton, and then Anna-Claire had started singing—

This was scary, but at the same time part of me was sure there was an explanation. Maybe Greer had taken him back down to the greenroom. She was baby crazy.

I was at the row now, and he was gone. Just gone. So was his diaper bag. His empty bottle lay abandoned on the floor. Beside it was a single sheet of white paper, folded in half.

I picked it up, my hands visibly trembling. I opened it. A note. Handwritten in large block print.

If you ever want to see your baby again, GO HOME—

The black ink went blurry. The paper rattled in my hands. I couldn't read. I couldn't see or breathe. My spine was glass, and all my blood was water. I found myself sitting on the floor beside his empty bottle. My dazed mind noted there was a little milk in it, maybe half an ounce. I blinked hard, trying to clear my vision. But I didn't need to read more of the note to know what had happened.

I had not dreamed a witch. I'd seen a real person, made of flesh and bone and a secret, dark agenda, peering in my window. I'd seen her again, hurrying through the parking lot toward the fire door that the kids kept propping open. She'd been stalking me.

No. She'd been stalking Robert. And now she had him.

3

AS MARSHALL PUT the leftover snacks in the greenroom refrigerator, he caught himself hoping Bree would walk in and see him handling this small task for her. It was like a dead mouse he could drop on her doorstep. It made him tired of himself. She was happily married. With three kids. Not to mention her husband was both a nice guy and one of his damn bosses.

He was digging a surprising number of fruit-snack wrappers out of the sofa cushions when Cara found him.

"Need some help?" she asked him, smiling

Every other middle-school human must have vacated the building; he was getting eye contact and everything. He smiled back.

"Thanks," he said, and then couldn't resist adding, "Sugar Peep," just to see her eyes dart around, making sure no lingering teen or tween had heard the silly nickname. God, he wouldn't be thirteen again for a hundred thousand dollars. Not even for a day. He stopped teasing her and added, serious, "I watched rehearsal from the balcony. You were great. I can't wait to see the whole show."

She looked down, tried to wave it away. "I don't do much in that scene."

"Are you kidding me? You were all I could look at." And to think he'd been so worried. At Cara's old school, drama club had been tiny and underfunded, but it was huge at St. Alban's. Less than a quarter of the kids who tried out made the casts. Cara'd worked so hard, practicing every afternoon in front of the hall mirror, her heart so clearly set. He'd been praying she'd make the ensemble. Instead she'd landed Marty, a Pink Lady, with a solo and a custom-made satin jacket that she got to keep. "I'm so proud of you. You have a presence that lights up the whole stage. Like your mom."

That made her smile, though it was not exactly true. Cara was better. Onstage, charismatic Betsy had always turned stiff and awkward, things she almost never was in life. Bree had been the actor who could make the real world disappear.

He'd gone to see *Sense and Sensibility* his sophomore year of high school because his English teacher offered extra credit. He'd been in school with Bree since sixth grade, but in the play she'd truly turned into another person, one who was magic and beautiful and twice as alive as any girl he'd ever seen. He'd barely noticed Betsy as the mother.

Later, at the standing weekend keg party by the tracks, he'd caught sight of Bree and another girl near the fire pit, both holding red Solo cups of tepid beer. He drifted over, trying to be cool, desperate to know her better.

It was as if she had a dimmer switch in her, and she'd turned it all the way down the second she stepped off the stage. The other girl? Was Betsy. She'd been around since sixth grade, too, but she'd grown up over the summer. He literally hadn't recognized her. In real life Bree became background next to Bets. Even Bree seemed to assume that he'd come over for her friend, and within five minutes she was right. Bets was flirty, fun as hell, with a whip-smart sense of humor that never quite got mean.

Cara had her mother's sharp fox's face and dark brown eyes, but inside she was more like him. Thoughtful and cautious. She did have Betsy's light, but like Bree's it kindled brightest when she was performing.

He meant it when he told her, "You killed up there today."

"You have to say that. You're my dad," she said, but she bumped his shoulder with hers, smiling. "I have my bag. Can you drop me at Yvonne's? Her mom says we'll stop for dinner on the drive."

She was going with a school friend to her family's lake house all weekend. He'd planned to take her out for burgers, just the two of them, first. Still, he said, "Sure."

It was hard to find time with Cara these days, but he didn't want to mess up this nice moment. She was pulling away, growing up, keeping small secrets. In another five years, she'd be off to college. Maybe by then his ancient suits and his southern accent wouldn't embarrass her, though compared to the way he'd talked when he was her age, he practically sounded like a TV news anchor. Most of the other parents here had no accent, though. Or they had that faint, vowel-rounding burr that said Old Atlanta Money.

She helped him turn the table onto its side and flip the legs down, and for a moment he considered inviting Bree to eat with him instead. Trey was working out of town. She might want grown-up company. It would be perfectly innocent with all three of her kids there.

He shook his head. Since Cara changed schools, they were thrown together all the time. Before, she'd always belonged to Betsy, which had made her sexless somehow. How had she gotten so damn beautiful?

Cara was humming "Freddy, My Love," her curls bouncing as they carried the table back into the storage room. He needed some serious distance from Bree, but his daughter was thriving at St. Alban's. He couldn't stop being involved in her activities or, worse, pull her from the school over a few stray pink heart-eyed feelings.

It was probably residue of his love for Betsy. She and Bree had been so close. He'd keep avoiding Bree until he stopped crushing like he was Cara's age. Maybe he should get back on Match. He'd tried it a couple of years ago. Nightmare. He hadn't been ready. Maybe this crush was proof that he was now.

"Hey, have you seen my mom?" Anna-Claire leaned in the

doorway, looking like the underage-Russian-supermodel version of her mother. Peyton slouched behind her, her face buried in a book.

Cara's hum abruptly cut out, and she straightened, her cheeks staining. She picked at her plaid skirt. Bree had dropped off a whole bag of the school's pricey uniforms after Cara got the scholarship, saying they were hand-me-downs from Anna-Claire. Bree was such a good actor that only the one price tag she'd missed had kept him from believing her.

The firm paid him well. He could have afforded the uniforms, if not the tuition. Still, he'd let Bree get away with it. Because she loved his kid. Betsy's kid. She'd been after him to let her take Cara for private voice lessons, too. Maybe he should, but it would mean seeing Bree more. Last thing he needed.

"Check the parking lot?" he said.

"The car's gone," Peyton said, not looking up.

That was strange, but before he could react, his phone buzzed. Bree. His stupid heart beat quickened when he saw her name on the screen.

He smiled at the girls. "This is her. Probably looking for you."

Anna-Claire's eyebrows came together, and she checked her own phone. "Why didn't she just text me?"

He pushed the button. "Hey. Where'd you get to?"

"Can you take the girls?" It had to be Bree. Caller ID said so, but he didn't recognize the voice. It was raspy-sounding, guttural.

"Bree?"

"I need you to take the girls." It was her, but sick and strained.

"Is it Mom?" Peyton asked.

"Do what, now?" He was careful to keep his voice calm and his face pleasant.

"Tell her I have a Skype study with Anderson at six. I need to get home," Anna-Claire said, grumpy.

"Where's the car?" Peyton asked.

At the same time, words were tumbling out of Bree. They were nonsense.

"The baby is . . . the baby is—I'm sick. I'm so sick. Please take the girls to your house." He blinked. Marshall lived a good half hour outside the city, way past Bree's own house. He heard her take a long, shuddering inhale. "No. I mean, take them to my mom's place."

He covered the mouthpiece, made himself sound calm and easy. "Girls, I can't hear with you talking. Out!" Cara shook her head at him, a frantic, minuscule no. He fixed all three with pure adult face. "Go on. Close the door."

Cara shot him an anguished look, but she went. Anna-Claire made her nervous. She was the school's It Girl, according to his daughter. She wasn't mean to Cara. He'd asked. Still, he was an ex-cop, with a feel for people. The air between the two girls always felt a little scratchy to him, like sandpaper. But it was kid stuff, and something serious and grown-up wasn't right with Bree. He waited until the door shut to ask, "How sick? Should I call an ambulance? Where are you?"

"No. No ambulance. Just take the girls to my mom's. I'm already on the way to the doctor." That explained the missing car. So why were the hairs on the back of his neck standing up? "Anna-Claire can tell you how to get there. It's close. Walk them in to the security desk and ask for Shelly Ann Kroger."

"Jesus, Bree, I know your mom's name." He and Bets had practically lived at Bree's house back in high school. Shelly Ann had served the punch at his wedding. What was wrong with her?

Bree talked over him. "She'll come down and sign them in. Don't scare her. It's just a stomach flu, but I don't want the girls to get it." She was lying. She was way too upset. Peyton was staring through the little square window in the door, her eyebrows anxious, as if she, too, knew her mom was lying. Out in the hall, he could hear Cara and Anna-Claire singing in harmony, some doowop thing from the play. Bree added, "And don't call my husband. I'll call him."

As if he would call his boss to inform him that his wife wasn't feeling well. "What's going on? You sound—"

She cut him off again. "I think you fucking owe me this." She almost snarled it. "Help me, or you can goddamn well explain to Trey why you wouldn't."

He'd been worried; now he was shocked. Bree almost never cursed, and even stranger, she was threatening his job, which was insane. He was very good at what he did. Two or three times a year, he turned away headhunters who wanted to shop him to other firms or corporations. It was partly loyalty to Bree that kept him at this firm. All this over a car-pool ride, something he would do every day if she needed it.

"Of course I'm going to help you." He meant it gently, but his surprise made it come out clipped.

"Don't tell anyone," she added.

"Don't tell anyone *what*?" He was confused again. A secret stomach flu?

He heard a slapping sound, one, two, three times. It sounded like she was banging the flat of her hand into her forehead.

"Anything. Jesus, anything," she said, so wild and high and crazy that her voice cracked.

"Bree, are you—"

She hung up.

4

I'D CALLED MARSHALL from my car on instinct, even though he lived so far and our girls were not close friends. Greer's mom was probably in the parking lot right now, and she'd have happily taken them.

But I didn't want Peyton and Anna-Claire to ride off with some *mommy*. I wanted fierce, smart Betsy. Marshall was the next-best thing. They were the only cops I'd ever really trusted, and like most ex-policemen, Marshall owned guns. I hoped he had a gun on him right now, breaking every single zero-tolerance school rule. I hoped he had a hundred guns, because he knew how to use them. I wanted him and all his guns and knowledge and training to escort the girls to my mother's secure building.

I pressed a shaking hand to my heart. It felt swollen, huge. It thumped and wheezed against the closing walls of my rib cage. At least the girls were with him. I'd heard their voices in the background. I didn't care if he resented me or thought I was cashing in as if he owed me, as long as they were safe.

I looked down at the watch Trey had given me last Christmas, the delicate gold links so real and solid, and it seemed like someone else's memory strapped to someone else's shaking hand. It was 5:03 now. I was halfway to my house.

The note was on my passenger seat. My vision was too blurry for me to read it, but it didn't matter. I knew exactly what it said.

> If you ever want to see your baby again, GO HOME.
> Tell no one.
> Do not call the police.
> Do not call your husband.
> Be at your house by 5:15 P.M.
> Or he's gone for good.

At first I'd thought it was a joke. Had to be. Any second, someone would pop out holding Robert, laughing, and then I would snap that person's neck. But I'd been all alone.

Then I'd found myself in the parking lot. I'd run down the stairs and out the back door, heedless. I'd spun in a circle, seeking a swirl of dark dress, the flash of sun on silvery gray hair. She was old, and the infant carrier was heavy, she could not have been moving fast. But she'd been nowhere in sight.

I'd known, hadn't I? From the moment I'd seen her peering in my bedroom window. I'd thought she was an omen. I'd hoped she was a dream. But she was real.

My logical brain kept saying I could not know that it was this specific woman who had taken my baby. Not for certain. The witch peering in my window still could have been a nightmare. The little old lady on the street could have been someone's nice nana, running errands.

But I did not believe it. I almost didn't want to believe it, because then anyone could have Robert. Any kind of monster.

GO HOME, her note said. Was she going to meet me? Was Robert with her? I was on the fastest route, speeding down a narrow road through a neighborhood, the street tightly lined with Craftsman bungalows. Most of the houses had pop tops and additions, making them too large for their lots. They loomed over me, crowding close, as if the world itself were squeezing in on me.

I caught up to a slow-moving Lexus and braked. I wanted to peel into the bike lane and go around it, running up on the curb, tearing up the manicured grass.

I couldn't risk being pulled over by the police, though. I had to be home by five-fifteen.

I met my own eyes in the rearview, and I was shocked to see that I'd been crying. Black mascara streaked down my face. My breasts ached and pulsed like they were heavy with milk, the way they had when the girls were little and I went too long without nursing. It was a phantom pain, because Robert was a bottle baby. He'd been three weeks early, and his suck reflex had been poor. Nursing had burned up more calories than he was getting, so I'd had to supplement. My lazy baby liked the bottle so much better. He started fussing and turning away when I offered my breast. It hurt my feelings, trying to get him to latch while he struggled and squalled. When I offered a bottle, he snuggled close and smacked and cooed.

"You could just give him formula," Trey told me, and we had, though it made me feel weepy and, in the swamp of my postpartum hormones, like I was failing at motherhood. Trey said I was too hard on myself. "Bottle-fed babies do just fine. Why not enjoy him? He's our last one." That was Trey, always on my side. God, I wanted him here now, confident and decisive, helping me know what to do. But the note said not to call him. I was too afraid to disobey.

It was my turn at the stop sign. I was sweating so hard the salt stung my eyes. Next I'd turn onto a four-lane road, and then I could go faster. I was bare minutes from my house.

I put one shaking hand up to wipe at my eyes. I'd come this far on such a wave of adrenaline I could barely remember the drive, but now my brain was beginning to work again. That woman, she had taken his diaper bag. Did that mean she meant to keep him? She had extra formula, diapers and wipes, a change of clothes, and a blanket that smelled like me. Surely she didn't mean to keep him? GO HOME, the note said, but I was finally asking, why take the diaper bag if she was going to meet me now? And, looming larger, why Robert? Of all the babies in the world, why mine?

The answer was obvious. It was money. Had to be. Trey made so much of it. His family had even more. She'd taken Robert because he was worth a lot of money.

I should call the police. Trey would have already. Any of the Cabbats would have. But—the note said not to. It said to GO HOME, and I was almost, almost there. I would see if she was waiting for me, meeting me now, because once I called them, it couldn't be undone. I had to think, be careful, do everything right. She had Robert.

If this was about money, I had to figure out exactly how much I could get my hands on. I wanted Trey with me again then, so fiercely. He would know. I ran our household budget, but he handled the big-picture stuff: investments, retirement, his trust. He could tell me how much cash we could lay hands on, but I couldn't call him. The note said not to, so I couldn't. She could have partners, watching me.

But after she told me how much, surely she would let me call my husband. To get the money. He could decide if we should call the police. Or some kind of professional. There were people whose job was to negotiate with kidnappers, freelancers who didn't care about catching bad guys or any of the rules. I'd seen a movie about one of them, or a TV show. They only cared about getting the baby back. Maybe it would be better, safer, smarter, to call that kind of person. Trey would know. I found my head nodding itself, up and down, and I could breathe better. Soon I wouldn't be alone in this. Together Trey and I were stronger. We'd get him back.

I was at the turn into my neighborhood, but the light was red. An outsize SUV was in front of me, blocking my way in. My watch said I had six more minutes. The light stayed red and stayed red, and I screamed, a long, harrowing howl, beating my hands against the wheel. A woman in the car beside me, a young mother with a toddler strapped in the back, turned to look at me, openmouthed.

The toddler looked, too, eyes as round as quarters. I stared back, and I hated her. She had her baby buckled in safe behind her. She had everything I wanted. Whatever she saw in my face made her hastily turn forward again. As soon as the light changed, she took off.

I was in my neighborhood now, but in my panic I'd forgotten about the girls. Safe with Marshall but on their way to my anxious little mother's place. If they showed up unannounced, if Marshall mentioned how odd I'd been on the phone, she would assume the worst. She always assumed the worst.

"Hey, Siri, call Mom."

She answered on the second ring. "Hi, sweetie!"

I had to sound normal. I had to do a better job than I had with Marshall anyway. I thought about Anna-Claire, the way she slipped so easily from role to role. I'd just watched her channel Rizzo, and yet her own essential self was alive under every line. She was a girl inside a girl, and both were true.

She'd gotten this from me. A bug, Trey called it fondly. *She got bit by your acting bug.* Now I had been boiled down to an animal, wild with terror and fury, wholly feral. But I also had to be Bree Cabbat, wife and mother, busy and happy. That person felt so distant, so foreign. I had to make her true. I felt myself nod, thinking. *In this scene Bree calls to ask for a favor, and nothing in her tone upsets her mother.*

"Hi, Mom! I was wondering if the girls could spend the night at your place—maybe even the weekend?" I was turning onto my street. I sounded good, though inside I was little more than something howling.

"Well, I would love that! But we didn't plan it. Is everything all right?" She sounded worried. That was all it took.

"I have a little stomach virus. It's going around, and it's so contagious. Robert's safe—he's too young to catch it, but if the girls come home, they'll have it in five minutes." I made myself laugh, a light little sound. I manufactured it inside my body, then released it.

"Oh, how awful. Should I go get them at school?" They stayed with her so often that they kept pj's and toothbrushes and even extra clothes and swimsuits there.

"No need. Marshall's dropping them off."

"Oh. How's he doing? How's Cara?" She always asked that, in exactly this tone, ever since Betsy went out on a routine domestic and did not come home.

"Fine, but, Mom? I really don't feel great. I need to go lie down."

"You poor thing! Do you want me to come get Robert?"

"No," I said, too fast, too hard. I forced myself to soften. "You know how contagious these things are. I don't want you to catch it either."

"Okay. Try to get some rest."

"I will. You're the sweetest," I said, and hung up fast.

My cheeks felt wet. I reached up and touched them, wondering when I'd started crying again. But at least I could see my house ahead.

As I pulled up, everything looked so still and quiet. The drive was empty, and no cars were parked out front. She was not here. Robert was not here. The very idea had been lunacy, driven by fear and hope. If Robert was here, why would we pay? But if no one was going to meet me, why had the note told me to go home? I couldn't make sense of it. Nothing made sense.

I was reaching for the button that would open the garage door when I caught a flash of bright color from the corner of my eye. I stopped the Escalade in the driveway.

A gift bag hung from my front doorknob. It was striped in hot pink and yellow, with lime green curling ribbons and tissue paper exploding out the top. It couldn't have been there long. It was so garish I would have noticed it when I was leaving.

Had she told me to go home so I'd see this? Perhaps inside the bag I'd find instructions, telling me when and where and how much. I shook my head. It felt random, so risky. We lived in Great Lakes, an old, established Decatur neighborhood, very safe but still urban. Anyone could have come along and taken the bag.

I turned off the car, then got out and ran to my door, hoping this was what she'd wanted me to see. Hoping this would tell me what she wanted. We could pay. If we didn't have enough, Trey's family would help. They had never fully warmed to me. They'd liked his first wife, Buckhead born and with the right last name, so much better. But they doted on my babies. Especially Robert, their last and littlest grandchild. The only boy, which mattered way more than it should to my father-in-law. But now I was glad. He would help us. We would pay, and she would give Robert back.

I pulled the bag off the knob. It was light, but I could feel items shifting in the bottom of it. If that old woman had left it, then she'd come in plain view of our front-door camera. The video would already be uploaded to my cell phone.

I let myself in, hurrying through the house, back into our great room, where I dumped the bag out onto my kitchen island. There was a cheaply made smartphone with no casing and no screen protector. This *was* from the woman who had Robert, then. Had to be. This was how she would tell me where to bring the money. There was also a charging cord and an old Bluetooth, the flat triangular kind that tucked up close beside the ear. The last thing in the bag was a bottle of prescription medication, which struck me as odd. Not related to the other things.

I got out my own cell phone and checked the app that linked to our security camera. One new video had been uploaded almost immediately after I left the house, according to the time stamp. I pressed play.

It was her. The witch I'd seen peering in my window when I was half dreaming. The meemaw I'd shown Marshall at the school. I'd known it all along, but it still sounded a bell of shock deep down inside me. She could have shaded her face with the hat, but instead she locked gazes with the camera. How blatant she was. How bold.

Her eyes were dark pits, deep-set under sparse brows, and her face was webbed in wrinkles. She had sagging jowls and a long, sharp nose. She had to be seventy, at least. I hit pause and used the capture feature to get a still shot. I pulled the picture up onto the screen, staring at her grainy face, looking for softness. She was all angles, with a grim set to her mouth.

I picked up the prescription bottle. It was made of opaque white plastic, and at the top it said, CONTROLLED DRUG. *Possession without authority illegal. Keep out of reach of children.* Under that was an orange rectangle with the word "HYPNODORM" printed in white block letters, then in smaller text, *Flunitrazepam.* There was no patient name, no doctor, no pharmacy listed, but the back was tacky, as if a sticker had been peeled away.

I blinked stupidly at it. She had left me a phone and what sounded like tranquilizers or maybe something for anxiety. I shook the bottle, and it rattled softly. Was this a courtesy drug? Illegal sedatives, meant to calm me through the experience so I wouldn't screw it up? That seemed insane, which was scary. I didn't want an insane person to have Robert. But it was also oddly polite. A twisted and somehow female kind of thoughtful.

I opened the bottle and tipped it over into my palm. Half a dozen dark blue capsules fell out. I dumped them back in, then traded the bottle for my phone. I was going to Google "Hypnodorm," but the old woman's face still stared up from the screen. It froze me for a second, and then the disposable cell phone rang, buzzing against the marble countertop like an insect. I jerked and dropped my own phone with a clatter. It knocked the pill bottle over, and the capsules spilled across the island. One fell onto the floor, rolling away.

The ringtone was calypso music, tinny and shrill, so cheery that it made me want to scream and smash the phone with my fists, my wrath, a hammer. Instead I picked it up. The screen showed me the caller's name.

Robert

A number and his name had already been programmed in, so that now it was as if my own baby were calling for me. God, how long had this been planned?

I pushed the green talk button and then hit Speaker, leaving the phone flat on the counter. My hands were shaking so hard I wasn't sure that I could hold it.

"Please, where is my baby?" But she was already talking, too, over me.

"Did you call anyone? Your husband?" Creaky. Growly. Old. She had a southern accent, thick and rural.

"No. Where is he?" I strained to listen for some sound, a snuffle or a sleepy gurgle, that would prove Robert was with her. All I heard was muffled traffic and the faint hum of an engine; she was driving. With every passing second, he was farther away.

"Or the police? Are you having someone trace this call?" she demanded.

"No, no, I swear," I said, glad to hear the way it rang with truth. I was glad I hadn't called, so I could please her. This woman, this stranger, had my baby.

Her words were still coming at me in a rush, tumbling over each other. "You could still call the police on your own phone. Right now. I'm going to talk as long as I need to, and what with technology these days, I'm sure they could find me. But I have your baby in a sling, tied to me. Can you hear him breathing? We're going to stay this close, me and him, until you and I are done. You do everything right, I'll give him back. But if sirens or lights come on behind me, I will finish this here and now. I'll break his flimsy neck. When I get where we're going, if they breach my door or throw in a gas canister, I'll twist his little head right around backward."

I was swamped in so much fear and hatred then that I could barely breathe. My whole body yearned toward an unknown place where my baby was in a moving vehicle, bound to her body.

"I didn't call the police." Talking to her made me feel so cold.

My teeth wanted to bang together. "Can you please at least put him in a car seat?"

She ignored that. "Who did you call."

Not a question. Did she know, or was she guessing?

"Are you watching me?"

"My daughter has eyes on you." I blinked, surprised she would tell me that. It was too bold, almost careless, like the way she'd stared into the camera. I didn't want the woman who had my baby to be careless. I was even more surprised to hear her say "my daughter." She was a mother? What mother could do this to another parent? "Who have you talked to?"

"I called a friend to take my girls. I didn't tell anyone about you, I swear. Is Robert all right?" I could barely pull air into my twisted-shut lungs. I needed to become another woman, one who wasn't too afraid to breathe. One who could think and be so careful and make all the right decisions.

"Please," I said, and I meant a thousand things. *Please give him back. Please tell me he's okay.* Most of all, *Please don't hurt him.*

"He's fine. Sleeping." Then she added, "He's . . . a good baby."

Her words were grudging, but it almost sounded as if she liked him, or at least liked babies. And now I knew she was a mother, like me. This was good, a good thing to know about her. It might be hard for a mother to actually hurt him. I wanted to believe, so much so that it was dangerous, that it would be much harder than she'd made it sound when she talked about his fragile neck. I appealed to the only part of her that I could fathom.

"He'll be hungry soon. He'll want my arms, my smell, my voice." Any mother would understand these things. "Just tell me what you want. I'll give it to you."

I meant, *How much?* but asking that way turned my baby into a commodity, a thing that could be bought or sold or thrown away. He was a person. A tiny person, so helpless and so dear. My person I had made inside my body, who had only been separate from me for ten short weeks. I could almost still feel him, kicking and spinning at my center. It felt as if she'd torn him out of me.

"We'll get to that," she said. "First I have to tell you the rules."

When she said that, I heard more than age in the shake and creak of her voice. I heard fear. She was afraid. Like me.

I wasn't sure if this was good or bad. Good, because it made her human. She had my child; I needed her to be human. Bad, because frightened people do such stupid things.

Which meant I had to stop being afraid. For Robert's sake. I had to help this woman—this other mother—not be scared, too. That almost made me laugh. It was as if I'd seen a way out, and all it would take would be for me to leap up in the air and fly. I did the only thing I could do.

I pretended I was a different woman. One who was not afraid. I pretended it so hard my hands clenched into fists, my nails digging painfully into my palms.

"The rules," I echoed. Rules were good. Rules made everybody safer.

"One. Tell no one. We keep this between us. I'm giving you a chance to get your baby back, but if you tell anyone, I'll end this. You understand?"

I didn't understand. Not what "end this" meant. I could not allow myself to know what she was saying. I was still building this new, less frightened character over myself, someone calm and helpful. A woman who could be trusted to keep rules. "Yes."

"Two. You keep this phone with you at all times. When I call, you answer. You take it with you to the bathroom, you hold it when you sleep."

My heart crashed. When I slept? Did they mean to keep Robert overnight? I couldn't live through that. I didn't think I could live through one more second, actually, but one second passed, and then another, and I kept on living.

"I understand."

"Three. Do exactly what I say. Nothing added, nothing skipped.

That's it. Three rules. Follow them and this will all be over tomorrow. For both of us."

I found myself nodding, as if she could see me. Maybe her daughter could. She might be in my backyard right now, watching.

I glanced at the window, but at some point I'd closed our wooden shutters without thinking. It was a habit left over from childhood, when my mom was constantly afraid that someone would see it was only her and me inside, small and vulnerable. Trey was a sunshine person, though. It shocked me to think that only two days ago I'd been laughing with him about how our marriage was a long series of laps around the house, undoing each other's window settings. Robert had been sleeping sweetly in my arms. Two days, but it felt a thousand years away.

Now I stared at the shutters like a feral thing, shivering, wondering if the daughter was out there. She could be three feet away, wishing me ill on the other side of my wall. She couldn't see me, and I couldn't see her. This was good. The old woman had looked right in the camera, showing me her face, but as a mother she'd feel protective toward her child. If I could identify the daughter, it might make it feel riskier for her to give Robert back.

Then I realized I might already have seen the daughter. She could have been the driver with the toddler who'd watched me scream and pound my steering wheel. Or driving the big SUV that had blocked the turn into my neighborhood. She could be anyone.

"I can follow rules," I said. "I want this to be over."

She sighed. "Mrs. Cabbat, that's what I want, too. For this to be over." She sounded almost sorry, which was so strange and foreign. I hated her with a black instinctual fear, huge and inadvertent, but I was also glad she had a child herself. Glad her child was female, too. It felt safer somehow. For Robert.

"How do I know he's okay now?"

A pause, and then I heard her say, "Hey, baby? Hey there." Her voice was gentle, almost sweet, and I heard his sleepy protest. I knew him from that sound, even under her voice and the noise of traffic. It was Robert. I felt relief, then horror. It was as if I'd had a knife in me this whole time, and she had pulled it out, then put it right back in.

"You have to burp him twice," I blurted, my calm shell cracking. I had a vision of him colicky, crying, keeping her awake. I didn't want her angry or resenting him. "At least twice, because otherwise he gets fussy."

There was an awkward pause, and then she said, "Mine was that way, too. When she was small." Her voice was gruff, but I felt a surge of hope. This tiny bit of information, one parent to another, felt like a filament stretched between us, tenuous as spiderweb, connecting us. "Say the rules back to me. I need to make sure you understand."

I nodded. Made myself breathe in and out. "I'll keep this between us. No police, or even family. I'll have the phone with me, every second, and answer when you call. I'll do exactly what you tell me to do."

"Good," she said. "Good."

"Can you please tell me how much now, though? I might have to move things around."

Whatever amount she said, I would get it. I would loot our accounts, sell everything we owned. I would steal my mother's pistol from her gun safe and rob a bank. I'd almost rather that than call Trey's parents for cash, but I would do that, too.

There was a small, shocked silence, and then she asked, "You think this is about money?"

"I . . . I thought—" I stammered. It had to be money. What else did we have?

"You think I'd take a baby to get money?" Her voice rose, incredulous, and Robert gave a protesting mewl. Immediately her voice softened into shushing noises. "Ch-ch-ch."

She understood babies, this mother, and she was being gentle with him. His cry subsided. It made me grateful to her, an involuntary golden gleam inside my fear and rage and hate. Our slim connection strengthened, running back from her to me.

"I'm sorry. It was an assumption. I can't know what you want. But I'll do whatever you say."

I wasn't trying to soothe her. There was no room for pretending between us. This was truth, raw and ugly. She owned me, and we both understood that. Somewhere, in a car that was moving farther away from me every second, I heard Robert sigh and stir in her arms.

"Hm." It was a little hum of sound, thoughtful. "I'm almost to a place where I can stop for a little. Hold on a minute."

I waited, listening to road sounds and her breathing. The traffic sounds faded, and then her car's engine went quiet.

Her voice dropped almost to a whisper. Intimate. Confessional. And then she told me what she wanted.

5

"Mrs. Cabbat, I'm old. You can likely hear that in my voice. What you can't hear is, I'm also sick. The kind of sick that means I got no energy to spare, and I don't have much time left. So I got nothing to lose. I could go to prison for the rest of my life and still be free before summer ends, you understand? I don't care what happens to me. I only care about my daughter."

I felt myself nod. I only cared about my son.

She went on. "Taking your baby, that was my plan, my choice. All my girl has done is watch, so this is on me, and finding me won't lead you to her. I won't even see her again until you and I are finished. Maybe not even then, depending on how it goes."

All these things sounded so personal. It made my skin crawl, and yet I leaned in.

"Tell me what you need."

The call lasted a long time. We spoke softly to each other, intimate as whispers in the night. I wanted to keep talking with her, keep the line open to wherever in the world she had my child. She was gentle with me, perhaps sensing how near the edge I was, and I was gentle back. I did not think of her as a witch, or a stalker, or a kidnapper. I tried to speak to the part of her that was like me. Mother to mother.

But when she was finished talking, she hung up. It closed my only live connection to my son. It was like the breaking of a spell.

I cried out, "Wait!"

She hadn't told me when or even how I would get Robert back. But she was already gone.

My legs stopped working. I fell down. I was no longer inside myself. I floated up until I pressed into the ceiling, watching my body writhe and beat at the floor. It spun and bucked, shoving and kicking its way into the den, where it rolled to scream and bite at the carpet.

When my body calmed enough to let me back inside it, I was in my bedroom. It was dim and quiet. I sprawled on the floor beside the bed, the cheap cell phone still clutched in my hand. Even in my fugue state, I had been obedient, keeping it close. It was my only link to my son.

I stood up, creaky and slow, and the Bree I saw in the full-length mirror was a monster. Eyes puffed nearly shut. A swollen face streaked with mucus and mascara. As I stared, and long seconds ticked past, I realized I'd stopped crying. My throat was raw, hoarse from screaming, but I was calmer. I was ready to do what I had to do.

"I've given you six Hypnodorm. It's the same thing as Rohypnol. You know this drug?"

"Isn't that roofies?" I paused, confused. "That's a date-rape drug."

She snorted, then said, "You think I want you to—" She sounded almost offended, as if in the hierarchy of evil, rape was a thousand times worse than snatching my child. My spine tensed, but her voice softened again on the next sentence. "Well. That is what it's known for. I picked it because Hypnodorm steals memories. On this drug people do things they don't remember. Things they'll never remember."

I washed my face, then spent a few minutes rolling an ice pack back and forth across my swollen eyes. I also texted Mom, needing to know the girls were safe inside her building for the night. She texted back a pic of them in her tidy kitchen, mixing up a batch of oatmeal scotchies. They were laughing, Peyton's cheek dusted with flour.

It looked like a window to another world, distant, impossible for me to reach. It was on the other side of a two- or three-minute window of time when I had looked away.

I went into my dressing room to rifle through my cocktail dresses with numb hands. I didn't want my usual colors or cuts. I needed something closer to a costume. Bree Cabbat had fallen entirely apart, so I could not be her. I had to be some other woman, smiling and calm. I'd begun to be her earlier, but that character had shattered when the old woman hung up. I could not shatter again. Not if I wanted Robert back.

Just the thought of him and I felt tears threatening again. I didn't understand how I had any left; I was desiccated, so wrung out that no water could possibly be left inside me. And yet I felt them welling.

I dashed them away, looking for the dress I wanted. It was shoved toward the back, the tags still on. I'd meant to return it. I favored springtime colors, floral prints in breezy fabrics, and this Erdem was jet-black, sleeveless, with pointed shoulder pads and a high collar. I'd bought it in a spasm of odd hormones, a day before I realized I was pregnant with Robert.

Now I found myself nodding stupidly and pulling it on. The stiff, shiny fabric felt like armor. It was a little tight, but not in a bad way. I had a pair of high-heeled black booties, dressy enough to read "cocktail party" and hide the aging pedicure I'd meant to fix this weekend.

"Your husband's firm has a party tonight. At the Botanical Garden. Yes?"

"Yes. But I never RSVP'd." I'd had secret plans to claim "cranky baby" and skip it in favor of microwave popcorn and streaming a movie with the girls, Robert sleeping in his pack-n-play nearby.

"Well, I need you there."

"I can just show up." I was Trey's wife. They'd let me in. But her request felt nonsensical. She took my baby to make me go to a party?

I sat down at the vanity, trying not to think of Robert. If I let myself feel his absence, I'd start screaming again. If I started, I didn't see how I could ever stop.

I turned on the mirror lights, flinching at my pinched, pale face. But the ice had helped. I looked like a woman who'd once been pretty. Maybe even myself, if I were ten hard years older.

The whites of my sunken eyes were crimson from crying. I tilted my head back to put in some Visine. I couldn't show up at the party looking like this. I'd been ordered not to draw attention or questions.

"Get there soon as you can. Smile and chat. Be like regular, you understand?"

"Yes." I didn't. It sounded bizarre, impossible. In the pause I heard Robert mutter and shift, and she drew a ragged breath. Was this the sickness that was killing her? Something respiratory? Or did her chest feel closed and tight from stress, like mine? I was seeking clues to her in every word and sigh, trapped in our terrible intimacy.

When she spoke next, her voice dropped. We were to it. The thing she wanted from me. *"Before ten o'clock, you need to get at least three of those pills down Spencer Shaw's throat."*

She'd taken Robert because I was close with Spence. Well, Trey was. Or partnered with him anyway. I smoothed a caffeinated cream over my eyelids to take down the swelling, feeling an irrational surge of rage at my husband.

How many times had I watched Trey rub his forehead, rueful,

over some mess of Spence's? And yet he kept on working with him. Spence landed clients, but Trey did most of the work that kept them. Spence was better at cocktail parties than contracts, and he was also willing to break rules that Trey would not so much as bend. Spence stayed within the lines of the law, Trey had assured me, but I got the feeling it was sometimes only barely. And now this was happening. I set the cream back in the drawer, then turned to check on Robert.

In the space of half a breath, I'd forgotten he was gone. It almost undid me. I froze, fighting back a wave of tears and panic. I'd read about something like this happening to people who had lost a limb. They would reach out with a hand that wasn't there or feel cramping in a foot they no longer owned.

I stood abruptly, turning to the built-in drawers behind me. I kept my jewelry in the top two. I opened the lower one, which held costume jewelry and some older pieces. The bracelet I wanted, a chunky gold thing meant to be worn above the elbow, was all the way in the back. It felt too young for me now, and ever since I'd had the girls, it was a little tight. I wanted that, though. The bite of that cold metal in my flesh.

I pushed it up my arm until it pinched, then nodded, calmer. I could not forget myself again. I could not keep reaching for him. It would break me down, and I would fail.

The bracelet would help. It was a trick I'd learned in a college acting class, what felt like a thousand years ago. If some real-life sorrow or anxiety was pulling me out of a role, I could use something physical to locate that distraction in my body. I'd pack my pain or worry inside the squeeze of a tight shoe or the tug of a ponytail holder. Then the rest of my body was free to become someone else.

I'd used a variation of the trick all three times I'd been in labor. I'd pinched the tender spot between my thumb and forefinger as each contraction hit, moving myself into the small pain while my body heaved and surged. The trick had worked in the early stages, until some animal inside me took over and I was nothing more than a will to push.

I was still a mother, but separated from all that made me so. I had to put Robert's absence into the constriction of the bracelet. I put my fear there, too, the whole choking cloud of it. And my anger with my husband, which was quickly changing into a pure, wild rage at Spence, as cold and clear and biting as grain alcohol. I added my desperate longing for Trey to be here with me, my surges of desire to call the police, and most of all my paralyzing love for my child. I had to let some other woman ride my body.

Be Betsy, I thought then. She'd been bolder than me, always, and dead calm in a crisis. Betsy had owned any room she'd entered. I could almost feel her presence closing over me. My best friend, gone but still saving me.

"You want me to roofie Spencer Shaw?" I sounded as incredulous as I felt. "You want Spence to . . . what? To not remember tonight? Why?"

"Don't you worry about that. Just you worry about your part."

Her voice was still gentle. We spoke softly to keep Robert asleep, but the near whispers seemed to pull us closer. Her voice, breathy in my ear, was so intimate, and I desperately wanted to please her. I wanted her to like me. Hell, a small, crazy part of me wanted to like her, too, because she had me wholly in her power. I needed to believe there was sweetness in her. That she liked babies and would be kind to mine. That if I did exactly what she said, she'd give him back.

I said, "Help me understand why you'd do this. I know it's not money. Can you please tell me what you really want?"

Her voice dropped even lower. "What I want, you can't give me. Not direct."

"Maybe I can help you get it. If you—"

"I want to put the world right. I want what's fair," she interrupted, and it was a cry right from the center of her. It shook her voice into something younger somehow, because the world was not fair, and

anyone her age already knew that. "If you drug Spencer Shaw, I can make him do right by us."

I felt the power between us shift, just a bit. I had asked, and she had answered. She had given me something. "But it's not fair to take Robert." I used her word. "He's innocent. I don't know you, but I don't think I ever did you wrong?" I made it a question, afraid of angering her.

I heard that thinking little hum she'd made before. "I am sorry for that." It sounded like she meant it. "This isn't about you, and I'm not without feeling. I know it's hard, especially for a girl like you. You were raised soft, everything laid out on a pillow. Most folks open their eyes onto a harsher world."

I had to protest this. "I'm not soft."

She didn't believe me. I could tell. She made a click noise with her tongue, almost a tutting sound, then said, "You married who you married, and he chose to work hand in glove with Spencer Shaw. So here we are. It's not fair to you. But I am nigh out of time, and what happened to me and my daughter—it's not fair either."

Her voice stayed quiet, but I heard steel beneath it as she spoke about her child. This was the part of her I understood most, feared least. The part that clearly loved her daughter. I had no name for this woman, but of all the things I'd seen her be—kidnapper, stalker, witch—she was somehow tying herself tightest to this one: mother. A warm word, but so cold and strange when it was touching her. My own sweet-hearted, timid little mother was never called that. I called her Mom. Mama when I was small. Peyton had only just this year given up Mommy.

This woman, this mother, said to me, "Before I leave this earth, I am going to set things right."

I smoothed on foundation, thinking hard. "Fair" might be the only word she'd said that truly mattered, if I wasn't going to be blindly obedient. It was a clue to who she was and why she'd done this awful thing, and yet my mind shied from pursuing these questions further. She had Robert in her arms. She'd told me if she saw or heard any sign of the police, she would twist his— The very thought brought me back to her heel, obedient and good.

I wanted to please her. I wanted to turn the things she'd said about fairness into a story that would make her into the kind of person who would do right by me and my son.

But what if this feeling of communion were only in my head? If I could figure out who she was, what wrong she was trying to set right, then I should. In case things went wrong. In case I couldn't get the pills down Spence, or she was lying, or she changed her mind.

Fairness. I turned the word over and over as I gave myself a smoky eye. Fairness was a thing people went to courtrooms to try to get, though Trey often joked that in his job cash trumped fairness every time. Was this about one of Trey and Spence's lawsuits? Had Spence bent or broken a rule?

They'd worked together on so many cases, including the large, uneasy merger that had taken Trey off to Chicago. What had Trey said about it? *This is not a marriage of equals we're officiating. Our groom is a cannibal.*

How many of their clients had been cannibals? Could I narrow it down?

I striped my lids in black liner, thinking. If this was about a case, she was not their client. A client could have simply made a date for drinks with Spence and doped him up herself. Also, she didn't talk like someone who'd be a main player in a multimillion-dollar lawsuit. Her accent sounded like my mom's. Like mine, before my college adviser told me, *No one is going to cast a redneck Juliet,* and registered me for dialect class.

She was from the small-town South, like me. Had her family been caught in the cross fire of something big and cold and corporate?

She was sick, she'd said. Was her daughter sick, too? Perhaps a client of Spence's had done something with chemicals or food or the groundwater that had *made* them sick. Or perhaps she'd lost her job in some merger and with it the health insurance that could have cured whatever was now killing her.

I shook my head. It could be one of a hundred cases, some decades old. Without more details, all I could do was hope she'd taken Robert to get something concrete from Spence—information, a file, a taped admission of wrongdoing—because I could help her do that. I could drug him so he wouldn't remember giving it to her. I could do it for Robert.

"Will the drug hurt Spence? Three seems like a lot." I was afraid to question her, but I didn't want to harm Spence.

Though if I had to roofie someone . . . Spence took advantage of my husband, skated close around ethical corners, and I didn't love how he treated women. There was a basic disrespect there, in the way he talked over us at dinner parties or let his eyes drop lower than our faces. He'd cheated on both his wives. If whatever she took from him during his lost time cost him money or embarrassment, even his career, I would not regret it. Not if I got Robert back.

She said, "He's a big man. Tall and broad, carrying some extra weight. One won't do it. Two might, but I can't play with 'might.' Three is sure, so make it three. My daughter will be watching, waiting for the drugs to hit."

Her daughter would be at the party? I asked a question without thinking. "If she's there, can't she just give him—"

She interrupted, her voice harsh. "You think we didn't try? We went to his office before. We couldn't even get past that receptionist. But you? He'll talk to you. He'll be sweet and drink whatever you give him. Because you matter."

"I only matter because I married Trey," I said, but she was still talking.

"That receptionist wouldn't so much as give us an appointment. I insisted, said I needed a lawyer, and she tried to pawn me off on some little bitty black girl who passed by. That child didn't look half old

enough to be a lawyer. He didn't have time for the likes of us. We don't blend with your kind of people."

"My kind of people?" She was saying I was soft again. A noise came out of me. Not a laugh, but related. "Everyone at this party belongs to Trey. I don't blend either." I faltered at the end, because in midsentence I knew that what I was saying wasn't true. I might not be fully at home with Trey's old-money Buckhead crowd, but I wasn't like her. Not anymore. "I know how to look the part. I've been married sixteen years. But I grew up in Hurd County, just me and my mom." She hadn't mentioned a husband, and I'd never met my father. Our families sounded similar. If she knew how much she had in common with my own mother, she might feel softer toward me. "I didn't have a college fund or private school. We lived in a two-bedroom ranch house that leaked every time it rained." I could also hear myself easing a little more South into my vowels. Nothing obvious. Not fake so much as regressive. One step closer to seventeen-year-old Sabreena Kroger's diction. "Every fall my mom would drive me two towns over to go to the Goodwill there, so my 'new' school clothes wouldn't be recognized by whoever threw them out."

All these things were true, but when Betsy died, I'd lost my strongest tie to the girl I'd been before my marriage. I had no reason to visit my old neighborhood since my mom's move. Perhaps I'd gotten soft, spoiled. These days Marshall sure treated me as if he thought I was an over-pampered deb. But I hoped she'd see the girl I used to be. That girl was likely not too different from her own child. I waited, barely breathing, until she answered.

"I did that Goodwill trick, too. When my daughter was small."

I felt the cord of connection thicken between us.

I sat back down at the vanity, the bracelet chafing me. The haunted rag doll I had picked up off the floor was gone, replaced by a pretty woman with high cheekbones and a glossy, pale mouth.

Trey loved me in a short dress and heels. If he were here, ready to take me to the party in his tuxedo, if everything were normal, he would dance me around, singing "Wonderful Tonight." How was it that my baby was missing and yet I could still make this woman in the mirror smile? It even lit her eyes.

Theatre, I thought, though I'd gotten married less than a year after college graduation. I'd been in exactly one professional play, at Actor's Express in Atlanta, winning the role of Syl in *Traps* over pros with Equity and SAG cards. I'd done it to prove that marrying Trey instead of going to New York was my actual choice, not simply fear that I didn't have what it took. Now I was grateful for every play I'd ever done, every class I'd taken, every workshop, because they let me be two things at once: a howling mother-monster, mad with fear, and this bold-eyed, smiling woman.

Or maybe the training and the practice didn't matter. This was my child. Tiny little women picked cars up off their babies. They sold their bodies. They killed. They died. I could smile at a goddamn party and get a spiked drink down a man who loved a cocktail.

"You sure look like you belong. I seen your car. Your shoes. You walk like you own everything you see." As she talked, Robert woke up. All at once it became so hard to concentrate. I heard him sigh, and then the little noises he made while stretching. "Just a minute."

I heard the clunk of the phone onto a hard surface. A dashboard? Robert fussed, and she was talking to him in a comforting murmur that ebbed and flowed as she rustled around. Then, in a place far from me, off a highway in a car that I could not imagine, I could hear Robert eating.

Listening to his happy smacks and grunts, I thought, He doesn't know enough to be afraid. As long as she feeds him and cuddles him and keeps him dry and warm, this could be no different for him than that night exactly six weeks after his birth, when he stayed with his sisters at my mom's place, so Trey and I could have a romantic overnight at the St. Regis.

I was grateful then, so grateful that it wasn't Peyton or Anna-Claire. Peyton had been born so anxious. I had a flash of her in a dark room, curled into a fetal ball, picking her fingernails bloody. Anna-Claire chose fight over flight every time. I saw her hurling her body against a locked door, screaming until someone came to drug her or hurt her or gag her. My body shuddered with a thousand feelings. Hate and rage and helplessness, but also this strange gratitude that Robert was so young. I could get him back undamaged, just himself.

I put the Bluetooth in my ear. I transferred my wallet, some cash, and the cheap cell phone into a black beaded bag. It was a little large for evening, but I had a lot to carry.

I reached for my own iPhone, and it felt like reaching for Trey. As my fingers closed around it, I was swamped again with that desperate need to call him. I wanted his arms around me so damn bad. I'd call Trey first, then the police, my father-in-law with his political connections and his money. Or I'd call Marshall, who was so gruff with me these days, but surely all our history could trump that. He had guns and understood crimes. Marshall could find her.

A picture flashed in my head. Me, peering through a crack in *her* drapes. I would shoot her right between her eyes with one of Marshall's pistols, then run in to pluck my baby out of her dead arms.

"I'm sorry! I'm sorry," I said out loud, apologizing as if she could feel the ripples of my imaginary rebellion. I couldn't stop seeing my son's small head, round and covered in a floss of pale hair, resting in her gnarled hands. His neck was such a slender stem, still wobbly when he held his head up. One twist. It would be so fast. So final. My own head shook back and forth in a silent, involuntary no.

I shoved the bracelet up higher on my arm, feeling the good bite of it into my flesh. I wasn't going to call anyone. I was going to follow the rules.

I grabbed the evening bag and headed toward the kitchen, careful not to turn my head as I passed the nursery. The animal inside me howled, but outside I was Betsy, bold and cool and street-smart, and the room through that open door was still an office. No giraffe wallpaper. No black hole like some essential organ missing from my middle.

Back in the kitchen, I picked up the capsule that had rolled away, dropping it back into the bottle.

I needed to leave, but I didn't trust myself to drive. I got my own phone out and opened the Lyft app. I could have a Lux Black here in ten minutes. Good enough. I hit the button to confirm.

Then I went to Google and typed in "Hypnodorm." I scanned the entry, reading about dosage and side effects. Roofies lowered inhibitions, made people suggestible, and stole their memory. I was going to feed them to the lawyer who worked with my husband on multimillion-dollar cases. Spence held the secrets of a host of rich and powerful people. People who made even Trey's father look like small potatoes.

The bottle said the capsules were one milligram each. Google told me a standard dose was one to two milligrams and warned that roofies could be dangerous if they were taken with alcohol. This was Spence, so they absolutely would be taken with plenty of alcohol.

I put my phone away and tipped two capsules into my hand. He was a large man, though, and maybe the pills were old. He might set his drink down unfinished. I tipped out a third, stuffed the bottle back into my purse, and went to Trey's office.

It was a masculine space with an exposed brick wall, leather chairs, and art deco prints of famous New York buildings. A French bar cart from the 1930s displayed Trey's mostly full bottle of Pappy Van Winkle between lesser bottles of Lagavulin and WhistlePig rye. The firm would be serving top-shelf tonight, but not Pappy. Pappy was so far over top-shelf that the atmosphere around it was thin. I'd paid almost two thousand dollars for this bottle, a present for Trey's fiftieth birthday.

In the smoked mirror, I watched as a tall, slim figure, dressed to cause trouble, poured a shot of Pappy into a rocks glass. She pulled three capsules apart, one by one, and tipped fine, white powder into the bourbon.

"You dose Shaw by ten, hear? The drugs work fast, so excuse yourself, quick as you can. Then you text me and say it's done."

"Yes. I'll text you." I couldn't hear Robert eating anymore. He must be finished. *"Remember, you have to burp him twice."*

"I will. I'll be sweet with your boy, as long as you are doing what I need. Now, you got any questions on it?"

I swallowed. If I succeeded, the girls might never know that he'd been missing. I wanted this. Innocence was permission to be bold. I'd been raised by a mom who saw monsters under every bed. If it weren't for Betsy, fearless and strong enough to drag me toward adventure, I might have grown up afraid of my own shadow. Had Mom been right about the world all along?

Maybe, but I didn't want the girls to know. If I got Robert back tomorrow, unchanged, unharmed, the girls blissfully ignorant, all their lives could continue, normal.

I'd tell Trey, because I wasn't sure who or what I would be in the wake of this. I had no chance of coming out of this unbroken. I was split in two already. But I hardly cared. Not if all three of my kids could be safe and the same.

"What do I do after I text you?"

"You leave. Don't stay to watch. Don't try to find my girl. I've left her out of the worst parts. She had no part in taking your baby, understand? That was all me. In the morning I'll call and tell you where to pick him up."

"Okay," I said.

And that was it. She disconnected.

I stirred the bourbon with the silver bar spoon. The drug dissolved easily, disappearing into the amber liquid. I nodded to myself. I could watch for when Spence's glass got low, then offer to top him off with a shot from Trey's best bottle. I couldn't imagine him saying no to Pappy. If he dared, I'd knock him down and pill him like a cat with the other three.

I was tempted to have a sip to make sure the taste didn't give anything away, but with all three dissolved in there, it must be strong; I needed a clear head. Besides, Google said that roofies were tasteless. It was why they were so dangerous. Girls kept sipping their Cokes or beer with no idea of what else they were getting.

There was a monogrammed silver flask on the bookshelf, right beside a framed photo of Trey on the porch of his frat house with his closest brothers. He looked so young and confident, but my hard gaze went to young Spencer, grinning beside him, one arm hooked around Trey's neck. This flask was from Spence, too, a gift when Trey made partner. I got it down and carefully poured the shot into it, not spilling a drop.

I screwed the cap on, tight. After Spence signed whatever they wanted him to sign or said whatever they needed him to say or gave them whatever files they wanted, I'd get Robert back. I'd have him in my arms tomorrow. I could peel away this grown-up version of Betsy, with her smoky eyes and bare legs. I would be myself, though I wasn't sure exactly what that would feel like after this. Perhaps I'd become my mother. I'd heard most women did eventually.

I slipped the flask into my beaded purse. The blinds were open. Of course they were; this was Trey's space. Even as I closed them, I saw headlights turning up the drive. My Lyft was here. It was time.

Inside, I felt a curtain rising. I was on.

6

WHEN I WAS fifteen years old, an outdoor mall opened up about thirty minutes away. It had a Gap, and a Claire's, and a Rave. Everyone at my school was wild to go. One Saturday, Betsy's mom dropped us off there. I had a little babysitting money, but a cute pair of earrings and an ice-cream cone for us to split cleaned me out. Bets was dead broke to begin with, and we had another two hours to kill.

"Five-finger discount?" Betsy said, eyes gleaming, and then laughed at the horror on my face. "I'm kidding. Mostly. Why don't we try on the sluttiest clothes in the universe?"

That sounded fun, but still, I shook my head. What if the girls working the stores somehow guessed we had no money and kicked us out? My cheeks burned with imagined shame.

Betsy knew me well enough to read my mind. She affected a snooty accent and said, "Come along, *Elizabeth*, we'll max out your daddy's Visa."

She reached into my purse and mimed pulling it out. It was as invisible and unpresent as my actual daddy, but I could almost see the faint outline of the card as she waved it at me. I was VP of the drama club; she knew this would work. She'd given me her own name, Elizabeth, and she was the boldest girl I knew. Plus, the long version sounded classy, a rich-girl name that put a swagger in my step.

As we blew through the doors into Rave as if we already owned everything inside, I proclaimed, "If I put more than two hundred on this card, Daddy'll kill me!"

Betsy laughed and answered just as loud. "He didn't kill you last time."

I don't know if we fooled anyone. I doubt that the minimum-wage girls working the store even cared. We had a blast, though, trying on bustiers and plaid microminis so short I felt daring taking two steps out of the dressing room.

I'd kept that imaginary Visa with Betsy's long-form name. I took it with me anywhere that I felt out of place, as if it could buy me tickets. I'd had it with me the day I met Trey.

Now, as the Lyft driver turned in to the Botanical Garden, I could feel it in the bottom of my bag, infused with Betsy's leftover magic. It felt realer tonight than the actual cards in my wallet. It turned me into my best friend, boldly wearing someone else's dress, smiling easy as I headed to a place where I did not belong to do something that I should not be doing.

The bracelet pinched. Somewhere far away, back in Decatur, that pain tethered me to a woman, some mother, I'd left screaming and writhing on the floor. She was not here. She could not be here.

The sedan was pulling up to the front entrance when the Bluetooth chimed in my ear. I answered on the first ring, one hand reaching up robotically to touch the button.

"Hello?"

I could hear Robert making small, snuffling noises. I could hear the breath of the mother who wasn't me, and yet she was the one who held him. It was almost panting, short and shallow. Three breaths and she still had not spoken.

"Hello?" I said again.

"Are you there yet?" She sounded urgent, but also tinnier, farther away. Had they reached her destination? I thought so. The air on the line sounded different. No traffic sounds. At least Robert was no longer rocketing down a highway in her lap. She'd taken him a few minutes before 5:00 P.M., which meant he could be no more than four hours away from me. No, less than that. She'd stopped for at least half an hour to talk with me.

"I am." I closed my eyes.

"You're not!" she insisted, as if she knew. Was the daughter in place already, watching for me, or was she only reacting to the quiet on my end of the line?

"I'm right outside. Getting dropped off now." A tremor had come into my voice. The car had stopped. "Thank you," I told the driver, and got out. Ahead, a group of four men emerged from a dark, sleek sedan, chatting and laughing. Faint music drifted toward me from inside.

"Bree!" someone called, and I waved in their direction, smiling wide.

"On the phone, sec!" I called back, then pointed to my ear to indicate the Bluetooth.

"Oh! Tell Trey we'll miss him tonight." It was Michael something, a young associate.

I nodded and turned away. "You hear?"

"All right, then." They were definitely somewhere else. Not in a car. "Maybe I should stay on the line with you. Listen in."

"No!" I'd pulled Betsy over my raw skin, but now I felt her shell trembling, and my voice shook. Those soft, sleepy baby sounds could crack me. "I'll text as soon as it's done. I can hear . . . I can't . . ." A small hysteria was rising in my voice. I was losing control of what my face was doing. I grabbed the bracelet, pressing it upward, feeling the good dig of it into my arm.

"All right, all right," she said. Her voice was trembling, too. "Go on, then, but remember, my daughter will have eyes on you. You'd best do this thing."

"I promise," I said.

She hung up.

I stood by the curb, head down, clutching my purse, until I was Betsy again, bold and calm. Then I strolled toward the entrance to give the man with the clipboard my name. Saying it felt like a lie.

He checked the list, then smiled. "Have a good time, Mrs. Cabbat."

I hurried through the Botanical Garden's winding paths, passing beds and buildings and huge, living statues made of wire frames covered in plants. They had a medieval theme happening this season, with a twenty-foot-high dragon in a thousand shades of green, leaves overlapping like scales. He faced a flowery knight on a blooming white horse's back.

I wound my way toward the sounds of a jazzy piano and a woman singing, torchy and low. Coming around a curve, I almost ran into a group of people. Three couples, the men in sleek suits, the women in cocktail dresses. I didn't recognize any of them, so they were probably clients.

"Excuse me," I said, passing them.

I was a little out of breath. I made myself slow down. I could not arrive sweaty and tumbled. God, this would be so much easier if Trey were with me. I wouldn't have to work so hard to be a woman who belonged here. Trey pulled me into conversations, his hand resting lightly on my hip, putting me at ease with his coworkers and clients. With him I didn't need Betsy's carte blanche Visa.

He'd always done this for me. His gaze had made me confident from the first time it landed on me. I'd been in the middle of an uncomfortable acting-class assignment, quaking inside, when our paths first crossed.

The assignment sheet said, "Choose a wholly unfamiliar place in which you feel YOU don't belong. Invent a self who does. Dress the part and go there. Interact. Feel it, live it, be it."

Most people in the class made up a new character, but I chose to take Elizabeth and her Visa to Atlanta's High Museum of Art. I'd never even been there on a school field trip. Definitely a place where I did not belong. Not back then. I knew nothing about art history or techniques. I wasn't even sure what kind of art I liked. I walked the halls, shivering, reminding myself that the Visa in my pocket had no limits. I could buy it all and burn it for firewood if I wanted.

That helped, but I still didn't want to "interact." It felt more like lying than theatre. The "audience" would not know that they were inside a performance. But the follow-up paper was a third of my grade. I straightened my shoulders and breezed down a hall, inhabiting Betsy's confident walk, trying to psych myself up to talk to someone. Trey always claimed he'd fallen for me then and there, watching me saunter past him toward a huge abstract painting at the hallway's end.

I used that same walk now, confident and unhurried.

One of the men called after me, "Are we going the right way?"

I smiled over my shoulder. "Sure are. Almost there!"

And we were. Another two turns and I saw the broad green courtyard in front of the Orchid Center. The piano was off to one side, the singer a glamorous forty-something with a jet bob and lipstick as red as her sequined dress.

I passed through the crowds, smiling and greeting people, matching up names with faces, saying the right words, always looking ahead to find Spencer. My husband's coworkers and friends were outlined sharply against the soft light of the paper lanterns strung all across the wide space, as if they'd all been drawn into the scene by CGI. None of them felt real. No realer than I was anyway.

The drugged bourbon in its silver flask, the three extra capsules rattling softly in their bottle—only these things were real. And Spence.

As I circled, I saw the party more clearly than I ever had before. I'd come here at least ten times over the years, but I'd never realized that it had a structure to it. The most important clients and the senior partners were scattered across the courtyard in front of the Orchid Center, this one near the piano, that one by the walk, and the party swirled around them. The more important the person, the less they had to move. Everything they wanted—conversations, little bites of food, drinks, fawning attention—came to them. Lesser beings orbited, looking for an in.

Spence had been right there in the center last year. But of course he'd been married then. The other named partners—and all five were men—each had his wife beside him. Did Spence feel out of place without Charlotte? I felt my heart seize up, cramping in my chest. Surely he hadn't skipped out early.

But no. If Spence had left or no-showed, the daughter would have told the mother.

I'd tried to put the daughter out of my mind. Once I'd thought of her, it was hard not to look for her, even though the mother had warned against it, and there were hundreds of people here. I knew less than half of them.

Would she stand out? I thought so, at least a little bit. If she could blend, they wouldn't need me. She would talk like her mother. Her dress would be wrong. A quick scan of the lawn gave me at least three possibilities: A silent thirty-something standing nearly invisible by a shadowed bench. An older, anxious blonde absentmindedly wringing her hands by the closest bar. A thin woman in a cheap blue dress standing silent at the edge of Mr. and Mrs. Aster's circle.

My gaze slid away as if these women had been coated in Teflon. The compulsion to please the mother was strong, and she'd told me not to look for her daughter. I looked instead for Spencer, but he wasn't up here.

I took the stairs down to the succulent garden. A huge buffet had been set up under the pavilion. Here were lesser clients, associates, and paralegals, all loading up plates with shrimp and tenderloin. On the stairs three young administrative assistants in recycled bridesmaid's dresses hovered, whispering. I made my way through the throng, greeting people but never stopping. I could not get caught up in conversation.

My urgency was rising as the minutes flew. It was hard to stay cool and confident, hard not to run and shove, calling for him. My breezy smile felt tight, almost painful to hold. I could feel that ruined woman in Decatur, feel all the things she held, coming for me.

I pushed on, longing for Trey. With him I would be able to breathe. Under stress he got calmer and more focused. It was part of what made him an excellent lawyer. It was the thing I'd found so immediately attractive when he came up to me that day in the High Museum.

I'd put on an expensive floral sundress I'd borrowed from the costume room. My hair was in a sleek chignon to make me look older, and my makeup was subtle. My sandals were the giveaway, although I didn't know it at the time. They were my own, knockoffs with too many straps. They wouldn't have fooled Trey's sister for a second, but Trey wasn't looking at my shoes.

I stared up thoughtfully at the huge painting of . . . I wasn't sure. It was a white field with bright blobs of color scattered at random, some overlapping as they reached the left edge. I knew that a man had joined me, but I pretended I didn't until he spoke.

"You really seem to like this one."

I glanced over at him. He was tall and thickly built, wearing a beautifully tailored suit. No tie. His sandy hair was freshly cut and gleaming. He was what my mom would call "boyishly handsome," even though he was at least a decade older than me. He stood in the hall like he belonged there. He stood like a man who believed he belonged anywhere.

"Don't you like it?" I asked, near toneless. I was too nervous to risk an opinion.

"Honestly? No." He grinned and added, "I think it looks like an amoeba orgy. And not in the good way."

I hadn't dared to say that I disliked the piece until his joke gave me permission. His ease was palpable, shining, large enough to envelope and include me. I'd laughed out loud.

God, I wanted him here now. Without him this was not my world and these were not my people.

I wound my way through the party back to the stairs, scanning the crowd with growing desperation.

A waitress with a tray of glittering crystal coupes stopped near me and said, "Gimlet?" in a thick southern drawl. I stared at her for a moment. Her black-and-white uniform and her tray made her anonymous.

The daughter! I thought, heart stuttering, convinced. Then I realized that if the daughter were a caterer, she could have dosed Spence at her leisure. I grabbed a drink and drained it. The woman's eyes went wide, but the warmth of the gin was already calming me. I set the empty glass back on her tray.

"Thank you," I said, and started up, conscious of time streaming by. One of the partners, Rick Janeway, was coming down. "Have you seen Spence?" I asked him.

"I saw him a little bit ago," Rick said. "Hey, come down and meet my niece! She's second year at Georgetown, and she's interning with us this summer."

"Sure, just let me grab a drink." I hurried up the stairs, ignoring Rick as he called after me that there was a bar downstairs as well.

My watch said it was already nine-thirty, and the only place I hadn't looked yet was inside the Orchid Center itself. But it was so hot in there. Spence was a big man, thick and florid. He kept his office like an icebox.

I went in anyway, and the humid air seemed to stick inside my lungs. The jazz singer's crooning was cut off by the closing door. Inside, I could hear the low tones of a cello leading a string quartet in the alcove opposite the door.

It was even dimmer inside. I had to wait a moment for my eyes to adjust. I began winding my way through the small rooms and hallways, all lined with stone-walled beds full of thousands of orchids, all shades and shapes, alien and lovely. They hung down in fantastical chains from lattices and arches.

I kept searching, smiling as I passed by the few people who had braved the humidity to see the flowers. I peered through a fall of pink blooms into a dead end and saw a couple in a tight embrace, half sheltered by the plants. His hand was under her short skirt. It was a Spence-type move, but not Spence. It was a paralegal. Chris or Craig. I didn't know the girl. I backed away silently and pressed on.

If Trey were here, he would bellow, "Spence, damn it, olly olly oxen free!" and be so good-humored about it that no one would be affronted by his nonsense.

It had been that way at the High Museum the day we met. He stuck by me as I turned and made my way back down the hall, this time pausing for each of the featured artist's paintings. He paused with me, his tone light as he confessed, "I'm not big on modern art. I want people or animals. Maybe boats. I can really get behind a good boat picture."

I tutted. "Very old-fashioned of you."

"I know. But these look like bad wallpaper to me."

That made me laugh again. We moved on, now in tandem. All the paintings in the hall were similar, white backgrounds with various shapes spattered across the canvas. He made up names as we passed them: *Rainbow McNuggets. The Diatom's Revenge. Dung Takes a Holiday.*

That one got us both giggling, and a stuffy-looking older couple shot us a glare. I grabbed his arm, almost pinching, shushing him, but he wasn't fussed. He put a hand over mine, walking again, my hand now tucked companionably into the crook of his elbow.

I liked the feel of him. Solid and muscular. I could smell some kind of aftershave, spicy and faint, and under that his own warm male smell. I liked that, too. *Interact*, the assignment said, but from the moment I touched him, it wasn't about the assignment anymore. Something real was happening.

We wandered the exhibit, chatting more than looking, until the halls let us out into the tall, round atrium.

He paused there and said, "I worry that that boring exhibition ruined your afternoon."

"Just a little." I smiled up at him.

He said, "Well, my mother is responsible for bringing it here," and for half a beat I was purely horrified. This man had the kind of family who sponsored art exhibits at the High, and I'd just insulted his terribly important mother. Before I could burst into a flaming blush, he added, "I think I owe you a better time. Can I buy you a coffee? A glass of wine?"

It was a pickup line, and a good one. The blush came fainter and for different reasons.

I'd been twenty-one for mere weeks, but I said, "I'd love a glass of wine," like any grown-up might.

"I'm Robert Cabbat. The third, no less. Everyone calls me Trey." He smiled and held his hand out to me.

When I took it, I felt like a piece of me had been waiting for this touch, this day, this man. He stared into my eyes, so frankly interested that I felt both comfortable and wholly myself, a strange juxtaposition; I'd been pretending to be Elizabeth with her Visa for so many years that I actually became her.

"Bree Kroger," I said.

We strolled to a nearby café on the grounds, and he ordered a pale French wine that I didn't know how to pronounce.

His easy conversation had put me more at ease than the alcohol did. He always put me at ease. If Trey were with me now, my job would already be done.

I found a round hub for multiple hallways that I'd seen before and spun slowly, close to despair. I had less than twenty minutes. I caught a flash of movement down one of the narrow paths. I hurried along it, and the familiar shape of Spencer Shaw, his back to me, emerged from the deep shadows at the end.

He had a mostly empty rocks glass in one hand, and he was talking to someone. His big body blocked my view, so I sidestepped, pushing into the plants. It was Gabrielle Baxter, a second-year associate. A standout in the newer hires, according to Trey, destined for the partner track.

She was also very pretty, with warm tones shining in her rich, brown skin, wide-set eyes, and a full mouth. Right now that mouth was twisted into the fakest smile I'd ever seen. Her gaze met mine over Spencer's shoulder, and I read a certain desperation there.

"Spence!" I said, too loud, as if I were tipsy and clueless. He startled, and as he turned toward me, I saw him pull his other hand off her waist. "And Gabrielle! You guys having fun?"

"Yes. It's a great party," Gabrielle said, but her eyes stayed locked on mine. In a language every woman spoke, she was asking me not to leave.

"Bree!" Spence said, smiling. "How's my best guy's best girl?"

He was bluff and hearty, but I had interrupted something that smelled an awful lot like a lawsuit. I was honestly surprised. When another local firm had been nearly destroyed by a series of harassment lawsuits, he'd said, "Even I know better than to shit where I eat," in his typical vulgar fashion.

At the same time, I was almost glad. I was going to drug him, after all, and let the daughter get whatever she needed out of him. Information, documents, some kind of an admission—I had no idea. It might cost Spence and my husband their big case. It could even cost Spence his law license. But even if it hurt Trey or crashed the whole firm and we lost everything, even if we had to move in with his chilly parents, I didn't care. Not considering the stakes. But it did make my job a little easier, to find Spence being such a predatory asshole.

I said to Gabrielle, "I'm glad I ran into you. Rick Janeway is looking for you."

Her smile was grateful. Rick was her direct supervisor. "I better go see what he needs. Please, excuse me?"

Spence didn't move, so she had to scrape her body past his. The contact set her mouth in an angry line.

As soon as she was gone, I whispered, "What was that, Spence?"

He had the grace to look a little bit embarrassed. "What was what?"

I gave him mom eyebrows, stern but much more loving than I

felt toward him. As if he were being nothing more than naughty. "I think you know."

He shrugged, faux sheepish. A boy with his hand in a cookie jar. "I was flirting. I'm six inches from single, so what's the harm?"

"You're her boss, for starters." Still not stern. More amused, though I wanted to smack him. Gabrielle was talented, but he was a named partner and a rainmaker. In a he said/she said, the firm's bottom line would listen to him. At the very least, he owed her an apology. But I had to get him in the mood to have a friendly drink with me, and quickly. Something irreplaceable, more precious than a woman's career or dignity, was at stake here. A life. Robert's life.

He blew out air like a frustrated horse. "Yeah. I know. I do know better. I was talking about the divorce, and she was being sympathetic. . . ." His ruddy cheeks flushed deeper red.

This felt like an opening. "Well, nothing happened, really. Let's have a drink and forget it." If the mother had her way, he would forget a lot of things tonight. And she was going to have her way. I pulled the flask out. "I packed a little of Trey's Pappy. I have a shot left. . . ." I shook it, tempting him with the slosh of it.

Spence blinked owlishly at the flask, and I realized he was drunker than I'd thought. He carried it well, I had to give him that. I held the flask out, my heart hammering, willing him to make this easy. But he shook his head. I paused, surprised and instantly afraid. I'd never seen Spence turn down a drink, least of all a truly high-end bourbon.

"I better not. Was I really out of line with her?"

"Yes," I said truthfully, before I could think better of it. Telling him the truth was the wrong way to get him to keep drinking.

"Shit. It's been a day. I had to meet with Charlotte and her lawyer, and she's being an unmitigated bitch." His mouth crumpled. His eyes looked wet. "Divorce is the worst damn thing. You don't know. You and Trey are lucky."

I wanted to scream at him as he rambled that no, we weren't. I wanted to pinch his nose shut until his mouth popped open and I could pour the bourbon in.

Instead I shrugged, casual. "It's a party. Forget about it. I bet she already has. She was drinking, too. Here, hold out your glass." I started unscrewing the cap.

He waved it away. "I really better not. I think I'm in bad shape, and I have yet to check in on half my clients. God. I better get to it. People are going to start leaving soon." He shook his head, then moved to go past me.

"Wait," I said, desperate. I grabbed his arm. "Want to sober up, fast? I can help with that. I have these pills . . ." The lie came out of nowhere.

"I need some food. And maybe a cup of coffee." He was trying to pull loose.

I shook my head, kept my hand on his arm. "These pills work so much faster. Charcoal pills."

That got his interest. "Charcoal pills? I think I've heard of that. Is it a prescription?"

"No, of course not. It's more like a vitamin. You can get them at CVS." I traded the flask for the pill bottle and rattled the capsules for him, careful to keep my hand over the label. "They line your stomach. They're for if your kid accidentally takes too much medicine or eats a Tide Pod."

This was true. I still had some at home, left over from when Peyton was a toddler on a mission to find something poisonous and shove it into her little pink mouth. Activated charcoal came in capsules much like the ones in the bottle. They were black instead of blue, but it was dark. If he ever saw a real charcoal pill, it wouldn't look that different.

At the same time, this was insanely risky. Hypnodorm, I assumed, would only wreck memories formed after it was in his system. He wouldn't remember the daughter, but he might very well remember me giving him these pills. That might be the last thing he remembered, actually. I had no idea what the mother wanted her girl to get from him, but all I could do was hope he was too drunk to connect it to this moment.

I opened the bottle, dumped the pills into my hand, and then quickly put it away. I was worried he might get it in his head to read the label. I held them out for him. "I bring them to parties in case I overdo it. A couple of these babies and I'm good to drive."

This was pure fantasy. Activated charcoal didn't absorb alcohol.

"They really work?"

"Sure," I said. "I mean, it isn't a miracle or anything, but they'll undo a couple of drinks."

I could see a faint shaking in my hand. I hoped he wouldn't notice.

Spence was interested. "I take three?"

God, I didn't want to hurt him. Roofies could interact with alcohol. Dangerously. Google had said so.

I said, "I usually take two."

I almost whispered it, hiding the words under the moan of the distant cello, in case the daughter was nearby. She might be hiding in the curvy paths of the Orchid Center, waiting to take Spence in hand. I said it as a sop to guilt, even as I rendered him helpless for a woman who wished him ill. And truthfully, I would have done much worse than this to Spence. To anyone. To save Robert.

"Yeah, but you weigh what? A buck-twenty?" He grabbed all three out of my hand and popped them into his mouth, then washed them down with the dregs of his drink.

I was instantly so relieved it made me dizzy. I felt myself sway, putting one hand on an arch to steady myself.

"Easy there, hon!" he said, smiling. "Maybe *you* needed those pills."

I smiled back, light-headed. I had obeyed, fully, and whatever happened now, my part was finished. I would get Robert back. She had promised. I was woozy with joy and a thousand other, fainter feelings: guilt and worry and mistrust and a sick, sick fear.

I said, "I took a Lyft here, no worries."

He smiled. "Then you can drink that Pappy. I'm jealous, but I need to go butter some clients. I haven't so much as said hello to the Clausens, and you better believe I will hear about it from Jim Astor if they escape before I do." He turned to go, lumbering up the narrow path. At the turn he paused. "Thanks, Bree. You and Trey, you always have my back."

Then he was gone. My spine sagged. I almost sat down right there on the hard stone floor. I leaned against the arch instead, digging in my purse for the cheap phone. The mother had told me to text her as soon as I got the pills down Spence, but I wanted to call. I wanted to hear my son breathing or eating or even crying.

There was only one number in the contacts. *Robert.* I stared at his name, as if the letters could bring me closer to him. I would have him soon, back in my arms. Tomorrow, she'd said. I pressed the message icon instead of the call button. I wanted to do everything perfectly. The hard part was over. I could not mess up now.

It's done.

It took an endless span of seconds for her to answer. I could see the dot-dot-dot in the window. My heart was still pounding, and I still felt dizzy, but I could not fall apart. Not yet. Not until I had him back.

Good. Now go home.

I didn't move. I couldn't. Not without more assurance.

When will you give him back? I felt my body shivering.

When it's finished. Go home.

I couldn't tell if she was being reassuring or threatening, or if she was scared, like me. The words could be read as cold, but I remembered the tremble in her voice. Her own child was here, up to something risky. The daughter had to intercept Spence now, tempt him away from the crowd. The mother had to be so frightened for her child. We were alike in this.

My clammy hands texted, I understand. I will get out of your daughter's way. But please, can you please tell me when I'll get Robert back?

STOP TEXTING ME AND GO HOME. I'll call you in the morning.

I felt my head shake back and forth. The morning was a thousand years from now. She'd said "tomorrow" from the start. But I had done what she asked, and I wanted Robert now.

Then a wild hope rose. What if the instructions for getting him back were at my house already? She could have left them there, the way she'd left the phone and the bottle of pills, hanging on my door. She could be setting Robert himself down in my backyard, his infant carrier crushing the basil plants by the window where I'd first seen her. It was a crazy thought, but that didn't change the effect. All at once I was moving, almost running, flushed with new urgency. Roofies worked fast. Ten minutes, fifteen, Google said. I had to get out, get home, and not see the face of the woman who came to gather up a reeling, slurring Spence. If the mother thought I was a threat to her child, she'd be a threat to mine.

I hurried toward the exit, shoving her phone back into my purse and grabbing for my own so I could summon a Lyft. I went blind around a corner and barreled into a man. We had to grab onto each other to keep from falling.

"Excuse me," I said, and at the same time, he said, "Sorry."

A familiar voice.

Marshall Chase stared down at me, surprised, and then his eyebrows pushed together and his steadying hand clamped onto my arm in a squeeze.

"Are you fucking kidding me?" he said.

7

A WOMAN BANGED into Marshall, throwing him off balance. His arms went around her, he inhaled sharply, and he knew instantly that it was Bree. He smelled her roses, not heavy or overly sweet. Roses undercut with earth and herbs that deepened the scent, the way good bitters deepened whiskey.

He'd had a few, so when they steadied, he wasn't altogether sure who had caught whom. He stared down into her shocked, pale face.

"Are you fucking kidding me?" The words popped out. He'd been thinking about how not to think about her, and here she was, in his arms.

She pulled free, surprised and maybe angry, tottering on precariously high heels that put them almost eye to eye. "Are you following me?"

Marshall blinked. "Am I what? I came in to get out of the crowd for a minute. What are you doing here?" Right exactly here, bowling him over.

She swiped a hand through the air, as if shooing him, then pushed past him, heading out of the building. "I can't talk to you."

He fell into step beside her, a wobble in his turn. He wasn't drunk, but he sure as hell wasn't sober. Now that there was a safe distance between her body and his, he remembered she'd told him she was sick. So sick that just this afternoon she'd cussed and yelled and threatened him to make him drive her girls. Now here she was at the party.

"Okay, well, can I do anything else for you today? Shine your shoes? Clean out your litter box?" He was ragging on her a little, buzzed enough to revert back to the old friend that he was.

She sped up, saying, "I have to get home."

Why was she here? He'd come because it was expected, and the food was always good, and it would fill the time with Cara out of town. It was better than sitting home alone thinking about Bree's odd behavior, and the curve of her hip, and the way her face had lit up with love today when she saw Cara. He'd assumed she would be home in bed. But here she was.

"Did you get the kind of flu that comes in waves?"

Again he was razzing her, but she wheeled instantly to face him. She put both hands on his chest, and then she shoved him. Hard. It rocked him back a step.

Marshall wasn't sure what shocked him more, the underlying unkindness of the jokes he'd made or that she'd laid such furious hands on him. He rubbed at his mouth, as if his words had galloped out without permission and now he didn't want to let out more.

"That was offsides," he said. And stupid, because he hadn't minded driving her girls at all.

Bree glared at him like she wanted nothing more than to punch him in the face. "Yes, it was." He started to apologize, but angry words came pouring out of her, unstoppable. "Why are you being such a shit to me?" Her voice was raw, a forced, furious whisper. "For weeks now you've cold-shouldered me, and you have no idea the unending hell this day has been. When I called you this afternoon, I treated you badly, I know, but God . . . I'm . . . I . . . I feel so fucking terrible." He felt the curse words like more shoves. Betsy had had a filthy mouth and a wonderfully filthy mind to match, but even in high school Bree only cussed in extremis. She stepped in so close that her earthy rose smell enveloped him again. "I'm a person, Marshall. Full of blood and organs and feelings, and I don't live my whole life trying to make yours suck more. You think I want to be here? I want to be home, with my kids. All three of them. That's all I want. That's all I want."

She stopped abruptly and turned away, shoving open the exit door. There was a moment of discordance, the cello moaning behind them and the torchy singer crooning along with the piano on the lawn ahead. The warm spring air felt cold as he followed her out of the humid orchid house.

He was thinking about Cara now, at the start of third grade. She'd been cute as a Muppet, all snappy brown eyes and skinny legs and corkscrew hair. A boy who sat behind her kept pinching her arm when she wouldn't talk to him in class.

"He probably likes you," Marshall said, and Bets had surreptitiously pinched the back of *his* arm, her face gone fierce.

She told their daughter, "If that's how he shows he likes you, Cara, then that right there is a little turd boy who thinks the world owes him a girl who likes him back." Cara wanted to move seats, and Betsy had shut that down, too. "You don't move. He moves. I'll go with you, but you have to talk to your teacher. We will sit down with her, and you will tell her what is happening. That boy has to learn that if he lays hands on a girl, there are consequences."

Then she'd stopped talking, her eyes so angry. Not with him. With the world. She was mad that she'd lied to their daughter. They were both cops. They knew how often boys laid hands on girls, consequence-free. Only a few months later, a man who believed he had the right to beat his wife to death had taken Betsy from them.

He still thought she'd been right to say it. He never wanted his daughter to think love excused poor treatment. Worse, he was letting his lonely, bitter heart turn him into that kind of man. He didn't want to be the guy who said bitchy things to a woman he was attracted to because he couldn't have her. Not even a little.

His silly crush wasn't Bree's fault, or her problem. It was not her fault he was lurking around in the orchid house to escape party small talk. Not her fault she'd accidentally rammed into him.

"I really am sorry," he said quietly.

"Fine." She kept walking, fast, zooming across the green, weaving through the crowd.

He stuck with her. "No, really. I've had a couple, not that that's a good excuse." He'd never thought about how the ways he tried to keep his distance might read to her. "I've been shitty to you for a while, huh? Believe me, it's not about you. I have some stuff to work out." That was true enough.

Her anger seemed to be receding. She paused and put a hand on his arm to pause him and looked up into his face, serious.

"Forget about it. Okay? It's fine. We're fine." She turned and hurried off again, clearly finished with the conversation.

Except . . .

She was drowning. He hadn't seen it when she was cursing at him, angry. But in that single, soft forgiving glance, he knew. Even buzzed, he could feel his old invisible cop antennae quivering.

He'd seen drowning eyes like Bree's before. A dozen-plus years back, when he was still in uniform and he and his partner took a routine noise-disturbance call. Someone had heard a scream inside a ground-floor apartment in a nice working-class neighborhood. He knocked, and a girl came to the door.

She was a cute little thing, fourteen tops, her hair in braids. She told them that everything was fine, smiling as wide as the Minnie Mouse on her T-shirt. But her eyes were deep, dark wells. She'd seen a spider, she said. She was sorry, she said. She promised to keep it down.

The second the door closed, he called for backup, and then he kicked open the door and he and his partner busted a serial who had raped eleven girls and women in their own homes. That asshole had been right behind the door with his knife pressing into the girl's spine the whole time she was smiling and saying how afraid she was of spiders.

That was the bust that had taught him to follow his instincts. It had also gotten him his detective's shield.

Bree's eyes over her smile had been as shadowed as that little girl's. Still, he hesitated. Maybe he wanted her to be in distress, damsel style, so he could save her. She'd made it pretty clear that she was finished with the conversation.

She was passing Trey's secretary now, Janice, who reached out to take her arm. Bree shrugged her off, pressing onward, and in the bright, apologetic smile she gave Janice, Marshall saw something purely ghastly.

"Fuck it," he muttered, and he hurried after her.

8

I WENT BACK to the same shaded path I had taken in. It was narrow and secluded, hemmed by arches of hanging vines. I hadn't called for my Lyft yet, though my phone was in my hand. Marshall had distracted me. I hurried forward a few feet, letting the darkness swallow me. If the daughter was watching me, she would think I was leaving the party, obedient. Then I paused to work the app.

"You're calling a car service?" Marshall asked behind me in the darkness. I almost jumped out of my skin. "I'd offer you a ride, but I've got no business driving. Cara is at her friend's lake house all weekend, and I've kinda tied one on."

"I don't mind Lyft," I told him. The car was on its way. Fifteen minutes. Hopefully, if the daughter was leading Spencer someplace secluded, or even off the grounds entirely, she would choose another path. There were so many.

"I want to ask . . ." Marshall's voice trailed off. Whatever it was, it was difficult for him.

"What?" I had time to listen. It was better than waiting alone with my thoughts. I might go mad. I would have Robert back, tomorrow at the latest, but I wasn't sure how I'd survive this night.

Behind him, back up the path, I saw Spencer Shaw and the

Clausens at a small bar on the edge of the green closest to us. I froze, feeling my eyes go wide and my mouth tighten. Marshall turned to see what had dismayed me.

Spencer passed a white wine to Mrs. Clausen. The daughter was not with them. No one was, unless I counted the bartender. I didn't. He was male. The three of them stepped away and stood in a triangle shape, chatting.

Marshall stared from me to Spencer Shaw's group with way too many questions rising in his eyes.

I wasn't sure exactly how much time had passed since I'd dosed Spence, but roofies worked fast. He could start reeling and slurring any minute. He already didn't look good. Sweaty and pale. He took a white linen handkerchief out of his pocket and mopped at his brow.

I was afraid to leave. Maybe something had gone wrong. If the daughter couldn't get Spencer off alone, would I be blamed?

Marshall said, "Bree, are you okay?"

It shocked me that this conversation with Marshall kept on happening. Life kept on happening. Robert had been brutally taken from me, and yet here, on the green, Spence was clapping Mr. Clausen's shoulder, a singer was crooning, waiters were passing signature gimlets and snacks. People were eating and gossiping and going to the bathroom and breathing in and out. It was wrong and crazy. I wanted everything to stop. I wanted the daughter to complete her business. I wanted my son.

"I'm fine," I said.

Marshall said, "Something's off. Talk to me."

A female figure turned onto our small path, blocking my view. The light was behind her, making her a curvy silhouette. My heart leaped up into my throat. Was it the daughter, come to shoo me home?

I grabbed Marshall's arm, saying, "Shhhh," trying to drag him backward.

"What are you . . . ?" he said.

I let go, ready to run for the entrance, my heart galloping, but the woman called out, "Bree?"

I recognized her voice. It was Gabrielle Baxter.

Gabrielle was not the daughter. She couldn't be. I'd met her parents at a party. They were black and sophisticated and quite well-off. The old woman I'd seen was white, and she didn't have a posh, rich-person's accent. Plus, the mother had told me they'd been unable to get in to see Spence. Gabrielle saw him every day.

"Are you hiding from Gabrielle?" Marshall whispered.

"No."

As she came to join us, I shifted so I could still see Spence. He was trying to charm the Clausens, leaning in to tell an animated story, but he looked downright sick now. He paused and swayed, and Mr. Clausen looked concerned. God, I hoped I hadn't over-dosed him.

"Hey, Marshall," Gabrielle said.

"Evening, Gabrielle." Marshall took his puzzled glance off me to greet her with an easy smile.

She turned to me. "I've been looking for you. Janice said you were heading out this way. I'm so glad I caught you."

"I can't stay. I'm on the way to meet my Lyft."

"I only need a minute." She looked anxious.

This was about Spence, I thought, my heart sinking. It had to be.

I had a sudden urge to tell her, *Don't sweat it. I just roofied him, and however uncomfortable he made you feel, I bet something worse is coming for him.*

"Maybe tomorrow you could call me," I said instead. "If you want to talk privately."

Marshall asked, "Should I give you two a minute?"

"No," Gabrielle said. She touched his arm lightly. "Marshall knows."

They were friends, I realized with a small shock. Marshall, who had gotten colder and colder toward me, was close with Gabrielle.

"Oh, this is about . . ." Marshall inclined his head back toward Spence, who was now waving an expansive hand a little too close to Mrs. Clausen's face. He looked like he was assuring them that he was fine. He did not look fine.

Gabrielle nodded. "She saw. So it isn't my word against his anymore." She turned back to me, chin up, almost challenging me, her hands twisting together. "If you're willing to back me up, that is."

If Marshall knew, then the inappropriate behavior I had seen in the Orchid Center was not an isolated incident. I ought to be shocked by this, and outraged, determined to make it stop. If Gabrielle made partner, she would be only the third woman to reach that pinnacle. The first African-American woman. Spence was putting all that at risk, using his seniority in ways that made me sick. If she spoke out, the blame would fall on her. Even post-#MeToo, the good-ol'-boy network was strong at old, established firms like this one. But right now I was busy watching Spence for my own reasons. Tomorrow, once Robert was safe home, I would care.

Gabrielle, her voice fierce, said, "This stuff with Spence, it's all him. He started it after things got bad with Charlotte. I want you to know I never flirted with him to get ahead, I never—" She broke off, but I knew what she meant.

"Of course not. I never thought that," I assured her. I should help her, but all I wanted was to get away and look at the cheap phone, see if the mother had texted me some new instructions. She might need me to intervene and separate Spence from the Clausens. I had to make sure all went well for them, so that it would go well for Robert. "But I can't really talk about this now."

Her lips curved down, and she blinked. Disappointed but not surprised. Spence worked so closely with my husband that talking to me at all had been a risk. Now she thought I was shutting her down, taking his side.

Marshall saw it, too. "Bree will back you. She's just sick," he explained. For all that he'd been so cold, he knew me well enough to know this and to vouch for me. It did my aching heart some good.

"Oh. Nothing serious, I hope?" Now she wasn't sure what to think.

"Just a bug. But I'm desperate to get home," I said. "Can we talk next week?"

She glanced at Marshall, and then she smiled, genuine. "Yes. I'd appreciate that."

I smiled back as best I could. The world refused to stop spinning, and all these things did matter. I simply couldn't care about them now.

Movement from the green. I looked back to Spence in time to see him double over in a fast, jerky spasm. He looked like a puppet with all his top strings cut. He vomited, violently, splashing Mrs. Clausen's shoes. She let out a loud cry and stepped back. Behind them the party was a moving backdrop, people turning and shifting, trying to see what was happening.

Gabrielle and Marshall stared, too. She froze, but Marshall started toward them. Lightning fast, my hand shot out and grabbed his arm.

"No!" I said. I should never have given Spencer all three capsules.

Spence straightened, but he could not keep his balance. He went reeling sideways, with Mr. Clausen reaching out almost comically, bounding forward to try to catch him. Spence slammed into the small bar. Bottles tumbled and fell in a chiming of glass on glass, and the bartender scrabbled, trying to catch them and right them.

A great wave of voices welled up from the party, people coalescing and hurrying forward. Spence spun and vomited again in a great, gushing arc that sent the Clausens and the bartender scuttling. It stopped the crowd. Spence staggered sideways, then went crashing to the ground.

A moment of near silence. Even the piano jangled to a discordant stop, the singer cutting off in mid-croon. Then everyone surged forward toward him again.

Mrs. Clausen called out, "Someone help!"

Mr. Clausen yelled, "Who here is a doctor?"

"Oh my God," Gabrielle said.

Dr. Charles, a longtime client, and another man I didn't know pushed out of the crowd and ran to Spence. Dr. Charles started barking orders over the hum of anxious voices, telling everyone to stay back.

"I should—" Marshall started.

"Stay with me!" I clutched his arm harder. Gabrielle paused, too.

A few people worked to hold back the others, one man bellowing, "Give the doctors room!"

Spence was thrashing, bucking and seizing, and more vomit spewed up from his mouth. It was brown and red, and red foam bubbled after from his lips. Was that blood? It was so bright against his pale skin, the green grass.

Dr. Charles and the other man turned him on his side to keep him from choking, one of them yelling more words that I couldn't understand.

"Oh my God," Gabrielle said again.

This was not an overdose. Nothing like. An overdose of roofies meant sleepiness. Unconsciousness. Maybe nausea, but not like this. Not these violent shudders and seizures, this eruption of bloody foam. Google would have mentioned this.

Which meant he was allergic? But I didn't believe that. My heart was telling me a darker truth.

Whatever I had given him, it wasn't roofies.

The mother had lied. Her daughter had never intended to get Spence alone. Maybe she wasn't even here. Or maybe she was, either in a cocktail dress moving with the crowd, or all in black standing on one of the bridges that looked down on the gardens, or hidden on a quiet, shady path, like me. Watching. Making sure.

On the grass Spence went suddenly still. So very still.

Dr. Charles was seeking a pulse now, and then he was barking more orders. He was facing away, so his words were lost to me, but he and the other man rolled Spence onto his back. Dr. Charles started chest compressions, and I saw Spence's blood-streaked face. His eyes stared up at the paper lanterns, blank and unblinking, as shiny as sea glass.

Panicked conversation swelled, the crowd edging forward, pushed from behind. Several people had their phones out. Calling 911, I hoped. I hoped not filming.

"Back up!" I heard a man yell in a high, frightened tone. "Please back up and give him room!"

"Is he breathing?" a woman called out. "Is he . . . is he . . ." She couldn't finish the sentence.

But Gabrielle could. "Is he dead?"

Watching the doctor's desperate chest compressions shaking Spencer's big body, watching his slack and unresponsive face, I knew the answer.

And I had handed him the pills. Whatever they'd been. Even now, tucked safe in my purse, I had the silver flask, monogrammed with my husband's initials, sloshing with whiskey I'd dosed with the same toxin.

"Oh God, oh God, oh God," I heard someone saying, and it was me. Everything the mother had told me was a lie, and what did this mean for Robert?

I found myself backing away, tugging Marshall and Gabrielle both with me. His gaze on mine was searching.

Gabrielle, concerned, said, "Bree?"

I shook my head. I had no control over my twisting features. The invisible Visa in my purse was gone and, with it, Betsy's bold and breezy smile. I'd killed Spencer. The woman who'd orchestrated it still had my baby.

"Bree?" Marshall echoed.

I let them both go. I was fumbling in my purse now. I pulled out the phone she'd left for me.

Nothing. No text, no missed calls.

I scrabbled farther, until my fingers found the cash I'd tucked into the bottom.

"I need help," I said to Marshall. I pulled out a bill. I wasn't sure what it was, even, but it was legal tender. I turned to Gabrielle and thrust it at her. "And, God, I need a lawyer."

She was still staring at Spence's inert form, stretched out heavy on the green lawn, but the money was in her peripheral vision. It trembled and wavered, and it took me a moment to understand that this was because my hand was shaking.

I'd been married to a lawyer long enough to know that if I told her about dosing Spence, privilege would not apply. We were at a cocktail party, on a dark path winding through shadowed beds and huge living statues. Any number of unseen ears could be nearby. We had no expectation of privacy. So I held the money out like a promise to be honest later, hoping she would help me.

She looked to Marshall first, silently asking something. I found myself looking at him, too, my eyes begging him to trust me. Betsy had, all her life.

"I don't know what it's about," he told her. "But . . ." He glanced at me and then gave Gabrielle a short, sharp nod. Again, it felt so good to be this known, this trusted by him.

She took the bill. "Okay. I'm your lawyer. Let's get out while we can and go someplace where we can talk."

We turned and hurried up the path to the exit. My Lyft was just arriving. We all got in, and as we sped away, I heard sirens in the distance. Coming for Spence, I thought. An ambulance or paramedics on a fire truck sent to help him.

Too late.

9

WE SAT IN silence the whole way home, Gabrielle, then me, then Marshall in a row in the backseat of the dark sedan. I could feel the tension in their bodies, a thousand silent questions pushing in on me from both sides.

I was going to answer those questions, too. All of them. As soon as we were alone. I'd stopped acting out of panic and blind obedience. Now I was thinking, deciding, and a vast black calm settled over me. The mother had lied about the pills. Maybe about everything. I could not face the conclusions I was drawing by myself.

I checked my messages. Mom had texted to ask if I'd seen Peyton's cell phone. The simple query made my heart twist. It was so precisely Peyton, a quiz-bowl MVP who never forgot a fact but could not remember where she'd put her phone, or her shoes, or even the Burt's Bees lip balm she claimed she'd die without. Anna-Claire had texted, too, telling me to check her Insta if I wanted to see the cookies. I had an immediate, fierce longing to feel my girls tucked up against me, one on either side, smelling of sugar and vanilla and coconut shampoo. But for now I needed them safe at Mom's.

Trey had texted, too. He'd talked to both girls. Stomach flu! No wonder I haven't heard from you. Rest up and feel better. Call me in the morning. Love you.

In the front seat, our young driver whispered into a headset, the nothing-talk of the newly in love. Something about a movie, but I could tell by the tone that the subject didn't matter. They only wanted to be talking to each other.

Trey and I had been like that, once upon a time. Every happy couple has that phase. For us it happened fast. He was so easy to talk to that the glass of wine led to a dinner date, then a play with drinks after. We made the world bigger for each other. He liked to feed me things I'd never tried before: marrow, quail, unpasteurized French cheeses. His theatre experience was limited to sleeping through *Phantom* until I introduced him to Pearl Cleage, Sam Shepard, Tom Stoppard. I was playing Babe in *Crimes of the Heart* at school, and he came to see me. Twice.

Once we started sleeping together, I was lost. I'd had a couple of serious boyfriends, but neither of them had ever seemed to know if sex was good for me or not. Trey? Trey tried things and asked things, until he knew. Sex felt like something he was inventing for me. I abandoned my dorm room, commuting from his bachelor apartment up in Buckhead, addicted.

In the wake of it, my body languorous and so sated I felt as stretchy and abandoned as a cat, we would whisper back and forth. I got a pretty clear picture of the life he wanted.

Kids topped the list. At least two, and soon. He was thirty-three, and he wanted to have them young enough to camp and ski and scuba-dive with them. He imagined a big Buckhead house with an outdoor kitchen. Family dinners, game nights, summers at a second home on Tybee. He worried that he wouldn't get these things with me.

"You're so young," he said over and over. At the museum, with my updo and understated makeup, he'd thought I must be twenty-five at least. "So young and so damn talented."

I was supposed to move to New York to pursue acting after

graduation, but the more time I spent with him, the sillier it seemed. New York had been Betsy's plan. In high school, and then at Georgia State, she'd spun tales of how we'd rent someone's walk-in closet, sleep in bunk beds, eat Top Ramen. We'd waitress, covering each other's shifts for auditions, until we got our breaks. I was holding on to a future she'd invented. One that she'd already lost interest in.

She and Marshall had been married two years by then. They'd finished the police academy and had full-time jobs and an apartment. They were grown-ups, talking about trying for a kid of their own. Watching them together, happy and bonded, taught me that the shape of love changed inside a marriage, but not necessarily for the worse. It could deepen. Get better and sweeter. They were building something real.

The things Trey wanted started sounding real to me as well. Real, but very specific. I wasn't sure if he would shift his detailed dreams enough to make them ours. I started editing them, out loud. Yes to a big house with an outdoor kitchen, but not in Buckhead. I'd met his family by then and felt their chill. I wanted Decatur, which was artsier and, back then, more diverse. Yes, hell yes, to kids, and yes to Robert Evan Cabbat IV, if we had a boy. But no to Ireland for a girl. I liked classic names: Eleanor, Rose, Claire. Also, I thought a Tybee house would tie us down. I wanted to travel, show our kids the world and see it myself. He liked my ideas, and our dreamy whispers started to sound more like plans. When he asked me, I said yes.

It had been such a good call. Sixteen years in and we loved each other still, rock solid. The spark of attraction between us waned at times, but it always flared again, strong and bright and somehow grounding. He was a great dad, patient and good-humored.

But in the quiet darkness of the Lyft sedan, listening to the young driver whisper nonsense with his lover, I was thinking clearly. About Spence, and the mother and her daughter, and lies, and my husband's job. Trey and Spence worked together on almost every case they did. Whatever Spence had done, Trey must have known about it. Maybe Trey had helped.

I'd push the thought away, only to have my husband's beloved face rise up again in my mind. Questions rose with it, brand-new and ugly.

What did you do?

And worse. *What will it cost us?*

We pulled into my driveway. I hustled Marshall and Gabrielle inside, then sent them on through to the great room and did a lap around my house, making sure all the blinds were closed. I had no idea where the daughter was. She might still be at the party, or off to meet her mother, or living some unimaginable life of her own. She would not be coming back here to watch me, though. I was terribly afraid that there was no reason to watch me anymore. I closed the blinds anyway, praying I was wrong.

The second I joined them, Marshall and Gabrielle began asking questions, talking over each other. I talked loudest. The words pushed out of me, silencing them.

"I killed him." Or the mother had, with my help. I wasn't sure. I wasn't even sure there was a difference. I didn't care right now, though surely there would be a reckoning for this. One day. Now all I could care about was Robert.

Whatever Marshall and Gabrielle had been expecting me to say, this wasn't it. Marshall's whole body jerked, as if I'd given him a small electric shock.

She asked, "You did what?" her disbelief writ large.

"I killed Spencer Shaw," I said, to be completely clear. Once that was out, the rest came fast, as if I had a million rancid words trapped in me and my admission released them. I started from the moment I'd first seen her, dreaming that a witch was peering in our bedroom window.

When I got to the part where she took Robert, Marshall's eyes widened, as if it had just occurred to him to wonder where my baby was. Or perhaps he was realizing he'd been in the building when my boy was taken. Gabrielle's hand came up to cover her mouth, pressing hard. She looked to Marshall, but he was staring at me, his lips gone white. When our eyes met, his were so, so sorry.

I kept on, telling them about the gift bag, the pills, my fraught phone conversations with the mother. We'd settled around the breakfast table, but as I talked, Marshall got up and began banging about in my cabinets searching for all the things he needed to make coffee. Gabrielle got out her phone and began rapid-fire thumb-typing into it. I wasn't sure if she was texting or taking notes, but it was clear that she was listening intensely, even though she didn't look up from her screen. It was easier without their eyes on me.

As the coffeepot burbled, Marshall gathered all the objects I'd told them about, first dumping the phone, the charging cord, the empty pill bottle, and the dosed flask out of my purse.

When I got to the part where I found Spence trapping Gabrielle in the Orchid Center, his hand on her hip, Marshall and Gabrielle exchanged a speaking glance. I pressed on as Marshall picked up the drifts of colored tissue paper, still scattered on the floor by my built-in desk, and tucked them back into the gaudy gift bag. He returned all this to the table as well. I plucked the Bluetooth from my ear, then set it beside the phone.

Now all the things the mother had given me were clustered in the center of the table. Marshall sat down on my other side, and the three of us huddled around the pile as I spoke, as if it were a tiny campfire on the coldest, darkest night of the year. I reached out and powered down the Bluetooth, then made sure the ringer was on. If she called, I'd want her on the speaker.

If. That word almost cracked the icy quiet that had come over me in the car. I didn't let it. My whole life was hinged on that short word. *If* she called, I needed to be clear and calm and perfect.

And if she didn't? That was an abyss that made me put the word away.

Even thinking it might be a cosmic betrayal. Not just of Robert or my hope in his small heartbeat. It felt like a betrayal of the mother herself, as if my doubt could reverberate through the universe and make her call her daughter back and throw away her own burner phone.

The phones were our only concrete connection, but there was another, stranger cord. Our sick intimacy echoed still, and even though I understood now how much she'd lied, I still believed in it. Perhaps because it was the only hope I had.

She'd promised to call in the morning, and it wasn't even midnight. I would not break yet.

I'd come to the place in the story where Gabrielle had found Marshall and me on the path to the Botanical Garden's exit. "And the rest you know. You saw what those capsules did to him."

Gabrielle looked up from her screen, the set of her pretty face so very serious. "How do you know it was the pills? Maybe it was a seizure."

Marshall shook his head. "That would be one hell of a coincidence."

I agreed with him. "Whatever she gave me, it wasn't roofies. It was meant to kill him."

Marshall glanced at the silver flask. "We'll find out. The cops can test the bourbon."

Instantly and urgently, my hand was on his arm. "We're not calling the cops."

He looked surprised. "We have to. This is way above my pay grade. Unless you think we should go straight to the FBI?"

"No!" My only chance was to wait for the call. Either the phone would ring or it was already too late for the police or the FBI or any force on earth to help me. I sat inside the black calm that had come over me in the car, waiting to know which way to tip.

"She's right," Gabrielle told Marshall. "No police until we talk to a criminal lawyer. I have a friend, Leticia Marks. She's excellent. I should call her."

"No point," I said. She still didn't understand, or she wouldn't be talking about these things that mattered not at all.

"Of course there's a point. It's to protect you!" Gabrielle's phone buzzed softly in her hands, and she glanced down at it. Her lips compressed, and when she looked up, she was close to crying. "I just heard from Rick Janeway. He followed the ambulance, and I've been texting with him. I didn't tell him anything about you, of course. Just asking for updates. He's with Spencer's brother. Bree, he's dead. Spence is dead."

I'd known already. I'd seen his slack face, his eyes glossy and blank. His body had had a boneless nonresistance as Dr. Charles had pumped at his chest. But still the confirmation hit me like a blow to the chest, caving my shoulders in. God, but the mother was ruthless. And she had Robert at her mercy.

"I really did believe that they were roofies," I told Gabrielle.

"Of course you did!" Gabrielle said. "But dosing someone with roofies is damn sure illegal. I think you've tripped the felony-murder rule. You didn't set out to kill him, but you did agree to drug him. He died during the commission of a crime, and that can be first-degree murder."

"I don't care," I said, fierce. "I just want Robert."

"I know. I know that. But I'm your lawyer. I have to think about you."

They still didn't understand. I could see it in their faces. I said, "She took Robert, out of every baby in the world. She had me kill Spence. Me. Me specifically."

Marshall stood abruptly, and I could almost see my words reverberating in him. "You think she picked Robert because he's Trey's son. Trey and Spence are partners. You think this is about some case that they worked on together."

I nodded. "I think that was the plan all along. Two birds, one stone. I was just the stone." There had to be a reason I'd been chosen as the weapon. *You married who you married*, the mother had told me. Again I thought to Trey, *What did you do?*

Gabrielle had been acting as my lawyer, but my words turned

her human again. She pressed her hand against her mouth once more.

Marshall was seeing the whole picture now, same as me. "Jesus. You think Robert is already—"

He did not finish the sentence. I was glad. I could not bear to hear the end, not yet. Not while there was still that small "if."

I said, "I still think she'll call, Marshall. But not if we bring the police in. She has her own kid to protect. So we sit tight."

A horrifying surge of pity crossed Gabrielle's face. Marshall turned away to walk over to the coffeepot. He did not want me to see what he was thinking. But I knew. They both were thinking it: The mother had never meant to give Robert back. A foolish corner of my heart hoped she'd drive my baby far away, give him to some nice childless couple in Canada. If he was alive, if he was cared for and loved, that would be enough. But if she hated Trey as much as she had hated Spencer, she would not risk us ever finding our boy. She played for keeps.

Marshall and Gabrielle believed now that Robert was already dead. But they had not talked to her. I had. I'd felt that small, strange chain running from me to her and back again, connecting us. Her family was much like mine when I was growing up. Just a mother and a daughter, barely getting by in the small-town South. I'd told her so. I'd known how to speak her language. Our connection was real.

She'd engineered Spencer's murder and she'd stolen Trey's son, but he was my son, too, and she *liked* me. It was too frail and slim and stupid a hope to say out loud, but I still felt tied to her, and whatever was between us felt unfinished. Anyway, it was the only hope I had.

Marshall came back and gave me a coffee mug. The ceramic felt boiling hot, and so did his fingers. He said, "Your hands are ice."

I set the mug down. "I don't want this."

"Drink it anyway. You need it. And so do I." He went back

to the coffeepot, and I heard him tell Gabrielle, "I think she's in shock."

I drank. The coffee had so much milk it was cool enough to bolt, and it was loaded with sugar. I drained half the cup. This was how I used to drink it in high school, senior year, when Marshall and Betsy and I would study late nights at Waffle House. I hadn't actually liked the taste of coffee then.

He came back with two more mugs and handed one to Gabrielle. He sat down again beside me, and his eyes were so kind. I recognized my old friend. Betsy's husband. All that cool reserve was gone. I let myself sag onto his shoulder, and he put his arm around me. He smelled like cedarwood and coffee and the past.

Marshall said, "Okay. If this is about a case that Trey and Spencer did, why bring you into it? Why not make Trey do the dirty work?"

I'd thought about this, too. "I haven't any idea how well, if at all, she knows Trey, but she knows men like him, like his father. The system works for them. Trey would call his father and the cops and the FBI and the governor. I think she had me pegged for a spoiled rich girl, but I'm also a mother. She put her money on me. It was a good bet."

I finished the coffee in another long, shuddering pull, hungry for any kind of sweetness.

Gabrielle was trying to get her cool and analytical attorney face back on. She almost had it. Lawyers, the kind who saw the insides of courtrooms, were like actors. They could be the job, tell the story, play the part. Most of Trey's colleagues worked on contracts and settlements, never getting out of a conference room. Gabrielle shared Trey's ability to litigate. It was one reason she was such an up-and-comer.

She asked, "Why not kill Spence herself and then take the baby. Do it all on her own?"

I thought this was rhetorical, Gabrielle thinking out loud, but I knew the answer. Knew it in my gut, and this was more proof, wasn't it? That the mother and I were in some real way still connected?

"Because she's sick—dying. She told me she won't live to see the end of summer, so I'm not sure she could have. Physically. And she's trying to keep her daughter's hands clean."

Marshall shook his head. "Wouldn't felony murder apply to the daughter, too?"

Gabrielle shrugged. "Oh, hell yeah, and accessory to kidnapping. The daughter is in it up to her neck, but they might not understand the law. Plus, a prosecutor would have to prove in court that the daughter staked you out or actively helped another way. No one has a legal obligation to report a crime, even if it hasn't happened yet. I think. We really need Leticia. May I please call her?"

"Fine," I said.

She hesitated. "If Leticia thinks you're safe to call the cops in, can I do that, too?"

"No!" I said, instantly angry, my slumped spine jerking up straight.

Her eyes were huge and dark and sorrowing. "I'm sorry, Bree, but if you're right, if this is about something Trey and Spencer did together, the chances of this woman calling you back at this point . . ."

I shook my head. "It's one thing to send me to kill a man she hates in a garden far away. It's another thing to—" I couldn't finish. I looked back and forth between her and Marshall, tears finally breaking out and spilling down my cheeks. "She's held him all day. Fed him. He's such a good baby, and he's lost that newborn scrawny look. He's fat and pink and sweet. He learned to smile last week, and it's all lopsided and toothless. I don't see how she could, no matter how much she hates Trey. She's a mother. It would be so personal."

"That's true," Gabrielle said, and I saw a little of my hope leach into her features. "Okay. But I am going to go call Leticia and ask a few hypotheticals. To know your liability."

She took her cell phone and headed out down the hall that led to my formal living room. I thought she'd agreed mostly because I was the client. I knew the firm's first rule from Trey: Keep the client happy.

"You should listen to her." Marshall looked grave. As an ex-cop, he'd seen levels of cruelty that Gabrielle and I had never known.

There was no way to explain my hope without sounding unhinged, so all I said was, "If I'm wrong, it doesn't matter." I could not stop there. I would have to say the most awful thing, out loud, to convince him. "If I'm wrong, she's already killed him, and I don't care what happens to me."

Marshall rubbed at his eyes, then nodded. He looked sick, but he stopped arguing. We would do this my way. He got up and gathered the coffee cups, taking them over to refill them. "It's going to be a long night."

It was. The longest. I was trying to decide what "morning" meant. A minute after midnight was the start. But midnight came and went with no call.

We got more coffee and went to sit on the big sectional sofa. Marshall moved the artifacts to the coffee table gingerly, hoping for fingerprints, I thought. But I'd already touched those things all over.

When Gabrielle finally finished her phone call and came back, I said, "We'll talk about it later," before she could begin.

She fell asleep around two, her bare feet propped on an ottoman. Marshall dozed as well, listing sideways on the sofa. I listed with him, until I looked up and saw Trey sitting across from me in his favorite chair. I wanted to run to him, hurl myself into his arms, but I was also instantly so angry.

What did you do? I yelled, and I was halfway to standing before I realized I'd been dreaming him.

Marshall snored lightly. Gabrielle didn't stir.

The clock ticked, the long hours passed, I waited. I could almost feel the mother, somewhere far from me. I thought she might be awake, too, still holding my son. Deciding.

When Gabrielle woke up around five, I got a couple of new toothbrushes from my pantry stash. I sent her to the master bedroom to shower and then borrow any of my clothes she wanted. Marshall was up before she got back, and I sent him to the guest bathroom.

When they returned, their eyes were full of questions that they didn't ask. It was almost sunrise. Gabrielle went back to staring at her phone, and Marshall took over pacing. Outside, the sky stayed dark, and I heard a growl of distant thunder. A storm was coming.

Dawn changed the blackness around the blinds to soft gray light. As the rain broke, patting and tapping at the roof, Gabrielle came over to sit down by me on the sofa. She'd borrowed some sweatpants and a T-shirt. She was both shorter and curvier than me, so my clothes simultaneously made her look very young and very sexy.

She took my hand. "Leticia said you could be liable, but she thinks you could claim necessity or duress. The threat of those defenses would help her get you a good deal, if they even want to prosecute. To be blunt, you're white and you're wealthy. We don't think you're risking prison time. We should talk to the police."

I hadn't considered prison. I should have. I'd killed a man. Not just any man. My husband's childhood friend, his partner, his second cousin who had spent endless hours with my family. I knew how Spence had liked his gin and tonics, knew he ate his steak rare and his bacon burned near to ash. I'd once borrowed a swimsuit from his soon-to-be-ex-wife—no, his widow—after a client dinner at his house. Charlotte and I had changed in their master bedroom, and I'd found myself peeking at her naked body with a faint, nostalgic envy. She was built like me, tall and slim, but her breasts had never been baby-chewed. She'd had no stretch marks creeping silver up her toned abs.

I wondered if she knew yet that Spence was dead. She hated him, or so he'd cried to Trey. Would she be sad or relieved? I doubted that Spence had thought to change his will. The police might suspect her of the poisoning, actually, but she ought to be safe. She hadn't been at the party.

I doubted I'd be a suspect either, if we stayed silent. I'd had no reason to want Spence dead. I still didn't want him dead. I only wanted Robert.

"I want to wait until nine at least," I told Gabrielle. "It's rude to call anyone before that."

I almost laughed when I heard myself say it. It was so surreal. As if the woman who'd stolen my baby and tricked me into killing Spence would be sitting by her phone, waiting out the clock for the sake of social mores.

A sound came from the coffee table, widening our eyes, stopping our breaths: the buzz of a phone against the antique brass.

I was up off the sofa, reaching, before I realized it was my own. I could see my husband's handsome face smiling up at me from the lit screen.

"Trey," I told them.

Marshall blew his breath out, his eyes on me kind and sorrowful, and in his gaze I understood that this was the end of it. The night was truly over, for all the storm was keeping us in darkness. She would not be calling.

I lifted the phone with shaking hands. Once I told my husband, it was real. Not just for me. For the girls. They would never trust anything again with the kind of innocence that they had now. It would change Trey, too, and our marriage. It would wreck my mom and leave Trey's family reeling as well. I couldn't see the world very clearly past this moment, but I saw enough to know it wasn't a place where I wanted to live.

My free hand, of its own volition, pressed the red circle that sent Trey to voice mail.

I was not ready to give up. "She could still call. It's still morning." Until noon I would leave the world intact for the people I loved most.

Gabrielle's voice was gentle. "You have to talk to your husband. He must know about Spence by now. My work-group texts are blowing up. If he doesn't hear from you, he'll call friends or family to come check on you."

She was right. God, if he called Mom! She would panic. She would come straight over and bring the girls. Here, to this house, where the world was as frightening as she had always believed. I didn't want the girls in this place, where life was dangerous and terrible and we were sheep, sweet and dumb, ready to be preyed on by monsters like the woman who'd taken Robert, or like my father. He was the one who'd made my mom see the world this way.

She'd started dating him when she was fourteen and he was twenty. When she was sixteen, she dropped out of school and they got married, left the state. She stayed with him, too, right up until she realized she was pregnant.

"I used to smoke. Did you know that?" she told me back when I was Peyton's age and asking pushy questions. All I knew about my dad was that he was in prison. She wouldn't tell me what state, much less the facility. I hadn't yet connected this information to her nerves, her deep mistrust, her many calls to the police about noises on the roof or at the windows. In my aggrieved adolescent imagination, my father yearned to know me. He probably wrote me long, hopeful letters from his cell. Letters that my mother kept from me, unjustly, the same way she made me keep a chore chart and a ridiculous sunset curfew.

"I don't see what smoking has to do with it," I told her, snotty-voiced, one insolent hip cocked at an angle my elder daughter would reinvent and throw at me before her age hit double digits.

My mother shrugged. "A pack a day, for years, right up until the test said I was pregnant. I knew that smoking killed people. It said so right on the package. I'd heard of lung cancer, emphysema. Still, I couldn't stop. Smoking only hurt *me*, and I was used to being hurt. My husband made sure of that."

Her gaze was so serious, her words so calm. She talked to me like I was a person. Not her kid. Like I was some adult she'd met on the bus, and she was telling me some factual information. It made my eyes ache and my mouth go dry.

"He hurt you?" I asked.

"Oh, yes. I had nine broken bones before I was old enough to order a cocktail. That was when people could order cocktails at eighteen. Then my period was so late. I took a home pregnancy test. Back then it was all test tubes, and you had to wait two hours. While I waited, I smoked. Chain-smoked, even. I'd just lit up a fresh one when I saw that the liquid had turned blue. I dropped the cigarette in the toilet, and I never smoked again. That blue color said the cigarette wouldn't only hurt me. It would hurt you. So I flushed it, and then I left your father. He was at work. I knew if I didn't go, he would beat you right out of me, maybe that very night. I could never be sure with him. I put as many of my things as I could carry into a Hefty bag and hitchhiked all the way to Georgia, to my mother's house. He never let me have a car. I was pretty sure he would come after me and kill me. He'd always said he would, if I left. I slept on her sofa for weeks with a loaded shotgun right by me, hoping I wouldn't be too scared to use it. What I didn't know was, he was cheating on me. He was actually glad to have me gone. He moved the other woman right on in. He loved her more than me, I guess. So much more that she was the one he eventually beat to death. That's why he's in prison. Do you have any other questions about when you're going to meet your dad?"

I hadn't. My mother had never been allowed to tell this story to the girls. I'd forbidden it. He'd died, still in prison, when I was in high school, so he wasn't real to them. The world he'd created for my mother wasn't real to them.

But if Mom brought them home, then what had happened to

Robert would be real. It would uproot them from that place I saw on Instagram, all innocence and laughter in Mom's apple-green kitchen, where Peyton grinned with flour dusting her cheek and Anna-Claire proudly lofted a plate of cookies. They had to stay away.

I sent a text to Trey. Tummy flu still raging! Yikes! I'll call later! I added four heart emojis, but not the four words I most wanted to send him.

What did you do?

I could see the little dots that meant Trey was texting back. I set the phone on the table, facedown. I didn't want to get into a conversation. I'd have to tell so many lies. My phone buzzed softly against the brass, over and over. Trey was texting up a storm.

Marshall pushed my phone toward me, gentle and encouraging. He wanted me to stop waiting. He wanted me to answer my husband. His grave expression told me that soon, in hours or minutes, I would have to open up my blinds and let the truth in.

"Bree," he began, but I turned away. Refused to look at him.

That was when the calypso ringtone started playing with thin, metallic urgency, rattling the cheap phone. It was the sweetest song I'd ever heard.

10

GABRIELLE STARTLED, STARING at the phone with wide, haunted eyes. I felt blinding hope and terror, both so strong that they threatened to crush me between them.

Marshall was suddenly right beside me, his deep blue eyes blazing, energized. "Keep her talking."

"Why? We can't trace it," Gabrielle said. "We need the cops! I told you!"

"Hush," I ordered them both, dropping to my knees beside the coffee table.

"Any information could help us," Marshall said, so fast that the words almost ran together. He was pulling out his own iPhone. He poked at it, then set it next to the chiming burner phone. I could see it was recording.

I nodded, then hit the button to put the phone on speaker.

"Hello?" My voice cracked, so that the greeting was hardly recognizable. "Hello?"

I could hear her breathing. That was all. Just her. No baby sounds.

"I wasn't going to call," she said.

"I know." I felt as if I were a glass vase that had already shattered, and yet all my pieces were still stacked onto each other into my usual shape. The lightest touch and I would fall into a million jangling shards. "But you did. You did call, and I'm so grateful."

Her voice turned a little grudging. "He's a good baby."

She used the present tense, as if Robert were right there with her. Hope squeezed my ribs shut tight, until it was hard for me to breathe. Until it was hard for my heart to keep on beating.

"He is. He is a very good baby."

I still could not hear him, though. I strained, listening. The silence wasn't really silence. It was white noise, tinny and airy, same as on our last call. If I had to guess, I would say she had not moved again. Marshall ducked his chin at me, encouraging. He had a little notebook and a pencil in his hands. I hadn't noticed him get those things. Maybe he'd had them with him the whole time, tucked away in his inside jacket pocket, as if he were still a cop.

"What was really in those capsules?" I asked. "Because I know it wasn't roofies."

"Hmm," she said, her thoughtful noise. "Cyanide, mostly. Or something close to it. I'm not a chemist." Her voice took on a hungry tone. "I take it you saw what happened? To Mr. Shaw?"

She didn't sound angry that I had disobeyed, more like she was actively hoping I had seen.

"I couldn't get away in time." That wasn't what she was after, though. I knew the words she wanted, and I had all of them in me. I let a few loose for her. "I was up on a little path, but yes, I saw. I saw him die."

She released a shuddering breath. Almost pleasure. "I wish I'd seen. But my daughter watched, at least. She was owed that."

She'd already heard details from her child, and still she was greedy for more. "It wasn't easy, if that's what you're asking. I wouldn't want to go out that way. It was hard to watch."

"Hmm." She made her little noise again. "Well, I told you to go home." Now her tone was matter-of-fact.

Marshall's eyes on mine stayed so steady, shoring me up.

I said, "I didn't call the police. Even after Spence died. I still haven't told Trey. I believed that you would call again. I hoped you would."

She snorted, almost angry, then asked, "That story you told, about your mama going to Goodwill two towns over. Was that true?"

"Yes," I said. Gabrielle's face was a question. I looked away, down at the phone. The caller ID said *Robert*. I couldn't look there either. I turned my gaze back to Marshall, so calm and serious. He was the safest place in the room. His pencil scratched softly against the notebook. I had her talking, like he wanted. I wondered what he could possibly be gleaning from the flat, small things she was saying, but I trusted that it was something. "Yes. It's true. Why do you ask?"

"Because I believed you," she said. The flash of anger was gone. Now she sounded tired. "That's not a thing a girl who grew up with money would ever think of. Not a thing a rich girl would guess. You and your mama, you said. Where was your daddy?"

Her interest in me felt so real. "Prison. I never knew him. He was a dangerous person. Angry. He'd lose control and hurt my mom. He hurt her a lot. He killed his next wife."

"Well now, that's hard," she said. "My husband, he was a more thoughtful type. He liked things his way, like most men, but I will say he never once lifted an angry hand."

We were falling back into that intimate rhythm we'd had earlier, almost whispering to each other. "Did he ever lift a hand when he was calm?"

She chuckled, and I felt our connection spark and strengthen. I'd understood her.

"He liked things how he liked them," she repeated. Then she added, "He was faithful, though. Never left us for some other woman." That wasn't exactly how it happened, but I let her assume. I liked the way she was aligning our histories, matching up her life with my own mother's. "Never would have either. He liked having me about. He had a good job working construction. Good benefits, so I got to stay home with our daughter for a couple years, though it made things tight. He didn't even want to be away from us while he was working. I'd make him a lunch every day and take it to his job sites. He liked me to sit with him while he ate. He'd play with the baby, tell me about his work. But then he died on me."

Marshall scribbled more words onto his notepad, his eyebrows raised. I think they were both surprised at how easily we were talking. Gabrielle had her hand over her mouth again, a gesture I was coming to recognize as characteristic. She covered her mouth when she had a strong feeling, as if otherwise it might get out.

I asked, "Did Robert keep you up? You sound tired." I wanted to say my son's name. Make him a person for her. Keep him a person. Keep him alive.

"Naw. He slept through pretty good. Needed a bottle at around four."

I felt my breath catch, and silent tears spilled down my face. He always wanted a bottle then. The fact that she had his early-morning feeding time right made me believe he'd been there to eat it. And then I heard him. Very close. A burbling baby noise, unmistakably my son.

"Robert!" My legs gave out, and I found myself rocking back onto my hips.

"He's here in the sling, tied to me," she said. "Like I told you."

I managed to lean toward the phone again. "But that's not what you planned." I said it flat. Resigned. Not an accusation or a challenge. Just the truth.

"Naw," she agreed. "That wasn't the plan."

I made myself be still. I made myself not scream. Marshall had said to keep her talking, and I clung to this idea. "What was supposed to happen?"

"I meant to drown him." It was so calm. The way I might say, *I meant to go to Publix* or *I meant to call Mom*, on a day when time had gotten away from me. "I was going to do it as soon as I knew that Spencer Shaw was dead. I was going to dope him so he'd sleep through it, though. He wouldn't have ever known."

My body rocked itself back and forth. Words spilled out of my mouth, breathy and urgent. "But you didn't. I hear him. I'm so glad. I'm so grateful. You didn't, and I hope you won't. I love him so much, and you don't have any reason to hate me. Please, please don't."

"Ch-ch-ch." It was the noise she'd made to soothe Robert. She was making it for me now. She swallowed and started to speak, then paused. I waited. She started again. She was full of a strange need. I could feel her wanting to talk. I could feel her wanting to talk to me particularly.

"Here's the thing," she said, and then stopped again. I waited. When she finally spoke, her words came very fast. She was almost defensive. "I read, like in my mystery novels and such, that it gets easier. I like suspense-type movies, too, and I've heard the same thing there. They all say it. You kill a person and it's hard, but then, you know, you get a callus. It builds up. Easier every time, they say." I heard Robert sighing as she shifted him. "I'm not finding that to be true."

I was nodding. As if she could see me. I understood her, and an awful, cold acceptance descended upon me. I made myself be so calm. She wasn't talking about killing Spence. He hardly counted. That hadn't been hands-on. That wasn't even mostly her. I'd done the dirty parts, and then I'd watched him die while she was far away, holding my son.

She meant she'd killed someone else.

"Was it a baby?" I sounded so flat and nonjudgmental that it shocked me. I wasn't sure what kind of character I was playing now. Not Betsy. Maybe a priest, behind a screen, hearing confession. Or a machine, heartless and hollow, taking data. "That might make a difference."

Marshall and Gabrielle understood her now as well. Gabrielle's whole face had disappeared behind her splayed hands. "He was older, but I'd still say a baby. He had a little blue backpack in his stroller when I took him. It said 'Gee-Off' on it in these fat bubble-cloth letters. Isn't that the dumbest thing you ever heard of? A backpack for a baby. But they had stupid amounts of money, so they spent it stupid."

I was rocking, a slow, soothing movement. Gabrielle left the room. I thought because she could not stay silent. I wanted to go with her, lie on my bed and press my face into a pillow that smelled like my husband. I wanted to scream and cry and kick.

Marshall stayed. He'd gone full cop on me, his eyes as flat as if the notes he was taking were a grocery list. Cops could do it, too, I realized, like lawyers and actors. They could tuck themselves away inside another person. Right now he was someone rock steady, and his calm gaze felt like the only thing that kept me chained to the earth. Forget gravity. If he looked away, I'd shoot up into space. I'd feel my whole body crumpling in that vacuum, imploding into itself.

Because she was not hiding anything or lying or manipulating me now. She was only saying true and awful things. Saying them with my baby in her arms.

"I didn't scare him, or hurt him. He wasn't scared for even a minute. I had a cat like that once. Mitzi. Some old mama cat had her in my carport and never came back. I brought her in. Bottle-fed her. She spent her whole life in my house after that, never cold or hungry or sad, not even once't. This little boy, he was like that cat. When he woke up in my car, I told him I was the new sitter, and he was just as nice as pie. I'd taken him from his mama, at the park. She was in a fuss with someone on her cell phone while he napped, and I moseyed away with the whole stroller. But he was used to waking up with sitters. His mama liked to go about. We followed her awhile, to get her pattern, you know." I stayed my flat, calm character, but inside I felt a flash of angry joy that Marshall was recording. She'd admitted that her daughter had assisted with a kidnapping, and the daughter was the only thing she cared about. It felt like leverage. "She was always running out to lunch, or getting her hair or nails fussed over, or doing hot yoga, whatever that is. No nanny, so her boy was used to different folks. He couldn't fathom a bad thing might be happening. When we got back here, I gave him a lot of Benadryl in juice, and he went right to sleep. He never even woke up when I put him in the water. I made sure it was warm, but not too hot. Like you do a bottle."

She was quiet for a little. It was a mercy. I felt as if she wanted me to say something. It was a waiting pause to see how I would take this. I made my voice stay low and calm and gentle.

"You didn't call his mother? Didn't put a gift bag with a phone on her door?"

"Hmm." She made that noise again. I could also hear Robert stretching, grunting a little. "Naw. I didn't need her help."

I couldn't swallow. But I had to speak. "Don't do it again. It won't get better or easier. I think the movies and the books all lie."

Marshall gave me a short, proud nod. I was saying good, right things. The best things, his eyes were telling me.

She said, "You know the strangest part? It wasn't until after that I realized those letters were his name. Gee-Off. It's a way to spell Jeff. I saw it spelled that way in a Agatha Christie book. I like those British mysteries where everyone's so calm. Cozies, they call them. But I never knew how to say it until I saw it spelled out on Gee-Off's backpack."

"Please," I said. I couldn't help myself. "Please don't do that to Robert."

Marshall's eyes flashed a warning. I nodded. Tried to calm myself.

"Well," she said, a noncommittal sound. "I don't want to. But I have to finish this. I don't have a lot of time, you understand. I'd told myself that the minute Spence was gone, I'd finish. But I never did give your boy the Benadryl. I think I already knew it would be hard to do again."

My eyes closed. "You don't have to. Let's think of something else, together."

"I'm past that. I already did my thinking. On and off while I was dozing in this chair all night. I wanted to keep your boy in my lap in case you had called the police. But I wouldn't have slept any better in a bed. I'm sick. My body hurts. Anyhow, I found us a third way."

My heart leaped in my chest, and Marshall leaned closer, intense. "Then tell me." I sounded eager now. Whatever she wanted from me, it felt already done.

But she was still talking, almost musing. "Before I started down this road, I tried to imagine the worst thing I could do to a person. That was easy. My husband died young, and that was hard, but it didn't break me. I'm dying now myself, and it's not so bad. When I learned I had a few months left, I went right to my daughter and told her, and she put her arms around me, and I knew she'd go on living, after. It's the natural order. She is my real comfort. I understood then that losing a child would be the worst thing. But Mr. Shaw didn't have any children. I had to get real direct with his bill. The most precious thing he had was his own sorry life. In some ways it felt like letting him off easy. I thought to myself, well, it's the best you can do. Now, though, between Mr. Shaw and Gee-Off. I think I liked what happened to Mr. Shaw better. It's so . . ." She paused, word hunting. "Relaxing. He's in hell before me, and that feels right. And I know I made the world better by taking him off it. I don't know if that baby, Gee-Off, would have made the world better or worse. No one will know now. That doesn't seem fair, and all I want is to make things come around fair before I die. I look at your boy here, and he's a sweet baby. I think maybe I ought to go another route."

"Yes," I said. "I want that."

Gabrielle reappeared in the doorway. She'd been listening from the hall, crying silently. Her large, dark eyes were swollen, and the whites shone pink.

"I do, too." Her voice turned musing. "Maybe I knew it even before I took your boy. Why else give you extra pills? Maybe I wanted to know if it would feel fair if Spencer Shaw was dead. It did. It does. And I don't want to put this baby in the water. So." She paused. "You see where I'm going."

"Yes." I did. My gaze fell to the silver flask holding that deadly shot of Pappy, gleaming on the table. *Cyanide, or something close to it*, she'd said. Marshall understood her, too, his eyebrows lowering, and Gabrielle looked close to being ill. She was already shaking her head in an emphatic no. "You want me to give Trey the other pills. You'll trade his life for Robert's." My voice was dead flat. Not even I could tell if I was considering this choice.

But she surprised me. "Naw. I think that was in the back of my mind when I gave you six, but it won't work. How would I know for sure when it was finished? You'd lie, try to fool me. You'd send me pictures of your husband playing possum with his face all powdered to look pale, maybe even bring an ambulance to your house for show, wheel out a body in a bag. I wouldn't blame you. Even if I could be sure, so much suspicion would come at you, your husband and Mr. Shaw dying the same way, and you right there both times. You'd end up in prison, and then who would raise your kids?"

Her concern for me sounded sincere. I believed it was sincere, and yet I also believed she would kill my child. Both these truths were alive inside her. Gabrielle crept a little closer. I could see that her lawyer's brain was still online, working behind her puffy eyes.

"I don't understand what you want, then," I said.

"I've been spooling this out in different directions all night, seeing how it might work. It's like that riddle about the river, where you have to get a fox and a goose and a bag of corn acrost without any one of them eating the other. I've put the puzzle pieces every which-a-way. And I only see one path. It's this: You bring your husband to me."

"Bring you Trey? Trey is in Chicago." I couldn't imagine bringing her my husband like he was a dove or a goat, a necessary blood sacrifice. Except I was imagining it, I realized. I would trade anything for Robert, except one of my girls. And at that thought, a third path lit up. One I could walk down. I blurted out, "What about me? I'll trade you me. Trey loves me. If I died—"

"Aw, now stop." She clucked her tongue at me. "You're a true mother. I seen it in you from the start, and I thought you might offer. It's because of that, me seeing that in you, that I'm making you this deal at all. Because I feel for you. But a man can always get another wife. Especially a rich man. They'd line up three deep to heal his sorrows, pretty as you and younger to boot. The only things your husband can give me to make things fair are his life or his son. The others who wronged my family didn't get to choose, but I'll give that choice now, to you. You decide. Which one."

Marshall jerked his head in a quick nod, but I didn't need his affirmation. I was already talking.

"Trey," I said. "I want Robert back."

I was lying. All three of us in the room knew it. Maybe even the woman on the phone knew. I wasn't giving her my husband. I was gaining time. But I was a good actor. The words rang true. So true that I might mean it after all. If it came down to it. And maybe she knew that, too.

"Good," she said. "It's what I would choose. Now, hush and listen here to me, because this is the last time we'll talk. I'm going to smash this phone up with a hammer, soon as I hang up. I thought and thought how to work this, and you'll only get one chance at it. First, call your husband home. You can tell him the truth if you like, or any lie that pleases you. Just get him on a plane. I'll give you the day. Tomorrow I'm going to leave Robert here and drive to the Funtime Carousel and Gold Mine. You can meet me there if you decide to trade. You know Funtime? You know the carousel?"

"I don't," I said. It sounded made up.

"Well, you're too young. It closed years ago. It's up north of the city. You bring your husband there to me, nine A.M. sharp, mind. I won't wait. Come together, in the same car. Then the two of you walk up and meet me at the carousel."

"Then what?" I asked, confused.

"Then you and me are done. I'll finish my business with your husband and this whole black world, and then I'll give you directions to go get your baby."

This I understood. She meant to kill Trey and then herself. Or both of them together. Marshall held his hand up, shaped like a gun, asking if I thought she was armed. I shrugged.

I asked, "So who will have Robert? Your daughter?"

She tsked. "Naw. I'm telling you, she's clean of anything that happens to your boy. I'm keeping her clean. I'll just leave him and come meet you."

"By himself?" Strange that this could shock me, considering everything she'd done. I had a vision of Robert alone in a dark place that smelled of mold. Maybe hungry. Maybe wet. Crying for me, every minute an erosion to his tiny trust that the world was warm and loving. "How far away is Funtime from where you'll leave him?"

Marshall gave me an approving nod. It was a smart question, but she wasn't stupid enough to answer.

"Not close, but he'll be safe enough. He may be mad before you get to him, but he won't die. I'll clip him in his car seat, and there's a good strong door between him and any coyotes." She said the last word with only two syllables. *Ky-oats*. My head shook, back and forth. No. I didn't want Robert waiting for me, alone in some abandoned gas station or a backwoods shed or a soundproofed city basement. "If you come without your husband, if you send police instead, I'll never tell where he is. He'll stay there, crying for you, until thirst gets him. He's in a place won't nobody find him. Not fast enough. I'll die knowing it'll finish fair without me. Hard on the baby, though."

I believed her. I could see it. It would be easier than putting him into the water. She wouldn't have to do anything but keep silent and die. She could tell herself that Trey and I had made our choice.

Far away, in a secret place with a locked door, I could hear Robert stirring, making hungry peeps.

"I'll see you tomorrow. Or not. It's on you now."

"Wait," I said. "Please tell me. What did he do? What did they do?" I meant Trey. And Spence. And Geoff's poor parents.

A pause, a breath, but she didn't answer. "I won't call again."

"What did he do?" I insisted, but she was gone. I was talking to dead air.

11

MARSHALL KNEW THAT the old woman had made some mistakes during the conversation, though he couldn't see them all clearly yet. He could feel them like little cracks, spidering and spreading in the veil that hid her from him.

She'd said too much. Why had she been so forthcoming?

Something was at work inside her, a strange tenderness aimed at Bree. Bree herself had a pretty serious case of Stockholm syndrome going, no doubt, but why was her softness being reciprocated? It made no sense.

Marshall scrubbed at his tired eyes, grateful that Cara was with Yvonne at the lake. She'd spend the day kayaking and swimming, hearing birdsong as sunlight sparked the blue water. How could the world be wide enough to hold that place and this one? Her live, young joy should not share a planet with what was happening here.

He'd been right there, too, in the building. Bree had even shown him the kidnapper, pointed at her through the greenroom window, agitated, and he hadn't followed up. He'd been so busy trying to keep his distance.

Now she was crumpled into herself on the sofa, rocking faintly. Whenever he looked her way, he wanted to rip the world in half and pull the old woman out through the boiling center for her.

But he could not muddy up his mind with rage or worry. Not even hope. Hope was too personal. In real life cops didn't work cases they were close to, and this was why. He needed to be thinking, cold and clear.

"She messed up," he told them, so calm. He'd found his old cop voice, rusty from disuse. "She gave us the other child's name and approximate age. There will be news stories about a missing toddler, and this one had an unusual name."

"How does that help?" Gabrielle said, overwhelmed.

"Until now we had only two points, Spence and Trey, connected by the line of a legal case. Geoff is a third point, a way to triangulate. When we find the lines connecting Geoff's parents, the right case file will be inside the shape they all make together. Inside that file we'll find the woman who took Robert. We need her real name."

With the real name, maybe, just maybe, he could get Robert back. If he was willing to be ruthless. He didn't have to mull it over. He was willing. He was past willing. He could feel a coming violence, like a prickling carbonation in his blood. This was yet another reason cops were not allowed to work on cases close to them.

Gabrielle burst into motion, pushing off the doorway. "We should have called the police. They would have traced that call. We'd know exactly where she is." Her words came blurting out, all rush and tumble, a road straight to regret.

"No," Marshall cut in, firm and cool. They could not indulge in woulda-coulda-shoulda. He saw only one path that might get them all the way to Robert. It was full of switchbacks and deadfalls, but it was a path, and he was on it. "We got this. I have a plan." Well, the seeds of one. "Remember, if Bree had called the cops first thing, Robert would be dead already."

Bree flinched, but it was good for her to hear these words. Like every parent living, she'd be looking for a way to make this her fault.

She looked up at him with drowning eyes. "Maybe we should call them now?"

"No," he said. He looked at Gabrielle and was glad to see her nodding, backing his play. Bree could end up in prison and still lose her baby. And as murder/suicide plans went, this one felt pretty tight. He could see six thousand ways it could go ass up if they called the cops. "She's tied the baby to her body, which makes snipers or gas or a breach too risky. She doesn't care if she lives, so they can't negotiate. That's every choice the cops have. They have to stay inside the law. They have limits." He held Bree's gaze. "We don't. All I need is her name. She has a weak point."

He saw it click in her, or perhaps she'd thought of it already and was only recognizing how far down into this thing he'd go with her. A light came into her eyes. She said, "You want her name so you can find the daughter. Get something to trade that isn't Trey."

He nodded, even as Gabrielle's jaw unhinged. He turned to her before she could speak. "We'll leave you out of anything illegal. I don't see another way." The daughter was the only thing she cared about. Finding her was the key.

Bree stood up, firming her lips and squaring her shoulders, her gaze burning into him. Gratitude and hope and something else, unreadable. "So what do we do first?"

She asked as if she were sure he knew, and he felt her faith like a jolt, pure energy crackling through him. This was that force she had in her, the thing that had made her so electric on the stage. She'd turned it on him like a beam.

"We send the phone and bag to a private lab. The pill bottle and the dosed flask incriminate you, so I'll hold them in case we need them. I know a lab that works Saturdays. I'll call them. A rush job will be expensive, but . . ." She was already waving that away, so he started packing the artifacts into the gaudy bag. "Not enough time for DNA, but if they can get fingerprints, maybe she has a record. Gabrielle, call a car service? As soon as we're done here, you need to go drop this stuff off." He handed her the sack, then unclipped his own phone from his belt. "I'll text you the lab's address."

"I can do that." She came down hard on the last word as she got her phone out. It was a warning; there were things she would not do.

Bree understood the warning as well. She turned to hold his gaze in what became a promise between them. No limits.

Then she looked down, her cheeks coloring, and changed the subject. "The mother said finding her wouldn't help me find the daughter."

Pushback was good. If he had to convince her, it made this idea more his. If it failed, at least Bree would have someone to blame besides herself.

"She meant finding her physical location wouldn't help. We know the daughter isn't with her. But her identity? If she didn't care about us knowing that, she would have answered your last question. She told you everything else you wanted to know. About herself, her family, her motivations. Geoff. But she wouldn't tell you her name, or her husband's name, or her daughter's. She wouldn't say what Trey and Spence did, and people with a grievance love to express their outrage. She didn't because if you knew which case had harmed her, then you could find her name. If she wants to hide her name, then it's worth finding." Bree was nodding, seeing it, so he pressed forward. "I need a water glass and a big Ziploc storage bag, please." She turned toward the kitchen, but his next words made her blanch. "Then you have to call Trey. Get him up to speed, so he'll hop the first plane home."

"I will." She hurried away to get the things he'd asked for.

He turned back to Gabrielle. "After you drop this stuff off, can you go into the office? I'll stay here and start the research. By the time you get there, I'll have emailed all my notes to you. You can use them to narrow down Spencer and Trey's cases."

Bree was already back. He took her hand and found it trembling so hard he had to steady it as he pressed her fingertips cleanly onto the water glass. "So the lab can rule your prints out." He dropped the glass in the bag and sealed it.

"Thank you," she said. That was all, but her eyes were full of unsaid things.

He nodded, feeling a sudden need, sharp and small and selfish, to be the one to make this happen. He would shake hands with Satan, trade anything, to be the one to get Robert back. He could almost feel the small, live weight of the baby, see how joy would crash through her as he put that weight into her arms.

He pushed it away, dirty from the want of it. Find the name. Get the daughter. That was all.

"My car is here." Gabrielle took the bagged glass. "Call the lab. Tell them I'll be there in half an hour."

"I'll walk you out," Bree said.

Marshall didn't want to be in the room when Bree returned. It would be hard enough for her to call her husband, tell him what she had to tell, without a witness in the room. Besides, there were things he needed to be doing.

He went into Trey's office. It felt strange to be in this room, alone. Or at all. Trey was his boss. They hadn't really socialized since he lost Betsy. But he remembered the place, with its spare, modern furniture and high bookshelves lining two of the walls. He sat down at Trey's desk, but Trey was shorter, so the chair didn't fit him. His knees jutted up. Still, he wasn't going to change the settings.

He called the lab and got lucky; the cute tech with the dimples, Jenna something, picked up. She always came through for him. He told her it was for the firm but made it plain it was more urgent than a regular rush job.

"I'll get it done. But only because you begged," she teased. "I'm going to be here until midnight, though." A dramatic, suffering sigh.

"I owe you," he told her.

"What kind of owe me?" she asked. "Six-pack of PBR or shrimp dinner?"

"Lobster, if you find me some fingerprints."

She laughed, and they disconnected.

He was swirling Trey's mouse to make Windows come up before he realized he'd probably just been asked out on a date. Worse, he'd probably accepted.

Betsy had always told him he was stupid about flirting. Once, at the grocery store, he'd left the cart to go grab a local lager from the refrigerated case in the back. A woman came up and asked what kind of beer went well with steak. He'd been telling her about his favorite brewery when Betsy came to find him. The woman left abruptly, and Betsy had almost choked to death laughing. She'd fluttered her eyelashes and fake-swooned into his shoulder. "Excuse me, kind sir, do you have any beer in your pants?"

Was it a date? Jesus. Jenna looked so young to him. Well, it was not a problem for today. He should go out with someone anyway. That swamping wave of sick desire to be the one to hand Bree her baby back told him so. It was different from simply wanting Robert safe and home. Very different. His stupid crush on Bree wasn't ever going to be a good idea, but it was downright dangerous now. Dangerous for Robert.

He opened up his Gmail and quickly typed in his notes, all he'd gleaned from Bree's story, the video, and that long, strange phone conversation. He organized them as he went. It wasn't much.

Witch: Widow. 70+. One child (F). A reader, esp British mystery novels. Likes suspense movies. Owns or owned house with carport. Terminally ill. Accent = Blue collar, rural. Georgia?

Husband: Died young. Construction worker. Controlling/abusive?

Daughter:

He had no facts about the daughter, only the understanding that she was in this up to her neck and that she was the mother's only weak point.

He would start with their strongest lead. Geoff. It only took four searches to find him in the online edition of an Alabama newspaper. Geoff Wilkerson, age three, had gone missing from a local park almost six weeks ago.

It hadn't spread beyond the local news. Partially because there'd been a deadly mass shooting at a Texas school earlier that same day, then another at a California nightclub not twelve hours later. These things had dominated the news cycle. But there was also enough in the Alabama stories for him to get the subtext: The cops thought one parent or maybe both were behind their son's disappearance. The case wasn't being treated like a kidnapping.

He shook his head. The cops had this one very, very wrong.

Geoff's father was Adam Wilkerson, a community-college professor. Marshall's eyebrows knit. He'd been expecting either another lawyer or someone rich enough to be a client. Adam Wilkerson was head of the business and legal-studies department, so maybe he had been a lawyer at one point. A disgraced one, if he'd fallen from Trey and Spence's level to teaching at a junior college in Gadsden, Alabama.

Adam wasn't on social media, but he found Geoff's mother, Kelly, on Facebook and Instagram. She listed her profession as SAHM, still, and that hit him like a fist.

Her profile pictures showed a cute, pug-nosed blonde in her mid-twenties. Her Insta was private, but she'd turned off her Facebook security settings. Her feed was filled with people posting thoughts and prayers. There was a 1-800 number and a plea for information pinned to the top, probably the reason her security was set so low. It had been set up by her sister, who'd posted a furious rant about how the police weren't looking for Geoff and asking "the Internet" to help bring him home.

Marshall scrolled down past all this. He was looking for the Wilkersons' regular life. Before. When he found it, it was hard to look at. It was so nice and normal. Pictures of avocado toast and a fat Siamese cat and fresh-cut flowers. Almost every other posting showed a smiling toddler. Geoff had had a short, round face like his mother's and a cap of blond hair in that bowl cut normally reserved for television children. His happy smile revealed baby teeth with gaps that made them look like little corn kernels.

He was a beautiful child. Again, very hard to look at.

Marshall scrolled further, until he found a good picture of the husband. He was a tweedy sort, older than his wife, with small round glasses and a bald head and some salt in his tidy beard. She was in a cocktail dress, tucked up under his arm. They were clearly heading someplace special.

Marshall pirated the shot and a good face shot of Geoff, too. Then he attached both to an email and sent them to Gabrielle and Bree along with his notes, the couple's names and address, and Kelly Wilkerson's social-media links.

He could hear Bree moving around the great room again. Pacing, he thought. Not talking. She must still be trying to get up the courage to call Trey. He felt for her, but his cop brain pointed out that if Trey was still ignorant, he was also likely in a calm state of mind. He could be useful.

Marshall took advantage of her hesitation, texting Trey pictures of all three Wilkersons. He'd forwarded himself the still shot of the old woman from Bree's phone earlier. Now he cropped it in close, so Trey wouldn't recognize his own porch, and sent that, too.

He texted, Do you know any of these people?

He saw the dots that meant Trey was answering, then, No. Did you hear about Spencer? Were you there?

He was clearly upset, answering so fast that there had not been time for him to do anything but glance at the pictures in passing.

Marshall thought fast, then replied, I'd already left the party, but I heard. I'm very sorry for your loss. I know it's a bad time, but this is for a case, and it won't wait, okay? Take a minute. Look carefully. Maybe even check your contact lists or emails or old case files, if you can access them remotely. The couple is Adam and Kelly Wilkerson. That's their son, Geoff. Her maiden name was Frier.

Marshall waited for a moment, but no further answer came. He'd give Trey a few minutes. Hopefully Trey would answer before Bree called him.

He couldn't imagine that conversation, or what Trey might think, say, feel. If they didn't find the daughter, would Trey go to the carousel and trade himself for Robert? Marshall would, for Cara. It wasn't even a question. He thought Trey would, too.

He knew Trey pretty well. Not just from work. Back when Betsy was alive, their families got together a few times a year. In summer especially. Trey would grill shrimp and steak and veggie skewers in the outdoor kitchen. Cara and Anna-Claire had played well together then, like same-age cousins who only met on holidays. Peyton, a year younger, tagged behind, and Trey would intervene nine times a night to make the older girls include her. Back then the yard had a swing set and a slide and a sandbox, nicer than the equipment at the park near his house. The sandbox even had a lid.

"I keep it shut unless they're using it. Religiously. Otherwise the girls would pretty much be romping in a giant litter box," Trey'd told him once, laughing.

When Marshall remembered those nights, it was usually in terms of Bets and Bree, drinking too much wine and talking like they hadn't seen each other in a year. The reality was, they'd probably been on the phone for half an hour earlier that very day. Still, they were seldom face-to-face, so those nights revolved around them.

Trey and Marshall were the cooks, the child minders, and the servers. They chatted about college football and grilling, the only places where their interests intersected. It had impressed him to see a big-time Buckhead lawyer type hosting and cooking and keeping the sandbox cat-shit-free so his wife could enjoy a rare night with her best friend.

Maybe that was a sad statement about men, that this could impress him. But it did. It had. He'd come away thinking that Trey was decent, in the best sense of the word, and crazy about his family.

Marshall ran a hand over his face. He felt scratchy and dirty and guilty and angry all at once.

He turned back to the computer and searched for "Funtime Carousel and Gold Mine." He clicked the Google Maps link first and found it northeast of the city. They could get there from Decatur in ninety minutes. It was tucked away in some hilly wilderness off an old country road leading up into the Blue Ridge Mountains.

He left that page open and went back to follow a link to a photo-heavy article called "Creepiest Dead Theme Parks in America." BuzzFeed blamed a new highway that was built in the eighties for Funtime's demise. It had never been enough of an attraction to be a destination. It was the kind of place families stopped by on the way to something better.

He began scrolling down through the pictures, reading, adding a few more notes as he went. Funtime had been owned by Larry and Mariah Denton. Perhaps it still was. There was a picture of them standing with their arms around each other by a cotton-candy booth.

Mariah Denton was not their perp. Wrong shape of face, wrong coloring. Still, he added Funtime and the Dentons to his notes, then sent a new email to Gabrielle, copying Bree, asking her to research them. They could be connected. People doing serious crimes often went back to their old places and friends. Crime was stressful, and familiarity was comfort. It was one way they got caught.

The next picture showed a terrifying, mossy cowboy figure standing by an equally scabby-looking blue pack mule. Both figures were coated in fine black fungus, and the skin of the cowboy's face was peeling away. It made him look leprous, or possibly undead. The caption said his name was Funtime Jack. The mule was Baby. That sounded familiar. Maybe Marshall had been there as a kid? But no, he realized, he was thinking of Paul Bunyan and Babe, his big blue ox. Probably the Funtime owners had done it on purpose. Animal-sidekick plagiarism.

In the den Bree was talking now. Too quietly for him to make out the words, but he knew how hard it must have been to even start this conversation with Trey. Good for her.

Last was a shot of the carousel. It had still been standing when BuzzFeed's photographer visited, though most of the animals were missing. There was a dragon and a griffin and an Aslan-type lion listing sadly on their poles. A few of those benches for parents to ride remained, too, covered in carved unicorns. Fantasy animals, not a match for the cowboy. Funtime must have picked their things up piecemeal from other failed fairs.

Bree's voice rose in distress. He heard her say, "I'm so sorry. . . ."

A molten rage filled him, preemptive and immediate. Trey was blaming her! He was across the room at the door before he could blink. She was already clinging to a cliff side. Marshall wanted to rip the phone out of her hands and tell Trey, *This is on you. What the hell did you get up to with Spencer?*

But the next thing he heard was Bree saying, "Thanks, Mom, but really, this is the best way for you to help. I feel better, I swear, but I think I'm still contagious. I'll get them tomorrow night."

She was checking on her girls. Making plans for them to stay at the condo again. Marshall blew a long breath out his nose, like a human balloon overfilled with unnecessary rage, offloading. Well, there were other places he could aim it.

He went back to the desk and sat down to text Trey again. Any of those photos ring a bell? Sorry to press. It's important.

In the den Bree was saying, "Please don't worry. It's just a bug."

She sounded so young and sad and sweet, working to reassure her anxious mother, much like the Bree he'd known decades ago. His crush on her back then had led him to his wife, and Bree had become his friend. A close one. In fact, he'd almost kissed her once.

It was about a month after Betsy ditched him. Bree came home from Georgia State for the weekend and dropped by his house. Because they were friends, sure, but he thought (rightly) that Betsy had sent Bree to check on him.

She brought a four-pack of Bartles & Jaymes, and he fronted

like everything was fine. He told her about the job he'd taken at his uncle's auto-parts shop, saving up for the police academy. He mentioned a girl who sat ahead of him in church. Maybe there even was one. Someone sat in front of him. It might be a girl.

The truth was, he'd hurled himself into a hum of busy misery to wait Betsy out. He was clocking overtime at the shop, weight training, running, anything to keep his heart from breaking while he waited for Betsy to come back to him.

If Bree reported he was wallowing and pining, she might not. No one comes back to sad-sack, lovelorn goons. So he made jokes and talked about how awesome post-high-school life was, until Bree put a hand on his arm and stared him down, serious.

"Marshall. I'm your friend," she said. No pity in her eyes. Only kindness.

He felt misery break out all over him like a sweat, visible and obvious. "Please don't tell Betsy, okay? Tell her I'm great. Tell her I have a date next week. I can't stand it if she's feeling sorry for me."

"Okay," she said. He glared, skeptical, but she raised three solemn former–Girl Scout fingers. "I promise."

After that they sat on the floor and watched MTV, drinking the sticky-sweet coolers. She quietly let him be unhappy, but not alone. It was the nicest gift he'd ever gotten. Better, in the moment, than the ten-year-old Chrysler LeBaron his dad had dropped off before skipping his high-school graduation.

Neither of them was a big drinker, so by the time all four bottles were empty, they were leaning on each other's shoulder watching *Celebrity Deathmatch*. She giggled until she snorted and then grinned at him, embarrassed.

He remembered then how pretty she was. He'd forgotten, cloaked as she'd been in Betsy's best-friendship. Her grin faded, and she bit her lip. They both were buzzed, and she smelled of roses. He leaned in a little. He could have kissed her. There was permission in the way she tilted up her face.

Instead he got up, then reached down to pull her to her feet, too. "You better eat something before you drive. Come on. I'll make you a Steak-umm sandwich."

She seemed as relieved as he was that the last inch had not closed between them.

Back then he'd thought of Betsy as a girl in an adjoining hotel room. She'd closed her door, but he didn't think she'd bolted it. His was wide open, waiting for her. Kissing Bree would nail both doors shut and drape them with bombs and poison frogs and fire. Betsy would forgive him any girl who happened in this gap, except for her best friend.

Even so, there were no other girls in those long months. How could there be? He and Betsy had invented what love should look like. His parents were divorced, hers hated each other, so they'd made up something different. They'd discovered sex together, too, the summer after junior year, and developed their own lexicon of looks and phrases that no one else could read or follow.

When Betsy did come back, they called her months at Georgia State her rumspringa, when they talked of it at all. They didn't, much. No need, once it was over. It had been a good thing. She'd needed that time, free, before she could choose a life with him and never wonder, never wander. He'd never had her restlessness, but the separation had taught him his own capacity for faith and patience. He didn't know everything she'd done in that year. It didn't matter. He'd simply waited through it, like a seed over a long winter.

He wondered if Bree ever thought about that long-ago kiss that didn't happen. Remembering it now, the shine of her eyes, the way her dark hair had smelled of roses even then, though some sweeter, simpler version, he understood the truth: This was not some silly crush.

He was in love with her.

He knew Bree better than he knew anyone on earth, except for Cara. He knew her, and he loved her for all the reasons Betsy had loved her. The big ones, like her loyalty and that fierce fight under her quiet, but also a host of tiny, intimate things. The way her nose got little wrinkles on the sides when she grinned or how she saved the bits of cookie dough in her ice cream to eat at the end.

No one else alive knew him and his history the way Bree did, because hers was all entwined in it. No other woman looked at Cara and recognized and cherished every bit of Betsy that was alive inside her only daughter.

Ironic. If he'd kissed Bree those many years ago, he'd have lost Betsy forever. Now that situation had completely reversed. Of all the women he could bring into his daughter's life, Bree might be the only one that Betsy would fully approve.

He ran a hand across his hair. No wonder he was hell-bent on this course, though it was dangerous, illegal, and in a flaming moral red zone. Not to mention this was the wrong time to realize he loved her. There was never going to be a good time, but this was the actual worst.

Once this was over—if this was ever over—he would have to get some distance. He would buy Jenna-from-the-lab her shrimp dinner, maybe get back on Match, definitely take himself off snack-mom rotation.

But for now he couldn't leave her side. For now he had work to do. Gabrielle had already sent an answer to his first notes.

M, I did a quick search, but nothing came up in our files on either Adam or Kelly Wilkerson. Not as cocounsels, witnesses, plaintiffs, or defendants. No mention in depos either. I'm going to go through every file Trey and Spence worked on together, one by one, starting with the oldest, but you know our search function is amazing. I'm concerned. —G

He emailed back, saying he was disappointed but to stick with the deep search. As he hit send, his phone buzzed. A text had landed. Trey.

I don't know any of these people.

Now, that was interesting. He'd taken Gabrielle's faith in the quick search functions with a grain of salt; he still believed that the Wilkersons were in those files. So either Trey was lying or he really, truly did not recognize them. Which meant . . .

He saw the conclusion Bree would want to jump toward, and it worried him. He went back into the great room.

She was folded up on the sofa, staring at her own cell phone like it was made of snakes.

"I'm not going to tell Trey." She said it loud, defensive, as if she'd been fighting with Marshall about it for a solid ten minutes before he came into the room. "I did text him, okay? I apologized for being out of touch but told him the little flu I had was awful. He knows about Spence, so he's already headed home. He got a seat on an eight-o'clock flight. I'm not going to call him when I can tell him at home, in person, tonight."

He didn't want to join her in the fight she'd started without him, but she had to talk to her husband. "You think face-to-face will make it easier?"

"No," she said, fierce. "God, not at all. But when I tell him, Marshall, when I ask him 'What did you do?' I need to be looking right into his eyes. It's the only way I'll know if his answer is the truth. Ever."

He understood her then. She wasn't fighting him. She was only fighting for her marriage as well as her child.

He said, "I texted Trey, too. Sent him some pics of Geoff's parents."

"You found them?" She was up and coming toward him then, so fast. "Show me!"

"I copied you on the email." She scrabbled for her phone, then paced away, staring down at their names, their faces. "Trey didn't recognize the old woman or the Wilkerson family, and Gabrielle can't find any Wilkersons in the files. Or at least she hasn't yet."

He could see her putting it together.

"I don't know them either, Marshall." For the first time since this had begun, she sounded genuinely hopeful. She'd seen what it might mean and was jumping to the exact conclusion he'd feared. "Trey doesn't recognize them?"

"That's what he said." Emphasis on the last word.

She smiled, though, a true wide smile, so beautiful it took his breath. He held his hands up, palms down in a calming gesture. But it was too late.

"It was Spence!" she said. "This is something Spencer caused, behind Trey's back! Spence was up to his neck in something really awful. Like bribing a judge or who knows what. Could be anything, but if it's not in the files, then it's nasty enough that Spencer didn't leave a paper trail. The mother thinks Trey was in on it. But he wasn't. He doesn't know them. If we can prove that Trey didn't know—"

"That's a big leap," Marshall said. "It's a lot of leaps. Gabrielle could still find—"

"It makes sense, though!"

It did, but her hope in this best possible explanation would close her mind to other possibilities. He could not afford that luxury. The problem was, with Spence gone and Gabrielle's searches coming up empty, there was only one way to uncover the connection. He'd have to talk to the Wilkersons.

It was the last thing he wanted to do. They would be reeling from their child's disappearance and the awful pressure of being wrongfully suspected. And for them Geoff was *missing*. Nothing on the wife's social media indicated they thought he was dead, but Marshall couldn't tell them the truth. They would want to know all the details, and he'd be implicating Bree. The whole thing was tricky as hell, but he didn't see another way. Not in the time they had.

"I have to go to Gadsden," he told her. "Now."

"Damn right we do," she said.

He blinked. "You have to talk to Trey."

She waved that off. "How far is Gadsden? Two hours? At most? Trey won't be home until late. I can't sit here alone all day, waiting for him. I swear to God, I'll go insane. The girls are with Mom, and I need to be doing something to help Robert. This is it."

He didn't know how to tell her no, but he should. "We can't tell them the truth. We have to be careful and hard on them at the same time. It will be difficult. Not comfortable or kind."

"I'm coming," she insisted. "I'll follow your lead. I know we can't go in honest. But I'm a good actor. This is something I can do."

Maybe she could. This was the woman who, with her baby freshly missing, had put on a fancy dress and lipstick and lied and lied and lied. Every word and glance and smile at the gala had been a separate deception. She'd fooled him for quite a while, and he had a damn good track record for spotting liars.

"Okay," he said.

"We're going to get Robert back," she said. She came to him then, eyes blazing with hope and so much boldness. She took him by the arms, and in the set lines of her face there was nothing of her anxious, rules-bound mother. This courage was a thing Betsy had fostered in her. It was like seeing a small piece of his wife, alive in her.

Betsy lived on inside him, too. She had formed him. She was the one who'd told him every day, with only her easy, unblinking faith, that he was nothing like his father. That he was the kind of man a person could count on.

"Yes," he said, against his better judgment. "We'll get him back."

PART II

SONS

12

BY THE TIME we got to Gadsden, I had half a hundred texts from Anna-Claire, asking to come by the house. The very idea was a horror to me, and not only because she'd find it empty and realize something so much worse than stomach flu was happening. The place felt gutted, pitted, its newly hollow center filled with danger. I told her in no uncertain terms to stay away, as if I believed that she could catch something, as if terror were contagious. Even if I had been at home to smile and lie to her, I did not want her breathing the air.

She pushed me, relentless. She had a global-studies report due Monday. She needed her laptop, and her copy of *I Am Malala*, and the soft blue hoodie that helped her think. I told her no again, that this bug was very contagious. She insisted with the invincible certainty of a thirteen-year-old that she would not get sick.

Grandma and Peyton can wait in the car. I'll bring Lysol and spray it in a cloud all around myself as I runrunrun up to my room. Mom. MOM. It will take one second!

"Dear God, this child," I said to Marshall. Texting with her about these small, real troubles made me feel disoriented, almost dizzy. I remembered that I used to be a woman who cared deeply about her daughter's book reports. I could not get there from here. I had no patience for her concerns, so far away and foolish.

Then she got my mother to text me, too. Honey? A-C is really worried. I have a surgical mask she can wear to run in. She needs her Malala. . . .

I told Mom to take them to Little Shop of Stories and buy another copy and any book that Peyton wanted. My treat. As for the laptop, Anna-Claire could go to Google Docs and work from Mom's old Dell.

But the HOODIE!!!!! my daughter texted.

Okay, I finally texted back. Come get it. But bring your phone to hand me when you arrive because the second you set foot in this house, you're grounded. Two weeks.

That, finally, ended it. She had always been this willful. Even as a newborn, she'd kept her days and nights reversed for weeks, beating every method for reorienting babies I could find in books or on the Internet.

I was the one who stayed up with her, because I had the breasts. I'd learned to nap when she did, lying on my side in our king-size bed with her in the center, one palm on her chest, feeling the rhythm of her small breaths even in my sleep. One afternoon when she was about two weeks old, I woke to find Trey stretched out on the other side of her, propped up on an elbow, watching us with an odd, small smile on his face.

"What are you thinking?" I asked, sleepy and happy to have him home early.

He smiled wider, as if I'd caught him out, but he answered.

"I was thinking how the shape of us has changed. In ways I didn't see coming." I gave him a puzzled look, and he went on. "It's like she's this little pink dot, and you're wrapped around her in a yellow warning circle. Then I'm wrapped around you, red. And nothing can get to you, much less her, unless it comes through me."

I laughed. "Well, that sounds like a lot of manly bullshit."

"I know, I know!" He chuckled. "Maybe it's a mammal thing.

Or maybe it's because she's so new and you're so tired. Look, I know you're not weak. I saw you push her out—you're a superhero. But I still have this crazy urge to go punch a bear to prove I can protect you. Maybe when she's older, and when you are up and about, I won't feel this way. But now? I look at that floppy little thing and your tired eyes, and the shape of us feels like a bull's-eye. The baby at the center, you around her, then me around you."

It *was* manly bullshit, but I also liked it. He could be outermost ring in his shape, I decided, as long as I was the outer ring in mine. I had to be willing to wrap all the way around him and our baby and protect them, just as fierce and true.

I had been willing. Then. Now Robert was gone from our safe concentric circles. We'd been cored.

Trey didn't even know it yet. I dreaded telling him. There were so many things we could say to each other, shattering, awful things that we would never be able to unhear. I'd been stupid, and I'd gotten so much wrong. I was the one who'd looked away from Robert. I'd been too afraid to call Trey or the police. I'd obeyed, blindly, and my decisions had led to Spence's death. I could not bear it if my husband came at me, using all these things I blamed myself for as weapons, and yet I had such an ugly, blame-soaked question aimed at him. It was sour as bile, bubbling in the back of my throat.

What did you do?

As we drove through spats of dark, gray rain, I prayed hard that the answer would be, *Nothing. It was Spencer.* It frightened me, how badly I wanted the Wilkersons to say, *Spencer Shaw? Oh, yes. We go way back, and we helped him do awful things. Illegal things to slant a court case his way, and of course, his partner, Trey, knew nothing.*

It wouldn't absolve me of my part in Spence's death, but it would make it a little easier to live with. More important, it killed the awful question that felt like a gun in my hand, aimed at my husband. If Trey's worst sin were being ignorant or blind to Spencer's doings, then I'd already forgiven him.

Ever since they'd gone their separate ways in law school, Spence had been more colleague than friend, but Trey couldn't cut Spence out entirely. They were family. They worked together at a firm where over half the partners were relatives of both by birth or marriage.

When we saw Spence socially, it was tied to a client dinner or some other work obligation. Trey sometimes hung out with Spence alone, especially as Spence's marriages had failed, but he steered clear of Spence's posse of hard-drinking male friends. That set went off on high-stakes Vegas weekends and booze-fueled hunting trips, and they were not averse to a little coke or speed or Adderall. Almost all of them were divorced. Some more than once, and for the same reasons that had broken up Spencer's marriages. Trey kept a clean line between himself and all that. I knew this. I had seen it. So it made sense to me that Trey would not be part of Spencer's darker legal doings either.

As we entered the Wilkersons' neighborhood, I tried to set all this aside. These thoughts belonged wholly to Bree Cabbat, and I could not be her now. I packed away my daughters, safe with my vigilant mother, and my husband, flying home early for all the wrong reasons. Hardest of all, I tucked Robert, safe and sleeping, into a warm sanctuary at the bottom of my brain. I also tried to forget that Geoff was dead. I would soon be face-to-face with his parents. The character I was playing did not know what had happened to their son.

The rain eased to a drizzle as Marshall's GPS guided us toward their house. The mother had spoken of the Wilkersons as if they were rich, but I'd taken that with a grain of salt. I knew from when I was little that even the lower rungs of the middle class looked pretty damn rich when you were poor. But this neighborhood was definitely upper-middle-class; gracious old Tudors and Colonials were mixed in with some outsize newer builds, all lining streets that spread out behind a country club, many with views of the golf course.

"How much do community-college professors make?" I asked.

"Not this much," Marshall said, giving me a one-sided smile.

I knew that the boxy McMansion with its three tiers of symmetrical windows belonged to the Wilkersons before I saw the house number. It was the only home on the street with untrimmed bushes and a ragged lawn. They must have forgotten to schedule their service.

We cruised past. There was an older-model BMW parked in the drive, and the dark sky let us see that there were lights on inside.

"Someone's home," I said.

Marshall hadn't called in advance. Calling would give them two hours to decide if they'd meet with us or what they'd tell us, and he wanted to see their reactions fresh. I'd worried that no one would be home, but if that were the case, Marshall planned to stake out the house while I took a rental car back to Decatur. No matter what, I had to be home before Trey. If he found our house empty, he might panic and call my mother or the police.

Marshall turned the corner before parking his old Taurus. We'd gotten a Lyft back to the Botanical Garden to pick it up. We left it out of sight and headed back down the street to the Wilkerson house; he didn't want them to see the make and model or, worse, think to write down his plate number.

The drizzle was now a mist. Not enough for umbrellas, just enough to make us hurry.

Marshall still wore his nicest suit, a dark gray with a subtle stripe that he'd had on at the party. I'd pressed it out for him and loaned him a fresh shirt and tie. It was an older shirt, too tight for Trey but still a bit too large for rangy Marshall.

Marshall's plan was to stay as close to the truth as possible without giving away who we were. My legal situation was too precarious, he felt, to allow us to be honest. He would say he was a freelance PI, no association with the firm. If they didn't look closely at his license, they might even assume we were from Alabama, too. He'd say we'd come to them because he was working a missing-child case that was similar to their own.

He'd introduce me as his partner, but he'd told me to talk as little as possible, as if I had the dual role of a PI and a stone statue, mute and pale. I'd thrown on a simple blue dress that was more suited to an afternoon fund-raiser, but it was the most businesslike thing in my closet.

As we went up the walk, I was already having a hard time keeping both our missing children fictional. I pinched the soft flesh between my thumb and index finger, hard. I was a person who did not know Geoff's face or his fate. There was no Robert in this story. I was not a mother.

I set my face to something neutral, then reached out and touched the bell.

Almost at once we heard slapping, angry footsteps, and then the door was jerked open. Kelly Wilkerson, wearing yoga pants covered in cat hair and a tight white T-shirt with food and coffee stains spattered across her breasts, sized us up in a hot, raking glance. Her blond hair hung in dirty hanks around her face.

"You came!" she said. "My husband said you wouldn't."

I felt myself spin into flux. She was expecting someone. Strangers. I exchanged a glance with Marshall; neither of us knew who we'd just become, but in that glance I knew we were both willing to be whoever she expected, if it got us in the door.

"May we come in?" Marshall asked in a neutral tone. Not overly friendly, but not coolly professional either.

"Sure." She opened the door wider, and as the gray daylight hit her face, I felt my heart bottom out. On Facebook she'd looked like a grown-up with her sleek hair and perfect makeup, but her soft jawline and the baby-plump skin around her eyes said she was closer to Anna-Claire's age than my own, barely legal to drink. Before we could step through, suspicion darkened her face, and she said, "Wait. You're not reporters, are you? My lawyer says you have to tell me if you are, and we're not talking to the press."

"We're not reporters," Marshall said.

"Okay, then," she said, pulling us inside a huge, vaulted foyer with a gaudy chandelier. "Adam says hiring a publicist is going to make us look more guilty, but it's what people do now. Because of Twitter. We'll be crucified on Twitter if they actually charge us. We have to get our side of the story out, but our stupid lawyer says we aren't allowed to talk to reporters, not at all, for any reason, and the police keep coming back to question us, and no one's looking for Geoff. That's the main thing. They won't look for Geoff because they think I did something to my own baby. Nobody believes me."

So I was a publicist. I felt my expression warming as I sank into the role. It helped that I, of all people, knew that the cops had it so very wrong. When I told her, "I believe you," it rang with truth.

Marshall said, "Is your husband home? We'd like to talk to both of you if we could."

"He went to the store. He said. To get bread and milk, like if a hurricane was coming." She snorted and passed a hand over her eyes. She was answering Marshall's question, but as her hand dropped, her gaze settled on me. Her eyes were bruise-blue and shiny as glass. They didn't belong in a living being's face. "That's some bullshit right there. Is it bad to lie to your publicist? Because I'm pretty sure he's actually off screwing his wife. Ex-wife. The other wife." She laughed, an abrupt and ugly sound. "He wouldn't want that in the press release, huh? But I don't care. You can put it right in. Say that while the police are circling me like sharks and not looking for my son, my husband is off finding comfort in the big fat bosom of his ex."

I was glad my job was to be quiet then, because I couldn't speak. I could barely breathe. Was I looking at the person I would become if we didn't get Robert back? She was feral and simmering, either drunk or high on something. Whatever she'd taken, it was not enough to push down her quaking fury at her husband, at the police, at the awful state of not-knowing she'd been left in for six weeks.

I had a strong maternal urge to pull her into my arms, as if she were one of my own girls. I wanted to rock her and let her scream out her rage. I wanted to scream with her. It was all I could do to keep my face in the plain, interested shape of Potential Publicist, trying to get hired.

"Do you think he'll be back soon?" Marshall asked. Her husband was the one we most wanted to talk to. He was a law professor, likely an ex-lawyer, and closer to Spencer's age.

"Sure. I mean, how long can that particular errand possibly take?" She snorted at her own joke, then extended one arm in a parody of gracious welcome. "Shall we await him in the living room?"

The foyer had wide arches on either side, showing me a dining room with a formal living room across from it. They looked like stage sets for an updated production of *A Doll's House*. Everything matched, perfectly. It was as if she'd gone to some upscale Rooms To Go and had them pack up entire staged areas for her, even the oversize stone vase and the painted wall fan and the mirror.

She started toward the living room but then paused, staring at her sofa and the matchy-matched floral chairs as if she'd never seen the room before.

"No. Let's go back to the kitchen. I could use a drink. You want a drink?" She didn't wait for an answer, though a drink was the very last thing she needed. As we followed her deeper into the house, Marshall shot me a warning look, though what he was warning me against, I could not fathom. "I hate that couch. I was pregnant when I picked it out. The house, too. It was the second house we looked at, and I said, 'This one, please,' like I was picking out an ice-cream flavor, and he bought it for me, just like that. His wife still lives in his real house. She got most of his real furniture, too."

"I'm very sorry," Marshall said, grave and truthful. I knew him well enough to recognize that for these three words at least, he was not in character.

We came into a huge kitchen with a dining nook and an open keeping room behind it. On the back wall was a stone fireplace with a large flat-screen TV over the mantel.

This room felt realer than the others, as if people actually lived here. At the same time, it looked gutted. The walls were bare, and a leather sectional sofa and a low coffee table were the only pieces of furniture in the large space. There was a faint smell of rot in the air, treacle-sweet and cloying.

"Maybe you could answer a few questions while we wait for him?" Marshall said.

"Drinks!" she said, ignoring this.

She was already pulling open a white cabinet. The whole kitchen was white-on-white, but right now it was filthy. Dishes were piled up in the farmhouse sink and along the counter. Three or four disposable aluminum casserole pans were in a stack, the sides encrusted with dried food. Beside me there was a set of stainless-steel flour and sugar canisters with a small army of prescription pill bottles standing in an amber row in front of them. A dozen or so fresh peaches were rotting down to sludge in a crystal bowl. A cloud of tiny fruit flies hovered around them.

"Do you have coffee?" I asked her.

She could use some, and I spotted a fancy Nespresso machine on the other side of the sink. She shook her head, though, dragging out a bottle of Hendrick's.

"I have room-temp gin or fuck off. Which would you prefer?"

"I'm good, thanks," Marshall answered.

She opened another cabinet, but it was empty. The glasses were scattered, used and dirty, around the room. She picked them up, one by one, smelling them and peering at the bottoms, until she found two that did not have visible mold growing inside. She banged them onto a clear space on the island so hard I was shocked they didn't shatter against the marble. Then she looked to me.

"No thanks." My smile felt sickly.

She sloshed gin into both glasses anyway, then picked up the fuller one and drank it off. She banged it down again, just as hard.

"You sure?" She picked up the other glass, waving it back and forth between us.

"We're good," Marshall repeated.

She wheeled on him. "Oh, you're good, are you? How nice for you." The gin sloshed in its glass. I was afraid that she was going to drink this second shot, too, and God only knew how many of the prescriptions lined up on the counter were already in her system.

"I'd love some." I reached for the glass.

"Offer rescinded." She jerked it back and gulped it down, open-throated. Her eyes were watering now, and her voice was raspy from raw liquor.

"We just need to ask you a few questions," Marshall began, but those were the exact wrong words.

She drew back, chest heaving. "Are you reporters? If you are, you have to tell me. Are you some kind of sneaky cops?"

"We're not reporters or cops," Marshall said, calm and easy, as if he were talking to a wild horse. "We're not publicists either."

I saw fear flash across her face, and then it was gone and she was laughing. "No? For a second I thought, oh God, they're here to rob and kill me, and then I realized I don't care. That seems fine, actually." She shrugged, then turned to me, waving a hand at my dress. "But I doubt robber-killers wear Max Mara."

"My name is Marshall." Marshall pulled out his wallet, flipping it open to show her his license. He was in the sitting area, across the breakfast counter, too far for her to see his details. Not that it mattered. She barely glanced at it. "I'm a private investigator."

Her too-bright doll's eyes pointed back at me. "I know that dress. Nine hundred dollars, right? I saw it at Saks just before Geoff—" Her voice cut out abruptly. Then she went on. "I was waiting for it to go on sale, but you have it already. You must be here to milk us for cash. Get a few more full-price dresses, huh? Well, we already have a PI milking us. Fat lot of good that happy asshole's done."

Marshall stayed in character, firm and kind. "I'm not looking for a payday. Not from you. I'm already on a case. It led me here."

She wasn't listening. She was in motion, herding me around the counter, staggering a little as she tried to gather him up as well, waving her arms. "Get out! Now! I will call the useless cops, and they'll come, too. Any excuse to poke around, ask me more endless questions. It's what they do instead of looking for people's missing children."

When Marshall didn't move, she shoved him. It broke my heart. She was so small and soft, shoving at a mountain. I felt a rush of fondness for Marshall as the mountain moved for her, as if her shove had power. As if it mattered. But I couldn't simply leave.

I grabbed her arm, hauling her around to face me. Her face was a parody of outrage, and she slapped at my hands. I held on tight.

"I'm not a PI. I'm a mother. My name is Bree Cabbat. He works for me."

"Bree," Marshall said, a warning bell.

I ignored him, holding her fast and saying, "I'm a mother. I'm a mother," again and again as she struggled and smacked at me. "They took my son, too."

She heard me then. She stilled, and her dead doll's eyes found my face. "The same people?"

"We think so. That's why we're here."

"He's still missing?" She swallowed, breathing hard. "Your son is missing?"

I nodded, and even as I said the next five words, I prayed that I was lying. "Yes. I'm just like you."

13

WE ENDED UP sitting on the sectional sofa with her between us, hungry to talk. To me at least. Her knees were angled my way, her back to Marshall. He shot me a look over her head, warning me to keep my mouth shut as questions came spraying out of her.

"The people who took Geoff, you think they did it again? To you? Why do you think that? Who are they? How do you know?"

Her hands clutched at my forearm, but I let Marshall answer. I thought he'd wring my neck if I didn't. I wished I could tell him not to worry. I'd dropped my assigned character, but I wasn't me. I was some other frightened mother, fictional. One who'd never spoken to the mother or killed a man while the daughter watched from some dark bridge or alcove. One who did not think of Robert and fall apart. One who definitely did not know what had happened to this woman's son.

I didn't regret telling her something closer to the truth. She'd been kicking us out, and without the Wilkersons I couldn't see a way to get Robert back. Still, if she told her lawyer that there was a parallel case, he'd come looking. We didn't want any kind of investigation, considering our plans for the daughter, but I wasn't worried. How would they find us? She was so drunk she wasn't likely to remember my name, and I hadn't said we were from Georgia. They would not know where to start.

"There are parallels between the cases that point to the same perpetrator," Marshall said.

"How old is your son? Like preschool age? Is he blond?" she asked, still focusing on me.

"The boys are similar, yes." Marshall spoke fast and loud, in case I thought of answering. "The method of abduction was the same as well."

She finally turned to him. "I'm shocked you found us. You must be good at your job. Are you from here? The national news didn't pick up our story, which our lawyer says is lucky. Lucky! Even he thinks that I did something to my son. And now the trail is cold, our PI says, and then he bills us again. I guess Adam can goddamn well afford it." She waved an angry hand at the house, as if showing us all the things Adam could afford. "Adam is the one who said he thinks the guy is milking us. What do you think? I have these nightmares where our investigator knows where Geoff is but he won't tell us because then we wouldn't pay him anymore. Do you think if you find her boy, you might find Geoff?"

That question would have killed Bree Cabbat. But I wasn't her. I was a woman with a black Visa that said "Elizabeth" on it. I could feel it, heavy in my purse, ready to charge more hours to keep my PI looking.

"I'm not sure," Marshall said, so gentle. "I know you have a lot of questions, but I want to get back on the trail. Can you answer a few of mine first?"

She nodded but still turned back to me to ask one more. "Have they contacted you?"

"Not so far," Marshall said, again coming in fast.

Kelly sucked in a breath, still facing me. "If our PI was any good, he would have found *you*, though, right? Your related-seeming case? Instead you came here. Adam must be right about our guy milking us. Except I don't really think that came from Adam. I think his wife, his ex, put it in his head. She wants to keep his money for her own kids."

I could feel Marshall willing me to silence, but she was talking to me, not him. Really me, not some character. I clutched my purse so hard, trying to feel a credit card that wasn't there through the thick leather.

My face twitched itself into a truer shape, and words got out, asking about the mother. "So you didn't get a call?" Marshall coughed, sharp, and I belatedly added, "Either?"

She shook her head. "No. No contact. In fact, no one calls us anymore. Not after six weeks. At first, we got a lot of visitors, a lot of food, but now it's like no one can stand to look at us." She whirled back to Marshall, desperate. "I think whoever took Geoff must have sold him. Maybe to someone who can't have babies? Someone nice, and they love him, and they don't know he's stolen. Do you think that's what happened?"

I understood her need to picture Geoff with some wealthy, childless couple, warm and fed and loved. She'd scraped my character off my skin; I was almost only me. She deserved to know her son was gone. This not-knowing—it was the only hell that looked worse than the one I was facing. But Marshall's eyes held a clear warning. If I wanted Robert back, I had to be quiet now.

It was hard to keep on looking at her; she had that right. I looked around the room instead, then wished I hadn't. My mother's eye picked out half a dozen pale rectangles on the walls where framed photos had once protected the paint from fading. Family photos, or perhaps prints from *Where the Wild Things Are* or *Pete the Cat*. In the carpet's indents, I could see the missing furniture: a toy chest, a low table with a toddler-size chair, a bookshelf that would have been stuffed with picture books and art supplies.

"I don't want to say too much about the other case until I get some information," Marshall said. "I don't want to influence your answers."

I could feel her trembling through the sofa. "Okay. That makes sense. Ask me anything. Clearly, I'll tell you. No filter. I already told you about Adam and his wife. His ex, and how she's trying to protect his money. But he's the one who wants to fire the PI, and wouldn't any decent person pay for a chance to get their only son back? My only son, I mean. Adam has three kids with her. Two boys. So not his only son. My only son. I'm babbling. I'm sorry. I will answer your questions, but . . ." She craned her neck over her shoulder, looking to me. "Can you bring the gin here?"

"Let me get you a glass of water," I said.

"Yes, okay. And an Ativan? They're on the counter." She was already turning to Marshall, asking again, "But it's possible that if you find this other boy, you'll find Geoffrey?"

"First I need to establish that these cases are connected," Marshall said, so very gentle.

"Yes," she said. Marshall reached for his phone to show her pictures of Spencer and my husband, but she got up and walked after me, into the kitchen, talking. "He was an accident. Geoff. I was only nineteen. Adam was my professor. Such a stupid cliché, except I really did fall in love with him, and then I was pregnant. His wife kicked him out. That means he didn't pick me. I didn't think about it that way at the time. But she kicked him out, so I got him. Like, by default. Just like I got Geoff." I was washing out one of her filthy glasses. She picked a pill bottle and dumped a couple of small white tablets, as innocuous as aspirin, into her hand. The glass I had was full of suds, so she tossed the pills into her mouth and dry-swallowed. She kept on talking, her volume rising with every fast, slurred word. "My whole life here is pretty much an accident. I got this house, and her husband, and dresses like yours if I shop off-season, but sometimes I wished I'd never had a baby. That's true. I'm not allowed to say that, because it makes me sound awful. But it's true. There were days I wished I was single again or in school and not a mom." She set the pill bottle down and pressed her hands hard into her head, Marshall's waiting questions forgotten, her words slurring and her shoulders shaking. "Not most of the time. Most of the time, I loved him so, so much. But on bad days, when he was crabby or tired, or I was, I might wish him away, so I must be being punished. It's my fault. I wished it, and now he's gone."

Marshall had risen, but he seemed helpless in the face of this storm. He shook his head at me, and I felt it was permission. Permission to be, if not myself, then at least human. I took her in my arms. She was brittle and small and shaking.

"Every mother has those days. Every mother. And you loved him, and you didn't mean it, and this is not your fault. Someone bad took him. It's their fault. Not yours, no matter what you did or thought or said." I wasn't speaking to her alone, I realized. I was saying these words for myself as well.

She clung to me like a drowning person. "Is he your only son?"

"Yes," I said. "My only son. So please, I know this is hard. But for the sake of both our boys, can you look at some pictures?"

She nodded, clutching my arm. "Stay close? I'm scared to look."

I walked her back to Marshall, and she was so little that it felt as if Anna-Claire or Peyton were tucked under my arm. She clung, letting me guide her to the sofa, so pliable I could have walked her anywhere. I sat her back down in between us.

Marshall passed her his phone, showing her a photo I'd sent. It had been taken last year, at a firm dinner. Spencer Shaw looked out from the screen with a shit-eating dog's grin on his face. Trey stood by him looking serious in the blue suit I liked best, the one that darkened his eyes to navy.

She stared for a long time before she said, "I don't know them. I want to say I do. I want to recognize one of them at least. But I've never seen either of those men."

I believed her. She was too messed up to lie. It did not hurl me into despair. I would have been surprised if she had recognized them. Her husband was the one we most wanted to question.

Marshall swiped again, showing her the grainy shot from my security camera.

"I don't think—" she began, then tilted her head to one side. "I don't know. Maybe I've seen her somewhere? I don't know her. But I could swear I've seen that face."

She'd probably spotted the mother the same way I had. A darkness in her peripheral vision. We were the same in this, and as she clutched my hand, I became wholly myself. Bree Cabbat, raw and hurting. I swore silently that when this was over, no matter what, I would find a way to let her know what had happened to Geoff. She'd pushed me past caring if I were caught. At this point I was the only one who could end up in prison. Marshall worked for Gabrielle, and her privilege covered him, right up until the point that we kidnapped the daughter. I'd leave him out of that, too, if I had to. I would do it all and tell this poor woman the truth, and I would go to jail. I wouldn't care, if Robert was safe.

Kelly asked, "If I don't recognize those men, does that mean the cases aren't connected?"

"Not necessarily," Marshall said, and at the same time, I said, "No. Don't worry about the men. It's the old woman. She took them, we think."

She stared at the picture, and Marshall mouthed, "Bree!" at me over her head, his nostrils flaring.

"Where do you think you saw her?" I asked, ignoring him.

"I'm not sure. Just, she looks familiar."

"If I can ask a question, now," Marshall said, tight, and then in softer tones, to her, "Your husband, is he a Ph.D.?"

She shrugged. "No. He's a lawyer." I felt a little flame light up in my very center. She was still talking, though the gin and pills had put a ramble in her voice. "They prefer people in the actual professions at the school. That's their big thing. Learn from real pros, not academics who—" Her voice cut out abruptly. Her drugged gaze sharpened, and she sat up straight. "Those other men you showed me, in the suits. They look like lawyers. Are they lawyers? You think that Adam knows them?"

"That's not the angle I'm pursuing," Marshall lied.

Of course he was thinking it. We both were. Adam had another house, and three more kids, and alimony, and still he'd bought her this place. Not possible on a professor's salary. His income must be bolstered, perhaps in illegal ways.

"You do!" She glared back and forth between us. "You think Adam knows them!" She got up, agitated, pacing away to the counter. She turned back to us, and when she spoke, it was the calmest, clearest thing she'd said so far. "If he made this happen, I will burn him up alive."

"No," I said, though Adam might well have been working with Spencer Shaw. And perhaps with Trey.

Her eyes were flat glass, no humanity in them. "I'll burn him up alive."

That was when we heard the front door opening. Adam was home.

She moved so fast. She was out of the room before Marshall or I was even standing. As she sprinted out of sight, a wail came from her mouth, inhuman, like a siren. Marshall took off after her, me running in his wake.

Ahead we heard a thud, then a crash. A man was grunting and yelling, "Jesus, Kelly, what the—"

I came into the foyer in time to see Marshall peel her writhing, shrieking body off her husband. Adam Wilkerson sat flat on his bottom in a heap of plastic grocery bags, one cheek bleeding from three long, parallel scratches.

Kelly flailed in Marshall's arms, still screaming. Her husband's mouth gaped open, and his glasses were askew. Eggs had fallen out and broken right beside him, leaching under one pant leg, so that it looked as if he'd been trying to hatch them when he was attacked.

"What did you do?" his wife shrieked, slapping at Marshall. Marshall simply carried her out of the room, back through the doorway, as if she were a child. As they disappeared, she yelled again, "What did you do?"

The very question I was desperate to ask Trey.

I stared at the sad little man, his dismayed mouth, the blue-black circles under his eyes. I didn't know if he'd really been at his ex-wife's house or only at the grocery store, but I recognized a person being eaten up by grief.

"I'm sorry," I said. I knelt by him and began putting his spilled groceries back into the bags.

"Who are you?" he asked, touching his cheek, pushing his glasses up onto his nose. I could see a ring of fine stubble, shining silver on the sides of his shaved head. He was so much older and smaller than he'd looked on Facebook. He was pitiful and bleeding and sitting in eggs. I felt such sorrow for him. Even if he had done something with Spence or Trey, Geoff's death was a hideous injustice. The mother and her daughter had invented this hell, for all of us. Nothing on earth justified what was happening to Robert either. Nothing. Our little boys were innocent.

It had taken this broken girl literally tearing her husband open to make me see it. In the ruin of Kelly, I saw all the things I did not want to be. Tonight my husband, the man I loved, the father of my children, would be home. I wasn't going to burn him up alive, no matter what his part in this. I couldn't blame Trey for what the mother had chosen. I felt myself rewrapping, all the way, around my husband. No conditions, no requirements, and no limits. Me, then him, and then our girls and Robert, whom we must bring back into the safety of the middle. Our bull's-eye.

"I'm Bree," I told him, tucking three unbroken eggs back into their carton. "The man with your wife is Marshall, a private detective investigating a case similar to yours. He needs to ask you some questions."

I helped him stand, though I wasn't sure he'd understood half of what I'd told him. He seemed bewildered. I carried his grocery bags through and dumped them on the filthy kitchen counter. Kelly was sprawled on the sofa, face blotchy from weeping. Marshall sat up straighter as we entered, but she only glared. Her adrenaline was spent, and gin and Ativan were hard at work in her.

I went to her and took her by the shoulders. I told my new and bedrock truth to her, as she trembled, icy, in my arms. "Nothing your husband did, no matter what, deserves this. That old woman is the one who took them. She took two little boys who never did a damn thing wrong. It's all on her."

Her eyes shuddered closed, and she collapsed back against the sofa. Her husband hovered in the doorway, anxious, his pants wet with egg, slow blood in little trickles drying already on his cheek.

"Is she all right?" he asked.

"She took two Ativan and drank two shots of gin since we arrived. I think she had something else before we got here. We should keep an eye on her," I told him.

He nodded, looking even more exhausted, and I got the sense that this was not the first time he'd seen his wife in this state. He turned to Marshall. "You know something about Geoff?"

The small flare of hope in his voice made me want out of the room. I believed with all my heart that he would recognize Spencer, be able to pinpoint the exact case that had started all this, but I didn't want to watch as Marshall made him confess. It would be brutal, and I couldn't bear it. Not knowing what I knew about his son, and with all my protective layers of character peeled off. I should get out of the way and let Marshall, untethered, press the truth out of him. I kept saying too much anyway, just as he'd feared.

I said, "Where do you keep your Band-Aids and Bactine? We need to disinfect those scratches."

He blinked at me, owlish and confused behind his glasses, then waved me toward a little hallway off the kitchen. "In the laundry room. There's a first-aid kit in the cabinets above the dryer."

I hurried away. Behind me I could hear Marshall beginning our cover story. He was saying we had a suspect, but since we felt that my son's safety depended on not involving the police, we would appreciate discretion. He didn't say their son's safety depended on it as well, but it was implied.

Ruthless, I thought, and yet I was so grateful to him. I was a better actor, but here we had no script, no fourth wall, no audience hungry only to be entertained. This was real. I sped up, and his voice faded as the hallway turned.

There were three doors in a horseshoe at the end. Adam Wilkerson hadn't specified. I opened the one on the right and found a small office. One of the others must be the laundry, but I wanted to give Marshall time. I flipped on the light, revealing deep cranberry paint and walnut furniture that was old and very good. It didn't go with what I'd seen in the rest of the house. The back wall was lined with shelves of leather-bound law books.

Like Trey, he had an office bar, built in behind the leather sofa. Blanton's instead of Pappy. I felt a sharp surge of want. My hands were shaking. My whole insides, too. I walked over, reaching for the bottle.

A vertical row of three small photographs ran down the wall between the window and the bar. The center one, a five-by-seven in a pewter frame, caught my eye. My hand froze. The photo had been taken in front of a white house with tall columns. Azaleas framed a long porch with a blue banner festooned with gold Greek letters hanging from the rail.

I knew these columns, this porch. Even the bushes. Trey had a picture of this place in his own office. It was his old frat house.

I ripped the photo from the wall, held it in two hands. A row of boys stood on the lawn, young, grinning, arms around one another. New pledges? Adam Wilkerson was on the end. No beard back then, but his hairline had already been receding. He'd tried to hide it with a buzz cut. I recognized the round egg of his head and his small, sharp nose. I leaned in close to peer at his new brothers lined up on the lawn.

No Trey. No Spence either. No one I knew. But all that mattered was that my husband wasn't there. I was dizzy with relief.

Then I looked past the pledges. To the place where my eyes did not want to go. The porch, where three older boys were grinning. *The officers*, I thought. Trey had been VP his senior year. Spence had been treasurer. Their faces were smaller than dimes, out of focus, but I knew my husband. I knew the shape of him, the body language. The young man to his right was Spencer Shaw.

This was a Trey I'd only seen in photos, young and cocky. Why was he here, small and blurry, grinning at me from the wall of Adam Wilkerson's office?

My husband's eyes were dark dots, unreadable. They held no answers. Meanwhile, up the hall, Marshall was asking Adam Wilkerson all the wrong questions.

This wasn't about a law case. This was something so much older. This was something personal.

14

MARSHALL SAW IT, the moment Adam Wilkerson recognized Spencer and Trey. A micro-tic of the head, too small to be a flinch, but it was the ghost of one. Adam knew exactly who they were. More than that, Adam knew what the three of them had done to jump-start every awful thing that was happening now. Marshall would have bet his house on it.

Still, Adam kept staring at the picture. He pressed his lips together deliberately, then pushed his eyebrows into a puzzled shape. Pure theater.

Marshall was glad to know he could still call bullshit with such inner certainty. Back in his cop days, sitting one-on-one in small gray rooms, Marshall could smell fear and worry and self-justification coming off the guilty. He could almost hear their brains scrabbling against their skulls like little mice, the frantic scritch of claw on bone.

He'd been worried he had lost his knack for sniffing out dishonesty, ever since Bree had snowed him so hard at the party. He thought if she lied to him again, he might catch it, though. Her face and body language sold her words, note perfect, but her old stage charisma leaked when she was lying.

He'd seen it when she was lying to Kelly Wilkerson and also

clocked the moment that the leak had closed and she'd become herself again, saying way too much. Onstage she'd always been a little more alive than other people. Last night, in the Orchid Center, he'd assumed she was shining because she was at a party with her husband's clients. Not to mention he'd been trying not to let his gaze drop to her long, bare legs. Plus, he hadn't seen her act since high school.

He still remembered, though. She'd played the killer in *The Mousetrap*. Emily in *Our Town*. Juliet and Blanche DuBois in weird, truncated high-school adaptations. Most people who'd seen her onstage remembered; they always brought it up at the reunions, how good she'd been in this play or that.

This guy, Adam, he was just a regular liar. Marshall watched him manufacture a shrug.

"Nope. No." He looked Marshall dead in the eye. "Can't say either of those faces rings a bell."

Marshall looked back, long and level. A cop stare, bolstered by cop silence, creating an expectant void.

Adam's face stayed quizzical. Here, his face said, was a man who wanted badly to be helpful but, regretfully, had nothing.

Such unmitigated bullshit. But subtle. Kelly was buying it. As Marshall had floated Bree's way-too-close-to-truth story by Adam, a little tension had come into Kelly's drug-slack spine. A little hope. Her husband's denial crushed about half of it out of her.

"Show him the other picture. The old lady," she demanded, slurry and querulous and not ready to give up. "She looked familiar to me. I think I saw her in the Piggly Wiggly. I was feeling the avocados, and I turned around and there she was, bent over the stroller. Geoff was asleep. I thought nothing of it at the time, because who wouldn't look? He was such a lovely boy."

Marshall was sure she'd just broken his pressure, but instead it was as if she'd piled more weight on Adam. The mention of a lady sped up Adam's blinks and paused his breathing. His expression remained polite and helpful, but Marshall got the sense that Adam had an idea of whose face would appear in the next picture. Moreover, he didn't want to see that face.

Marshall flipped to the grainy photo from Bree's security camera. Held out the phone.

Sure enough, Adam had a hard time pointing his eyes that way. He glanced nervously at his wife, the ceiling, the window, but finally he had to look.

Micro-surprise, micro-relief. Whatever woman's face he'd been expecting to see, it wasn't this one. Interesting.

"I don't know her." He really didn't.

Kelly Wilkerson deflated, listing sideways, her head lolling on the sofa back, as if his words had rendered her unable to hold it upright any longer. "Maybe look again? I really think I saw her. Avocados."

Her husband patted her leg. "I'm sorry, honey. I don't know her at all." Marshall heard a subtle shade of vindication. It was true.

"Maybe you should look at the pictures of the men again," Marshall said. "They're both lawyers. Aren't you a lawyer, too?"

"I'm a professor," Adam said.

"But you went to law school. You passed the bar," Marshall said, inexorable.

"It didn't suit me. I'm better here, in academia. I like the life of the mind."

Beside him Kelly continued to sag down, her eyes drifting shut.

"You live more like a lawyer," Marshall said, looking pointedly around at the vaulted ceilings and marble counters.

"I have some family money," Adam said. He waved at Marshall's phone like he was shooing it away. "I told you. I don't know them."

Marshall wanted to follow up, but Kelly appeared to be fully unconscious now. She'd faded out so fast it worried him. "Kelly?"

"M'yes," she slurred, so slack as to appear boneless. "M'up."

She wasn't. As they watched, her lips parted, mouth falling open. Marshall was about to get somewhere with this asshole, but he couldn't keep pushing while this girl slid into a coma and died.

"Kelly? Hey, Kelly?" Nothing. He turned to her husband. "Maybe we should—"

"She's fine," Adam cut him off, making Marshall's eyebrows rise. "I saw her like this yesterday. And the day before that. This is what three P.M. looks like here."

A little drool had collected in one corner of her mouth. But she was breathing, shallow and steady.

Marshall leaned toward Adam and dropped his voice to a conspiratorial whisper. "Well, she's definitely out. If that helps you change your answer."

"What does that mean?" Adam asked, but a flush came to his cheeks, visible above the beard.

"You tell me," Marshall said. "No judgment. There are plenty of questions I wouldn't want to answer in front of my wife." He was good cop now, inviting Adam into a world where men kept confidences with each other. It smelled like that might work on this guy. "Remember the stakes. The cops are on the wrong scent, and I don't think your PI has any leads. I do. This could be your shot." Shitty, considering what the mother had told them about Geoff, but there it was.

He could feel Adam shifting, but he didn't break. "I told you, I don't know those men. I'm sorry for your client. She's in hell. Believe me, I know. But it can't have anything to do with me."

Marshall caught the tiny emphasis on "can't." The guy was in denial. He couldn't bear for it to have anything to do with him.

"He's lying," Bree said from the doorway. Adam jerked like he'd been shot, twisting at the waist to see her. Kelly stirred at his sharp movement. She made a small moan, but her eyes stayed closed. Bree held up a small framed photo, stabbing her finger at the faces in the picture. "That's you, with the pledges. That's my husband, in his senior year. That's Spencer Shaw."

Marshall shot her a quelling look. She'd pretty much handed this sober asshole her identity.

"Oh," said Adam, very unconvincingly. "Was that Spence? I didn't recognize him. I haven't seen Spence or Trey in years."

Marshall glanced at the picture as Bree came over closer. A frat house? Yes. Spencer and Trey were tiny figures with round baby faces and shaggy college-boy hair. He had a blinding moment of clarity, anger at himself hard on its heels.

Not a lawsuit. Something earlier. He could feel all his assumptions washing away. He shouldn't have made such assumptions in the first place. A rookie mistake, not being open to everything. He was too close, as he'd feared.

Too close to the family, the situation, way too close to Bree. He knew too much about Spence and Trey, their job and how connected they were. It had made him myopic, blinded him to the idea that this might be old, old business.

Underneath his anger, he was thinking. *Three boys, same frat.*

That put this thirty years ago. But when Adam saw the current photos of Trey and Spence, he'd instantly remembered some piece of their history. Something bad enough to make him lie and say he'd never known them. When he'd heard that the next photo was of a woman, a face had come into his mind. Not the old woman, though. Adam had expected a different face.

The daughter? That was the most likely explanation. The mother was in her seventies, and she'd told Bree she had one female child. He did quick math. Yes, the daughter could be the right age to have been at school with Trey and Spencer and this jackal.

It made sense. So, say Adam was expecting to see the face of the daughter when Marshall asked him to look at a photo of a woman.

A young, drunk Spencer Shaw, frat brothers, and a woman spelled a certain kind of trouble. He knew what Spencer was. Or to be more correct, what he had been when he was living. He didn't know this guy, Adam, and he couldn't figure Trey fitting into the scenario he was imagining. But Spencer? Please.

Not two weeks ago, he'd gone to make some copies of a printed report only to find that Spencer had Gabrielle hemmed in the long, thin tenth-floor copy room. She was at the very back by some shelving, a good two feet away from him, but he'd put his big body between her and the door. He had one arm stretched across the aisle, resting his hand on the largest machine. Her exit was blocked, and the air felt wrong.

Spence was saying, "I'm genuinely curious, and who else can I ask?" There was something naughty-schoolboy in his tone. "It's just a question."

Gabrielle's mouth was set in a mild, pleasant smile, but over it her eyes blazed, furious.

"I need to get back to work," she said.

"Come on, tell me." Spence sounded like he was asking to wheedle a piece of candy off a secretary's desk, the kind she'd set out in a dish for anyone. Faux naughty.

"What's the question?" Marshall asked, coming all the way in. Spencer whirled around, surprised, and Gabrielle's face flashed a huge relief.

"You walk like a cat for such a tall guy," Spencer said, laughing, then clocked the folder in Marshall's hand. "Is that for the Price case? You know you can get my girl to copy that shit for you. Do you even know how to use this machine?"

"I do," Marshall said. He moved closer to the wall so he could see them both, turning their line into a triangle.

"Well, good on ya," Spence said, overly hearty. "If I tried to mess with that behemoth, the whole building could take off like a rocket ship, crash into the sun." He laughed at his own joke and looked to Gabrielle.

She forced a chuckle, but Marshall could see a red wash of anger retoning her skin.

He put on a puzzled look, like a hayseed yokel with a stupid question. "So what are you doing in the copy room? If you can't work the machine." His voice had an edge that belied his empty-eyed smile.

Gabrielle drew her breath in, short and sharp.

"Funny guy," Spence said. "I'm talking with my colleague." He said it in a way that drew a line between him and Gabrielle, both lawyers from wealthy families, and Marshall, a blue-collar hick who ran a team of investigators for a decent living wage. "But I have to go prep for that meeting."

His gaze went flat, heavy-lidded, staring Marshall down. Unlike Gabrielle, Spencer wasn't trapped. There was plenty of room for him to pass. But he wanted to make Marshall move, so Marshall stepped up against the wall. He felt no need to measure dicks with the guy.

When Spence's footsteps were out of earshot, Marshall turned to Gabrielle. Her spine was stiff, her expression now guarded. He stayed by the wall, so she could leave at any moment she chose.

"Do I want to know the question he was so weirdly keen for you to answer?" He said it quiet and wry, no pressure. Like commiserating.

She softened. A little. "You didn't hear?"

"No," he said. "I felt that something was off, but I don't know how off."

He liked Gabrielle. They'd had lunch, together with a third-year associate and three paralegals, quite a bit last year, when they'd been part of the support team on the same big case. She was funny and sharp and more than pulled her weight.

"I thought you'd heard but didn't want to—" She faltered.

"Take on Spence? I don't, particularly. That said, does someone need to?"

Her eyes went pure acid. "You tell me. It's hard to know if I'm being 'oversensitive.'" She was quoting Spencer. He was sure from the inflection.

"Okay," he said.

She swallowed and pressed her lips together. She didn't look at him as she said, "He wanted to know if black women could have pink nipples. Or if they were always brown."

Marshall's eyebrows went up. Way up. "You're not being oversensitive."

She knew that, of course. He said it anyway, so she could feel sure that he knew; women, black women especially, often had to prove they hadn't somehow caused the crime against them before anyone would help or even listen. He'd learned this from Betsy, who'd made him a better cop in so many ways. She'd made him a better man, too.

Gabrielle said, "He's curious about a lot of things. He's been getting curiouser and curiouser. Ever since Charlotte left him."

"What do you want to do about it?" Marshall held her gaze, steady, with no expectations or pressure. Ready to follow whatever lead she took.

She shook her head, both disgusted and angry. With herself, in part, he thought. Of course she wanted to call Spencer to account. If she did, though, she could tank her whole career. He saw the complications, same as she did.

"I don't know yet," she said, her look daring him to judge her. When he didn't, she added, "He was always the kind who would call a woman 'hon,' but he was never this offsides. Maybe he'll calm down when the divorce stuff does? Or when he gets an actual girlfriend. For now I'm trying to stay out of his way. But if it gets worse . . ."

"If it gets worse, what?" Marshall tried to keep the same tone, but her temper sparked.

"Oh, what do you know about it?"

"Nothing," he said, holding up his hands. "All I mean is, if it gets worse, I saw what I saw. And I'll back you, whatever you decide."

"And get fired with me? That sounds chummy," she said.

He shrugged. "I'll land okay. You have more to lose than me. To be honest, though, you need a better witness. Someone with more juice."

Bree had that juice, and she'd seen Spence harassing Gabrielle in the Orchid Center. That felt like it was a thousand years ago, and it was moot now. Spence would not be bothering Gabrielle, or any woman, ever again.

Marshall looked at Adam, the liar, who'd expected to recognize the woman in Marshall's final picture. He could feel sorry for a guy whose child was missing and still think him an asshole. His years as a cop had taught him how. Awful things happened to shitty people all the time.

The thing he couldn't figure here was Trey. When he added Spence and this guy with his too-young second wife up to everything the mother had said about her daughter, it felt like simple math. It would be, if Trey were not in the equation.

At least his mind was open now. He'd wasted so much time looking for a lawsuit.

Bree leaned over the sofa, all fury, her voice a hoarse whisper. "What did you do?"

Here was bad cop. That made him good cop. The "we're all boys together" approach had felt like it was working, so he said, "Don't overreact, Bree. He's worried. I get it. He didn't want to say anything in front of his wife, but he's got no reason not to talk to us now. He wants to find his son." He turned to Adam, commiserating and kind. "When I said I had a picture of a woman, you expected to see someone other than the old lady we showed you. Someone younger, yes? Probably this woman's daughter. Who?"

Adam flinched, surprised. He wasn't used to being read so easily. "I never said any of that."

"Sure you did," Marshall said, still chummy. Adam's gaze slid sideways to his wife. She was motionless, her breathing light and shallow.

"Who did you hurt?" Bree demanded, ice.

"No one," he said, fast enough for it to have the ring of truth. Conviction in his tone. Interesting. Bree looked unconvinced, and he came back even harder, and still, Marshall thought, truthful. "I didn't hurt anyone."

"Then who has a grievance?" Marshall asked. "Fair or not. Just give us the name. It could lead us to your son. You remembered a face. You have a person in your head. Give her to us."

That was the right question. Asked the right way. It was like steaming oysters. He could feel Adam popping open.

"Lexie Pine." It was practically a whisper.

He heard Bree's sharp inhale, saw hope igniting her features. He felt it, too. This was a toehold. Not the mother's name, no, but he really did think now that Adam had expected to see the daughter's face looking out at him from the photo Marshall had shown him. If Lexie Pine was the daughter, then all they had to do was find her and take her, and they would own the mother.

Marshall was very good at finding people. If he thought of it as an arrest, then he was very good at taking people, too.

"Good," he said.

Adam touched his arm, rushing in with a defense. "But it can't be related. It was her idea. Lexie Pine can't be connected to . . ." His voice faltered. "To my son."

"Who's Lexa Pin?" It was Kelly. Against all odds her eyes were open. "Who did you hurt?" A slurred echo of Bree. "Did you do this? Is it because of you?"

"Jesus, now look!" Adam hissed at Bree, and then to his wife, he said, "Of course not. I didn't do anything. These people are insane."

Kelly struggled to sit up, eyes blazing, hands curled into claws that scrabbled feebly at her husband's chest. "Who's Luxie Pime?"

"Please leave," Adam Wilkerson told them, catching her wrists. "I need to see to my wife."

Kelly was still trying to claw at him, held fast by her husband. Bree looked ready to leap in and help her.

Marshall jumped up and caught Bree by the arm, hauling her back toward the foyer, though part of him wanted to get out of the way and let these mothers rip Adam Wilkerson to flinders. "Let's go."

"The hell," she said, pulling.

"Bree. No time. We have what we need."

A name. A state. A location. Even an exact year for the inciting incident, since Trey and Spencer had been seniors when this worm was a pledge. Marshall could find Lexie Pine, no doubt. The only question was, could he find her fast enough? He had no more time to waste here.

"I'm going to call the cops if you don't leave," Adam snapped. He was still awkwardly wrestling Kelly. She was floppy and slow, fighting at him as if she were underwater.

Bree breathed in sharp, but Marshall held his eyes. "I don't think you will call the cops."

They stared each other down. Adam had been so self-righteous when he'd told his wife, "I didn't do anything." But Adam's gaze dropped first.

"Just go!" he said. They did. They were almost through the doorway when he added, "But you will tell us what you find?"

This guy was such a weasel. He was only now considering what it would mean if the name helped after all. That they might find his son.

It was only for Kelly's sake that Marshall answered. They would never find good news for her, but they could perhaps give her a measure of peace. Her husband's question had stopped her underwater battling. She sagged in his hands, her chalky face turned toward them.

"Yes," Marshall said, just as Bree said, "Of course we will."

As they let themselves out, they could hear Kelly braying at her husband, ungainly and unsober. "What did you do? What did you do? What did you do?"

As soon as the front door closed, Bree sagged against it, her eyes welling. "God, Marshall. That question. 'What did you do?' It's what I have to ask my husband. It's what I have to ask Trey."

"You drive," Marshall told her, fishing out his keys. "It's two hours. I'll have the answer long before we're home."

15

I DROVE SO Marshall could work on his phone and laptop, searching for Lexie Pine. We agreed to go forward as if she were the daughter. It was the only thing that made sense, we told each other. What we didn't say, not out loud, was that she was also our only lead. If we were wrong, or if we couldn't find her, then Robert was lost to me.

Once I had us on the highway, I asked Siri to read my messages. According to Trey's texts, he'd gotten the hotel to ship his suitcase and gone to the airport to sit standby, hoping to get on an earlier flight. While we were in the Wilkerson house, he snagged the last seat on the four-o'clock. Spence had died less than twenty-four hours ago, but Trey was desperate to get home to support his parents and extended family and also check in with key clients, most of whom Spence had wooed. I glanced at my watch, then set the cruise control a little faster; he was already in the air.

In coach. Right by the toilet, but at least I'll be home soon. Pour bleach on everything, please? Sorry, but I can't get your flu. Mom is wrecked. She practically thought of Spence as a second son.

Siri read the messages with no inflection, but I could hear my husband in the phrasing. He also asked if I was feeling any better and if I'd talked to the girls. He told me he loved me and to kiss

Robert for him, and he asked me to check in as soon as I could. My silence was beginning to worry him, I could tell.

I couldn't risk having him connect to the plane's Wi-Fi, seeing no answers, and texting concerned questions to my mom. I used voice-to-text to send a slew of reassuring lies. I told him I felt fine, now, just resting to recover. I also told him how sorry I was about Spence's death. Marshall shot me a sideways glance. I suppose I should have said how sorry I was *to hear* about Spence's death, but what I'd said had more truth in it. I told Siri to send.

Mom had texted also, asking how I was feeling and telling me that Anna-Claire had finished her report. Her last message said, Honey, don't be mad, but it looks like Peyton's left her keys as well. Her purse has nothing in it but nine kinds of lip balm. ☺! Can you check around the house?

Understanding flashed, and then I was swamped with rage aimed at my middle child. Marshall must have come to the same conclusion, because he gave me a rueful glance and said, "I know. I know. But she's just a kid."

No way in hell Peyton's keys were at the house. The mother had them! How else had a seventy-something-year-old woman in poor health gotten inside our eight-foot wooden privacy fence? She'd had keys. To the back gate and all the doors. She could have come inside and taken Robert in the night. Perhaps she had come inside, creeping around, touching our things. She would have seen Trey's gun safe and the deer guns in the locked glass case, making me, alone, outside the house, a safer target. She'd left her gaudy gift bag hanging on my door, when she could have dumped it brazenly down on the center of my bed.

But then I would have known she had the keys. I swallowed, realizing she still did. We were vulnerable in more ways than I knew, and the rage still washing through me became half fear. Peyton had looked away, making—

That thought cut out before it could finish. I'd looked away, too. I'd lost so much more than keys.

My anger did not abate, it only turned, aiming itself at the mother. She or her daughter had been that close to at least one of my girls. To my Peyton. Close enough to smell her coconut shampoo. Close enough to slip a creepy hand inside her purse.

Peyton wouldn't have noticed. Trey always joked that our middle child practically kept her eyes flipped around backward to peer deep into her own inventive brain. Either that or she had them pointed at a book.

I voice-texted Mom, Tell Peyton not to worry. I've got them.

If this was ever over, if Marshall's plan worked and we got Robert back, if I ever had my whole family safe at home, I'd tell Peyton that she was too young for her own set and that she could have them back next year. Meanwhile I'd replace them, right down to her Poké Ball key chain. I'd find a used one on eBay or beat a new one up a little bit myself. She must never, never know. Her soft heart would break; she'd blame herself. I would not allow it.

I checked my watch, then gave the cruise control another bump.

Marshall looked up from his laptop. "Done? I need to make some calls."

I nodded, and he put his cell on speaker so I could hear.

First up he asked a friend on the force to see if Lexie Pine had an arrest record. She did, starting from when she was barely twenty, the charges escalating over the years: petty larceny, possession, solicitation, assault, possession with intent to distribute. She'd been in and out of jail for most of her adult life.

I found her criminal history oddly comforting, more proof that this woman who'd staked out Geoff Wilkerson and possibly my children, too, who had lurked in the shadows of the Botanical Garden to watch Spencer Shaw die, was no angel.

Marshall also showed me her most recent mug shot when it landed. It was six years old; her last arrest had sent her to state prison for almost four years. She had a small, elfin face that might have once been pretty but was now creased and puffy, the skin picked raw in places. Dingy blond hair. Gray-pearl teeth in her slack mouth. Her eyes were wide and angry. I was so caught by that flat, furious gaze that I drifted onto the shoulder and the rumble strip growled at me. I jerked the Taurus straight and centered us, then took another glance. Her slightness surprised me. She had the narrow shoulders of a young girl, frail bird bones at her collar exposed by her peasant shirt.

"Meth?" I asked.

She looked like a person on a poster about meth, which made me understand fully why Lexie and her mother hadn't made it past reception when they went to the firm to see Spencer. No way Lexie Pine could have passed as either a guest or a caterer at the party. She must have entered the gardens early and then hidden while they closed and set up for the event. She'd stayed in the darkness, an avid goblin, watching Spencer convulse from a shadowed bridge or a winding dark path, or perhaps even secreted in the heart of one of the lush beds of taller plants, like a worm in an apple.

"Oh, yeah. Meth or maybe opioids," Marshall said, then fell silent, the soft tap of his fingers on the keys setting a rhythm. I had a thousand questions, but I kept quiet so he could check in with Gabrielle and run some searches. His cop friend had passed along a list of her "known associates" with the arrest record, and he was working those leads. I just drove.

When we got back to my house, I pulled boldly up into the driveway. Lexie was a lurker, but she would not be here. Given her mother's ultimatum, watching me was a risk they didn't have to take. I would bring Trey tomorrow or I would never again see Robert. Either way they won.

We'd beaten Trey home, but probably not by much. I needed to go inside, and yet I stayed in my seat. Marshall stayed in his, too, perhaps sensing my hesitation.

I said, "I want to apologize. For what happened in Gadsden. I know I said I could keep in character, and you didn't want to give the Wilkersons our real names—"

He interrupted me. "It was the right call. We got what we needed."

"But now they know who we are." Worse, we'd shown them a picture of Spencer Shaw only a day after he'd been poisoned. If the Wilkersons told their Alabama police detectives about the second missing kid, gave them my name, they would make connections. Right now, though, I couldn't care. Not with Robert missing. But I hoped with everything in my heart I'd care tomorrow, when Robert was home with his sisters, all three needing their mother.

"I'm not sure how much Kelly will remember," Marshall said, cocking a wry eyebrow. "As for Adam, he won't say a damn thing. It killed him to tell us that name. You think he's going to talk to the cops and remind his wife that their son's death is connected to his—" He paused, searching for the right word, careful, because whatever word he chose applied to Trey as well. He finally settled on, "Past?"

I buried my face in my hands. "But they don't know about his death."

"They know," Marshall said quietly. I peeked out, a question in my eyes. "Kelly does anyway. She kept using the past tense. All the photos were down. They pulled out half the furniture, too. Kid things, I'd guess, going by the imprints in the carpet. You don't do that if you think your kid is coming back." His mouth pressed into a thin line that looked angry, but I knew it wasn't. This conversation, it hit him in his fatherhood. He'd checked in with Cara on the drive, too. I'd heard her yelling joyfully through his phone. Something about a Jet Ski. He added, "Even if Adam is less certain, he won't say anything to the police. Not even behind his wife's back."

"Why?" I asked. He sounded so certain.

Marshall paused, but he wasn't thinking. He had an answer. I could almost see it in his mouth. He didn't look at me when he said it. "Shame."

We sat for another minute, silence building between us. I agreed with him. Adam struck me as a small person. Pompous and self-protecting. My heart went out to him anyway. To both of the Wilkersons, trapped in their terrible loss.

I said, "Promise me, when this is over, no matter what, we'll let them know about Geoff. I keep thinking about Kelly especially. And the police suspect her, on top of everything. We have to take that pressure off her and let her know what really happened. She deserves to know for certain. So she can . . ." I didn't know what. Recover? She wouldn't. Not in the way that word implied. You don't lose a child and come back to the world the same. "Grieve. Grieve in peace." That she could do. That she deserved.

"We'll find a way. Let's get Robert home. Then we'll do right by them," he promised. I could live with that. He said, "But first I have to track down Lexie Pine."

He looked so tired, though. He'd barely slept last night, and here he was, charging off into another sleepless night to track her down.

"What will you do with her?" I asked.

He looked at me, an appraising, very Marshall look, as if trying to decide how much I wanted to know. "I'll bring her back to your house. Until it's time to meet her mother." He made it sound so simple, so easy. As if he'd offer her an arm like a wedding usher and escort her here.

"Don't baby me," I said. "I'm in this with you. God, you're only in it at all because of me."

He tipped his head in an acknowledging nod. "Okay. I have a badge that will work if she doesn't look close. I'll play cop. Tell her I need to talk to her down at the station. If she declines to get quietly into my car, I'll bring her anyway. I have handcuffs. My car has a trunk, and it's old enough to not have that inside release. In other words, I'll do what it takes, Bree. If I find her in time, I'll bring her to you. Period."

My mouth was dry. I swallowed anyway, looking at his arms, his shoulders. If this man wanted to put me in a trunk, he could, with little trouble, and I was tall and fit. Lexie looked to be a tiny thing.

I forgot sometimes how strong men were, because on television, hundred-pound actresses fended off huge men with well-placed kicks, and because no man had ever laid harsh hands on me. Trey at fifty could still pick me up and swing me around, easily, while I laughed and kissed him. Sometimes, when I was feeling playful and romantic, I'd start wrestling him in bed. He'd let me pin him; he liked the way my hair tumbled in a tent around his face. I never once thought about how, if he wanted to, Trey could flip me and hold me down. He could hurt me. I'd be helpless. Those thoughts belonged to my mom. I never had to think of that. It was not a thing he'd ever do.

I couldn't fully imagine Marshall grabbing me either, pushing and folding and quelling me. He wouldn't. He was Marshall, so tied to Betsy in my mind that I sometimes forgot he had his own body. But he did, and it was tall and ropy with muscle. My soft-spoken friend rode around inside a beast that could twist my body into any shape, if he chose to, and my body could not stop his.

I understood this, but I was not afraid. His body was my beast tonight. He would unleash it and let it do things that were wrong and frightening and illegal. For me. To save my son.

"Thank you." My voice trembled. My words were woefully inadequate.

He rolled past that with typical Marshall pragmatism, saying, "Get everything you can from Trey. Not just what happened. Any facts or locations or objects he associates with Lexie Pine."

I nodded. It was hard to keep my gaze on his face. I wanted to keep looking at his shoulders, his arms, these weapons being sent into the world on my behalf. "I'll tell you anything he says that could help. He'll be home soon. I need to go in." I did, but I had to ask him, one more time, "Can you really find her?"

He glanced over, and I could see his conflict written on his face. He wanted to reassure me, but he didn't want to lie. "Yeah, I can find her. Gabrielle will be looking, too, online." God, I loved his certainty. But then he added, "The trick is getting it done before tomorrow morning. And we're assuming that Lexie Pine's mother intends to keep her deal with you and show up at Funtime."

"She will." Now I was the one who sounded certain. The mother and I had connected; I'd felt truth in her proposal. She would trade Robert for Trey. I also believed she'd trade Robert for her own child, though Lexie was a middle-aged woman now, and an angry and damaged addict. She would trade because Lexie was still her baby. Any mother would.

"Okay, then. Good luck." He meant with Trey.

"Good luck," I echoed. Sweet God, this thread we were following to get to Robert felt as fine as gossamer. If any of us went wrong, in any tiny thing, for even a moment, it would break. We would lose. We'd lose my son. I couldn't think like that, though. I had to keep pushing forward.

I unbuckled my seat belt, but I was still loath to leave him. Marshall loved the law, but he was in this with me, law be damned. I was swamped in gratefulness. On impulse I leaned across and grabbed him in an awkward, sideways hug. He stiffened, surprised, but then he hugged me back.

He felt as sure and solid as an edifice. I didn't want to let go. But we had separate work to do now. I got out and hurried up the walk, inside. I didn't want to watch him drive away.

Exactly seven more minutes passed. I watched them happen, one by one. The little winding clock hung by the mantel had never ticked so loud or so slowly, and then I heard the garage door rising. Trey was home.

I wasn't sure what I would do when I saw him. I owed him a story. He owed me one, too, much older.

I was afraid of who he would find when he came through the door. Some version of Betsy, furious and bold enough to say so? A stranger, locked down and cold? But I heard his dear, familiar voice call out my name, and I remembered who I was. I remembered how well I knew him; I loved my husband. I was the outermost ring around our family bull's-eye, and I would be gentle and only myself as he walked blindly in to find his son gone and the hardest conversation of our marriage locked and loaded, waiting for him. Even before my mind could make this feeling into words, I was up and running for the side door, and then I was in his arms. The smell of him was safety, it was comfort.

"Hi, sweetheart," he said, smiling down at me, though his eyes looked sad and very tired. I could see how deeply Spencer's death had shaken him. Well, Spence had been family. Problematic family, and not much liked at times, but loved and soaked in history. He was already grieving, and I was here to grieve him more.

"Trey," I said, and my grave tone was enough to make his smile falter. "It's worse than you think. Spence was only the start. I have a lot to tell you."

I felt how still he became, his whole body pausing, even his breath. He didn't panic or clot the air up with a thousand questions, though. Trey, in a crisis, got quiet and decisive. He said, "Okay. Tell me."

I led him to the great-room couch and sat him down, and I started at the beginning. It was easier than I'd thought. I'd had practice, telling this story to Marshall and Gabrielle. He didn't interrupt me until I got to the part where Robert went missing, and then he started asking, "What? What?" Once he was past the shock, he got even quieter, reaching to grip my hands. His were shaking. I told him about my long conversation with the mother. The party, the pills. He was thinking, hard, but I saw no realizations or dawning understanding cross his face. Perhaps he was stuck on the idea of a lawsuit, just as we'd been.

In the light of Robert's disappearance, Spence's death became smaller than it would have at any other time. When I got to the Wilkersons, our trip to Gadsden, he spoke again.

"Adam Wilkerson. I've heard that name?" He looked down, thinking. And then he had it. "Marshall asked me about him. Earlier today. But I don't know him, Bree." There were no tells, no twitches. His gaze on mine was anguished and sincere.

"You do," I said. "But it was a long time ago." I'd kept the small framed photo I'd ripped off Adam's wall. I pulled it out of my purse and showed it to him. He stared down, uncomprehending. Then he blinked and raised his eyes to mine.

"That's senior year, I think?" he said. "I'm with Spence and Justin Weller, the president. But . . ."

I pointed at Adam Wilkerson. He looked, and then his eyebrows came together, and he shrugged. "That's Ansel." As soon as he said the name out loud, his furrowed brow cleared. "Ansel Adams. We called him Ansel because his name was Adam and because he was a pretentious little shit with an old Nikon. Like a shutter stop kind of thing. He was always taking pictures. Even turned his dorm into a darkroom. He only got a bid because he was a legacy."

Then understanding hit him, and his eyes met mine, horrified. He'd made the connection between Ansel/Adam and his own past and what was happening now. He knew. I could see it. He understood the trade the mother had offered me, exactly as Adam had when he saw the pictures of Spence and Trey. I could feel my largest question hanging in the silence between us.

What did you do?

Its words and shapes kept forming in my mouth, and they tasted so accusing. I clamped my lips shut tight against them. I would not ask him in that tone. I didn't have to ask at all. He would tell me. I knew he would, because I knew him. And how many blaming questions was he holding back? Before he told me how he and Spence and Adam were connected, I wanted him to know I was carrying my share.

I said, "I looked away. I was watching the rehearsal. I should have—"

He cut me off, near instantly. "This is not your fault. No person sits inside a fortress staring at their kids. You were at the school. Where you felt safe. Where you and the kids damn well should have been safe." He was defending me in the brooks-no-bullshit lawyer's voice I usually heard only when he was practicing a closing argument. A tiny piece of me, very tiny, wondered if this was a performance, too, covering how much he blamed me at his core. Then his professional voice cracked, and a raw and naked pain leaked through. "You didn't do a damn thing wrong, Bree. Even with Spence, you didn't do wrong, and I don't care what the law says. His death is on the woman who took our child and lied to you and tricked you. Any mother would do what you did."

God, but that forgiveness, granted before I even asked, just waiting for me, felt so sweet. I did blame myself for Spencer, terribly, and tears started in my eyes. It hit me all over again, how deeply I knew this man: his strength, his character, our history. My fear of his answer lost volume in my heart.

This was Trey, who had gone with me into labor rooms, three times. The one who'd held me up at Betsy's funeral. Those were the only other times I'd been reduced down to an animal, as I was now, and three of those occasions had ended in such joy. He'd always given me exactly what I needed in my hardest moments, and his instant grace now felt like a promise. He would give me what I needed now.

"Tell me," I said. He knew what I meant.

"Lexie Pine." My heart sank to hear her name again. "What did Ansel—Adam tell you?" Now he was the one looking anxious, trying to find judgment in my eyes. I had none for him, though. All I had was love and waiting.

"Just that name," I said. "His son is missing, too. He and his wife aren't doing well. She's medicating heavily, and she lost it. He gave us the name and threw us out."

Trey stood up and walked away, and I could see fury in his back and spine. "So Lexie Pine took Robert? Lexie Pine was the woman you saw outside our window?"

"No," I said. "We believe the old woman is her mother. It's the only thing that makes sense."

He scrubbed at his face with both hands, and I saw that his eyes were leaking. The knowledge that Robert was in the hands of a crazy, vicious woman who had already harmed one child and that it was connected to his own past, it had wrecked him.

"I should have believed you when you first said there was a witch in our yard. I should have gone out and found her, held her, had her arrested."

"Stop it," I said.

He didn't. "And it's my history. Mine and Spencer's, and Ansel's, too, that caused all this."

"You can tell me." I went to him and took his hands, squeezing hard.

"It's not a good story. I don't look good in it. But it's not—" He squeezed my hands back, more tears leaking. "I didn't do anything that would justify her taking Robert."

"Nothing on earth justifies that," I said. Robert had yet to take a step or speak a word. "I blame her. Not you. But I have to understand how this began. So we can end it. You have to tell me. You have to tell me all of it."

He closed his eyes. He swallowed. And he did.

16

BEFORE I MET Kelly Wilkerson, *What did you do?* was such an angry question that the dear, familiar shape of my husband twisted into a monster when I tried to look at him through the lens of it. I'd had crazy ideas about how to know if his answer was the truth.

I would hold his hand, feeling for a pulse jump when he lied. Or I'd make him swear on his daughters' lives after every sentence that each word had been gospel. Robert's life, actually hanging in the balance, was too frail a thing to swear on. I'd watch for his lawyer tells, the confidential lean-in or the skeptical cocked eyebrow that I'd seen him practice for his closing arguments. On some cop show, the main detective said that people look up toward the right when they lied, trying to access the creative side of the brain. People telling the truth looked up and left, toward where their memories were stored. I'd planned to watch his eyes when I finally asked. I would convict him with his own glances.

But as he spoke, he barely looked up at all. We sat down together, and he told the story to his hands, clasped tightly in his lap, and I understood how foolish those ideas had been.

As if truth ever gave itself away so cheaply.

Back in high school, I'd played Blanche DuBois in a version of *Streetcar Named Desire* that was edited for teens. Our Stanley genuinely had no idea why he was yelling *"Stelllllaaaaa!"* in the road. He shook his fist and screamed the name because the script said it was time. But I'd read the unredacted play. I knew what happened in the lines and moments we were deemed too young to say or even know. As Blanche I lied like it was breathing, a necessary thing she didn't even notice she was doing. In that show I'd been Bree, pretending to be Blanche, who was pretending to be truthful, even to herself.

So I knew that people could tell lies in layers, and yet as Trey spoke, I thought that he was being genuine. Only a monster, a sociopath, could rack himself with such deep-set shame over a lie. And I had not married a monster.

When he did meet my gaze, I let my face show all my love and faith. I wanted him to understand that he was safe. I might not like his story, but I had accepted that no matter what Trey had done and no matter the mistakes I'd made, Robert's absence, the danger he was in, was on the mother's tab. Not ours. Now I simply wanted the truth.

"Do you remember 1992?" he asked. I nodded, but I shrugged at the same time. I'd been nine or so. "The Internet had just opened to the public. It didn't have pictures yet, much less video. There were very few women online, or frat boys either. I think it was just scientists and nerds. I knew people who had cell phones, but they were still these chunky blocks. Nothing with a screen or Internet."

"And this matters?" I asked, because even though his shame was palpable, this did not feel like the answer to my question. He nodded, though.

"What happened—what we did to Lexie Pine—it's different now," he told his hands.

I silenced myself. I listened. I let him set the scene.

In the early nineties, the Greeks whom Trey knew drank a lot and gobbled No Doz like it was PEZ during exams, but at Trey's frat particularly drugs were seen as "hippie shit." X was for Eurotrash, pot was for losers. Coke was the exception, because it felt so

Wall Street. A real man's drug, and many of his brothers were not averse to bumping up their weekends, privately in their rooms or bunched up in a bathroom stall. Never in the open. The norm was beer or swamp punch plus plenty of wine coolers for the ladies.

Spence was more chemically adventurous than most of his brothers, and he didn't have a regular girlfriend. These things were probably what kept him from being the frat's president. He dabbled in thoroughbred blondes, but he also went slumming with the patchouli-smelling girls who hung around the theatre department. The "Boho Hos," he called them, not to be confused with the kind of uptight, bow-headed sorority girls who only did oral. Those were "Bow Hos." Two syllables. Spence bounced back and forth between these types like the ball in Pong.

Senior year Spence was dating Lexie Pine, a scholarship freshman who lived across the campus in the older dorms. "Dating" was the nice word for it. They were not exclusive. Spence was a BMOC with a high-limit Amex, his dad's old Jaguar, and a rep for bringing the fun to any gathering. A lot of girls ran around with him. But he kept circling back to Lexie.

She was everything he liked: discreet and sexually adventurous and very, very pretty. She was "skint," as Spence put it, and maybe he liked that, too. She was also smart as hell and witty, and though these things were not on Spencer's list, they were probably why he kept seeing her. He liked talking with her almost as much as he liked sleeping with her.

As for Spence, he could be an ass, but he was fun and charming. When he asked her out, she went. He was also generous, and this mattered. Lexie had a work-study job that got her up at 6:00 A.M. to wipe down tables and wash dishes in one of the food halls. Her clothes all had that musty thrift-store smell deep in the seams. She had no car, so she didn't get to leave campus unless someone took her. Dates were the only time she didn't eat with the prepaid meal card her work-study provided. She'd wear a cardigan with big pockets to lunch, so she could illegally tuck away fruit and cheese and cookies for later.

Crazy Lexie, Spence called her, but not as a pejorative, or even literally. It was almost a compliment. He'd had non-Greek adventures with girls he'd called Crazy Janie, Crazy Amy, Crazy Lynn. He meant that she was wild, up for anything. Like Betsy had been. This I understood.

At Georgia State, Betsy was often out all night, meeting nocturnal people, talking for hours in bars like smoky holes, listening to start-up bands. She dabbled in drugs, even trying absinthe in a Waffle House parking lot at 4:00 A.M. The real thing, illegal and life-threatening, smuggled in from France. Or so the motorcycle boy who passed her the bottle said.

She'd come home smelling of mango hookah smoke and cumin, lips chapped from kissing, her eyes as puffy as they could get, given that she was nineteen. She'd stare at herself in the mirror, laughing, saying, "Hag," before bouncing off to a new adventure. Like Lexie, she kept her wildest moments on the down-low, telling only me, as if freshman year were her personal Vegas. I think even then she knew she would go back to Marshall. She told me stories that he would not want to know. Stories she would not want anyone else to know.

Lexie was the same. She didn't go to Greek parties. She barely drank. Quiet Lexie had to protect her scholarships. The one that bought her books was for winning a Christian essay contest. The one that covered the gap between the school's financial aid and her housing costs was from a church organization. It came with a morals clause.

Her discretion meant Spence could slip off with her and do "loser shit" that would have hurt his status with his brothers had it been known. He and Lexie would smoke pot and go to the midnight showing of *Rocky Horror*, or eat shrooms and sit on her dorm roof blowing bubbles.

They test-drove harder drugs together, Ecstasy and acid and Special K. Spence had the funding and Lexie had the hookups. These were experiments, not habits, though. They also tried a few things, sexual in nature, that Spence had only seen on the small collection of VHS porn the brothers kept hidden in the basement.

In October he bought her a pricey silver slip dress and took her to a French bistro downtown that had live jazz and twenty-dollar entrées. It was a *Pretty Woman* move, and she loved it. The next weekend she instigated a threesome with her pot dealer, a lush brunette whom Spence called Crazy Bonnie.

Bonnie wasn't a student. She lived in a ramshackle house on the outskirts of Charlottesville. She was at least twenty-five, and though she was overly wise in how threesomes worked, she was not a pro. Nothing Spencer did with Lexie was directly transactional. But he'd given her a special night. She wanted to give him something special back, and a threesome was a thing Spence had been talking about with a gross and hopeful fervor since middle school.

All that fall, at any all-male gathering, Spence would tell the story of the threesome. When guys asked who the girls had been, Spence would scoff and say, "Please. I'm a gentleman," and then go into extremely ungentlemanly and graphic detail. Trey heard the story often, and each time, in the way of such things, it got a little kinkier, a little more mind-blowing.

"*Barbarella* sex," Spence said. "Sex in motherfucking *space*. Two girls, no gravity." Never names, though. Just, "So, there's this crazy girl I know. . . ."

Some of the brothers might have guessed Lexie, but if so it stayed a boys'-club secret. Maybe they'd exchange a knowing look before offering her coffee on the rare mornings she slept over in Spence's room. But they were sweet to her. She was under Spencer's broad wingspan. By then she and Spence were seeing each other every week at least, though never at the frat's official mixers. He stayed at her place, mostly.

He liked visiting her world. He even dragged Trey to an open-mike poetry night at a run-down coffeehouse. Sober. The whole place stank of mothballs and jasmine incense. But Lexie was reading, so he was there, whooping and clapping when she finished.

Lexie herself developed a small, hungry way of glancing at Spence when she felt unobserved. Trey thought she'd agree to be his bona fide in a heartbeat. He also thought a steady girlfriend would be good for Spence. Settle him, or at least channel all his wild in one direction. But it never came to that. She didn't have the pedigree, and that mattered to Spence. Probably because it sure as hell would matter to his parents.

There was a diner near her dorm, a hippie spot with vegan sausage and a lot of tea choices, where Spence often met Lexie after her breakfast shift. He'd buy her café au lait and a chocolate croissant. Once she showed up when Spence was sleeping off a bender. It was not a frat hangout, but Trey was there, avoiding friends and grunt-pumping coffee, trying to care about fall finals with a bad case of senioritis.

He waved her over, happy for an excuse to close his textbook. She shook her head, a pink flush coming to her cheeks.

He understood at once that it was a money thing. He called, "Come on! It's my cousin who stood you up. The family honor is besmirched. I have to buy you breakfast."

He called the order to a passing waitress, not really giving Lexie a choice. She came and perched lightly opposite him, shy but pleased, he thought. He learned she wanted to study English lit and be a teacher. That surprised him. He realized how little he knew about her. Only what Spence had told him. That was mostly weird sex stories, but he'd gleaned a few facts. Like, he knew that her mother was a religious fanatic who'd hounded Lexie about both her grades and her virginity all her life. If she ever got a B, it was as bad as being pregnant. If she ever got pregnant, she might as well be dead.

"Her mom told her she'd been born in a little white dress that she could never take off. It would grow with her, and anything she did to stain that dress would stay. On her wedding day, she would have to wear it as she walked down the aisle at church. God and her husband would see it clear as day, so she must keep it free of blood and filth. Crazy, huh?" Spence had told him, and then cocked an eyebrow, grinning. "I gotta tell you, Trey. I have done some damage to that dress."

Spence thought the mother was the reason she was both so wild and so damn stealthy about it. Also why she never skipped a single class and studied more than any girl he knew. As if an A were not enough. She needed 100s.

Trey didn't learn much else that morning. He'd ask her things, but she'd answer short and then ask a question of her own. She had a way of cocking her head sideways, alert as a little squirrel, looking into his eyes with such attention that he felt worldly and interesting. It made him chatty. When she got up to go, Trey stood, too, and helped her into her patched jean jacket. It smelled like Swisher Sweets and almond oil, and she startled when she felt him sliding it onto her narrow shoulders.

Spencer told him later how much that simple gesture had impressed her.

"She's like, 'Oh! He's such a gentleman!'" Spence batted his eyelashes, doing a swoony-girl voice. "Which translates to she kinda wants to bone you."

He didn't say it seriously, much less as if it made him jealous. Just in the bawdy, overconfident way the brothers all talked about sex. As if they were jaded forty-year-olds with orgies and opium in their long and sordid pasts, when really they were kids. Kids who had sex the same way they had beer: as much as they could get and mostly of low quality.

"Well, yeah," Trey said, in the same tone, laughing. "I mean, who wouldn't?"

He patted his belly. He was built thick and muscular, but senior year he had a little pot. He really liked his beer back then. He still liked beer.

They were down in the frat house's rec room, a shoddy basement hole with a sectional sofa, a pool table, an English-pub-style dartboard, and five or six fat leather armchairs. The furniture was sprung, and the room stank of cigar smoke and the feet of a thousand young men, nothing like the formal living room with its grand oak furniture where they entertained alums upstairs.

Spence leaned in, lowering his voice. "She wants a devil's threesome. Says I owe her for that time with Crazy Bonnie. And she's got a point. That night really was all about me." He grinned and puffed his chest out, miming pulling on suspenders with his thumbs. Trey was too embarrassed to say he did not know the term. He shrugged, trying for cool, but Spence saw through him, all the way down to his curiosity. Spence made his hand into a devil's head, a loose fist with his index and pinkie fingers sticking up. "You know. A devil's threesome? Two horns." When Trey, with 1990s naïveté, still didn't get it, he added, "You're the other horn."

"You mean you and me? With her?" Trey said, then laughed again, but now with a nervous edge. He had his private fantasies, like anyone. Exactly none of them included Spencer.

"No, really." Spence raised an eyebrow, looking skeptical, even a little grossed out. "She keeps bringing it up. I got to tell you, I'm not the one bringing you into that conversation."

"Aw, I'm hurt," Trey said. Spencer's laughing tone had set him more at ease.

"Maybe we should take her up on it. I hear that as long as we keep her in the middle, it won't turn us gay." Spence was grinning now, clearly joking.

"But we're related. The babies would have two heads, maybe bat wings," Trey joked back, waving a lazy hand to cover his discomfort.

He didn't think Spence was actually suggesting anything. Plus, he'd been dating Maura for eighteen months by then. They were applying to all the same law schools, and Maura practically had their life mapped out from graduation all the way to death. Mini-orgies, with or without her, weren't on her map.

Neither were kids, but that didn't worry Trey. He wanted a family, but fatherhood felt vague and far away. He assumed that Maura would change her mind when the time was right. All girls wanted babies eventually, said 1992 Frat Wisdom. For now he was in love and also glad to be exclusive. She'd gone on the pill. He'd never had sex without a condom before, and it felt amazing and grown-up and illicit.

Spence kept slyly referencing the devil's threesome, though, as Thanksgiving and Christmas came and went. Sometimes he'd make that devil sign at Trey, waggling his eyebrows. It was a running joke, but private, like everything involving Lexie. The repe-tition and tone made it seem both impossible and funny, wearing away Trey's unease.

Right before Christmas break, he ran into Spence and Lexie at their diner. He joined them, though it felt weird to sit in this particular triangle. She smiled at him, eyes extra bright. She actu-ally talked, and what she said felt flirty. He grew awkward, almost shy, though Trey was never shy.

He'd imagined having a threesome in passing, like most guys, but it had been pure fantasy, involving Michelle Pfeiffer and her twin. But Lexie was so pretty. She even looked a little like Pfeiffer. He had to admit to himself the idea made him feel . . . not turned on, exactly. Curious.

Then he messed up with Maura. He'd spent New Year's with her at her family home in Charleston. She'd expected him to pro-pose. She'd been expecting it all year, actually, tossing hints he hadn't caught. She was usually so direct, so explicit about what she wanted. He liked that about her. But in Maura's mind it was obvious he should propose so they could get married immediately after graduation. That would give them the whole summer for a honeymoon. They could wander Europe, see Venice and Paris and

Madrid before law school started and they had to become serious adults.

Every week that passed without a ring was one less week she and her mother had to plan the wedding. As January rolled on, Maura got angrier and more sullen. Trey had no idea why. Then she dumped him, and Trey found himself in the middle of the first real heartbreak of his life.

He didn't handle it well. He started drinking more. His little pot expanded. His grades slipped. He stomped around the house picking petty fights with his frat brothers. A few of them went to Spence, asking him to calm Trey down.

So Spence invited Lexie Pine over on a night when their sister sorority was hosting a winter semiformal downtown. Maura was sure to be there, so Trey planned to sulk and drink at the frat house. He should have clocked that something was up when Spence, who never missed a party, stayed back to commiserate with him. He took it as a sign that Spence was growing up.

No one else was at the house except Vic Billings, in bed with a terrible cold, and the freshman pledge everyone called Ansel Adams. Ansel lived in the dorms still. There were no rooms for freshmen at the house, but he seemed to be there every minute anyway. He was already on academic probation, which meant he was banned from parties until his grades came up. Some of the brothers hoped they wouldn't. The general consensus was that this mandatory legacy was a dork, pretentious and sniffy.

Ansel drooped disconsolately in the rec room with Spence and Trey, not studying, bemoaning the loss of the party until they threw a barrage of crushed empties at him. He shut up and busied himself taking pictures of the raindrops on the basement's high-set, narrow windows.

Trey and Spence were both halfway to blasted by the time Lexie showed up. Trey hadn't known she was coming over, but Spence's Cheshire-cat grin, the way he said, "Oh, look. It's Lexie," made it clear that he was not surprised.

She accepted a beer to hold and gave Trey her tip-tilted smile, lips closed. She always smiled like that because her teeth were a little crooked and the canine on the right was chipped. Her musty clothes were damp with rain and her blond hair had darkened with it. She was so pretty.

The three of them sat on the sectional talking. Trey was too drunk to feel awkward, even though Lexie was between them, and whenever she turned to Trey, Spence flashed that devil hand sign over her head. Across the room Ansel was snapping shots of the crushed beer cans they had chucked at him. When that got old, he drifted closer, but he was smart enough to keep his mouth shut; they had accumulated quite a bit more ammo.

Then Spence asked her, "Did you bring us a present?"

When she nodded, he went rummaging in Lexie's jeans pockets, making her giggle. He pulled out a Baggie of dried mushrooms, and he and Lexie each ate a couple. Trey, whose entire drug experience was limited to three bumper snorts of coke, was drunk enough to eat one, too. Spence, who'd hit the magnanimous stage of his inebriation, even offered one to Ansel. He turned them down.

The colors in the room grew brighter and louder and more luminous. Trey had never seen so many colors. He couldn't quite remember the names of some of them. Lexie set her beer aside— she'd barely touched it anyway—and started swishing her hands through the air, dancing them, leaving trails of a thousand hands, all rainbow-colored. She smiled that tilted, closed-mouth smile, eyes shining.

"I like your hair," Lexie said to Trey. She touched it, tentatively, then petted it, then let her fingers ripple through it. "It's so gold. It feels like something Rumplestumpskin spun."

"Rumblestilskit," Trey corrected, then realized that was also wrong.

"Rump-pump-bump-skin," Spence said, and they all laughed, a slow kind of underwater sound.

Lexie's hands kept petting Trey's hair, and he could feel the

colors her touch left on his scalp. He reached out and touched her
hair. It had dried, and it felt flossy and fine, and there was Spence,
behind her, his hands on her waist. At that moment the devil's
threesome moved from a joke to something possible. Then Spence
bent her head back and kissed her while her fingers were still twin-
ing in Trey's hair. When Spence released her mouth to trail kisses
down her neck, she looked directly at Trey, her gaze brazen and
inviting. It stopped being possible and became a thing that was
absolutely going to happen.

"My room," Spence said, and Lexie nodded, dreamy, drifting
toward the stairs.

"Come on," she said to Trey, and his legs pushed him upright.
Ansel got up, too.

Spence said, "Not you, numbnuts," and Ansel sat back down.

Spence followed Lexie and caught her on the stairs, his hands
running up her thighs to her waist, and she was arching into his
touch even as they navigated up. Trey followed behind, as if pulled
by the long, almost visible locks of her rainbow hair that had entwined him. He could hear Ansel's camera whirring sadly as they
left him, documenting his abandonment.

Spence had an officer's room, with its own bathroom, but it
was on the third floor. Getting there took so damn many stairs,
and they seemed to stretch as Trey swam slowly up them. The
other two had started before Trey got into the room, but Lexie
reached her arms out to him, an invitation that pulled him over to
join them.

He didn't remember much of the act itself. It was dim; the only
light came from Spencer's ironic red lava lamp. His clothes came
off or were off or she took them off, and he sank into a red and
velvet darkness. Outside, the rain picked up, a drumming he felt in
his body, all over and inside him.

Lightning flashed, and thunder growled in after. The three of
them stopped drifting and became a storm. Lightning lit the room
in blue-white moments, and those moments were mostly what he

remembered, like a slideshow. Lexie on her hands and knees. Lexie on her back. Lexie on her side, facing Trey but wrapped in Spence's arms. The arch of her spine, the curve of her hip, her tiny pink-tipped breasts. Time stopped making sense, but at a certain point he felt himself, quite clearly, becoming third. Peripheral. The two of them were locked together, eye to eye, mouth to mouth. He found himself across the room, watching, dropping back into the normal time stream, back into his body. This was Spence, he realized. Not some anonymous extension of himself.

When he left, they didn't notice. He went back to his room and passed out naked in his own bed.

In the morning he woke up grainy-eyed but less hungover than he would have thought. The whole night felt unreal. He lay in bed, wishing it were the next day or the next week. He wanted distance.

He thought, *This will fade. In a few months, I'll graduate, and then I'll go to law school. This will become my wildest college memory. Embarrassing. Weird. Definitely drug-fueled. But an experience. And maybe,* he thought for the first time, *this is the sort of thing that happens to people who are close with Spencer Shaw. Maybe I ought not be that close.*

He went downstairs to the kitchen. Spence was already there, drinking coffee with a couple of their brothers, all of them hungover. Trey hesitated in the doorway. He was relieved that Lexie wasn't there. She must already have gone home. Even so, it was difficult to meet Spencer's eyes.

Spence grinned right at him, unabashed, saying, "It lives! Me, I feel pretty good, except I think a cat snuck in and shit in my mouth while I was sleeping. Want to go to Waffle House with us?" Like everything was normal.

No jokes, no references. Like it hadn't happened, which was what Trey wished. Perhaps Spence knew Trey well enough to understand he had regrets. Or perhaps it was only his regular discretion around all things Lexie.

They all went to Waffle House to sop their hangovers in grease. It was so normal. It reassured him, made his discomfort fade.

That should have been the end of it. A pebble dropped in a lake, disappearing at once, with ripples too small to rock anybody's boat. And so it might have been. Except for the pictures.

There had been rain that night, but not a storm. No lightning. The flashes had been Ansel's Nikon camera. Trey didn't remember Ansel coming into the room, but then again he also didn't remember shutting the door behind himself. Ansel had gotten really busy in his darkroom, too. There were a lot of copies getting passed around. They were everywhere.

The campus stayed the same for Trey and Spence, but it changed almost instantly for Lexie. Her job especially became hell. Young men came to her as if she were made of magnets. They looked at her with avid eyes, as if they could see right through her clothes. Every one of them knew exactly what was under there, after all. They told her so. They made suggestions and asked questions. When she bent to wipe a table, they would dash to stand behind her and mime pumping. The boldest and the meanest came in twos and threes to surround her, hem her in, put their hands on her. When she slapped the hands away, they'd laugh and offer train rides.

The girls were awful, too. She was slut-coughed in a wave that followed her around the dining hall as she bussed tables. Her friends stopped hanging out with her. She had multiple nicknames catcalled at her when she crossed the quad. Choo-Choo. Corn on the Cob. Double Horny. The one that stuck was Knotty Pine. Because she'd had all her holes filled.

Trey and Spence knew nothing of this at first. Lexie didn't show up at the diner or the coffeehouse for a span, but that happened sometimes. Trey got a few elbows in his ribs, but these were more like attaboys, and only from brothers. He assumed that Ansel had dropped some hints. He shrugged it off until a couple of weeks later, at a party, when he caught two sorority girls staring directly at him over the rim of a picture. They were flushed and giggling.

"What?" he asked. They only giggled harder, until he held out his hand. "Can I see?"

One gaped, blushing, but the other said slyly, "Sure. We're trying to figure out who this is right here."

She passed it over, her finger pointing to the trunk and upper legs of a man, kneeling and headless. Trey's whole body flushed with red shame as he recognized his own small potbelly, the trio of freckles on his hip.

Spence was also kneeling, headless, but not anonymous to Trey. Lexie was between them, legs splayed open, the photo taken from a gynecologist's brutal angle. It was not artful or even attractive, nothing like his memories of the night. It was clearly Lexie, halfway into a sit-up, so her face was still visible in profile. Her pretty features were distorted by the things she was doing, but not enough to shield her identity.

Trey left with the picture and went immediately to the frat house, storming down into the rec room. Ansel was there, alone, still on probation. Trey yanked him up off the couch and punched him so hard he collapsed back onto it. He went to hit him again, but Ansel curled into a ball and cried out, a high-pitched scream like a child's. He stayed in a defensive ball until Trey finished cussing him out. Then Trey threw the picture down onto his quaking body.

"I didn't print any of the ones with *your* face in them. Or Spence's," Ansel sniveled when Trey finally let him up. He added, "You're my *brothers*," in a way that made Trey itch to punch him again. He frog-marched Ansel all the way back to his dorm room and burned the negatives in the metal dorm trash can. Trey made Ansel throw in every print he still had, too. He didn't look at them. The one had been quite enough.

It was too late. The multiple copies Ansel had already passed out had assumed a life of their own, moving from person to person, all over campus. The one Trey had taken from the girls had been bent-cornered and floppy from handling.

This was the dawn of 1993. Most of the girls Trey knew had

never seen anything more pornographic than a *Playboy* center-fold, where beautifully lit girls, airbrushed to perfection, lay on rose petals or silk sheets or perched on horses. Most guys had seen blue movies on VHS, but the women in those films seemed far away and almost fictional.

Lexie was real. Lexie was right there.

Trey went to the registrar's to finagle a copy of Lexie's schedule. To his chagrin he learned that the student intern already had a couple of copies printed out, and he was happy to slip one to Trey for five dollars. He was a dorky nobody, non-Greek, with no idea who Trey was.

He said, with a sly grin, "You're the third guy who's come by to get this, and that's just today."

Trey waited outside every one of her classes. She never showed, even though her scholarships depended on her grades. She didn't show up in the dining hall for her shifts either. She hadn't, a cashier told him, for more than a week. That floored him. He knew she had no other way to eat.

He finally found her by accident, very early one morning. He'd tamped down his drinking, and he was getting up early and running every day, ridding himself of his beer belly. The soft pooch in the single shot he'd seen was a tiny shame that stacked on top of his others like a cherry.

Lexie came scuttling out of her dorm building as he jogged past. She had a big black garbage bag slung over her shoulder. Already thin, she'd lost weight, moving from gamine to gaunt. Her eyes were dull, her skin was broken out, and her pale hair was janked back in a greasy pony.

"Lexie?" he called.

She turned, and when she saw his face, she froze, then shot him a look of such pure pain and hatred that it stopped him in his tracks.

"Leave me alone," she said in a fierce, low voice.

"Lexie—" he started again, but she talked over him.

"One of those little-sister bitches you pal around with gave the pictures to the dean. I know it was a girl. He accidentally said 'she.'"

He knew then she'd lost at least some of her scholarships. The morals clause. He felt a weird surge of chivalry. For a moment, he thought, *I'll get my parents to help her. Pay the gap in her tuition.* They had the money. What would it mean to them? But then he imagined them seeing that same shot he'd seen. His mother surely knew that trio of freckles on his hip, from when he was little. He couldn't stand the thought of his father's disappointment or, worse, his mother understanding, even vaguely, why he owed Lexie Pine help. The words died in his throat.

She'd already turned away and started off, the bag jouncing against her back.

"Can I carry that at least?" he asked, jogging to catch her.

She stared at him, eyes widening in surprise, and then rage contorted her features. Furious tears rose in her eyes. She dashed them away one-handed, chest heaving with savage breaths as she worked to calm herself. When she finally got herself enough under control to speak, her eyes went blank and dull. She spoke in a fast monotone.

"Do you have any cash? I can't go home. My mom . . . my mom will . . ." She flushed an ugly red. "I want to go stay with my cousin Angela in Memphis. I think she's in Memphis. I need money for the bus."

He pulled out everything he had in his wallet and passed it over without counting, his face as red as hers.

"Thanks," she said, clipped and unironic, and then she turned and left him there.

He still wanted to carry her bag. Drive her to the bus station. Buy her a ticket on his Visa. But he could not make himself follow her.

He went home and started grunt-pumping beer, belly and reform be damned. At some point Spence found him, and when he caught Spence up on everything that had happened—Ansel, the pictures, Lexie's exit—Spence started drinking, too, silent and sorry.

The whole day was lost inside a blackout drunk, but apparently at sunset Trey showed up at Maura's sorority house with a ring he did not remember buying, holding up a boom box that was blasting Peter Gabriel. The next morning he was hungover and engaged.

He mostly felt relieved. His life was back on track. Maura had a path mapped out, tidy and morally upright. He'd stepped off it, and everything had gone weird and wrong.

Their law-school acceptances came in. For the most part, it was yes across the board. The one exception was that Trey and Maura got into Stanford and Spence didn't.

Trey had a strong, immediate intuition that Stanford was the school for him. Period. He didn't say Lexie Pine's name as he made this decision. He didn't even really think it. But perhaps he felt the ghost of her pushing him west. It was a prestigious choice, so Maura was an easy sell. She was thrilled he'd consider it after Spence got his no.

He worried Spence would fight him on it or be angry. He couldn't let it get ugly. Spence was family, and they would one day work at the same firm. He framed Stanford as what Maura wanted, and Spence was surprisingly cool. Maybe he wanted a break from Trey, too. He'd felt something for Lexie, and he had failed her. Trey was part of that.

"I'll miss you, cuz, but I get it. You have to follow the pussy," he said. "I'm going to stay at UVA, I think. I'll see you back at home."

That was that. Trey and Maura got married after graduation and spent the summer roaming Europe, exactly as she'd wanted. He didn't think about Lexie often, and when he did, the accompanying shame made him shove it away. He never considered what had become of her, or at least not realistically. He was young, and he had grown up wealthy; he didn't have the context. In his head she'd faced the consequences he would have had to face. Embarrassment. An angry parent. A different, maybe less impressive school. He was not from a place where people got only one shot or were allowed only one mistake. In his world there were infinite chances.

He finished law school. He came home to Georgia and passed the bar. He started his job, working crazy hours to earn his partnership. He realized Maura had meant it the thousand times she'd said she never wanted kids, and they began letting go of each other, working toward an amicable split. By the time he met me in the High Museum, Lexie Pine was a lost night that had happened more than a decade in his past.

He left her there, and there she stayed. Until right now. He set the whole story down before me, every detail, bleak and ugly. Then he looked at me, ashamed and sorry, afraid and defensive, to see if I still loved him after this.

17

ON THE WAY back to Atlanta, with Bree driving, Marshall began calling in markers and burning stored-up favors. Before he was done, he might be in favor debt. But this was Bree. This was her baby. No regrets.

The first thing he did was call his old partner on the ATL PD to give him Lexie Pine's name and approximate age. He asked him for any and all information, as fast as possible. Then he called Gabrielle to update her so she wouldn't waste more time on Trey and Spencer's old case files. She moved to tracking down the family that had owned Funtime, back when it was open. The Dentons. She agreed with Marshall that the mother had picked Funtime for a reason. The Dentons might know her, even have good guesses about where she'd go to ground.

"If you find them, tell them you're a lawyer and you're looking for her with news about an inheritance," he said.

"But I am a lawyer. Which means I probably don't need help coming up with a good story," she shot back, tart.

"Of course not," he said. "Sorry."

She blew all her breath out, slow. "No, I am. It's a good idea. I'm just . . ."

Tired, probably, and stressed out and horrified.

"Me, too," he assured her, and they got off the phone.

By then his partner had sent back an email with several files attached. Lexie Pine's prison and arrest records. She'd gone off parole seven months ago. That was a disappointment. He did have her last known address, though, plus a list of known associates and family.

Father, Preston Early Pine, deceased. And then her mother. Now he had the enemy's real name. Coral Lee Pine, age seventy-two, address unknown.

Marshall's investigator's license gave him access to some powerful search engines, but they couldn't provide everything he needed. Not legally. He had a contact number for a pair of computer "researchers" who were willing to operate outside those constraints. James and Tiana Weaver. He'd never used them. Marshall was a straight shooter, and the Weavers' brand of back-channel info was seldom admissible in court. But he'd heard that they could find out almost anything.

With a faint shock of irony, he remembered that Spence had given him the number. The connection was a sour taste in his mouth.

Favors weren't their currency, but Bree had Venmo. Marshall called James, offering twice their normal rate for answers on a timer. James seemed hesitant until Marshall mentioned that he had worked for Spencer Shaw. He said that even though Spence, as they might have heard, had passed away quite suddenly, his cases went on.

James did a brief confab with his wife. Marshall could hear the low buzz of his voice and then her keys clacking in answer. Spence had told him that Tiana was an autist, nonverbal, who could play a QWERTY keyboard "like Bootsy Collins played the bass."

James fell silent, but the keys kept clicking. He wondered if they were checking him out. Then James came back and agreed to take the job, but asking for triple if they got what he wanted in less than an hour. Marshall agreed.

While he waited, he had a too-brief, surreal check-in with his daughter, all sunshine and stories about getting to drive a Jet Ski, and then went to Google Earth to survey the area where Coral Lee Pine had set the meet. What he saw confirmed his instinct. She must have history with the place. She had to know its layout, intimately. Because it was perfect. For her. Not them.

First, it was private. There was nothing, literally nothing, left nearby. It was a dead zone from the highway exit all the way to the small park's entrance, which was ten miles down a rural road lined in fields and forests. He saw no houses or gas stations or small, open stores that might make the sagging carousel or ticket booth tempting to squatters. There would be no electricity, no plumbing, no access to food or clean water.

A single turnoff led to Funtime's rectangular parking lot. It had maybe thirty spaces. All of them were dead empty, or had been the last time the satellite had passed over. A wide concrete staircase led up the steep hill to the entrance where mossy Funtime Jack and Baby loomed. The ruined carousel was just beyond, on a peak; Coral would see them coming long before they saw her.

He tried to imagine that old woman at the top of the steps with a sniper's gun, aiming down to take out Trey, but that was soldier stuff. Old country people had shotguns and pistols. Even with a deer rifle, Trey would be out of range, unless she was an Olympic-level marksman. He couldn't see it; this woman was a poisoner. She'd put a baby in the water. His spine shuddered at the memory of the hunger that had leaked into her voice when she'd understood that Bree had witnessed Spencer's death. She'd wanted details. If he had to guess, and he did, she wouldn't have the skill. She was a close-in kind of killer.

He went back through his notes. Nothing Coral Lee Pine had said gave him a single clue to their location now. If they met her without anything to trade—Lexie or Trey—her plan would work. They could have her arrested, put on suicide watch and interrogated, but if she kept her mouth shut, there was no way they'd find Robert. Not in time.

There was almost a four-hour gap between Bree's first, long conversation with her, when Coral Lee had been driving, and the short one at the party, when she'd been holed up someplace stationary. Robert could be tucked away in a north Georgia mountain cabin, stashed inside some shed in Alabama or a farmhouse in South Carolina, or in a soundproofed urban motel room in South Atlanta. All those landscapes and more were in range.

If it came down to a search, Robert would die of dehydration long before he was found. They didn't have a starting point. Not even a state. His own tears and stress as he got hungrier and wetter and more lonely would burn up his reserves. A baby wouldn't last long in those circumstances. Two days, maybe. Three at most.

Even if Marshall gambled, narrowed the search down to the mountains within two hours of Funtime, they wouldn't find Robert. Not even with a hundred volunteers and a helicopter. Maybe not with a thousand. Not in time anyway. There were hiking trails and gravel drives and a million one-lane switchback roads up there. Tiny cabins and hunting blinds and sheds so overgrown with kudzu they looked like landscape. No, calling the cops to start a search once Coral had unbound the baby from her chest and left him to go meet Bree would be an impossible Hail Mary.

Outside the car the green and gold of Alabama was a blur, scrolling past his window, unheeded. He was supremely conscious of Bree beside him. She'd been quiet after sending her own texts, letting him search and compile and connect. He could smell her faint, herbal rose scent. If he couldn't find Lexie, he'd go with her to meet Coral. Maybe he could get Coral to tell them where the baby was. Maye he could *make* her. Even as he thought this, he was hoping that there were limits in him, limits on what he might do for Bree. Right now, searching inside himself, he could not find them.

So there really was no backup plan. He had to find Lexie. Period. He opened a new browser and started searching for the Pine family's digital footprint, taking callbacks from his sources as they came. Neither of them was on social media, and neither had credit cards. In spite of these limits, between his old partner and the Weavers and Gabrielle and his own research, Marshall had a pretty good file going by the time Bree hit the Georgia state line.

Coral Lee Pine had indeed owned a house with a carport, and it was located in the mountains of north Georgia. It was maybe half an hour north of Funtime, which made him glad Gabrielle was working that angle. Coral must know it, well. She'd sold her house for thirty-five thousand in cash about five months ago. Then she'd closed out her bank account and disappeared. This was just after her diagnosis.

Cancer, according to Tiana Weaver's emailed report, which included copies of Coral Lee Pine's medical records. Started in the ovaries, but it was everywhere before they found it. Lung fluid. Intestines. Liver. And brain.

That one paused him. He'd heard that brain-cancer patients could suffer personality changes. Some even became aggressive, lost their social inhibitions. And she was stage four.

She had no insurance, and her doctors had given her nine months, if she was lucky, without treatment. She hadn't lied to Bree about the seriousness of her illness. She was definitely on her way out. He didn't ask, and James Weaver didn't tell him how Tiana had gotten this private information. He Venmo'd their hefty fee and got back to work.

Then the lab called.

"You owe me that shrimp dinner." It was the cute tech, Jenna, again, flirty and exulting. There was no reason not to flirt back. Gain goodwill. He might need her help again, and he'd already decided he should keep the date he'd accidentally made. But he found he absolutely could not flirt with her in front of Bree.

Who would not care.

And yet.

"Good," he said. Curt. Professional. He felt confusion in her silence. "My boss is right here, waiting for these results. So. Perfect timing." He was rewarded both by Bree's quick sideways smile at being called his boss and Jenna's soft laughter.

"Gotcha. We can discuss your crustacean-based debt later," she said, then told him they'd found fingerprints that were not Bree's. A full thumb and a partial index.

He thanked her and asked her to send everything to Gabrielle at the firm ASAP and got off the phone. He had the names already, but the fingerprints might be useful as confirmation. Or defense exhibits if Bree was ever prosecuted.

The next step was tracing Lexie Pine's known associates. Not hard. They all had records.

Two were in prison and one was dead, shot during a drug deal gone bad. But Toby Leland, her on-and-off boyfriend and maybe pimp, was on probation and had so far been compliant. That would make him very easy to find. When Marshall checked Leland's registered address, he heard the cold interior click he'd always loved in an investigation. The sound of a case coming together.

It was the same as Lexie Pine's last known address.

He studied Leland's most recent mug shot as Bree turned in to her neighborhood. Leland had a pale addict's face, his skin picked and marred, his round eyes pink-rimmed. His hair was white-blond cotton floss, and he had a neck tattoo of a Jesus face over an eagle wing that went running up behind his ear. Marshall stared long and hard, until he was sure he would know the guy when he saw him, even if Leland'd shaved or dyed his hair and grown a beard to hide the tat.

When Bree pulled in to the drive, he'd already shut down and packed his laptop. He was ready to go, but Bree put a hand on his arm, stopping him. She wanted assurances that when this was over, they would let the Wilkersons know what had happened to Geoff and that he could find Lexie. He gave them, though he was more sure of the former.

That should have been it. He had work to do. He stayed in his seat, though. She was about to have one hell of an ugly conversation with her husband. He was trying not to think about that. What Trey's story might be. He knew Spence. He'd seen Gabrielle's face when Spence had trapped her in that copy room. Spence had never, to his knowledge, behaved that way to another female associate, but they were not likely to confide in Marshall. Not to mention, all the others were white and most were from wealthy families.

Gabrielle came from money, but she was a black woman, and the partners were almost universally white and male. There was one woman, but she was a junior partner. The only black partner was male and very conservative.

That made Gabrielle a pioneer, and as such she was vulnerable. Now he was wondering if some paralegals and administrative assistants might have seen a side of Spence that he kept hidden from the elegant white daughters of wealthy men. Spence married women like that. And cheated on them. And lost them. His pent aggression, his anger as his divorce had gotten uglier, it had to have gone somewhere.

Lexie Pine had been poor. Vulnerable. Unconnected. Meanwhile there was probably a Shaw law-library wing or building on that campus. So while he had ideas about what Lexie's story might entail, he couldn't make the most obvious explanations line up with what he knew of Trey.

Moreover, if he was a decent human being, he couldn't want Trey to be a bad guy. If Trey was, at his root, just another Spencer Shaw, then Bree would leave him. She would not want her daughters in the care of such a man. She would not want her son raised in that mind-set. Though that might not be up to her, if she left him.

Trey was wealthy, and his parents were one-percenters. Bree had a B.A. in theater from a state university and no real employment record or family resources. She'd be vivisected by the best lawyers in the country; she'd lose everything. If Trey was angry enough, if he let those lawyers take the gloves off, she could lose custody of her kids.

Marshall couldn't want any of that, which meant that he could not want Bree. Any good person would hope and pray her husband was as decent as he seemed and that he had an explanation she could live with.

So he said, "Good luck," to Bree and tried like hell to mean it. To his surprise it was easy. He loved her. He wanted her to be safe and happy more than he wanted her to be his.

"Good luck," she echoed.

He undid his seat belt, ready to go, but she lurched at him, and then she was in his arms, her hands clutching him, her rose-scented hair pressing against his face. It was the last thing he needed. It was the only thing he wanted. For a moment the pressure lifted. He might as well have been on Cara's lake. Sunshine and Jet Skis.

When she pulled away, he had to send a conscious message to his arms, telling them to release her.

She got out of his car, already gone from him. Her mind was on her son and her husband and all that the next few hours would bring. He wanted to stay with her, help her through it. Hear what Trey had to say for himself. But once he was back in the driver's seat, once he was in motion, reality settled back around him like a darkness falling. It was not his place. It never would be. Time to get to work.

First stop his house, to raid his gun safe. He was heading into Lexie's world now. The Methlands. He wanted to be armed. He took his .38 in his shoulder holster, plus a Beretta Nano at his ankle. Then on to the place Lexie had shared with Toby when she was on parole.

It was a rental with peeling paint and sagging shutters, set close to the road on a block down in southwest Atlanta that had yet to gentrify.

It was full dark now. He could see that the lights were on, and there was a shit-colored Civic in the driveway. He got up, and as he came close, he heard music playing. Creedence. Someone was home.

He stepped up onto the low porch, the boards bowing to his weight, and knocked.

The music cut off, and then Toby Leland cracked the door. Same cotton-fluff hair, but longer. Same neck tat. Marshall could see it through the gap as Toby peered out. The stink of old cigarettes wafted by in a puff of escaping air. It almost hid the skunky whiff of pot.

Toby's fingers, holding the door, were stained yellow from nicotine. He rolled his own, Marshall thought. It went with the slicked-back rockabilly hair and the white T-shirt. The only visible sleeve was rolled up, as if this man in his fifties had mistaken his age for the decade.

Greaser, Marshall thought. An aging S. E. Hinton character. But not Ponyboy or Soda. Someone harder. *Rumble Fish* gone wrong.

Toby's upper lip peeled back, revealing soft, gray teeth in a dog's smile that did not reach his eyes.

Marshall knew why. He had retained his cop look. A habitual offender like Toby would clock Marshall as a cop if Marshall were a hundred years old and dead in a coffin.

"Hi, Toby. I just got off the phone with Stewart Dobbs," Marshall said. A lie. Dobbs was Toby's probation officer. At his name Toby's lip-curl smile widened, trying to look friendlier. It did not go well. "I'm not here for you. So if you're hiding a piece behind this door, I suggest you put it someplace I won't see it and then talk to me."

Toby's eyebrows puzzled up. After a brief, slack stare, he stepped back from the door, leaving it cracked. Marshall heard him rustling around. Maybe shoving a pistol under a chair cushion or down the waistband of his pants. Toby reappeared and swung the door open a little wider.

"You alone in there?" Marshall asked.

"Yeah?" Hesitant but truthful. He wasn't acting like a man protecting someone inside. Lexie wasn't here. Still, due diligence.

"So let's assume you just hid a gun," Marshall said. Toby started to protest, but Marshall talked over him. "And I smell pot. I could call Stewart, wait here, get you violated six ways from Sunday. Or you could answer a question."

"Okay. Sure. Fine, what?" Toby was even more nerved up now.

"Where can I find Lexie Pine?" Marshall asked.

Toby looked relieved. A flash of true emotion, and Marshall's heart sank. The guy didn't know.

"I ain't seen Lexie in almost half a year."

"Can I come in?" Marshall said.

"What for?" Toby asked, bristling, that feral dog's smile back.

"I want you to tell me about the last time you saw her. I want some good guesses about where she might be now."

Instead Toby stepped out onto the porch. His feet were bare and bony, pale against the old, gray wood.

"Yeah. Okay. What's in it for me?" Toby asked.

Marshall had a fifty ready, clipped between two fingers. He waved it. Toby licked at his lips, eyes kindling.

Marshall had more cash. Quite a bit more. He'd pulled it out of his safe when he got the guns. But this guy was ready to sell Lexie out at the first offer. He was excited to do it, and why not? He had in the past sold Lexie herself. He'd turned her body over to multiple men, strangers, to feed his own hungers. Marshall had to work to keep *his* upper lip from curling in answer.

He told Marshall his story, darting little glances at the money.

They'd been living here since he got out, the two of them, renting the third bedroom as a crash pad when they could. That room had been empty the night Lexie's mother showed up. Very late. He and Lexie were dead asleep on the living-room floor in front of the TV.

"The front door banged open, I mean, BAM, like a thumper," Toby told him, his pink-rimmed eyes wide. "We'd forgot to lock it, I guess, but anyway, we hadn't heard no knocking. So I sit bolt upright, and there's this figure in the doorway. At first I didn't realize it was a person. I thought it was some kind of mummy or a witch, ropy silver hair lit up from that streetlight, and I couldn't hardly make out her face much except to tell she looked a thousand years old. I let out a holler, and I reached for—" Toby stopped, licked his lips. *Gun*, Marshall thought. Toby didn't want to say that part to a guy he assumed was a cop. "Anyway, Lex sat up yelling stuff, like, 'What the hell are you doing here?' The woman ran right at her and grabbed her by one elbow and hauled her up onto her feet. By then I'd realized it was some little old frail lady, and I was like, 'Bitch, you better step out.'

"But Lexie said, 'It's my mother, asshole,' and at the same time that old woman fixed me with the meanest eye I ever saw. She said, 'Look to your business, young man.' I'd been woke from a dead sleep, and I was jacked up mad as hell, but when she said it that way, it kinda stopped me. Dead in my tracks. Like, I don't want to say I was scared of some old granny, but Jesus.

"I was all like, 'Whoa, okay, now, Mawmaw, what'd'ya think you're doing?' and she fixed me with those big old spooky eyes and stepped right to me and said, 'Dying, son. I'm dying.' She said it all serious. I caught the stink of it on her breath. I don't know if you've ever smelled cancer, but it took my own ma. She had breath like that at the end. Death in it. I could smell it on that old lady so damn strong it kinda froze me. Then Lexie said, 'Mama,' all quavery and started crying."

He was so into the story that he'd even stopped glancing at the bill in Marshall's hand. High as he was, he'd almost forgotten who Marshall was.

Marshall asked, "So what did you do?"

"I did what any man would when his lady friend starts in with the serious waterworks. I got the hell out. Went and shot pool with my buddy Harv, and when I got back, Lex was gone."

"That's it?" Marshall said. He acted like he might put the fifty away.

"Hey, now, man, that's what happened!" Indignant. Eyes back on the bill.

"And you have no idea where she might be now," Marshall said. Not a question. A statement, flat and thick with disbelief.

Toby licked his lips. "While I was getting my stuff together, putting on some jeans and shoes and such, they was talking. She had a place for Lex all set up, she said. Rehab. Paid for and everything. It had one of those dumb-ass names, like a nature-camp name. Shady Oaks or Oaky Shades or some shit."

Marshall retracted the bill another inch, and Toby stepped in closer, saying, "And I remember one more thing, though. It was in Tucker. Oak something, for sure in Tucker, Georgia. That woman, her mom, she told Lexie, 'Before I die, all I want in this whole world is to see you clean.' When I left, Lexie was promising all kinds of things, but shit. I didn't think it meant nothing. Lexie been through the state program twice, and before that her mom put her through another place, plus she went to NA four times a week in prison."

"Her mother was never dying before," Marshall said. Mostly to himself.

"Yeah, well, that's all I got for you, man, swear. I will say this, though. She ain't come back. She went off with her ma like poof. I figured in a week or so she'd peace out on rehab and come tap-tap-tapping at my window. Or I'd see her at any of our hangouts and we'd drift back together-like, the way we always done. But damned if I have." Toby shook his head and made a spitting gesture. "Shit, maybe she did get clean. For now. But I know that girl. You want to find her, wait for her mom to kick it. She'll be back with me before the body hits the ground." He shrugged.

Marshall was already getting his phone out. He showed Toby the grainy picture from Bree's security camera. The old woman, her eyes like black holes, stared boldly up into the camera. "You recognize this woman?"

Toby nodded. "Fuck, yeah. That's her. Lexie's mom. Spooky old bat, eh?"

Marshall had been almost sure, but now he knew. Lexie Pine was the daughter. He was on the right trail, for all that it was cold here. Time to go. He passed the bill over and let Toby disappear back inside. Then he went out and sat in his car to check his phone, setting his .38 out in easy reach beside him because he knew the neighborhood.

The first thing he opened was an email from Bree. It was long. Detailed. He sat in the car, looking up and checking his perimeter every few sentences, scanning the story Trey had told her.

Scanning wasn't enough. He went back to the start and read it slow and careful, the way he would a witness statement, with his brain in neutral. As if it were possible to kill off every warring bias in his head.

It wasn't possible. He finished it, then went back to the beginning again. This time he tried to read it the way Bree might. With a different, more believing bias. He read it as if Bree herself had witnessed these things and was telling him this story.

Even assuming it was gospel, he felt a deep fury growing toward Trey, singular and separate from any other feelings he had about Trey's wife. The girl, Lexie-that-was, must have been so bright and so driven to parlay a high-school diploma from a public school in Eastern Jesus, Georgia, to a full ride at UVA. She'd grown herself a single, shining opportunity in a wasteland with no seeds or soil or light. She'd been driven out and lost it, while the boys suffered no consequences at all. He could see how, in Coral Lee's eyes, her daughter's life had been stolen. He could admit that her anger was righteous.

Her response to that anger, what she'd done to three families, was pure evil, though. This was a woman who, according to Trey's story, had always had a dark bent toward Old Testament judgment. The images she'd put in her child's head—Lexie walking down the aisle in a little white dress that bore the stain of her every sin for all to see—it gave him the shudders. He hated Coral Lee Pine for everything she'd done. Even so, he found he had room to hate Trey, just a little, too.

It was getting late. He sat quietly, breathing, letting all the emotional backwash flow out and through him. He did not have time for it. When he was calm, he called James Weaver again. He had one more question for Tiana, and he needed the answer now. Sooner than now.

"Shoot," James said, and after Marshall asked, he named a fee.

"Fine," Marshall said, and hung up. Then he got his phone to find him a diner close by. He needed protein and caffeine.

He'd bolted his sandwich and was heading out to his car with more coffee in a to-go cup when James called back. His wife was magic on that keyboard, just as Spence had said.

"Oakbrook Treatment Center, just outside of Tucker. Lexie Ann Pine, same DOB. She completed a six-week program and was released to her mother, Coral Lee Pine." The dates matched up with Toby Leland's story and Marshall's own timeline. Lexie had gotten out a scant eight weeks before Geoffrey Wilkerson went missing. So she'd finished the program, and they'd started planning this revenge while her mother still could act. Nothing like a goal with a deadline to keep a person on the straight and narrow.

"Thanks," Marshall said, but Weaver wasn't quite done.

"They marked her as a no-show for her follow-up therapy, though. She never came back for the outpatient care. Poof."

"Good work," Marshall said, and hung up. He transferred their money, then sat, stewing.

He didn't believe she'd no-showed for her appointments because she'd slipped. If she had, she'd be back in Toby's orbit. No, she'd ditched because she was invested in helping her mother complete her final task.

Sober, she'd be tougher and smarter and stronger than the Lexie he'd been hunting. This person had once forced open a slot for herself at one of the best colleges in the nation. Considering what she and her mother had done so far—child murder, kidnapping, expert manipulation, making or acquiring poison—she'd gotten back a good deal of her will and drive. She would see this through.

Worst of all, clean Lexie had a separate past, separate places, separate memories and comforts. He knew nothing of these, and he had no source he could tap to learn more. All his research so far, all his connections, only showed him a life she had abandoned.

His leads were ashes, and she might as well be air.

18

TREY WAS WAITING for a reaction, but I didn't have one. Not yet. I said, "I have to tell Marshall. Now. He needs to know all this. It could help him find Lexie."

Suddenly Robert was in the room with us. His small, urgent heartbeat was so much bigger than this history.

"Of course," Trey said, relieved, I thought, that I would handle this. That he wouldn't have to say it all again. He didn't object when I left the room to do it.

I needed time away from his questioning, anxious gaze, and more important, I didn't know how to tell his own story in front of him. I might say something to Marshall that would reveal my faith or lack of it, before I knew how I felt. I went to Trey's office.

Marshall's phone sent me to voice mail, so I sat down at the desk and emailed him. It felt good to write the whole thing out. It took almost an hour, and that was good, too. Typing it, seeing the story unspool in black and white, made it feel a little truer. At the same time, it felt strange to be talking to another man, even Marshall, so intimately about my husband and his failings.

Every time I paused to think, my eyes were drawn to Trey's own picture from his frat days, still sitting on the bookshelf. He was so young. In this shot no pledges were lined up on the lawn in front of him. Ansel/Adam had yet to rush. Lexie Pine had not crossed his path. She was probably unpacking her thrift-store jeans into her dorm's dresser, nervously rechecking her class schedule, meeting her roommate.

In my head the roommate was a lot like Trey's sister, a Vanderbilt grad who was cool and kind and distant with me. I even pictured them the same, blondes with bright, white, straightened smiles and too many shoes for a dorm closet. She would have a new bedspread and framed posters and a fancy coffeemaker and a minifridge. I added a pretty mother, much like my own mother-in-law, wearing one of her million lightweight silk sweater sets, helping her child arrange throw pillows and her old pink bear from home.

I was probably close. This was UVA in the nineties after all. What would this girl and her family have made of Lexie? She was not the roomie they'd expected.

I read my email over twice before I hit send, making sure the story I'd laid out for Marshall was as close as I could come to re-creating Trey's. I was glad to see I hadn't wasted lines defending my husband or making excuses for him. I was equally relieved to see I hadn't typed "Trey said" or, worse, "According to Trey" too many times. I'd written it plain, as if I believed it. That must mean I did. I hoped I did.

Growing up the way I had, both the story and the way he'd described Lexie, her behavior at that posh university, made sense to me. She must have felt how I had when I visited the UGA campus over in Athens. My scholarship would have paid my tuition at any in-state school that accepted me, and UGA had the most prestigious theatre program. I'd gone for a campus tour that included a dorm stay and a student guide.

They'd paired me with a sorority girl who drove me around campus in her brand-new VW Bug convertible. She had a Lowcountry accent and perfect teeth, and she assumed I'd rather go with her to a local Italian place than eat the free sandwiches at the meet-and-greet.

I ordered a side salad and water and white-knuckled it, my hand in my purse, fisted around Betsy's invisible, no-limit Visa, giving the rich girl her own accent and inflections back. It was pure performance, and she bought it enough to push me to rush, swearing I was sure to get a bid. The whole thing left me exhausted. I'd chosen Georgia State, grittier and grungier and smaller. Betsy's first choice, too. UVA was upscale and elite. I understood, in ways my husband at twenty-one years old could not have, how this one event could ruin a girl like Lexie. She'd had no safety net, no backup opportunities. It was awful what had happened to her, and my husband's part in it wasn't pretty.

But it also did not make him Spencer Shaw.

I hoped Marshall would agree. He knew Trey pretty well from work, plus they'd been thrown together quite a bit socially back when Betsy was alive. But Marshall had a cop mind, naturally suspicious. I wondered if he would ask the same question that was plaguing me.

Why had Trey never told me this, not any of it, before?

Perhaps he'd hinted at it.

"I was such an ass in college," he'd said more than once, shaking his head. Rueful, but also, I thought, fond.

I stared at the picture, at my husband's boyish, smiling face. I wanted to meet that young Trey. I wanted him to tell me the story, in his own words, fresh. My husband described his younger self as "a typical frat boy," yet I hoped to God that what had happened to Lexie Pine was anything but typical.

Why had he never told me?

When Trey and I started dating, he didn't earnestly detail his long-past college years, just as I didn't breathlessly tell him all about my time in middle school. We'd talked much more about current things. Of course we discussed our childhoods, our families, our romantic histories, like any new couple getting serious. On his part, his marriage and divorce had loomed largest in our conversations. My own sexual history was recent and short and bland.

Trey was the first man to ever be devoted to my pleasure. His own seemed tied to it. Ladies first, and often ladies again. Before him I'd had only two serious boyfriends, so I had no war stories per se. But I'd talked to him about Betsy's wild year, told him Crazy Betsy stories in the same way he'd told me a few Crazy Spencer tales. Surely he'd had openings to bring up Lexie Pine?

I'd even told him about the time Betsy frenched a girl, freshman year. She'd come whirling into our dorm room, bright-eyed and bursting with story. I'd closed my books to listen. It sounded like more than a kiss, actually. A mini-make-out session with pretty, petite Dai-tai from algebra.

"Do you *like* her?" I'd asked. "Does she like you?"

"Not like-like, either one of us. It was more of an experiment," she'd said. "But her boyfriend kept scooting closer and closer. I got creeped out and bounced."

I'd been horrified. "Her boyfriend was there? What if he hadn't let you leave?"

She'd waved that way, overconfident and immortal. "We were on that flowered sofa at that coffeehouse place with the pool table. What was he going to do, drop trou and pin us both down in front of the waitress?"

My mouth had dropped open, literally, to hear that this had happened in public. I'd also been relieved. It felt safer. Less serious. When I told Trey this story, he'd laughed at my tone, telling me that back in his day Spencer's Boho Hos danced sexy with each other, would even make out, looking coyly around to see what boys were watching.

"I think you must be the only girl who didn't at least try kissing another girl at college," he'd said. "Or the only one who wasn't a Kappa anyway." That was his ex-wife's sorority, which I gathered had been Waspy and uptight.

That was all he'd said. Nothing about Lexie Pine or his own sad, related history. Not until now. I wanted to know why. I carried the question back into the den after I'd sent the email.

He was sitting stiffly on the sofa. He'd made coffee. I could smell it, though I'd been gone so long that the mug in front of him was empty. I couldn't stand what the waiting had done to his face, lining it with stress and shame and impatience. He was braced, anxious to hear whatever I would say. So I simply asked.

"Why did you never tell me?"

He blinked, surprised. "It's not something I'm proud of."

"I get that. But still." Even as I said it, I realized that my faint disapproval about Betsy's much milder experiment wouldn't have encouraged him to open up.

He looked away, and I felt his impatience growing along with his discomfort. "It's not something I wanted to remember. Ever. It's certainly not a thing you tell a woman you hope to marry."

I didn't like that. It was too close to saying, *Not a thing you tell your wife*. We told each other everything. We were partners. I had kept nothing from him.

Fresh on the heels of that thought came another. *You never told him about kissing Marshall.*

Instantly my mind filled with excuses. It had happened three years before I even met Trey, when I was a freshman myself. It had meant nothing. Telling him would have made it seem more important than it was and perhaps strained the couples friendship Betsy and I were working to grow between us and our husbands.

But it had happened. The old, trace memory was alive in the soap and cedarwood smell that I'd caught earlier, when I hugged him. Marshall and I were never huggy or touchy with each other. Perhaps that kiss was why.

It had happened on a long weekend when Bets and I came home to do our laundry in her mom's big washer, free. She asked if I would go over to Marshall's house and check on him. The idea made me uncomfortable, but he was my friend, and I could see how much it mattered to her. She was still in love with him, I thought, which made me wonder what the hell she was doing, going wild at Georgia State. It wasn't like she'd traded a boyfriend for an education; she almost never went to class.

I agreed, on the condition that Bets would use her fake ID and get me some wine coolers. I couldn't imagine being dead sober and asking stoic Marshall how his broken heart was mending.

He was a mess, of course. He tried his quiet, tough-guy thing on me, but I'd never seen such sad eyes.

We ended up hanging out, watching game shows, drinking until we both had a good buzz on. He made me promise to tell Betsy he was fine. I agreed, even though I knew I wouldn't lie to Bets. When I got back, I told her he'd been a complete wreck. I think it was a relief for her to hear that. It meant that he still loved her, too. She left Georgia State a couple of months later, mid–second semester, instead of getting every penny's worth of adventure by waiting to officially fail out.

Her time at college had been like an acting job, I thought when it was over and she was packing cheerfully for home. Maybe college was that way for a lot of people. A chance to try on different selves. I'd done my experimenting with fresh identities from the safety of a stage, but Bets had had to do it in real time. For months I'd watched her try on a hundred girls, one after another, like slip dresses. And yes, some of those girls were selfish or rash or thoughtless. Pleasure seekers. Rule breakers. They had also been her best performances; she had a spark and a sizzle in life that didn't translate to the stage.

In the end she remembered herself. I could almost see her stepping away from a pile of discarded costumes. She hugged me tight good-bye, and it was my old Betsy in my arms. Herself, but grown. Done playing. Ready for something real.

But on that long laundry weekend when she sent me to check on Marshall, he didn't know that within three months he'd have her back. He was so sad that I kept patting him, squeezing his hand, leaning into his shoulder as we watched TV.

When the wine coolers were gone, I got up and said I needed to get home. He thanked me for coming, then got up, too, and pulled me into a real hug. It was strange to feel his tall, muscular body shaking, so weak. I wondered if he was actually crying. I'd grown up in the rural South with no father, no brothers. I'd never seen a grown-up male person cry. I pulled back far enough to see his eyes, and yes, they were wet. I was moved by this, and our faces were so close that I could smell wine coolers on his breath, sweet and tangy. I think we leaned in at the same time.

It wasn't much of a kiss. Lip on lip, our mouths only slightly open. Our tongues brushed, just barely, but I learned the blackberry taste of him.

Then we jerked apart.

"Too much to drink," he said, and shook himself like a bear. "You can't drive home just yet. You'll kill a deer or a tree or a pedestrian."

He grabbed my hand and toted me along to the kitchen, as if I were a Thanksgiving parade balloon. I felt like one. Light and bobbing along. He made me a sandwich that was crazy good. He buttered the bread and put it facedown to toast in the same pan where he'd cooked onions and some paper-thin steaks his mom kept in the freezer. I'd described that sandwich to a dozen people over the years. Never the kiss.

I did not tell Betsy, and I knew without asking that Marshall hadn't either. It was a moment born of alcohol and youth and his compelling sorrow. Telling would have hurt her for no reason. I'd been ashamed and sorry, but I'd learned from that moment, piling good decisions on top of it until I was no longer the girl who had kissed him. Until I was a woman who would not, in the same situation, make that same mistake.

I understood then that Trey's story was a larger, darker version of my own. He hadn't lied or worked hard to hide this. It was a thing of his past that had pushed him to become the man he was. It had changed him, so that it was no longer his. He'd distanced himself from Spencer in the wake of it, and from the boy he'd been. He was a better man now.

He was still looking at me, his last words hanging in the air. *Not a thing you tell a woman you hope to marry.*

"Okay," I said. There was a wealth of meaning in the simple word.

He heard it. His face crumpled, and then we were in each other's arms, and he was kissing me with such relief, such pain, such awful desperation. We fell back on the sofa, and what happened between us then was quick and rough and necessary.

My body wasn't ready. It hurt as he came into me. He heard my gasp and tried to stop, but I would not let him. I pulled him in, legs and arms tightening around him. I wanted the urgent re-connection, and I wanted the pain, too. It was like the bite of the too-tight gold bracelet I'd shoved high on my arm before I'd gone to that ill-fated party. It was a place to hide my larger pain and be with him. I forgave him with my body and my pain, and he held me so tight, moving in me.

In this way we'd made our girls, so different from each other and yet both so clearly ours. In this way we'd made Robert. I was aware of that, every second as I rocked him, his face hidden in my shoulder. I felt his tears on my neck, and then he was shuddering into me, and even as his body shook, I regretted his vasectomy. Robert's absence emptied out the act in such strange ways.

He turned me, turned us both, still mostly dressed, until he was on his back and I lay sideways with my head resting on his chest. He had one arm around me, my leg thrown over both of his. His free hand slid between us, touching me, precisely, correctly. This was Trey, who knew me. This was a man I knew.

He always made it good for me. For sixteen years now, Trey worked to make everything in our life good for me. Part of me was thinking, *Tomorrow I may lose him. Or we could lose our boy, which will break us in a thousand ways. This might be the last time I am with him.* And so I let it happen. I let him make it happen. Then I cried and cried and cried, and he held me, until the crying was more of a release than the sex had been.

In the quiet dark that followed, I listened to him breathing for a while. Then I whispered, "If Marshall can't find Lexie—"

"He will," Trey said.

"I have to meet her mother, whether he finds her or not. I have to go."

"I know," Trey said. "I'm going with you."

"No," I said, not sure if I meant no. We could not lose Robert. But how could we trade Trey? I should go alone. She liked me. I could beg.

"I'm going," he repeated.

I said nothing. I was so grateful and afraid. We held each other, and I think we dozed. I did at least. I was so tired, and there was nothing we could do. Nothing but hope, and pray, and hold each other through the long darkness, waiting for Marshall to arrive with Lexie Pine. Or not.

19

ANIMALS GO TO ground where they feel safe, Marshall knew, and humans were animals. It was instinct, operating underneath all the fancy curls of gray matter, down in the low parts of the brain. Home territory was so fundamental a concept, so basic, that it could trip up even the cleverest of criminals.

But there was an exception to this rule: addicts.

Addicts couldn't go back. Once in their old haunts, they started using again. His leads would not take him anywhere that clean and sober Lexie might be found.

He had to look earlier. Thirty to fifty years earlier. He had to find her in her childhood.

Impossible. But what else did he have? He could not tuck tail, give up, slink back to Bree, and sit with her through the long hours of the night. Unendurable.

So he did his due diligence, driving to the neighborhood where Lexie'd grown up. Coral's house, in person, looked so innocuous. Just a tidy frame ranch with a carport, like most of the others in this speck of a town crouched low between two mountains.

It was past nine-thirty, and knocking on doors this late in the country was a good way to get himself shot. He knocked anyway, starting with Coral's old house. The new resident was a small, grumpy woman in her forties. Marshall could hear two or three other voices inside. Teenagers or older kids, squabbling.

He flashed his PI's license and used the same lie he'd offered Gabrielle, about working for a law firm seeking the Pines with news about an inheritance. Both the story and the heavier southern accent he unleashed to tell it played well with her. It would be good for most anyone in this working-class, rural neighborhood with its tidy lawns and older, well-kept cars. He knew, because he'd grown up on a street much like this.

Back on Toby Leland's block, folks would have assumed he was a cop or a bounty hunter or a loan shark, lying, seeking the Pines with bad intentions. Here the woman warmed near instantly. She'd only met Coral at the closing, she said, but she pointed out the houses of the residents who had lived here longest.

Marshall hit those houses first, talking to about ten neighbors in total. They'd all known the Pines well enough, as one said, "to borrow sugar from," but none were truly close with Coral. She had left no forwarding address. Only one couple had even known she was ill, and she'd downplayed it with them. They had no idea where she might be now.

He was grinding. If this led him to Lexie, it would take a level of luck most lottery winners didn't get. Maybe he should ask around at the sparse local businesses? He'd seen a DQ and a gas station with a hot bar in it on the way. Close. Perhaps someone working in one of those places had known the Pines. He should hurry. They would close soon, and every minute that passed felt like time shaved off of Robert's already so-brief life.

He was walking back to his car when his phone rang.

Bree. He knew it, heartsick. He didn't want to answer. She was a single, exposed nerve. She would know from his hello how poorly things were going. He looked at the caller ID and saw it was Gabrielle. Her name was a reprieve.

"Hey," he said.

"They knew the Dentons!" She yelled it, almost.

He'd been so deep in his own failure it took him a sec to re-member who the Dentons were. The owners of Funtime. Her ex-citement sparked his.

"Tell me," he said.

"They were members at the same church. When Lexie's father was alive, the Pine family went to Funtime almost every Sunday. They'd have a picnic, let Lexie ride the carousel, and eat pink and yellow cotton candy. She didn't like the blue. The families were close. So close they gave Coral a job at Funtime after her husband died."

Her information was so detailed. "You talked to them."

"I talked to her. Mariah. Her husband is deceased. I did use your inheritance story, so thanks for that. She's in her eighties but still has her own apartment in an assisted-living place in Dawson-ville. You know where that is?"

"I do," he said, but she was still talking.

"She moved there to be near her sister's children and grands. That's all I got, because she has a hard time on the phone. Her hearing isn't good. But she knows that Coral is sick. You under-stand? That means she talked to her after the diagnosis. If you drive over, she says she'll talk to you."

He was already turning the car around. "This late?"

"Yes. Her place has its own entry, and she sets her own hours, she says. She's feisty! She told me, 'Honey, don't you know old la-dies never sleep?' She'll be up if you can get there before midnight."

He could be there by eleven-thirty if he gunned it.

"You are amazing," he told her.

"I know," she said, cocky. It made him grin, reenergized. "So are you. We're going to get Robert back, Marshall."

As he got off the phone, he was praying she was right. He drove southwest in the darkness, and her hope stayed with him. Gabrielle had found a close family friend. A former employer. One who had known child Lexie. Sober Lexie. One who'd been in contact with Coral Pine after her diagnosis. She might straight-up know or at least have a damn good guess where Lexie was. She would definitely know Lexie's pre-addiction safe spots, friends, contacts. His odds had just dropped from lotto level to a long shot in a horse race. He could work with that.

Speeding toward an interview that seemed like something solid, he felt as if a heavy cloud of fog had cleared. In the space he found himself thinking of Trey's story.

The events Trey had recounted were more than enough to send a vulnerable girl—one already prone to self-medication and away for the first time from the sharp judgment and rigid rules of a difficult mother—into a spiral that would end in addiction and prison time. The story confirmed that Spence was exactly the asshole that Marshall had known. So Lexie's history *could* have played out that way. Bree clearly believed it.

But deep in the logical left side of his brain, the chilly piece that housed his inner cop was calling bullshit. The tale left Trey's hands too clean. Trey, who was a good guy, came off as absolutely the goodest guy humanly possible, given the circumstances.

The drugs, the threesome, none of these things had been Trey's idea. He'd been tempted and pulled in, like some dewy maiden being coaxed inch by inch off her unicorn. In Trey's version the deepest moral blame belonged to Adam, the guy that Trey liked the least. Spence, who was dead, got thrown a little ways under a bus, too, for pushing and orchestrating. Lexie came off sympathetic, which made Trey sympathetic for presenting her that way, but still, she'd instigated the whole night and brought the drugs. And yet Trey was such a good guy in this tale that he didn't point a judgey finger at her. Instead he'd done some straight-up hero work. First punching Adam, who had dearly needed punching, then burning the pictures, seeking out Lexie, giving her the money.

The more Marshall thought about the story, the more it curdled in his guts. If a perp had tried to float this fairy tale by him in a small gray room?

Bullshit, bullshit, bullshit.

But then Trey was not some perp. Trey was, by any measure, a decent person. He had his faults, like anyone. Impatient at times. Definitely used to getting his way. But he was a loving dad and a faithful husband, generous with friends and charities. An excellent employer, fair and good-humored. So yeah. There was all that.

What if the story, then, was simply . . . mostly true?

The mind revises, Marshall knew. He'd always believe a fingerprint over an eyewitness. As time passed, events became mutable. People justified their actions, and the more shame they felt about a memory, the more they chewed it over, fretting and defending and editing, until they could live with it. Trey's very decency made him more apt to reframe a story like the one he'd told Bree. At least a little.

Or a lot. Or maybe Marshall only thought that because he was so stupid in love with Trey's wife.

He was in Dawsonville proper now, getting close. He had to pay attention to his GPS. Anyway, his reaction to Trey's story would not help him find Lexie, so screw it. It was a problem for tomorrow, or the next day. When Robert was safe home.

Bickford Independent Living Community was three long, slightly run-down buildings full of single-floor apartments, each with its own door. There was a shabby clubhouse and a small pool, but no office where he had to check in. The parking spaces were numbered, but every five slots or so there was a space marked VISITOR. He found an empty one close to Mariah Denton's place and went to knock on her door.

It opened almost at once. She'd been waiting for him. He recognized her from the picture. Clearly the same woman, but shorter and rounder. Her brown hair had thinned and silvered, but it was still long, wound up in a crown of slender braids. She wore a hotpink lounge set that could have been pajamas or a tracksuit and had bright green reading glasses on a string around her neck.

"Mrs. Denton? I'm Marshall Chase," he said, holding out his hand to shake. Instead she grasped his forearm and pulled him in, smiling.

"Come in, come in, young man. Anything I can do to help Lexie and Coral Lee! I've been racking my poor brains, trying to think where they might be staying. I'm sure I don't know."

A disappointment, but not a huge one. He hadn't expected it would be that easy. Just hoped. Mariah Denton was assuming that the two of them were together, though. They weren't. Coral, who read mysteries and thrillers, would be too smart to let her daughter stick a toe inside the room or house where she was holding a kidnapped infant. Lexie was a felon, with fingerprints and probably DNA logged in the system. Coral wouldn't want Lexie anywhere near Funtime tomorrow either. She had no way to know if Bree would bring Trey or the cops to meet her.

Mrs. Denton was still talking. "Oh, the bad luck that family has had, I tell you. It's so nice a good thing is happening, and with Coral Lee so sick, I know they could use the money." She was a chatterbox. That could be good or bad, depending on how well he could keep her on topic. He let himself be tugboated to the small kitchen behind the breakfast bar while she nattered on about the fictional inheritance. Gabrielle had prepped her well. A three-seater table with a floral plastic cover was pushed against the wall. She deposited him by one of the ladder-back chairs, and he obediently sat down. She hovered by him. "I was thinking I might make myself some cocoa, if you give me the excuse?"

"I'd love some." It was late, and she was elderly. Sugar and caffeine would buy him more time with her. "Do you have a way to contact either of the Pines?" he asked before she could start up her monologue again.

She went toward the fridge and got the milk out. "Well, I thought I did. As soon as I got off the phone with the young lady at your law firm, I tried the number Coral Lee left. It's not connected anymore. I thought for a moment she must have passed on.

She was very ill. But Lexie surely would have contacted me about the funeral. More likely it's off because of money troubles, so an inheritance would be an answered prayer. Is it enough money to be useful?"

She had bright black eyes, shiny as buttons, and she hardly paused for breath or answers.

"I can't give you specifics, but it's a comfortable amount. Can I see the phone number?" he asked. "When did she give it to you?"

"Why, it must be five or six months back, at least. When she was staying here. I have a guest room, you know. . . ." As she told him every detail of her small apartment's layout, she opened a kitchen drawer and got an old-fashioned paper address book, the kind with three-hole punch pages that could be changed out. It looked almost as old as she was. She flipped through the crackly, yellowed pages, then set it down in front of him, wishing aloud that she had a two-bath unit instead of just a half bath in the front. Coral Lee had had to come through the master to shower.

The address was for the old house with the carport, the one he'd so recently visited. A phone number was crossed out and a new one had been written above in fresher, brighter ink. Area code 762. Was that Georgia? It was probably a burner, but he took a picture of the whole page anyway and sent it in a text to Gabrielle that said, CLP's most recent number. What's this area code? Cell phone? Traceable?

While he was doing this, Mariah got out a pan and poured milk into it, not measuring, talking on, unchecked. Something about a cat now. He wasn't sure how she'd gotten there.

At the first sign of a pause, he put in, "Does Lexie have any close friends around here? Or in her old neighborhood?"

She was adding Dutch cocoa and sugar to her pan, again not measuring, but she paused to say carefully, "You know Lexie had some troubles."

He nodded, grave. "I am familiar with her history."

She went to work with a whisk, her dark eyes gleaming

whenever she glanced at him. "Well, good, then. I wouldn't want to gossip. When Coral Lee showed up six months back, I knew it was about Lexie." Mariah Denton lived right behind her eyes, and every word falling from her crinkly pink mouth had the ring of gospel. If he could ask the right questions, she would tell him what he needed to know.

"Had you stayed in touch?" he asked.

"Not really. Just Christmas cards after the church split. I try to get my cards out by—"

"The church that you went to together split?" he interrupted. He needed to get a rhythm going with her. Question, answer.

"Yes. Over doctrine. The congregation simply shattered. Pastor Farley left town in the dead of night like a criminal, and the bank took the building. After that Larry and I got our preaching off the radio. Now that he's passed, I take the shuttle bus to the Methodist church. It's nice. They have a dedicated minister for seniors."

He nudged her gently back on track. "The church you attended with Mrs. Pine, was it Methodist, too?"

That made her laugh. "Oh, Lord, no! Larry said the Methodists were full of nonsense." Her whisk paused. "I hope that doesn't offend you?"

"No, ma'am. Though I am a Methodist," Marshall said, smiling. He liked her, overshares and all. But he did not have the time to indulge her much.

She smiled back. "We went to a nondenominational church called Christ Redeemer. That was Larry's pick. He was a good, dear man, but he needed things a certain way. None of it bothered me enough to want to make it a bone of contention."

"A certain way?" Marshall asked, to get a sense of it.

"Oh, he didn't think there ought to be musical instruments in the church, and he didn't hold with dancing or wine or mixed bathing or card games, even Crazy Eights. Larry used to say, 'Give me a church that's just plain Bible, nothing added, nothing took away.'" Her tone was wry but fond. "Never mind King David in the Psalms talking all about drums and lyres and dancing. If I pointed that out, though, he'd get all foamy and preach at me. And I like a cappella singing fine."

She was drifting off topic again. "Mrs. Pine was like Larry in her beliefs?"

"I suppose," she said, still whisking and whisking. "Except Larry was easy to live with. I love Coral Lee dearly, but that woman is Jesus-bit clean through." Her tone made it plain that this was not a compliment. She must have seen Marshall's surprise, because she added, "The Jesus that got his teeth in Coral Lee is not the Jesus I know. Even sterner than Larry's. Truth be told, I felt sorry for Lexie. Coral Lee would put her braids in so tight you could see the hairs a-pulling at her scalp, like to pop." She shot him a mischievous glance. "And that right there, young man, is a metaphor."

It made Marshall chuckle, in spite of everything. "Were you a teacher, ma'am?"

"No, no," she said. "Unless you count Sunday school. I just like a book in the evenings."

"Maybe someone else from your old church would have better contact information?" Marshall prompted.

Her mouth turned down. "Might be so, but I mostly went there for Larry. I've lost touch with those folks over the years."

Marshall was learning a lot, but not the right things. Nothing that told him where Lexie might be holed up now. "Did Lexie have a close friend when she was a girl? Someone she might be with now? So far my investigation indicates that she and her mother are not currently together."

"Oh, no! I hope that doesn't mean she's back to her old ways?" She looked genuinely upset at the thought.

He reassured her. "I have no reason to believe she's fallen off the wagon."

She turned back to her cocoa. "That's all right, then. No, Lexie didn't have friends growing up. Not like you mean. I was her friend." Mariah was musing almost to herself now as she turned the stovetop off and poured the cocoa into two ceramic mugs, filling both perfectly. "She was homeschooled until after her daddy died and Coral Lee had to go to work. I don't mean in a co-op or group like they have now. Just her and her mama. That child had no idea how to socialize by the time she got to real school. She was like one of those puppy-mill dogs. She didn't know how to play."

He looked at her, very serious. "So you were her friend. But you haven't heard from her directly? Just her mother?"

She came over and passed him one of the mugs. His said TODAY I NEED A WHOLE LOT OF CHRIST and then in tiny letters under AND A LITTLE BIT OF COFFEE. Hers was yellow and said BLESSED in curly script.

"I meant I was her friend when she was little," she said, and sat down across from him. "Please understand, I hadn't seen Coral Lee for years until she showed up here a few months back. I knew her at once, though she looked awful. She told me she'd just dropped Lexie off at a rehab. Sold her house to get the money, which shocked me. It was not Lexie's first time through, you understand. But then she told me her own diagnosis, so I thought, well, why *not* sell the house? She hadn't much time."

The cocoa was creamy and rich, foamy from all the whisking. The real thing. "No indication where she meant to go? No thoughts about where Lexie could be now?"

"No. I'm sorry. When Lexie went into treatment, Coral Lee stayed with me for a few days, until it looked like Lexie would stick it out. Then she said she wanted to rent herself a place closer to the facility and visit every day. I told her she was welcome back anytime, and Lexie, too," she said. "We'd taken them in before, you may know."

"You mean the job at Funtime?" he asked.

"You have done your research! Yes. Lexie was such a cute little thing back then. I was taken with her. Hair like a buttercup, smile like sunshine. Larry and I never did have our own kids. It wasn't in the cards for us. So I spent time with Lexie. She was sweet and quiet and neat as a pin. Loved books. I connected with her on that, but I felt bad she was so anxious about her grades. I think because her mother never was satisfied. If Lexie got an A, Coral Lee wondered why it wasn't an A-plus. Lexie liked things peaceful, and I'm the same. As a littl'un, she would wring her hands and cry when Coral Lee got mad."

Marshall nodded. This Lexie tracked with the girl Trey had described, confirming a corner of Trey's story. A small corner. "Did she have any other friends at the church?"

"Not really. She'd go to Sunday school and sit quiet, listen to the lesson, make her craft. She didn't wiggle around or whisper. A dog-mill puppy, like I said. It was why I started inviting her family up for Sunday lunch. To give Lexie a little fun. How she loved that carousel! Coral Lee can be . . . a challenge, and Lexie's daddy was a stern man, too. But Preston was in construction, just like Larry, and they had similar politics and church thoughts, so the boys had things to talk about. After a couple years, a foreman job came up with Larry's outfit, and Larry helped Preston get it. Two months later he was dead. Freak accident. He fell at a job site and cracked his skull open. Before Larry got him hired on, he'd been working demo for years, which is so much more dangerous! Larry felt responsible, I think."

"So he offered her a job." Not a question, just keeping her on track.

"Not just the job. A place to live, so she could rent her house out for some income and keep homeschooling." She finally took a sip of her drink. He'd already finished his. "Her husband had insurance, thank God. Enough to pay off the mortgage, but she didn't want to stay there. Hard, you know, looking every day at all those places where she'd see the shape of her husband and him not there. I understood it after Larry died. I moved right in here. Then, a couple years later, I regretted it so. All I wanted was to see his places and shapes. She must have been the same, because after a year and change she did get a full-time job and move home. Lexie was eleven or maybe twelve when she finally went to school."

He had a sense of something she wasn't saying or that he hadn't understood. Something important. He leaned in. "They were living with you?"

She laughed. "No, no. A single woman? Larry said we'd look like Mormons! We let her live on the property, at Funtime. In Larry's hidey-hole."

He felt himself get very still. "Hidey-hole. You mean, like a bomb shelter?"

She shook her head. "Not exactly. More like a cabin, but built back into the hill. It was for Armageddon."

She was so matter-of-fact, blinking at him with those dark-bright eyes. He leached all judgment from his voice, made his tone mild and interested. "So Larry was a survivalist."

She made a pish noise. "Not really. Just our church preached a pretty immediate Gospel. Now, mind, I wasn't fussed myself too much about Armageddon. Jesus himself said, 'But of that day and hour no one knows, not even the angels of heaven, but My Father only.' So why do all that math? But the folks at Christ Redeemer thought it was soon. They were bracing for a world war, and famine, and disease, and Satan ruling for a thousand years of torment. They had a whole chart with Revelation matching up to politics and world events and whatnot. That's why we bought the property with the Funtime Gold Mine on it. Larry liked how it was up on a hill, out of all the main ways, with well water instead of being on a city system. Larry added the carousel, and he also built his hidey-hole behind it. Kept it stocked with these awful freeze-dried dinners-in-a-bag he got at Army Surplus, and he put in a gas genny and a compost toilet. He figured if things got bad, we could wait for the Rapture there, snug as bugs. But of course the Rapture didn't happen. That was what split the church, having the day come and go." She shrugged. "Revelation is a tricky book."

Marshall's heart was pounding. He could feel it in his fingers, his ears. This got him no closer to Lexie. But it might not matter. Not if he was right. "How far behind Funtime?" His voice had a creak in it. Misdirection, he was thinking. That was what Coral Lee Pine did best. Every cop hair on his body was standing straight up.

"A half a mile, if that, back through the woods, up a little trail that I bet by now is grown over. They built a new highway so no one had to pass the road to Funtime to get up to Highlands anymore. The power and such was costing more than we made. We had to close it down. We put it up for sale, too, but no one ever bought it, so there it sits. I'm going to leave it to my sister's middle girl. She might could do something with it."

She was off again then on another tangent, but Marshall let her go down it. His blood was singing in his veins, as if it had been heated. Nothing she'd said would get him to Lexie. It didn't matter. They didn't need her. He thought. He was sure. He was almost sure.

He knew where Robert was.

20

MARSHALL ARRIVED AN hour before sunrise. He'd gone home to shower, shave, and change. Trey and I did the same, putting on jeans and good walking shoes. Then I started a fresh pot of coffee, and I made us all eggs with fruit and toast. We needed fuel, whether or not any of us felt like eating.

We sat at the breakfast table dutifully putting food into our stomachs, and Marshall told us that he now believed Coral Lee was holed up at Funtime with Robert. That she'd been at Funtime since the second time she called me.

"She knows the place. She feels safe there, and she understands, better than anyone, how completely isolated it is," Marshall said. He was tearing through the food. "Plus, she's sick, so how much energy does she have to travel? Not to mention Lexie's rehab must have close to wiped her out. Squatting there is free."

His new plan was simple. When I walked up to the carousel to meet her, Coral would have to leave Robert alone. I would distract her long enough for Marshall to sneak up the hill past us and find the hidey-hole. He'd spent time learning the area on Google Earth and in his maps app with the help of Mariah Denton.

"That was . . . challenging," he said, and his tone made it clear this was an understatement. "She doesn't own a computer, never has, and she couldn't get her head around the idea that satellites are taking pictures of . . . well, everything. Wanted me to zoom in on her old house, then the Kroger." He buried his face in his hands briefly. "Anyway. Once I got her on task, she pretty much pinpointed it for me. I'll find Robert and evacuate him while you keep Coral busy."

"No," Trey said. "I don't want Bree to meet her at all. That woman is insane. She could be armed. She could—"

"She has no interest in hurting me," I interrupted. She didn't. She wouldn't. I was a mother, like her. I reminded her of her own child. I was the mother Lexie had never gotten to be. No, she wanted Trey. She'd take Robert. But not me. More important, he was arguing the wrong things. Marshall's plan was too easy and too reckless both. "Robert can't be there, Marshall. She wouldn't hide him so close. Her whole leverage is that if I send the cops instead of bringing Trey to her, she'll kill herself and leave Robert to—" I blinked back tears. "If he's that close, the police would surely find him." I remembered Spencer, spasming and foaming, and I shuddered. "She wouldn't bluff about this. She means him harm if I don't give her Trey."

Marshall swallowed the last of his toast. "I agree it's not a bluff. She's after blood." He was remembering Spence, too, I thought. The pills she'd convinced me were roofies. "But she knows this place intimately. With the bird's-eye view she has, she can see the parking lot. I bet she can see the road, too, for miles, and it's the only way in. Maybe there's hiking trails, but she knows those, too. Meanwhile she's told us she's leaving the baby elsewhere and driving to meet us. So if we, for example, send cops in early to set up an ambush, she's already there, watching them arrive. If she sees or hears anyone but you and Trey, she has plenty of time to—" His voice cut out abruptly. He didn't want to say what she would do, but he didn't have to. By the time the police made their way to the hidey-hole, they would find only the bodies.

Trey had gotten up while Marshall spoke. He was pacing, jittery from caffeine and sleeplessness and waiting. "You think she would leave Robert alone in that cabin when she comes to meet Bree? What if you get to the cabin and Lexie is there. Armed. With our kid."

I answered first. "She won't have Lexie anywhere nearby. Period."

Not only because we could send the police and she wanted to keep Lexie's hands clean. Of all the things she'd told me, that one had the most of my faith. But because she wouldn't ask Lexie to harm a baby. What Coral had done to Geoff had a ricochet. Coral had felt it. She wouldn't want her frail, newly sober child to do that. I knew it deep in my own motherhood, so solid and strong that I'd bet Robert's life on it. Not that I had another choice.

We spent our last hours chewing it over, the three of us, back and forth and around and around. Trey was mutinous. He hated the idea of me walking up alone to meet with her while he sat all the way down the hill in the car in relative safety.

I didn't want Trey to come, period. I was afraid she'd kill him outright, but Marshall said she would have to be a marine sharpshooter to pick Trey off from the top of the hill. But what if she got lucky? Or what if she saw us coming and walked down to the parking lot to meet us with a shotgun? Trey said there was no way in hell he was sitting home, though, and Marshall agreed. Coral needed to see Trey arrive. We had to look like we were complying. We argued about that until it was almost time to go, recycling the same points and fears and hopes without making any headway, churning fruitlessly. Marshall's plan won out.

Marshall looked relieved and also a little sick. We were betting so much on his gut instinct. If he was wrong . . . Still, his gut instinct had gotten us this far. I couldn't see clearly past any moment where Marshall was wrong, so he wasn't wrong, and that was all. Our course was set.

As we got up to leave, Trey said, "We should take your car. It has the base of Robert's car seat."

I nodded, moved to near tears by his implication. Taking the

car-seat base was an act of such deliberate hope that it made me
think of Kelly Wilkerson, with her past-tense verbs, her bare walls,
her empty, indented carpet. Her son's small life was over, and he
was already wiped entirely away. She seemed almost wiped away
as well. Trey was saying I would not become like her, just a body,
too full of rage and drugs and grief to hold anything else. Trey was
saying we were going to bring our son home.

Marshall got in the backseat, and I put a stack of dark blankets,
gray and navy, in beside him. Trey drove. Once we were on the
highway, I reached over the gap between the seats to hold his hand.
He gripped mine so tight it almost hurt. We didn't talk much on
the drive. No need. We all knew the plan. It was crazy and thin and
the only thing we had.

There was little traffic leaving Atlanta this early on a Sunday
morning. People were either still in bed or at church. My mother
had skipped her own service to let the girls sleep in. She'd forgotten
to tell them to put their phones away when she went to bed, and
she thought they'd stayed up late. I texted with her a little bit,
sending cheery missives about my recovery. She was hoping to keep
them long enough for pancake brunch before I came to take them
back. I told her that sounded perfect. Both girls slept until eleven,
sometimes noon, on weekends. This would all be over before they
had so much as stirred.

Thinking of them, tucked up safe together in Mom's guest
room, sleeping in the boneless way of young and growing things,
made me long for them, so fierce. I wanted to wake them myself
and offer pancakes, smell their warm, sleepy skin and pet their
tousled hair back. Their absence felt both normal and insane. They
often spent weekends with my mom or with Trey's parents, getting spoiled while Trey and I ducked out to the Biltmore or up to
New York. Now, though, I felt as if a month had passed since I'd
seen them, as if I'd abandoned them while focused solely on their
brother. I wanted to make it up to them, though they had no idea
that there was something to make up.

It would be better to keep it that way. If we could. If we got Robert back. If, if, if. I was so tired of that word.

We made excellent time, getting so ahead of schedule that as we pulled off the interstate, I worried we'd arrive too early. I wanted to do everything exactly right. There was a cluster of stores and gas stations at this exit: Krystal, Chick-fil-A, Dollar General. I asked Trey to pull in at a gas station to use the bathroom and get coffee, but mostly to kill time.

Trey didn't need the restroom. He stayed by the pumps, topping off my car. Marshall and I headed in. There was a young woman outside by the door. She leaned against the ice machine smoking, though she looked way too young to buy cigarettes legally. She had lank brown hair and a rash of pimples on her forehead that her straggly bangs failed to hide. She straightened as we drew close.

"Hey, ma'am?" she said, to me, only me, and her eyes twitched nervously toward Marshall. I understood why. He looked like a cop. And yet she was desperate enough to talk to me, and so I stopped. "Could you maybe get me something to eat?"

"Sure," I said. She smiled, and I saw a large black cavity, oval shaped, growing between her two front teeth. "What would you like?"

Marshall cleared his throat, a neutral sound. I ignored it.

She licked her chapped lips. "If you gave me a little money, I could pick. They'll let me come inside if I can show them I have money."

"We'll get you a sandwich," Marshall said, and instantly her eyes dropped and she stepped back. He took my arm, and I let him tote me inside. When the swinging glass door had swished closed behind us, he told me, "If you give her money, she'll just buy drugs."

"Oh, you think?" I said, tart. I took my arm back and went to the bathroom.

When I got out, Marshall was already paying for our coffee by the register. I went to the refrigerated case, looking for soft things, because of her teeth. I didn't see anything I'd want to feed my girls. Not for a meal. In the end I picked out two different kinds of Lunchables, a carton of milk, and a bottle of orange juice. I headed for the register, passing through the snack aisle to add a plain Hershey's chocolate bar and a four-pack of Dole fruit cups, so old they had a fine layer of dust on the cardboard shell. The date stamp said they were still good, though.

When I handed her the bag, she smiled at the weight of it, showing me again the oval of rot between her front teeth. It was striated like an agate, a darkness that deepened in concentric circles, telling me there was a lack of money or a lack of love or both in this child's life.

"Thank you!" she said.

Marshall started forward, but I didn't. Trey was back in the driver's seat, the engine running, but we were still ahead of schedule. This girl, she could have been Lexie thirty years ago. She was only three or four years older than Anna-Claire.

"Do you have someplace to sleep tonight?" I asked, and Marshall stopped, waiting for me.

She shook her head. "I could get a bed at this shelter I know, if I had twelve dollars." She looked at me, hopeful and guarded, pressing her lips together.

I opened my wallet and pulled out all the cash I had, seven or eight bills. I had no idea how much. I handed it to her, and it felt like some kind of offering. She was an altar. I wished I had more.

I could feel all the things that Marshall wasn't saying, but he held his peace.

"Thank you," she said again, blinking very fast. The money disappeared into her pocket quickly, as if she was afraid I'd change my mind.

"Take care of yourself," I told her.

We got back into the car. Trey seemed about to say something, but he got one look at my face and put us in drive and headed out. I grabbed his hand again.

With every passing mile, I could feel us getting closer to Coral

Lee Pine. I could feel her waiting. Our strange connection crackled, as slim as a filament but strong and live with current. I wondered if she sensed me coming as well, catching the ozone smell of our shared electricity rising in the wind.

The roads were old, and the closer we got, the worse they became. My SUV shuddered and jolted over the pitted, ash-gray asphalt. My cell phone lost its signal.

Ten minutes out Marshall opened his seat belt and lay down across the floorboards. Trey was driving, so I unclipped mine as well and leaned between the seats to help cover him with the blankets. The Escalade had a flat floor with a good amount of legroom, but long, tall Marshall still had to lie half on his back, half on his side, his knees at an awkward angle.

As I layered the blankets over his body, making sure his feet were covered, I felt as if I were tucking him in. His eyes met mine, determined, encouraging. I touched his cheek and nodded, though he hadn't said a thing. I pulled the covers over his face.

If all went well, Coral would be up the hill, on the grounds of Funtime itself. From her perch she'd be able to see us arrive. She would not come down, Marshall had assured me over and over. It would be bad tactics to give up the high ground before making sure Trey and I really had come alone, with no police. But did old ladies think like cops, in terms of tactics?

The sparse woods grew thicker as the hills grew steeper. There was still a faded sign standing at the turnoff. It featured a tall, cowboy-shaped human figure wielding a lasso. His face and body were covered in graffiti almost as old and faded as the sign itself. I could see that the coils of his rope spelled out FUNTIME, but only because I already knew the place's name.

A mile past the sign, another directed us left into the parking lot. It was empty except for an ancient Honda, the white paint coated in filth and the back bumper crumpled in and rusted. Trey crept toward it, avoiding the largest potholes. He looked pale as he parked beside it, just left of the wide concrete double staircase.

"You ready?" I asked the heap of blankets. I heard a muffled yes. I got my phone out and put it on vibrate, then opened up my stopwatch app and set it for seven minutes. The blankets tented and shifted as Marshall did the same. When the timer went off, I would have thirty seconds to make sure Coral was not watching the lot so Marshall could slip out of the car unseen and get into the cover of the woods. If Coral Lee spotted him, she'd hurry back to the hidey-hole and get to Robert first. If she was armed, I might not be able to stop her.

Trey said, "I still don't like you going up there alone."

"She probably expects me to come up first." I sounded sure, because I was. I could feel her above us, watching. Wanting to talk to me again. The strange thing was, I wanted it, too. I was almost hungry for it, this chance to clearly see the face that went with the voice I knew so well. I wanted her to look right at me, too, and really see me. I wanted the chance to change her mind. "Just stay here."

"Bree," my husband said, but this was the plan.

"One, two, three," I said to the heap of blankets, then hit the timer on my phone.

"Got it," Marshall said.

The numbers began counting down. I slid the phone into my back pocket to muffle the vibration.

"Bree," Trey said again.

Our eyes met. The world could change in so many different awful ways in the next hour.

I was conscious of Marshall, lying prone on the floor, and the tick of each second. I leaned over to press my mouth against my husband's, hard and fast.

"Trust me," I said. I could feel how tough it was for him to let me get out of the car, close the door, and leave him there, but he did it.

I hurried toward the entrance. I had just shy of seven minutes. The concrete stairs were wide and steep, with four metal railings breaking them into three sections. I went straight up the middle, fast and steady. As I ascended, I thought, *Get into character.* But who was this person climbing up to see Coral Lee Pine?

Betsy's black Visa could not help me here. I could almost feel it fall away. So many things were falling away. For this meeting, our first, our last, I had to be a mother, like her. A woman from small-town Georgia. Like Lexie, the only daughter of a hardscrabble single mom. This was the person who might move her to relent.

Going up, it did not feel like I was putting on a role. It felt like being peeled. I shrugged off anything that wouldn't help me. The corporate wife with her closetful of thousand-dollar dresses. The stay-at-home mom with a cleaning lady and the luxury of no job beyond her family, able to help at every rehearsal and robotics meet. The wealthy woman on the board of two prominent non-profits. Even the young, pretty Bree who'd gone strolling through the High Museum, so confident, catching Trey's eye in her expensive, borrowed sundress.

It all fell away, until I felt like little more than a child. I was a girl who'd never had dialect classes to sand her accent away; I could feel my mouth resetting itself for extended vowels and dropped *g*'s. I was Betsy's friend, tearing down the pitted, pale gray asphalt of our street on a hand-me-down Big Wheel. I was Shelly Ann Kroger's daughter, making tuna casserole with crumbled potato chips on top after school, because my mom worked two jobs and she would come home so tired and hungry.

This was where we had connected, Coral and I, and it wasn't a character. It was only me. My most basic, beginning self.

The steep stairs shortened my breath. Above me a huge blue cowboy hat appeared over the crest of the hill. As I hurried up, the rest of Funtime Jack rose, his face splotched black with mold that turned his wide smile into a threat. His blue pack mule stood beside him, one eye a fuzzy black pit. The end of its round nose had fallen off. The ticket booth came into view last. It had rotted in on itself, deflating into a pile of wood and shingles and signage.

At the top a path snaked between Jack and its remains, leading to the carousel.

I had to stop for a moment to catch my breath. Most of the animals and poles were gone, I saw. On the far side, the roof had fallen, so it was almost like a cave. I peered into the shadowy recesses, and there she was. Coral Lee Pine, who owned that whispery voice I'd learned so well.

She sat on one of the bench seats for tired parents. It was loose from the base, canted to face the stairs. I could not make out her features in the shadows. I walked forward, conscious of the phone in my pocket, the seconds ticking away. How long had the climb taken? Four minutes? Less?

The bench's sides were carved into the shape of a stampede of horses. They faced me, too. Their mouths yawped open, and their eyes were wide. As I got close, I saw they were actually unicorns, with faded wreaths of roses around their necks and short spiral horns.

One of the rideable animals, a lion, was lying on his side to Coral Lee's left. The pole was still attached, so it looked as if he'd been run through. He had carved roses in a wreath around his neck, too, but the paint had faded and peeled away until the blooms looked like odd, spongy growths.

I was at the edge of the platform now. I stepped up, finally close enough to see her deep-set eyes. Here was the face I'd first seen peering through my bedroom window, with that pointed chin, the turned-down mouth. Here also was the meemaw of the school's parking lot, wearing the same dark knit cap with its small peak. Her long hair straggled down her shoulders in thin, silvery ropes.

She was no older than my mother-in-law, but she had not had Margaret Cabbat's regimen of moisturizers and doctors to roll back time; the years sat heavy on her. She was pale, and a sheen of sweat had broken on her brow. Her eyes met mine, wide and anxious and too intense for me to hold the gaze.

Just to her right, she'd placed a small card table. It was set for tea with a woven mat, a flowered china pot, and two matching cups on pink-flowered saucers, the delicate handles edged in gold. They were full of dark liquid, and all at once I could not swallow. The brimming cups were harder to look at than she was.

Her baggy, shapeless dress was ash-colored. She had a brown-and-orange afghan on her lap, hand-crocheted by the look of it. The folds of it pooled on the bench beside her. One hand was hidden under the blanket. Holding a gun? I had no way to tell. But that possibility did not make me nearly as anxious as those delicate cups or the intensity in her hooded eyes.

"Hello, Mrs. Cabbat," she said, quite formal. The voice from the phone. It made my jaw tighten but also pulled me one step closer. We knew each other, she and I. She gestured toward the path behind me. "That's your husband in the driver's seat down there?" I nodded, glancing back. The stairs were too steep for her to have watched my ascent, but I could see the lot, and the cars, and the gray road snaking away through the hills and trees. Trey was a shadowy shape in the driver's seat. "He needs to come up now."

"In a little. I told him I'd wave when it was time." Sabreena Kroger's voice, shaky and unconfident. Southern. Shy. I hadn't been this girl in two decades, but I wasn't acting. This was a true creature, pulled out from the deepest places inside the woman I'd grown into. This was the girl Coral Lee Pine felt for, connected with. At the same time, I was Robert's mother, here to fight her tooth and claw. I could hold both. I knew I could. It was the most important thing the theatre had ever taught me. "I wanted to talk to you first. Just us."

"I thought you might. Please, pull up a seat." There was another bench, sitting aslant, nearby. I came closer and sat down on it. "I'd offer you tea, but . . ." She smiled for the first time, wide, almost a grimace. I was shocked by all the dark gaps in her mouth. So many of her teeth were gone. She gestured at the china cups. "This is not for you."

I felt my skin trying to shudder itself off my body. "I know. It's for Trey. And you." She dipped her chin in a small acknowledg-ment. "Is it the same drug I gave Spencer?" She nodded, and I made myself meet her gaze as I told her, "It's not a good way to go."

She shrugged. "I used a lot. It will be faster. It will be very, very fast." She picked up the cup closer to her, considering its dark contents. "Call Mr. Cabbat up now, please. He can have his tea, and we'll wait a little. Then I tell you where to find your boy and have a drink myself."

Time felt as if it were moving so slowly. Too slowly. I wondered if my timer had somehow turned itself off in my pocket. Surely seven minutes had passed? "I want to talk to you first."

She shrugged. "You don't have much time." She lifted her cup to me in a mock toast, as if readying to drink it, Trey or no Trey.

I felt a chill of doubt in my spine. Marshall had convinced me that Robert was here, but if so, if she killed herself now, we would find him easily. She would never allow that. I knew it. Was Marshall wrong?

I opened my mouth to speak, and in my back pocket I finally felt the gentle buzz of the phone.

In thirty seconds Marshall would be sprinting for the woods. If he was right, he'd find Robert, snug in his little car seat. He would go in, get him, and take him down to Trey. Trey would drive the baby out of reach of any gunfire, and Marshall would come up the stairs to get me. Armed, dangerous, ready. But first Marshall had to get out of her field of vision to the shelter of the trees, unseen.

I stood abruptly, staring at the spine of the carousel, behind her.

"Is someone else here?" I asked, my voice sharpening.

"No!" she said, alarmed. "Not unless you brung 'em." She still held her tea, but her other hand moved under the afghan.

I hurried past her, past her bench, heading to the hollow center spine of the carousel. The boards sagged under my steps, creaking audibly. She turned to track me, now facing away from the lot.

"Be careful," she said. "You could bring the rest of the roof down."

I ignored her, going directly to the carousel house. The door panel had been ripped away. Inside I could see the remains of all its workings. It was a dank and musty space, cold and dark, like a cave inside a cave. Dead empty.

I looked back at her, shrugging. "I think it was settling. Or maybe a rat. Are there rats?"

She was still twisted around, peering into the darkness with me. I walked toward her so she couldn't face the road without giving me her back. Her shoulders stiffened, and she set her tea down, turning as far as she could to watch me approach. Her free hand came up to rest on the bench's back. It was old and gnarled, twisted by arthritis.

I reached out, very slowly, so as not to startle her, and I put my hand on top of hers. Her skin was cool and dry and papery. I felt such a strange tenderness for her as our hands touched. I could not explain it. But I saw in her eyes my same feelings reflected. My touch had opened up a well of small regret inside her. Maybe even mercy?

"I came to beg," I said. I knelt, my hand still on hers.

I looked up into her face, and I could smell her now. Baby powder layered over the sour smell of a person who had not washed thoroughly in days. Marshall must be right. In the Dentons' hidey-hole, she'd be using baby wipes or a basin of water warmed on the stove. Her hair, this close, was thick with grease.

Her eyes were not black after all. They were a dark, deep brown, flecked with gold. The whites around them were yellowed, veined in red. She had an old woman's downy mustache. I could see how sick she was in her pallor, feel that her hand had a shake in it.

I said, "I came to beg you for my baby."

She looked down at me. Thinking, I hoped. Considering, her gaze full of a thousand things, but one of them was close to mercy. I could see it.

Finally she said, "You're so pretty, up close. Real pretty. Taller than I thought, too."

"I want my son," I said. "And what you're asking me to trade is impossible. You're punishing me more than any other person. Me, and Geoff's mother. What did we do?"

She glanced at her watch, a utilitarian thing, digital, then shook her head, her eyes on me so tender. "We do not have the time it would take me to explain. This is going to finish in my next hundred breaths, one way or another. Still, I want you to know I thought about what you said to me. About how this path I had to take was so hard on you, and Geoff's mother as well. Did your husband tell you what he done?"

I blinked, unsure how to answer. "He told me a little," I said at last. "But . . ." I had no excuses for him, no way to finish.

"I thought as much. Anything he said, I'm sure he made it soft, for you. So yesterday I wrote some things. Hard, true things. An explanation, if you will. Then I drove down to the post office. When you get my letter, you'll understand what's happened here, and why. You'll know who Geoff's mother is then. I added her name and address. Maybe the two of you ought to talk. You maybe can help each other cope."

My breath caught. "You mailed me a letter?" I tried to imagine seeing Kelly Wilkerson again, reading Coral's twisted version of the ugly story Trey had told me.

"Yes. It's the best I can do. Now, for your boy's sake, call your husband up. It's time."

Surely Marshall was safely out of view by now? Still I knelt, holding her gaze. "The best thing you could do is stop this. Tell me where my son is." This soft woman, begging like a child, this was true and truly me. At the same time, I spoke slowly, buying Marshall precious seconds.

She made that short, small hum noise that I knew so well. Her eyes on me stayed kind. "You remind me of my own girl. Not that you look like her. But you're so smart and pretty, and I think you have a sweet heart." She swallowed audibly and blinked hard, clearly in the grip of some deep feeling. "You're the woman I hoped she'd grow to be when I sent her off to college. Maybe that surprises you, that a woman like me would have a girl who went to college, but she did."

"I did, too," I said, soft, drawing another line between me and Lexie. She didn't seem to hear me, though.

"Even when she was little, she was so booky and so smart. She applied for every scholarship you ever heard of, and she got a slew of them. So many people, her teachers, our pastor, they wrote letters like you wouldn't believe on her behalf. Such a bright future, all those letters said." Her gold-brown eyes were so tender and so sad, but her next words came out harder. "It didn't work out that way. Not for her. Not like it did for you."

She started to turn away, and I clutched at her hand with both of mine, almost tugging. "I did nothing to you."

"I know. But the world ain't fair, Mrs. Cabbat. I sent my girl off in good faith, and your husband and his friends ruint her. They stole away every bright future that my family might have had." I had misread her softness. It wasn't mercy. It was more like regret. As if her plan had already played out to the finish. I understood then, there was no changing her. Everything was over already, in her mind. Done. This was just us working out a last small detail. Trey or Robert.

I let go of her hand and stood, looking past her down into the lot. All I saw was the SUV, all doors closed, Trey in the driver's seat. Surely Marshall was almost to Robert. I had to hold her attention a little longer. If he was right, if all went well, in five or six more minutes, maybe less, my son would be safe in his arms.

That word, haunting me again. It was too much hope and terror for two letters to hold. If.

21

MARSHALL RAN, QUICK and quiet, angling up through the thin trees at the base of the hill. His heart was pounding, but not from the run. He had missed something. Something wasn't right.

He could almost feel his wife moving with him through the trees. Betsy's ghost, who just after her death had come to haunt him every shift. Reminding him, *You have a kid. You have* our *kid. You have no backup.* It was the reason he'd changed jobs.

Strange to feel her presence now, so close that he could almost smell her jasmine lotion. The crazy corkscrews of her hair were in the breeze that touched his face as he ran.

But he was not in danger. Bree was. Bree, alone with Coral Lee Pine. That was probably what was bothering him.

He glanced at his phone. Bree and Trey had both lost signal, but his shittier carrier somehow still had a faint connection. He was navigating with the map on his phone and some still shots he'd taken off Google Earth. All aerial views, looking down on his location from space. It had been fall the last time the satellite passed over. The pictures made this place look lonely and cold, with brownish red clay the only warmth threading through dark granite and the thick cover of the turning leaves.

Today, though, was all sunlight filtered through the vivid green.

There was birdsong, and to his left something small, a squirrel or a rabbit, dashed away. Down here it was a beautiful spring day, and he had missed something. He knew it. He'd made a mistake. But what?

He ran as lightly as he could, avoiding twigs that might snap and the low, leafy branches that might rustle. If Coral Lee heard him, if she realized what they were doing, she might decide it was better to take Trey's wife away from him than take nothing. That must be why he felt Betsy brushing through him as he hurried up and up, the hill so steep that he was already a little winded. But they'd known this risk going in. Bree believed that Coral would not hurt her, and if she was wrong, she didn't care. All she wanted was for him to find the baby. Get Robert out safe. That was his only job.

He was skirting close to Funtime, but the woods were thick and well shaded, widespread branches reaching for the sun in competition with one another. That would make him harder to see, plus it meant that there was not a lot of ground cover. The time he was saving felt worth the risk.

He caught a flash of electric blue through the trees far off to his right. Funtime Jack's hat. He was already flanking the entrance. The carousel was just beyond. Was he too close? He had on his good hiking boots and dark jeans with a green-patterned shirt he hoped might blend with the woods. Now he must stay fast and yet be so quiet. He said it over and over to himself, like a mantra. *Fast and quiet, fast and quiet.*

The top edge of the carousel's collapsed roof came into view. He angled out, though he was too far to clearly see Bree or Coral. If they were talking, he could not hear their voices, and this was good. He hoped to God this meant they could not see or hear him.

Then he was past the carousel roofline, heading northwest on an angle farther up the slope. If this was not officially the Blue Ridge Mountains yet, it was damn close. It was plenty hilly here. His breath came short.

There was no fence around Funtime proper. He had to guess

how far he needed to go to get around the old gold-panning site. In the aerial pictures, it had been two matched squares of dirt, wood-framed, behind the carousel. Gold-mine attractions like these were often nothing but large planting boxes full of sandy earth. He and Bets had taken Cara to one up near Dahlonega when she was little. The owners seeded the loose soil with souvenir "nuggets" and let kids pan until they got something. The pits did not take up a lot of room. He must be past them now.

He angled back the other way, skirting the back edge of Fun-time. According to Mrs. Denton, there had once been a path lead-ing directly from the gold mine to the hidey-hole. He scanned for gaps in the trees that felt deliberate, but the woods were thinner here. Any of the spaces through the trees could be parts of a former path.

He turned back up the slope and pressed on, no longer run-ning. Now he was searching. There should be a cleared space up nearby, the remains of the Dentons' old garden. Past that was the hidey-hole, which might be hard to see. He hadn't been able to see it at all on Google Earth.

He felt that it was close. He also felt his unease rising, the smell of danger. He'd missed something. He was so tired. He felt that he'd aged years, as if the last two days had been a shortcut straight to middle age.

The earth was red with clay, the spring leaves and needles shad-ing everything. He pulled himself up a small, steep incline. It lev-eled off into a shelf, and when he stood, he found himself in the open.

The garden. It was on a rare level place, the hill rising up again behind it. Over half of it was still skirted by the remains of a low rail fence. Some rails were missing. Other sections had been pulled over or coated by blackberry vines. Just to his left, a rusty gleam of silver caught his eye. An old bale of chicken wire, lying on its side.

His heart was pounding. The hidey-hole must be very, very close. He started across. The sun hit this cleared space directly, so bushes and wildflowers and vines had taken hold. Blackberry and wild-rose thorns snagged at his pants as he pushed through. On the far side, an improbable stand of bright sunflowers towered, off-season, tall, and crazy.

He scanned the hill ahead, and a flash of light pulled his attention. The gleam of heavy glass shining through the trees.

A window. The Dentons' hidey-hole was right in front of him. He'd practically been looking at it, but only now did the shapes resolve. There was a weathered wall of gray siding built into the hillside. The cabin was narrow and tucked under a rocky overhang, in shadow. It had a heavy door and a single window. It had been built to blend, and as Mrs. Denton had said, the bulk of the house had been dug out from the hill itself.

His heart thumped hard, a booming in his chest. If he was right about anything, then it was this: Robert was here. Robert was fifty feet away, on the other side of that ancient wooden door. He knew it. He felt it. So why did he hesitate?

She wouldn't bluff about this. She means him harm, Bree had said.

He felt Betsy's fingers brush the back of his neck in warning, making the small hairs rise. Was someone with Robert after all? Lexie?

He unholstered his .38 and crept parallel to the cabin, moving out of the view from that single filthy window. Then he started forward again, angling his path to approach from the side.

He felt stupid doing it. Lexie wasn't up here. Coral, who read mysteries and thrillers, would not let Lexie deposit forensic evidence at the scene of a kidnapping. Still, he felt watched. Still, he kept sneaking gingerly toward the window from the side, silent. If Robert was not alone, then it had to be Lexie. Who else would love Coral Lee Pine enough to help her steal a baby? Engineer Spence's death? Coldly murder a toddler? There wasn't anybody else.

If he looked through the window and saw Lexie holding the baby, he would have to make a choice. He could put a bullet in her eye, then kick the door down and dig the baby out from underneath her body. Or he could hope she would not have her mother's ruth-lessness and kick the door down first, commanding her to put her hands up, away from Robert's frail, small neck.

He stepped soft along the wall, crouching, and then peeped up through the window.

There was only sunlight to brighten the dim room, and this single window's glass was dirty, but the first thing he saw was the shape of the car seat with the small form blanketed snugly inside it. Robert. Alive. Not unhappy. He was stirring from a nap, yawning and stretching, bowing his small spine, eyes shut. Lexie was not there.

The second thing Marshall saw answered all his questions. Who else would help Coral take such a dark revenge? No one but Lexie's own father. Who was dead. Who had long been dead. And yet. His hand was at work, here, too.

My husband had a good job in construction, Coral had told Bree. She'd been around the sites. Taking him his lunch each day. Mariah Denton had said, *He worked demo for years*. Marshall had filed that information away; he had not applied it.

The dynamite piled around the car seat was old. Very old. So old it was sweating, and the papery layers had begun peeling away. It must be as unstable as all hell, and there was a lot of it, stacked in a horseshoe around the baby.

Almost too scared to move, Marshall sucked in a shallow breath. He didn't know shit about explosives. He wondered how much Coral knew. He didn't see an obvious sleek black box with helpful numbers counting down in bright digital red. Instead he saw wires or cables or perhaps twisted fuses running in lines over and around the heaped dynamite.

Robert's eyes were open now. He kicked one of his feet out from under the blanket, waving it around. The movement brought his puppy-covered sock quite near the old sweating explosives. Marshall's mouth went dry.

He shielded his eyes with his hands, peering in, trying to make out details. The cabin was one room with a poured-concrete floor. There was a large camp stove next to a couple of folding chairs and a square table, plus a large, deep metal sink, like the kind in his laundry room. An ancient double bed sagged by the back wall, flanked by a sizable storage cabinet on one side and what looked a chest freezer on the other. That was all.

His gaze was pulled inexorably back to the explosives, his mouth too dry for him to swallow. One of the thick wires or cables ran in a looping coil that disappeared around the back of the pile of dynamite closest to Robert's head.

What was at the end of that? A timer? A detonator? The baby was looking around now, awake, waving his limbs bare inches from the ancient, sweating stacks. It could all blow any second. If he were dumb enough to kick the door down, it would blow for sure. Even breaking out this window was a huge risk. Jesus.

At the other end of the state, his daughter was packing up her things, getting in the car. He wanted to be there when she got home. *You have a kid. You have our kid. You have no backup.*

And yet that was such bullshit. He knew his wife. The ghost he felt was nothing but his nerves. If Bets were really here? His bold and mighty wife? She would damn well go in there and get Bree's boy.

He said a quick and silent prayer, then stood up straight, reaching for the glass.

22

I BEGGED. I kept begging, long after I knew that it would do no good. She was unshiftable, but still I wept and groveled, trying to buy Marshall enough time to find the hidden cabin. It was a one-note role for me; it was Coral who changed as I pleaded and cried. She grew sadder and softer and more and more at peace. Almost relaxed. Or fatalistic. Her sweaty sheen had gone.

I begged until she held up her hand, silencing me. "You aren't going to call him up. I understand. Deep down in you, you must know that he won't come. He won't walk up those steps and do what must be done." Her voice was gentle, gentle with me, but I could hear scorn for Trey in her tone.

With a wild flash of hope, I thought, *Maybe this is a test. If Trey comes up to face her, maybe that will be enough. Or he'll have to actually drink the cup, to prove his courage, his goodness. It will turn out to be only English Breakfast, brewed strong and black and scary.*

But I did not believe it. I was not in the after-school-special version of revenge, here to learn a valuable lesson and then go home with my son and my husband to live a more virtuous life. I'd woken up in the world my mother had always believed in, where strangers had the worst intentions and disaster crouched a breath away, waiting for me to blink.

Only two days had passed since I'd watched Spencer redden and heave and spew bloody foam onto the grass. This woman had engineered that death. She was genuinely sorry she hadn't been there to see him buck and die in agony. This was a woman who had spoken with simple, sad authority about the difficulties of pushing a three-year-old under the water and holding him there.

I argued anyway, feeling each good second I was buying creep past. "You don't know him. He will come, if I go to the edge and wave. He'll come right up."

She shook her head, then glanced at her watch again. "You're a good mother. You'd trade yourself for your child, just like I would. You walked up those stairs already. But now you're out of time. You should call Mr. Cabbat anyway, though. Just so you know the truth. It would be good for you, moving forward, to know. I want you to see him cowering in the car. Or maybe he'll try. He might even get partway up the steps, dragging his feet. Before this is over, you should know for sure what you married. So you can choose better next time. You have your girls to think about."

She'd said a lot of things, but only one phrase truly landed for me. "What do you mean I'm out of time?"

She ignored the question, barely pausing to let me finish it. "Or go ahead on down to your husband now. Take him home, if you find you still want him." She tilted her head to gaze at me with a horrifying pity. As if Robert were already gone. "If you don't mind a little advice, from one mother to another? Get your girls away from him. My letter will come. You'll see then. When you do, I hope you'll get them away."

I took a step back, toward the stairs. "I'll call him up. He'll come. You'll see. He'll trade himself. You don't know him."

"It's too late," she said. "The time has passed. And I have no desire to look into his face. I'll see him in hell eventually. I'll go on ahead and start my wait for him there. I want you to know—" Her voice hitched. "I'm truly sorry for your loss."

"How can time—"

And then my voice cut out, because she lifted the closer cup to her lips and drank it off in four long swallows. She set the cup down, flinching and shaking her head at the taste.

"So bitter." Her eyes were dark pits.

"My God, what did you do?" I asked. How long had it taken before Spencer was sick and convulsing and dead? Fifteen or twenty minutes? But his dose had been in capsules. This was pure liquid.

Coral cleared her throat. Her cheeks had already pinked. She smiled a soft, sad smile.

"What did you do?" I asked again.

That was when the explosion came, a huge reverberating boom, as if God were answering my question. Orange light flashed around the edges of the carousel. The frame shook and rattled. I felt as if a giant hand had reached into my body and grabbed my spine to shake me, too.

The old roof groaned and metal squealed. My hands flew up stupidly to cover my head as I cowered on the bench, sure the roof would come down on us. The china cups rattled on their saucers, dark liquid sloshing up over the rim of the full one. The one that had been meant for Trey.

The heaving earth beneath us stilled. The roof had held. I sat on my bench, blinking in the sudden silence. There had been birdsong all around us, but I had not realized it until they went so quiet.

I could not understand. I looked to Coral, and her face had changed. The afghan had fallen to the floor, and I saw that her hidden hand clutched a small black metal box. Sorrow and ecstasy were at war across her features. Her nostrils flared. Her skin was very red now. She coughed.

"It's done," she rasped, so voiceless that I read the words off her lips more than I heard them. "God, it hurts. It hurts me."

She tipped forward then, landing on her knees in front of her bench, a strangling sound coming from her mouth.

I stood up, blinking, stupid as a cow. "I don't understand." My
voice sounded trapped inside my head. I didn't want to understand.
Robert? I didn't want to understand.

I heard Trey's voice, tinny and faint, screaming my name from
very far away. I looked down the hill. He was out of the car, his face
a featureless white disk turned up toward us.

Coral was heaving now, writhing and gurgling, her skin red-
dening in a frightening crimson blush. Then I was running without knowing or remembering when my feet had started moving. I
banged into the stampeding unicorns on the arm of another of the
heavy wooden benches, and sharp pain bit into my thigh and hip.
I shoved myself away and kept on going, leaping off the platform,
sprinting around the edge of the carousel. A plume of gray smoke
was pillaring up into the blue, blue sky, high above the trees.

I ran around the carousel and toward it, through what used to
be the gold mine, my feet sinking in mounds of still-soft earth that
filled the framed boxes. I could see an orange glare growing up and
ahead of me.

I reached the woods, and I realized I was screaming. It was a
word, this scream. The word was *"Robert!"* and this made no sense.
I didn't want it to make sense. I could not stop screaming for him,
stumbling up a steep slope through the trees, screaming in the
wake of that, screaming into the stink of chemical-burn smoke rising in front of me, a black column marking an altar.

I pulled myself up onto a flat cleared space, and ahead of me,
way on the other side of a small open field, I saw the smoking
remains of a hole in the rock wall. There were bits of wood and
twisted metal scattered about, and a few small fires burned inside
and around it. Ash drifted down in flakes and specks.

I leaped forward, running toward it, as if there were still a reason
to run toward it. As if I might find him there, pink and sweet and
fat and gurgling, unharmed in all that wreckage. Thorns grabbed at
me, trying to slow me, and I ripped through them. My feet tangled
in a low rail fence. I went sprawling into brambles and sun-warmed

earth. I could barely breathe. There could be nothing living in that smoking, blackened cave. I knew that. I couldn't make myself not know. I felt blackness rushing through me. Coming for me somehow, though its root was in me. It was coming. I could not stop it.

I said, "Robert. Robert," quietly, into the dirt.

That was when I heard him. A thin, unhappy wail. I knew his voice, upset and singular and uncertain and perfect. I felt a sharp pain in my breasts and then a release, as if the milk from all the weeks I hadn't nursed him had let down at once.

I rose up on my knees, looking all around. Behind me Marshall was coming over the rise, red-faced and breathless with the car seat in his arms. He ran across the thorny field toward me. He must already have been on the way down to Trey when the blast hit. He must have heard me screaming.

I got up, ignoring the thorns that were ripping at my clothes and my skin, and I ran toward them. I got to them and grabbed them, both of them, hauling them to me, the car seat banging hard into my chest between us. Marshall grabbed me, too, holding my arms as I clutched the seat and stared down into Robert's dear, red, angry face, his eyes now screwing up, his mouth opening in a perfect, furious circle, his volume building.

I dropped to my knees, and they came with me to the ground. I had never loved anything more on this earth than I loved the tiny life we held between us. The car seat's base touched the dirt, and I bent over it, hands scrabbling to unlatch him, to feel him all over, making sure he was moving and whole and unburned and unhurt and exactly himself. And he was. I pulled him out and held the dense, warm weight of him against my chest. His whole body was a clenched fist now. He screamed in my ear, and I loved his living, perfect fury.

My eyes met Marshall's, and he was looking back, whispering, over and over, "I got him, I got him."

I drew Marshall to me, his dear face, and I pressed my mouth against his forehead, his ear, his hair.

"You got him," I said back.

To our right a little patch of fire had caught in a dead rosebush. It glowed orange, growing, and smoke rose, and Robert yelled and squirmed in my arms.

Now I could feel where the thorns had torn my skin. My hip pulsed pain from where I'd slammed into the bench. I understood that I was still in Coral's world. I might live here forever, from now on, in this fear-soaked place my mother had always known existed. She'd tried to tell me. She'd tried, but I refused to listen. Robert's tiny heartbeat fluttered against my own, his breath and tears hot against my neck, so even now, even knowing she had always seen things right, I could not care.

My husband was calling my name from far away, below us.

"Up here!" I called back. "We got Robert! We're up here!"

"We got Robert," Marshall echoed, and his eyes were an animal's eyes, wild and wide.

Somewhere, watching close or waiting far, Lexie Pine still walked. She was an enigma, who might be as angry and as dangerous as her mother or just something small and broken, wanting only to return to the deadly balm of her addiction. But in this moment my heart was so full I could not spare the room to fear or pity her, not in any incarnation. Nearby, so close we felt the heat of it, the rosebush burned and flakes of gray ash drifted down on us, gentle as snow.

Marshall and I clung to each other, Robert between us, calling loud so Trey could find us, "We got him, we got him!" At the same time, we were saying it most truly to each other, back and forth, back and forth, his arms tight around me with Robert, perfectly angry and alive, held safe and whole between us.

PART III

DAUGHTERS

23

OUTSIDE MY WALLS, in the dangerous world, Coral's letter was moving through the postal system. It passed from hand to hand, being sorted and loaded and carried ever closer, as three slow days crawled past. In the aftermath of our meeting, I didn't think much about the paper words she'd aimed at me. She'd left a legacy that was far more dangerous. Lexie. I could feel her making her way closer, too.

Lexie was a broad-spectrum anxiety, a darkness stretched so wide on my horizon that I could not see how my family would ever find our way through to normal. I wanted her arrested for her part in Geoff's death, but she knew I'd given Spence her mother's poison. I truly believed that Coral was his murderer, but I couldn't deny that I'd been her instrument. I had obeyed her every command. If Lexie were found, she would tell the police. Everyone would know. My children, my mother, all our friends and Trey's colleagues. I might go to prison.

Having her loose in the world was worse, though. On Monday the story hit the news, so Lexie must now know that her mother's plan was incomplete. In the darkest hours of the night, I wondered if Coral were also watching. Did she know she'd failed? Did her daughter feel her distant rage like arrows, slivering through space and time to find her heart?

As of Wednesday morning, the story had stayed local. Nothing national. A political sex scandal and the murder contract a Buckhead housewife had put out on her cheating husband had more traction. Or so Trey told me. I couldn't bear to watch any of it.

The early reports were calling it a thwarted kidnapping, with no mention of revenge or Lexie or even the Wilkerson family. The press had not made those connections yet, though they still might, when Lexie was caught, or when Geoff's body was found, or when the police released the information that Coral Lee Pine was also implicated in the murder of Spencer Shaw.

They knew that because I'd told them so myself.

That day, in the wake of the explosion, I huddled on the smoky hillside with Marshall, my son cradled so close. In that moment I could not believe that Coral was truly dead. Back at the carousel, I'd seen her drink, seen her drop to her knees, seen her face mottle and flush, just like Spencer's at the party. But I had not seen her die. I kept thinking, *She was still alive when I left her,* even as Trey found a way up the hill to us, red-faced and panting.

He fell to his knees beside me, saying, "Thank God, thank God," and running his hands over Robert's soft, bald head, then down his spine, then feeling every limb, just as I had.

When he found no injuries, his short breaths changed to great, heaving gulps. He rocked back on his hips, still holding us. I had no bottle, no binky to offer angry Robert, so I gave him the tip of my finger to suck. I hummed and bounced him, leaning against my husband's broad chest. I could feel the pounding of Trey's heart quieting and easing. I don't know how long the three of us stayed that way, relearning how to breathe in the sweetest moment I'd ever known.

And yet I could not believe that it was truly over.

Marshall had moved away without my noticing. I looked around and found him facing back toward the amusement park, scanning the woods, alert, as if he thought that at any moment Coral herself would come running at us from the carousel.

I told him, "I don't think she's coming. She might be dead."

"Good," Trey said, vehement, and at the same time Marshall asked, "How?"

"She drank tea. She drank the tea she'd made for Trey."

Trey said, "We have to get out of here, then. We should go straight down the hillside. Now."

He was rising, pulling me up as well, already turning toward the downslope, though it was jagged and steep. I planted my feet, bracing against his tug. "No. I have to see."

By then Robert had calmed enough for me to tuck him back into his car seat. I bent to buckle him in, and Trey picked it up by the handle, swinging it in gentle half circles to soothe him.

"See what?" Trey asked.

"I have to see *her*. I need to know for certain." I began hiking perpendicular along the slope, heading back to the carousel.

"No time. We have to get out of here," Trey said. He and Marshall were following, though. From far away I heard the thin wail of coming sirens. Trey heard them, too. "The police are coming? Already? How?"

Marshall squinted up at the sky. "Gotta be fire trucks. I bet people can see smoke rising off this hilltop for miles and miles."

I had a different answer, though. "Or Lexie called 911." She could be close. Close enough to hear the blast, which would tell her that the trade hadn't happened after all. For Lexie that booming was a bell that tolled Robert's death and, shortly after that, her mother's. Right now Lexie Pine thought it was over, but that would not last. I hurried on.

Behind me I could hear Marshall explaining to Trey that it was too late for us to leave. There was only one road out, and it was long. If we passed the firefighters before the first intersection, it would be obvious that we were fleeing the scene. Instead Marshall said we had to get our stories straight.

"*You* get our stories straight," I called over my shoulder, my voice sharp. "I have to see."

"Okay," he said, hurrying to keep up. "You have to edit the truth. Just a little bit. If either of you says the wrong thing, Bree could end up in jail."

"I'm a goddamn lawyer," Trey said, irritated. "I know not to incriminate my wife."

Marshall persevered. "Don't outclever yourself, Trey. Lawyers are used to talking. Don't. Avoid details and definitive answers, even yes and no, if you can. Say, 'I think so' and 'I'm not sure' and 'I'm so upset it's hard to think.' Only talk about the things you witnessed personally. It's fine to say, 'I was still in Chicago, then.' Meanwhile, Bree, you have to tell them that Coral was at the party. That Coral herself poisoned Spencer. You saw her there, okay?"

"Okay," I said. I would do whatever he said, but right now I just cared about seeing her, being sure. I was a little turned around, though. The woods all looked the same. I had to trust the angle of the slope to lead me back.

Marshall said, "She looked different, tell them. Black dress, makeup, a dark wig. That will explain why other guests don't recognize her from her photos. Although with that description a few people might say they saw her. I think it's likely, even. Eyewitness accounts are trash, and people like to feel important. Other than that, tell the truth. Tell them about seeing her, twice, and how she snatched Robert from the school. All you have to change are her instructions on the phone. Say she told you to get Spencer to the Orchid Center, where she would be waiting to confront him. The office log should show her trying to get that appointment earlier. Say you got him to the Orchid Center, introduced them, and then left, just as instructed. Do you understand?"

We came out of the trees by the gold mine. I hurried between the boxes this time, not wanting to be slowed by that loose soil. "I understand."

He kept talking anyway. "Don't mention the pills. You introduced Spence to her, and then you left them alone, because your instructions were to go straight home and wait for Robert. Everything else, you tell the truth."

"Jesus," Trey said. "Everything?"

"Yes," Marshall said. "Our trip to Gadsden, Bree's email, your story. The fewer lies we tell, the better."

"Jesus," Trey said again. "If the press—"

Marshall ignored him. "Bree? You could go to prison. Are you listening?"

"I got it," I said, and I did. I'd almost reached the collapsed side of the carousel. I started running, hurrying around to the front.

There was something like a heap of crumpled laundry, gray and brown and orange, on the platform. It was mostly in shade. It was very, very still.

I ran toward it, saying, "Stay here," over my shoulder.

Trey said, "The hell I will!"

I snapped, "Don't bring Robert near her!"

That made Trey stop. It was Marshall who trailed me, all the way to the edge. I stepped up onto the carousel's tilted floor, and the heap resolved itself into her form.

"Bree!" my husband called, a warning tone.

"I have to," I said. I went closer.

She lay coiled on her side by the felled lion with his paint-peeled rose wreath, and her body had that heavy stillness that only comes to the dead. One arm was hooked around his pole, the hand a gnarled bird's claw, clutching nothing. Her mouth hung slack, her cheek resting in a pool of bloody foam that was already drying. Her face was red, and her gold-brown eyes were shiny and open and empty.

I was filled with such a savage joy then. I wanted to scream until my raw throat gave out entirely. I wanted to kick at her corpse and beat her helpless stillness with my hands. I did none of this. I only looked down, my chest heaving. Looked closer.

Her dress had come up as she flailed. Her naked legs were pale, mottled with age spots and thick veins. One foot had kicked out far enough to be in sunlight, which lit up a floss of thin hairs on her shin. She wore old-fashioned cotton drawers. They were white, with small pink flowers, like a child might wear.

All the violence left me. This lifeless shape had once owned the raspy voice I'd obeyed. This lifeless shape had once owned me. She was truly gone, and if there was a hell, then she was writhing in it, trapped in an eternal rage at the sight of my son and my husband standing together near the edge of the woods, whole.

I hoped God was more merciful than that. I didn't want her ghostly eyes watching from any kind of beyond. I hoped she was in a quiet darkness. I hoped she was at last at peace.

The sirens were close, now. I reached out and pulled her dress down, gently, covering her underwear and the sad, wattled flesh of her thighs, hanging loose from her frail bones.

"Don't touch her," Marshall said, too late.

"Bree," Trey said again, and this time I got up and went to wait with him.

Marshall stuck by me, talking. "You know what to tell them?" I nodded. "Short sentences. Answer only what they ask. It's good to cry and ask for breaks. It's good to say 'I'm not sure' and 'I'm so upset and tired' and that it's all a blur."

I turned to him. "Marshall. I got it."

He nodded, but he looked sick with worry. His sweetness registered; he cared so much about these details. I could not, yet. I felt as if my entire body had been filled with waiting. It stretched out in front of me as far as I could see. We were on the hilltop waiting for the first responders. Once we were home, I would be waiting for Coral's letter. And her daughter. I was waiting for Lexie most of all, even then.

In my mind she wasn't the woman from the mug shot, with her picked, grayed skin and thin hair, middle-aged and brittle. She was the fresh-faced, pretty girl that Trey had known. I half expected her to come at us right now, screaming out of the trees, her wide-set eyes lamplit by rage.

Robert and I both had to go and get checked out at the hospital. Everyone was so kind to me. We were the victims after all. A policeman talked to me there, but just a little. A few questions. There would be more later. By then I'd have a lawyer with me. Trey had called to put Leticia Marks, Gabrielle's friend, on retainer. He'd called his family, too, and his father was mobilizing a fleet of lawyers and publicists. The Cabbats had a vested interest in keeping details out of the press. This distant flurry of activity mattered little to me in the moment, and yet I thought that one day I'd be grateful for it.

Trey was the one who called my mother. She brought the girls home, and he sat them down and told them all an extremely expurgated version of the weekend, while I sat quiet, Robert in my lap, my daughters pressing in close against my sides.

That night Leticia sat by me in my own great room as I gave my statement to the police. Marshall had already given his. I stuck to his story, truthful about all things except that one, my answers short and broken. It was easy to follow his instructions, because I could not stop crying.

The whole time Lexie Pine was a blur of motion that kept catching in the corner of my eye. I felt her breath in every breeze that touched my neck. I heard the whisper of her feet in every hallway.

After Leticia and the cops left, I couldn't sleep. I lay in our big bed staring at the window. The drapes were open, the way Trey liked them, because once the lights were off, I needed to see out. Lexie Pine had Peyton's house keys. Or at least no one had found them up at Funtime. Trey had already called a locksmith, who was going to redo all our doors, even our back gate, tomorrow morning. As for tonight I hoped Lexie Pine had not yet learned that her mother's business was unfinished, but I had to see for myself that

she was not standing in her mother's old footprints, bending my
basil plants to press her nose against our glass.

Robert slept between us, my hand on his chest, so that I could
feel him breathing. I looked at him, then out the window to our
moon-drenched, peaceful yard, back and forth, again and again.
The simple act of closing my eyes started a panic attack. So I
watched over him until almost dawn, when I was tired enough to
drift off without noticing.

I dreamed the concrete stairs that led to Funtime. Coral was
waiting for me there. Carousel music drifted down, a garish, joyous
waltz. I climbed up to find the painted animals whole again, rising
and falling on golden posts. Coral rode astride a perfect lion, noble
as Aslan, wreathed in living roses. As I reached the edge of the ride,
she smiled at me and checked her cheap watch, and all around me
the world exploded into fire and ash. I bolted upright to find a regular sunny Monday. Well, almost regular.

Peyton and Anna-Claire were in the kitchen, arguing over coconut milk yogurt flavors, as if a pair of bulky, silent ex-soldiers
from the private security firm that Trey had hired weren't sitting
nearby at the kitchen table. They knew that their brother had been
taken by the same woman who the police believed had snuck into
the gala and murdered Spencer Shaw, and yet here they were, fussing over the last honey-vanilla. Perhaps the presence of these large
armed men relaxed my anxious middle child. My oldest, I thought,
was a little bit excited by it all. The drama of having bodyguards
appealed to her. She lost out on the yogurt in the end because she
was too involved in nine simultaneous group chats to fight for it.

I had to remind myself that they hadn't known about Robert's
absence until it was over. They'd been at their grandma's, making
cookies, sleeping in. He was safe before they ever knew he'd been
in danger.

My mother was still upstairs, asleep in a guest room. She'd been
more upset than the girls. Too upset to go home. But also strangely
vindicated. She didn't say out loud that this proved the world was

as blackhearted as she'd always said; she didn't have to. I'd made her promise to go home this morning and make an appointment with her doctor, maybe go back on her antianxiety medication for a little. I thought I ought to find us all therapists. Ones who specialized in trauma. I wanted mine to have an M.D., so she could write prescriptions. Prescriptions sounded pretty good.

I made avocado toast for Anna-Claire, wondering how I could stand to let them go to school. I wanted to keep things normal for them, as much as I could. In the end I put Robert in his car seat and drove them myself.

An ex–Army Ranger named Mills went with us. His partner, Maxwell, discreetly followed in a dark sedan. It was a strange ride. Mills was young and beautiful, built like a movie star with a low fade haircut and a gun. Anna-Claire kept leaning up between the seats to ask him questions about his job and his military service and whether or not he was a dog person. She was both overconfidently flirty and thirteen years old, which made poor Mills wildly uncomfortable. He kept cutting his eyes at me, giving short, awkward answers while Peyton giggled.

I couldn't help him. The closer we got to St. Alban's, the tighter my chest screwed shut around my lungs. Robert had been stolen from this very campus. In the car-pool line, I gripped the wheel so tight that the blood drained from my hands. It was all I could do to let the girls get out and go inside. Then I sat frozen until the cars stuck behind me started tapping their horns in brief, polite peeps. I pulled forward, out of the way, but leaving wasn't possible.

I parked on the road across from the main entrance and turned the car off, in spite of Mills's puzzled glances. I told him we would go home soon. He texted his partner, and Maxwell parked behind me.

We waited. I don't know what they were doing, but I was watching for Lexie Pine. After a while I turned the car on to crack my windows and let the pleasant air circulate. I wasn't going anywhere.

Mills and I lived out of Robert's diaper bag all day. I had protein bars and fresh diapers and formula and bottled water. I downloaded a light, sweet audiobook about misunderstandings at a wedding and played it to pass the time. Mills probably hated it. Around one, Maxwell had pizza and soft drinks delivered right to our cars. It was from some chain, thick with plastic-looking pepperoni and cheap, rubbery cheese. It tasted better than it looked.

Marshall called around two. Just to check on me, he said. I'd been texting with Trey on and off, but I hadn't told my husband I was hanging around outside the school like a sex offender. I told Marshall, though.

"When I try to leave, or even look away from the building, I panic. It's ridiculous. There's an armed ex-marine in the car behind me who'll be here all day. But apparently I think it's my magic presence that keeps them safe."

Mills sat beside me, stoic, trying to pretend he wasn't listening.

"So don't drive them tomorrow," Marshall said. "Let Trey handle it."

It was simple and pragmatic, and it worked. Tuesday I kissed them good-bye and let them go on to the school with their father and Maxwell. Mills stayed with me.

After that I couldn't leave the house. Panic trilled up my spine at the very idea of stepping outside, being visible and exposed. I wanted walls around me and my son. I wanted more ex-soldiers, dotted around my yard like points on a compass.

I called the school office to make sure the girls had been checked in to the system at homeroom. I couldn't let Robert out of my sight. I liked him best bound to me in his sling. I tried not to think about how Coral's body had so recently been in place of mine, how my son had been tied to her, his flutter-fast heart beating beside hers.

The only thing that got me out the door was the arrival of the mail around eleven. I left Robert asleep in a bouncy chair by Mills and went to get it. I wanted to be the one to intercept Coral's letter. By then I wasn't waiting for it so much as I was resigned to it.

It wasn't there, though. Not yet. Just a stack of junk.

I closed the mailbox, impatience and relief at war in me, and my cell phone rang. I juggled the pile of mail into one arm, then pulled it out of my back jeans pocket. It was Marshall.

He was mostly checking up on me, but he also had updates he'd gleaned from his sources about the ongoing investigation. Coral hadn't used the detonator she'd had hidden under her afghan. That had been her backup. The explosion had been caused by a chemical timer.

"I told you she wasn't bluffing," I said, sitting down on one of the wrought-iron chairs on my front porch. "At the end she kept saying I was out of time, that it was too late to call Trey up. I didn't understand."

There was more. He remembered his promise that we would contact Kelly Wilkerson once this was all over. He now thought we shouldn't. Kelly was no longer a person of interest; we'd told the police that Coral had taken Geoff, though no body had been found. I wondered what explanation her husband would offer. How well would it match Trey's? He wouldn't make himself the villain, surely. In his story would he follow Trey and Spence upstairs at all? We agreed there was no need to bother Kelly. She had grief enough, and whatever her husband's story, I didn't want to hear it.

Depressing topic, but I wanted to keep talking. Marshall had gotten Robert back. Listening to his voice, even as we discussed these awful things, was the safest I'd felt since we got home. But he needed to call Trey and update him, too. I let him go and went back inside to check on Robert, though I'd scarcely been away from him five minutes.

I went to the kitchen to sort out bills and put the junk mail in recycling, thinking. Coral had mailed her letter from in-state. It should come in the next day or two. I hadn't told anyone about it. Not Trey, or the police, or Gabrielle, or even Leticia, who insisted that she was my lawyer and I should tell her everything. I hadn't even told Marshall.

I had a decision to make first. Would I open it or burn it?

No story that Coral would tell could possibly match Trey's. How could it, considering the source? Coral could know only what Lexie had shared with her. By all accounts Coral Lee Pine had been a strict and difficult parent. In the expurgated-for-Mother version, Lexie would not have confessed that she was the source for the drugs, or about the first threesome with Spence and Bonnie, or that she'd been the one to suggest another one with Trey. Nothing Lexie told her mother would mitigate what those three boys had done.

I hoped that I would burn it. The letter would not contain anything I could believe. Why give Coral's version any space inside my head? Coral Lee Pine was a poisoner, and she had dripped enough darkness into me already. And yet I could still feel the cord of our strange connection. She'd written to me. I wanted to read it.

All this churning, and still the letter was only paper. Lexie was her mother's flesh and blood, her will and fury. Until they found Lexie, I could not feel safe or believe that this was truly over. I wanted her caught, even if it meant she exposed my ugly role in Spence's death. Marshall had told me to lie if that happened. Deny it. Accuse Lexie of protecting her mother's memory or still trying to lash out at my family. It would be my word against hers, and I was a Cabbat. She was a junkie. My lie held more weight than her truth, but that echoed back against her history and my own in ways that sickened me. Nevertheless I had told him I would do it.

"She's probably left the state anyway," Trey said late that night, when he woke at two to find me mulling all this over, my hand resting on Robert's busy little heart. "The guys I've hired are a precaution. If she has any sense, she's long gone."

"I'm sure you're right," I'd whispered back, with absolutely no conviction.

For all Coral had said she was leaving her child out of it, I knew how dirty Lexie's hands were. She had helped her mother stalk a toddler. Maybe she hadn't known Coral's plan in the beginning, but after Geoff's murder she'd still helped Coral watch me. She'd let her mother take my child, too. Now Coral was dead with her plan only two-thirds complete. Would Lexie feel she had to finish it? She didn't come from a family who let things go.

The next day the mail came at eleven, right on time. I put Robert into his bouncy chair and left him with Mills again. I walked down the drive, feeling Lexie's eyes on me with every step I took.

I opened the mailbox, and there it was. I knew it at once. It was a white cardboard thing, the size of a sheet of paper, tucked between the smaller bills and larger catalogs. The only words on it were my name and address, the handwriting small and spidery, the letters crabbed together. No return address.

I grabbed the whole stack and hurried back inside. In my head, in the two minutes I'd been gone, Lexie had vaulted over the back fence, kicked down my back door, and taken Robert. It was a relief to see him peacefully napping in his chair, his pink mouth working a dream bottle.

Mills looked up from his book. "Everything okay?"

"Uh-huh," I said, trying to calm my breathing. "Can you sit with him? I'd love to grab a shower. He should sleep at least until noon, and I'll have the baby monitor in case he wakes."

"Sure," Mills said. He was good with Robert, I'd discovered. Giant Mills with his eight-pack and his hooded eyes liked babies. His sister had two kids, he said. I found it touching, even sweet, and these days I took sweetness anywhere I found it.

I brought the mail back to my bedroom. I locked the door and leaned against it.

I would not read the letter. I'd decided. There was nothing Coral Lee Pine could tell me that was true. It would do me no good at all. I would take it to the master bath and burn it in the sink. I had a lighter in there for my scented candles. Trey had told me he saw our family as a bull's-eye after Anna-Claire was born. The baby in the middle. Us around the baby in concentric circles. I realized now a bull's-eye was a target. I could not weaken us with Lexie still unfound—and maybe aimed at us. I had to keep Robert and his sisters safe, at center, and I wanted Trey wrapped tight around them. To not read was to choose to wrap around them all, my husband included.

I dropped the pile of mail on the bed, then fished her envelope out from between the bills and glossy catalogs.

I was halfway to the bathroom before I registered the small red stamps running in a chain along the edge. A long envelope from Visa had hidden the words before.

PHOTOGRAPHS, DO NOT BEND. PHOTOGRAPHS, DO NOT BEND. PHOTOGRAPHS, DO NOT BEND.

24

THIS WAS HOW affairs began. Marshall should not be standing on Bree's porch, readying to meet her one-on-one to talk about her problems with her husband. That was the first step in the *How to Screw Up Someone's Marriage* handbook.

On the other hand, there wasn't a universe where she called him weeping that way and he didn't go to her. It didn't feel physically possible.

She'd been so upset on the phone that he'd had a hard time understanding anything beyond the bare facts. Coral had sent a letter. An explanation, apparently, for all the damage she and her daughter had done. He hadn't been able to make out much beyond that, she'd been sobbing so hard.

Bree *had* asked, "How can I stay married?" He'd heard that question loud and very damn clear. So here he was to talk with Bree about leaving her husband, and he was . . . what? Supposed to be objective?

Trey's story about Lexie Pine had smelled off to him from minute one, but standing on the porch, he swore to himself that no matter what Coral's letter said, he would be fair. He would be more than fair. He would go in there a hundred percent Team Trey. Not only because the other team was headed by a dead murderess who lied, and tricked, and poisoned. But because Bree loved her husband. They had three kids who'd only known a happy, intact family so far. Unless Coral had sent actual footage of Trey assassinating Lincoln, he wasn't going to do anything to bust that up. This he promised God, the universe, and himself before he pressed the doorbell.

Bree opened the door so fast she must have been waiting in the foyer. She wore faded jeans and an old Tori Amos T-shirt she'd had since college. Her hair was pulled back in a loose, low ponytail. Barefoot, with no makeup, she looked so young, like the girl he'd grown up with. Her nose and even her lips were puffy and pink from crying, her eyes red-rimmed, but she was so lovely and so sad that he had to put his hands in his pockets to keep from reaching for her, pulling her into his arms.

Something had broken in him, some resolve, that day up on the mountain, when he'd put her baby back into her arms and she had clung to him. Her tears had wet his face, and she'd rained kisses on his head, his hands. Some essential barrier had crumbled, so that now he had to work to keep space between them. This was not the right time. There never would be a right time. She was not the right woman. Just the one he wanted.

She held up a large white envelope, the stiff cardboard kind they sold at the post office. She had Robert in a baby sling, crunched up into a wad like a little frog, sideways against her chest. It looked uncomfortable, but he seemed happy, peering cheerfully out. Marshall was glad the baby wasn't in his crib. It would be hard to forget that Trey existed with his small, helpless son right there, tied to Bree's body, always between them.

Bree grabbed his hand and tugged him inside. She hurried him back to the master bedroom, but at the door she stopped so abruptly he almost bumped into her. She pulled him back the other way, calling, "Mills? My friend is here. We're in Trey's office if you need us."

"All good, Ms. Cabbat," a young male voice called back from the great room.

"Today's ex-marine. Except Mills was an Army Ranger," she said by way of explanation. "Anna-Claire has a little crush on him." She was calmer than she'd been on the phone. Talking about her daughter, a smile ghosted across her face.

He followed her to Trey's office. The room would not let him forget Trey either. He was present in the pictures, the stark, masculine furniture, the law books, and the bar cart full of pricey brown liquor.

She closed the door behind them before she spoke again. "Did you tell anyone at work you were coming here?"

So this was a *secret* meeting. Great. "My job keeps me on the move. No one's going to find it strange that I left the office."

"Good. Mills won't mention it. He barely speaks. Strong, silent type."

"Show me," he said.

She held out the envelope. It was technically evidence, but he was untechnically going to do everything he could to conceal it from the cops, so there was no reason not to take it. He did so, and her empty hand immediately went to cup Robert, petting his back. He made a soft, happy sound.

She said, "I keep seeing her. Lexie Pine. I'm so tired that the edges of my vision feel all blurry. She's in my peripheral vision, peering in my windows. But when I go look directly, there's no one. The weirdest part? I'm not seeing the woman in the mug shot. Not that middle-aged person. It's Lexie when Trey knew her. The one in that envelope."

He was still examining the outside, reading the red-stamped words. "Coral sent pictures?"

"Not just any pictures. *The* pictures. The ones that Adam Wilkerson took that night," she said.

"How?" he asked, walking quickly to Trey's desk to empty the contents. At least twenty photos fell out, along with a single sheet of college-ruled paper, filled front and back with crabbed, spidery writing. The note was new, but the photos were very old, the corners bent, the paper soft from years of handling.

Bree was looking deliberately away, her arms loosely around her swaddled son. "It's in the letter. When Lexie left school and went running off to Memphis, she stopped all contact with her mother. Coral got worried, and she did the things any mother would do. She called the roommate and the dean's office. When she learned that Lexie hadn't been going to class and some of her things were gone from her room, she went straight to UVA, demanding to meet with someone in administration. They had a couple of the pictures by then. They showed her. The man who sat down with her made it clear that Lexie wasn't welcome back. Coral stayed in Virginia, though, looking for her kid. She also tried to collect the pictures. She couldn't stand the thought of them, her daughter's body trapped on paper, being passed around forever. She tracked down as many copies as she could, shaming or threatening or begging kids all over campus. There were complaints, of course. Security started watching for her. Eventually they called the real police, who told her they would arrest her if she came back. She wrote it all down for me."

He didn't read the letter, though. Instead, as she spoke, he sorted the pictures. There were only five shots, multiple copies of each. He understood what was troubling Bree almost at once.

Four he could dismiss. They were only raw, ugly pornography, graphic and unkind. In all of them, Lexie Pine's face was visible, but peripheral. The person holding the camera had had little interest in her face. The two young men in the shots, always headless or with their backs to the camera, swarmed her slight body, using it and filling it. Her expressions in the first four, from what he could see . . . well. She was having sex. Her face twisted into unflattering shapes that might be pleasure or pain or simply bad angles.

The fifth photograph was different. Significantly different.

There were three copies. He picked up the least damaged, studying it closer. He looked to Bree. She shrugged, tears leaking from her swollen eyes again.

The shot had been taken over one of the participating boys' shoulders, so his body obscured Lexie's below the waist. Lexie was on her back, her arms over her head to show the vulnerable hollows of her armpits, shoulders crunched up. Her small breasts were centered in the shot, lifted by her stretched, taut arms. The other young man was barely in the photo at all. Only the ends of his knees appeared, framing the crown of her head. Lexie's hands and wrists weren't visible, but her arms were stretched tightly, as if they were being pulled. As if the boy kneeling at her head was holding them, keeping them out of his friend's way.

In this shot, and this shot only, she stared directly into the camera. Her pale eyebrows pressed up and together, distressed. Her eyes were wide. To Marshall her gaze looked frightened, even distraught, but the rest of her expression was not visible; the young man at work between her legs had his hand over her mouth. Hard enough for his fingers to indent her cheek, for his palm to flatten her nose.

"That's Trey's hand." Bree's voice had almost no inflection. She was all the way across the room, but she knew which picture he'd lifted. "I know my husband's back, his fingers. That's him."

Marshall kept his face as neutral as possible.

On the phone she'd asked how she could stay married. Looking at the picture, he understood the question. But he was a cop, a realist who worked for lawyers now. He couldn't help but see what would unfold if she did leave Trey. He knew how these things played out.

Trey was a Cabbat. The family had so much money, so many connections, and they had never fully warmed to Bree. God, they loved her children, though, and that kind of family was used to getting its way. If Trey was hurt enough, angry enough, they would take everything from her. They would take her kids.

Of course, she had these pictures. Good blackmail material, if she could bring herself to fight that dirty. He should keep the extra copies someplace safe, use them for her if he had to. Make Trey back down. Except as soon as he came up with that plan, he saw the flaw. The pictures had small, soft teeth. First, they didn't show his face, so even if she was willing to release them, Trey could lie. Or worse, he could admit everything. Including Bree's part in Spencer's murder.

"Well?" she asked. "What do I do?"

He kept his expression neutral, but she knew him so well that his lack of reaction was telling. Her face crumpled back into tears, and her hands moved over Robert, restless.

"Maybe it started like he said. Maybe it was her idea. I can't tell what she's feeling in the other shots. But that one, when she sees the camera, it's so clear. She wanted it to stop. They didn't stop. Or maybe she didn't want any of it, ever. I don't know. I only know what I see." Her voice was a raw, ugly whisper. He had yet to speak, but she stepped toward him as if he'd argued with her. "He's not a predator. He never did anything like this again in his whole life. I'd swear to it. I think on some level he must be so ashamed. He must be sorry. Because he distanced himself from Spence and got back with Maura. He lied to me, or he kept silent, but maybe anybody would. He did an awful thing. Years ago. But he is not an awful man."

"He's not an awful man," Marshall echoed, relieved to have something he could say, a way to agree with her.

She nodded, vehement. "He's a good man. A good father. So good to me." Her eyes on his were pleading. "He did an awful thing."

"Yeah. He did," Marshall said. "So what's the fix? You love him. You have three kids together. You're not going to head right to a divorce lawyer's office. What do you want to happen next? How does this get mended?" He sounded pragmatic and cool. Inside he was shaking. He hated Trey for putting her in this position. He felt as if he was playing devil's advocate. Literally. "You can't blame him for

what Coral did. Hell, if he and Adam Wilkerson were mass mur-
derers, it doesn't justify her stealing children. You can only blame
him for this one moment, right here." He turned the picture toward
her, and she flinched. "He did this. It happened, but so did the next
thirty years. So did all the years of your marriage. All the good he's
done in his community and for you, his kids. So what now?"

Her face had cleared as he spoke. "When you put it that way, it
gets so simple."

That shocked him. "It does?"

"Yes!" she said. "He has to make it right. He has to make it
right with Lexie. He should have done it way back then, when she
was leaving for the bus. God, he gave her whatever little bit of cash
he had in his wallet." She shook her head, this thought profoundly
distasteful to her. "That must have made her feel worse, and yet she
was desperate enough to take it. That speaks volumes. We have to
find her. She's out there. There's still time to make it right. He has
to do now what he should have done then. Apologize. Make reparations. Help her with rehab, her mother's funeral, whatever she
needs. He derailed her life, Marshall. He owes her. So we find her
now, and he does everything he can to make it right."

Her eyes were shining. She'd seen a way through that she could
live with.

Marshall had his doubts. "You think he'll do that?"

In his experience wealthy, powerful men, even the nicest ones,
were bad at admissions and apologies. Hell, rich men were bad at
shame in general. Not to mention Trey'd had a chance already to
tell Bree this story. His son's life had been at stake, and Trey had
lied to her.

Her tears had stopped entirely, though. She was pacing, talking
faster now, her hands smoothing over the baby as he stretched and
cooed.

"Yes. He will. I know him. He's a good man. We find Lexie.
Maybe she won't be open to his amends, but we do have to try. He
should give money to help fix the larger problem, too. I mean, this

still happens. We can donate to campus awareness at UVA, rape hotlines, women's centers. But we start with an apology."

"Privately," Marshall said. Because that, maybe, Trey would do. A public admission? No. But he clearly still carried guilt over this, and if he did apologize to Lexie, make reparations? Bree was sweet, and she was forgiving, and she adored him. Maybe it could work?

"I hope privately. I don't want the girls to ever, ever know about this, if it can be helped," she said. "That's up to Lexie, though. I think? In my head I've been thinking of her as this terrifying thing. We've got ex-marines all over the place. I've been so scared. But that picture. She's so small, and scared, and hurting."

Marshall shook his head. "We don't know how deeply Lexie was embroiled in her mother's plan. She could very well be a threat."

Bree nodded. "We won't know until we find her." She paused, sucked in a breath. "If Lexie helped with Geoff—I don't know. We can't know until you track her down."

"I'm working on it," Marshall said. His whole team was. Gabrielle was on it, too, and cops in two states.

She smiled, though her mouth trembled. "All I know for sure now is what Trey did. That's what he has to fix. What do you tell Cara? Same as Trey and I tell our girls. If you do a bad thing, you don't say, 'Oh, but she did something worse.' You aren't in control of that. You aren't responsible for that. If you do it, it's yours. You apologize. You make amends. Maybe if Trey steps up, Lexie will realize she has to take responsibility, too. For whatever her part was in her mother's plan. It's the only way to fix this."

By "fix this," Marshall understood, Bree meant much more than the moment of Trey's history that the old Nikon camera had captured. She meant her marriage. She meant the world.

The world that he knew was huge and broken in a million unfixable ways, but in spite of all that had happened in the last few days, she still saw brightness, found a way to hope. He loved that she was going to try. It was . . . the word was "valiant." She was going to grab a lance and run at a windmill. Fine. But he was going to have her back. In case the windmill was a monster after all.

He sorted the pictures again, leaving one copy of each on the desk. The rest he packed up with the letter in the envelope; he could not risk Trey destroying them. If this did go sour, get ugly, the other copies and the letter were the only decent card they had. The letter especially. It linked Trey to the photos.

"I'll keep these," he said. "Just in case."

"Just in case what?" she said, but it was a distracted question. She was pacing, thinking, hoping, her essential optimism shining. She'd always been like this, the deliberate opposite of her mother. Shelly Ann saw danger in every dark spot. Bree saw restful shade. Marshall thought that they were both wrong to a degree. But if he was being honest, he believed that Bree was wronger.

Or maybe he was cynical. He could not have her faith in Trey. But if it were Betsy? Impossible to imagine Betsy in this position. But if it were? Yes. He'd have faith that his wife, the mother of his child, would do what was right. Even if it was hard.

Bree was set on this path, and if she was correct, if people were essentially good and love could win and hope was blah-blah-blah, she might save her marriage. Hell, she might save her husband. She might be the making of him. Marshall had to hope that it could happen, for her sake. For the sake of her kids.

He said the only thing he could say and still be completely honest with her.

"I'm right here if you need me."

25

AFTER MARSHALL LEFT, I ground out the hours by tidying every bit of flotsam I could find, keeping Robert with me in his sling. When the house looked ready for a photo shoot, I started in on the closets. Mills stayed on the same floor as me, amiably toting his novel and his giant bag of high-protein snacks. Around five-thirty his partner brought the girls home from rehearsal and quiz-bowl practice, then headed back out to escort Trey home from work.

I told the girls to heat up frozen pizza in the rec-room kitchenette, and there was a salad to go with it in the fridge.

"Head downstairs and do your homework. Then you can stream a movie, if you like. Trade off the babysitting. You are in complete charge of your brother," I told them. "Your dad and I need a little privacy."

"Gross," Anna-Claire said.

I handed her Robert, who was cheery but peckish, then gave Peyton his diaper bag, freshly restocked with everything he'd need. "Stay downstairs unless it's an emergency. Make it a double feature."

"Super gross," Peyton echoed, slinging the bag over her shoulder.

"Mills, can you go with them?" I asked.

"Yeah, Mills!" Anna-Claire said, visibly brightening. "Come watch a movie with us."

Mills looked so alarmed that I had mercy on him. "Homework first, and, Anna-Claire, Mills is in the middle of a book."

"I'll sit on the stairs and read so I won't disturb you," Mills said.

"You won't bother me!" Anna-Claire said, starting down.

Peyton had been visibly antsy all week, but none of this seemed to be touching my eldest. "Seemed" was the operative word. She was an actor, like me, with a talent for appearing Instagram-perfect even in the worst of storms. But I could see the pale lavender circles under her luminous eyes. Her friends pinged her phone relentlessly, caught up in the adolescent drama of being tragedy-adjacent. Outwardly she lapped up the attention, but her old stuffed dog, Bendo, long banished to the bookshelf, was back in her bed.

Peyton lingered until Mills went down, picking at her cuticles. "Mom. How much longer are the bodyguards going to be here?"

I wanted these nice, quiet professionals out of my house, too. They were here until Lexie Pine was found, though. She might be as dangerous as her mother, but I hoped Coral had acted, at least in the worst parts, truly on her own. Maybe, if this were so, she would be open to Trey's attempt to make amends. My secret, sweetest prayer was that there was a way for all of us to find a little peace.

Marshall thought this was naïve, or even stupid. He hadn't said so, but I knew his face. I agreed it was one hell of a long shot, actually, but this very week I'd had such good luck with long shots.

I said exactly none of this to my nervous middle child. Instead I smiled and brushed her hair back off her face. "Not long, honey. We're being overcautious. Your dad and I had a terrible fright. But Robert is home and you are safe, okay?"

"Okay." She didn't sound convinced, but she followed her sister down the stairs.

As I closed the door to the basement behind them, I saw that my own hands had a shake in them. I'd never been a nervous person, but the last few days had ignited all the anxiety-prone recessives I'd passed to Peyton, courtesy of Mom. I hated being on a different floor from Robert, even with a bodyguard present. I hadn't been away from my baby for more than a few minutes since Marshall had placed the perfect, angry miracle of him, kicking and squalling, back in my arms. His physical absence now left me shivery.

It was good to force this break, though. After all, he couldn't sleep between me and his dad forever. By middle school it would be so awkward. His college dormmate would not know how to handle a ferocious mother, curled up like a guard dog at the foot of Robert's bed. More immediately, keeping a baby in the bed between my husband and me every, every minute would soon start wedging our marriage apart.

I wanted to mend it. That had to start right now. I didn't want anyone, even Robert, in the room for this conversation. I had such ugly things to say. I didn't want his lovely clean slate of a brain absorbing them. And yet I felt that Trey and I would not be alone. The ghost of Lexie in her girlhood waited in our bedroom, hoping to be finally, truly seen.

Around seven the night-shift guys came to relieve Mills. I sent them down to the basement with the girls. Mills's partner dropped Trey off at home fifteen minutes later, waiting in the car for Trey to get safely inside. I met my husband at the door, and my expression was enough to panic him.

"What?" he said. "Where are the kids?"

"The kids are fine. In the basement with the security team."

"So what's wrong? You look . . ."

I put a reassuring hand on his arm. "I needed some time to talk with you. Alone." Trey remained on edge as I led him back to our bedroom. Perhaps he, too, felt the presence of Lexie's younger self. That girl was buried inside a harder woman, lost to years of addiction and rough living, and yet she was here, too, caught and preserved on paper, in the middle of the moment that would change her life. I closed the door behind us. Locked it. "Sit down."

He did, perching stiff and tense on the edge of the bed. I went to my dresser and got the photos out of my top drawer. I'd shoved Lexie back behind my underwear and socks, as if she were as innocent a thing as a pink diary with a heart-shaped lock. I came to join him, leaving a little space between us on the bed.

I sat down, and into this space I dealt her pictures out for Trey. One, two, three, four, Trey scanning each in turn, his lips going paler and paler, as I said, "Coral mailed these to me. She dropped them at the post office the day before we met her at the carousel. Trey, they came this morning." I set the last one down, and she was with us. I could feel her.

"Jesus." His hand came up to rub at his mouth. When he saw the final picture, his gaze skated away. Fast. He looked around, still rubbing his mouth, distressed. He did not look back down at the pictures. He did not look at me. "I never saw most of these. I didn't look when I made Ansel burn them. I didn't want to see—"

My eyebrows came together. He'd said, when he told me the ugly story, that he hadn't looked at the pictures when he went to Ansel's room to burn them. I hadn't questioned it. But now I knew personally how hard a thing that was to do.

I was trying to find the words to say this to him when he asked, "When did Coral Lee Pine get these pictures? How?"

I told him everything I'd told Marshall. As I spoke, his gaze roamed the room, avoiding my face and the photos both. His hands rubbed restlessly together.

When I finished, he finally glanced down. He reached for the second picture in the line, as if he were going to pick it up, but he didn't quite touch it. He looked away again, so sad.

"That's the one I've seen. The one I took from those sorority girls at the party." He swallowed, but it sounded dry. "I don't want to look at the rest. It's too ugly from the outside. Uglier than I remember. I hate that she sent these to you." His voice shook. He took a moment to collect himself. I waited, hoping he would meet my gaze. Hoping he would see my love and my compassion for him. Instead he looked down at his hands, and anger twisted his mouth. "I keep thinking, how dare she. How dare she send these to you. My wife. The mother of my children. Which is foolish. This woman stole our child. She had no conscience. No boundaries or decency. But still I think, how dare she." He gave a shuddering sigh, and then finally, finally, he met my gaze. His eyes were shining bright with unshed tears. "God, poor Lexie. This should have been nothing but a night in college. For her especially. A wild night that maybe we'd remember with that kind of"—he paused, searching for a word or phrase—"fond horror? One of those things you can't believe you did when you were young and dumb. I hate that these got passed around the school and hurt her so. I also hate her mother, but I'm still sorry she saw these. God, I didn't punch that kid enough. Ansel. Adam. Whatever his name is. I should have hit him more and harder. I half want to go hit him again now, except he lost his son. I guess, on top of everything, I'm grateful. I'm grateful Robert is home."

He wiped at his eyes, then shrugged helplessly. I saw nothing in him but sincerity and shame, but I couldn't help wondering at the way he'd processed it all so fast. His words, the arc of his feelings— the actor in me thought that it would make a good audition piece, and then I hated myself immediately for thinking that. Trey was a litigator, smart and articulate, his brain honed by years of work to process information fast. He'd been thinking of little other than Lexie for days now. His sorrow felt genuine, and I knew him. I loved him.

Still, I couldn't leave it be. Lexie would not let me, and I would not let him. I touched the last photo in the line. It felt cool and smooth, like nothing with a heartbeat, and yet I felt her there.

"This is the one where I . . ." I paused. "Where I have trouble."

He didn't look at it. He'd never seen them before, he said. And yet he did not look.

"What kind of trouble?" he asked. Interested. Concerned. He

reached past the photos to put his hand on mine. This was the Trey I knew. I said I had trouble, and he instantly wanted to fix it for me.

"I think Spence is holding her arms. Holding her down. And your hand is . . . Trey, she sees the camera." His eyebrows were going up. He still didn't look back at the picture, though. He kept his eyes on me. He kept his hand on my hand. I said, "I love you. And I know you. You can tell me what happened."

"I did tell you," he said, calm and even. "I don't particularly remember Spence grabbing her arms, but I also don't remember who all grabbed what and when." He smiled, a wry sad smile, shaking his head. "You can't see her hands, or Spencer's anyway." He said all this without once looking back down at the photo. That he had barely glanced at. That he had never seen before.

"I can see your hand." He kept eye contact, but he stopped touching me, folding his arms over his chest. His eyebrows went up, interested, faintly puzzled. I said, "Your hand is over her mouth."

"Okay. But, Bree, the camera catches a fraction of a second. So my hand was on her face. For that tiny captured moment at least. What are you saying?"

I swallowed. "I'm saying I want you to look at it. Really look."

"Okay," he said, a small impatience in his tone now. He glanced at the shot again, and then he shook his head. When he looked back to me, I saw a little anger in his eyes.

"I don't know what you want me to say. It's awful. They're all awful. But we were high. And drunk. Maybe she was being loud. Or my hand landed there accidentally. Maybe she was kissing it. It's a fraction of a fraction of a second, Bree."

I didn't like the irritated way he said my name. "I know, but, sweetheart, no matter how many times I looked at it, no matter the angle, I see a fraction of a second of a rape."

It was the first time I'd said the word. It was like a small electric shock inside my mouth. He must have felt it, too. He stood up, rising so fast that I flinched. I never would have thought any move my husband made could cause me to flinch. Never in a thousand years.

"I told you what happened," he said. "Everything, exactly as I remember it."

He stared at me. Not the picture. His eyes refused to turn that way again. When I first saw the photos, I had not been able to look away. I'd stared and stared at the last shot, the pleading eyes, her blond hair in a matted tumble, trying to make Lexie tell me a different story. She had not.

I pointed to her. "Trey. Look. Really look."

Instead he snatched the picture up, only that one, on the end, and began tearing at it. "I told you what happened. And sure, I was pretty high. Lexie got me high, remember? But I didn't rape anyone. I would never rape someone." He paused before the word "rape," both times, as if it were too ugly to be allowed into his mouth. Much less his history.

I made myself stay seated and calm. I made my gaze stay only loving. This was my husband, my best friend, the father of my children. And this was hard for him. It had to be.

"You can tear it up, but you can't unsee it. I can't either. That photo shows me a girl who wanted out. If the evening happened like you said, even if she started it, in that shot I see a girl who changed her mind."

"If?" he almost yelled. His chest heaved with fury or some other tightly leashed emotion. "If it happened like I said?"

I didn't stop, though. "Maybe you don't remember this part. Maybe she only changed her mind when she saw the camera. I could believe that. But you have to see. Even if you don't remember it that way, even if you thought it was all fine the next morning, and every morning, up until this minute. That's fine. I can believe that. But you have to see now. You have to face it. You have to fix it."

"I cannot fucking believe—" He choked on the words.

I kept talking, calm, relentless, loving. "There's a way past this. For you and me, maybe even for Lexie. We won't know until we

find her. She may be a murderer, in this hip-deep with her mother.
Or she may not have known the things her mother planned to do.
We can't control that. We can only choose what we do. You can
only choose what you do. Please don't be too afraid to look and
admit and try to make it right. Think if it was Anna-Claire in that
photo. Think if it was Peyton."

Something broke inside him then. His face flushed so dark it
nearly purpled. I rose, too, reaching for him, worried he would have
a stroke. He jerked away from my hands. He bent and snatched up
the other pictures, tearing into all those small, trapped Lexies as he
spoke, his voice graveled with fury.

"That would never happen to my girls. That would never happen."

I said his name, but he talked over me, tearing and tearing at
the photos, little flecks of destroyed paper drifting down.

"Neither of my daughters would be buying drugs, inviting boys
for threesomes. My daughters would never be in that room in the
first goddamn place. This was her fucking idea, Bree. Lexie's. Her
idea, her drugs, her choice. She wasn't raised like my girls have been
raised."

My reaching hands dropped to my sides. Coral was dead, and I
was fiercely glad, and yet, as my husband said these things to me,
cursed me, spoke to me with such fury that flecks of spittle hit my
face, I felt the tug of our old connection. From back when she had
owned me. From back when I was hers.

I said quietly, "You're right. Lexie Pine was raised like me."

That pushed all his breath out again. He tilted his head back,
staring down his nose at me, his nostrils flaring. Then he threw the
pictures at me. They were shredded so small that the air caught
them. They sprinkled down slowly between us in a fall like snow.

"You are nothing like Lexie Pine," he said. "You never were."

In those words I felt the whole world shift. Because he was
wrong. I had been. Her own mother had seen it, so much so she
changed her ruthless plan to make a deal with me. She'd given

Spencer and Adam no choices; she'd shown poor Kelly Wilkerson no mercy. She had bent for me alone, and that bending had let me save my son. His words did more than shift our past. It rewrote history.

What if I had not been in character that day in the High Museum? No theatre-department-borrowed dress, no Betsy-borrowed confidence. Sabreena Kroger, in her thrift-store jeans and faded madras top, hair undone, face bare, skate-walking through the museum in flip-flops, would not have caught his eye. Instead I'd been playing the exact girl he should have married in the first place. Impeccably groomed and expensively clothed, like Maura, but family-oriented, not career-ambitious. I looked like the girl that fit the dreams he used to whisper about back when we started dating, the kind who wanted private-school children and a beach house on Tybee and to live in the old part of Buckhead, two blocks down from his parents.

Or when we started dating, what if my history with men had been more like Betsy's? Betsy on her rumspringa, pushing boundaries in a way I hadn't ever needed to try. If I had, would he have kept seeing me, or would I have been a pleasant weekend?

Most of all, if I had ever gotten into trouble, like Lexie Pine in that last picture, would he believe that I'd caused it? Lexie's body had been passed around, splayed out and stolen onto paper, shown to everyone she knew, shaming her. She'd said no, or tried, with her covered-over mouth. His actions had erased that no, and his choices had erased her future.

He was right in one particular. Our girls were safer than Lexie Pine had ever been. Trey, with his money and connections and powerful family, would destroy anyone who treated his daughters even a fraction so poorly. But he never extended that protection to Lexie, even though he owed it to her. He hadn't then. He should have stopped when she wanted to stop. If he had, he would have seen Ansel. He could have gone ahead and punched him and taken the negatives then, skipping so many steps and saving Lexie's future. Instead he'd chosen not to see. He was choosing not to see again, now. He really could not imagine his daughters in her place.

"Because our girls are Cabbats?" I asked, trying anyway. My voice was low. Quiet. Not at all angry. "Trey, you're a Cabbat. And you were there. You tried the drugs. You wanted the experience. It could happen to Ann—"

"Oh, fuck you," he said, flushing even darker. "How can you say these things, in our own house? In our bedroom. You know me. You know me." He paced all the way to the door, waving his arms. "Why are you asking me these things?" It was like he was asking the ceiling or God. He finally looked back to me and said, "You think it's my fault Robert almost died. You think it's my fault Spencer—"

"No! Not at all. Not at all, I swear," I said over him. "That's all on her. I would never blame you. And we can get through this, I promise. I love you. You're a good husband, a good father, a good man. Nothing in the past can erase the good I see in you. I love you so much. I'll stay with you and support you. But you cannot keep on lying to me and to yourself. You have to face it."

My words had begun to mollify him, right up until the end. Then he hit a level of rage I'd never seen in him. It was worse than the yelling, this ice-white stoic fury. The dark blood color leached from his face. His blue eyes went vacant and cold.

"Are you actually fucking threatening to leave me? Over a thirty-year-old picture of a passing fucking gas pain some shitty girl felt for a fraction of a second in the middle of her own damn orgy?"

It was the "shitty girl" that got me. He didn't even hear himself say it. I kept my voice calm and repeated, "You have to face it."

He came back toward me, fast, looming over me, and in his icy glare I understood that tearing up those pictures had not banished her. Lexie was here. She was in me; I was her. A shitty girl from Eastern Jesus, Georgia, who grew up in a tiny ranch house. A shitty girl who never would have earned his second glance. A girl Coral had recognized as one of her own. I put my hands up, defensive, scared. He stopped short, bare inches from me, breathing hard.

"I'm done," he said. He swiped a furious hand at the tattered pictures sprinkled across our area rug. "Clean this up. Burn those goddamn pieces. I don't want our nosy, innocent daughters playing jigsaw puzzle with them."

His fury was a wall. On the other side of that wall I stood, a truth he would not face. I could feel it between us, implacable and unbreachable. He would not look. His whole life had made it easy not to look. No one had ever asked him to before.

Lexie *had* changed him. He'd distanced himself from Spencer, married Maura. He'd been done with "shitty girls" forever. He was still done, staring me down like I was one of them.

"That's the last time you threaten to leave me, Bree. If you love me so little, trust me so little, then pack a bag. See how that goes for you." He said it cool and furious, with all the weight of his family money and his name, and then he stood looking down at me, waiting to see what I would say.

I couldn't speak. Tears welled in my eyes. My whole body was shaking, love and fear and sorrow all at war. He seemed to see all that. It seemed to soften him. He walked away toward the bathroom door, rubbing at his forehead.

"I need a shower. I need to wash this conversation off me. Then I'm going down to watch movies with the girls and hold my son. I'm sleeping in Robert's room tonight, on the daybed, so you can get some rest. Take one of my Ambien. You've been sitting up all night every night since Sunday. You're a wreck. That must be where this is coming from." He paused, as if waiting for an answer. I didn't have one for him. Not one he would hear right now. He swallowed and nodded, as if my silence were confirmation. "We'll talk tomorrow, okay? Because if I let you keep on tonight, you'll break us. I don't want that. We have three kids. We love each other. I'm not going to let you break us. We will not put our girls through the ugliest divorce this city has ever seen. Think about it, Bree. You don't want to publicly accuse their father of being a rapist. You know what that will do to them. You'll tear us apart and make them hate you, and for what? An imaginary story you made up from a photo. You know me. And I know you. I honestly think you only need to get some sleep. Real sleep. It will all look different. We've had the most hellish week any parents could ever live through. Let's not make things worse."

He went into the bathroom, closing the door deliberately and gently behind him. I heard the lock turn, and then I heard the water running. I knelt down, weeping, and started picking up the pieces of the pictures. He was wrong to worry about the girls finding them. The photographs were shreds and specks. Some things were too broken and too torn to ever again be mended.

26

I DIDN'T TAKE the Ambien. I'd never tried it before, and I was afraid. Not because of the black label warnings about sleepwalking and memory loss. I was afraid that if the flesh-and-blood Lexie Pine came for us, her will as implacable as her mother's, her anger more direct and righteous, I would not wake up.

Trey would not make peace with her. Trey refused to be sorry, and I was irrationally fearful that she had somehow heard him say all those awful things, same as I had. In my mind her fury honed itself against his words and his willful denial, sharpening.

I lay all night in our king-size bed, alone. I'd never realized how wide it was, the white expanse of sheets going on seemingly forever. I stared out the window, the drapes pulled open and the back-yard floodlights on, listening through the baby monitor to Trey and Robert breathing. I slept in snatches, my mind too busy and worried and unhappy to let me rest.

I did not think that Trey had *lied* to me. I believed he had told me the story the way he remembered it. He believed every word he'd said. That was the problem. Belief and memory couldn't make Lexie Pine any less a victim of rape, couldn't justify his refusals to give that damning picture more than a glance. His belief and his memories also didn't make me into the girl he'd first seen and fallen for at the High. I'd known him seventeen years, and all that time didn't make my early history any less like Lexie's.

A little after four, Robert woke up for his bottle. I listened to my husband feeding his son. He talked so soft and sweet to him, saying, "Is that good, Bumper? Yeah, buddy, there ya go," and then hummed in a soft rumble. After, the familiar thump of his hand on Robert's back. "Let's get that extra burp out."

Once Robert was back down, Trey crept into our room to get fresh clothes. He took them into the master bath. I feigned sleep as he got ready for work, unready to argue again. I wanted to give him time and space to think, to remember, before I tried to get through to him again. He loved me. I believed that my words would stay with him today. He left early, before six, without trying to wake me.

I went to the nursery as soon as Trey was gone. I didn't want Robert left alone. Not even in his own room with the baby monitor on. I found him deeply asleep, arms thrown over his head. I felt grainy-eyed and hollow, so tired that my peripheral vision had gone fuzzy and dark spots swam before my eyes.

I sat down in the rocker to wait for him to wake. Down the hall I could hear whichever night-shift bodyguard had not gone with Trey walking heavy-footed to the kitchen. Getting coffee, I assumed. I closed my eyes and rested my head back, limp and faintly nauseous, until Robert stirred, making his stretchy, waking-up sounds.

I opened my eyes, and there, at the foot of his crib, glowing in the pale light of new morning, stood Lexie Pine. She was young and lovely and wrecked and angry in her white dress. I realized it was *the* white dress. The one her mother believed that every girl was issued at birth, that would show every stain and that she would be wearing on her wedding day. Her wedding day had never come, though. She'd never had a marriage or children, a connected family life, so she had come to show the dress to me. It was torn, streaked with blood and grime. I knew that my husband had helped ruin it. Her mouth twisted down, and her eyes shone with avid hunger as she stared at my son.

I was on my feet, a scream stuck in my throat, before I could so much as blink. When I did blink, she was gone.

I sat back down so abruptly it was almost a collapse, my whole body breaking out in icy sweat. Dust motes danced in the sunlight where I'd seen her standing. There was no girl in Robert's room. There was no girl period. Lexie was almost fifty now; she'd looked closer to sixty in her mug shot. I scrubbed at my aching eyes, clearing the last of her away.

I went to pick up Robert and smell his downy head, whispering, "We're safe, you're safe, we're safe," as I changed him, but I did not believe it.

I walked over to his dresser, inspecting myself in the mirror. It took me a little while to find Bree Cabbat's face. I practiced her relaxed shoulders, easy posture, all her regular expressions. I manufactured a soft, unworried gaze and pushed my mouth into a happy shape. I held that cheery smile until I could see it light my eyes. Only then did I go to make sure that the girls were up and getting ready for school. For the next half hour, I played the role of their mother, fixing breakfast and checking homework.

As soon as they left with the same ex-soldier who'd taken Trey, I let my face do whatever it wanted. I let my body slouch and huddle. I longed for Trey to call or text, give me any indication of his thoughts today.

I needed sleep. I lay down with Robert for all his naps, but sleep would not come. The day floated by us in a fog, and the slim shape of young Lexie lurked in every shadow. She woke me from every faint doze I fell into, touching my cheek with chilly fingers. When Robert was up and playing or eating or fussing, she coalesced at every window, staring in with wide, accusing eyes. I would whip to face her and find nothing.

I decided that tonight I would take one of Trey's pills after all.

It was past four when I finally heard from my husband. He sent a text.

Things got out of hand last night. We're sleep-deprived and so on edge. And who can blame us? I love you. You know that. Can we talk?

I texted back immediately. I'd like that.

Good. Not at home, though. Meet me for a drink after work at Haven?

South City Haven was a chic gastropub on the ground floor of the Midtown high-rise that housed his firm. The building was up on a hill, putting Haven at least a floor above Tenth Avenue's traffic sounds. Trey's building shared the block with a luxury hotel and a huge parking garage, the rest of the space taken by a rare Midtown green space that stretched between the buildings.

Haven's portion of the lawn had a bocce-ball court and little bistro tables, all set far enough from each other to afford some privacy. It was a perfect place to talk. Being in public would keep us calm and quiet. We would be forced to be gentle with each other. A drink wouldn't hurt either.

I texted back. Good idea. I'll reserve an outside table. Six o'clock?

He thumbsed-up my text, and that was all.

By the time the girls got home from rehearsal and Robotics Club, I had my happy-mommy face back on. I'd called Mom over to sit with all three kids. I knew it would be hard on her nerves, but I couldn't leave the house without her there. My mother was more vigilant than any fifty ex-marines. She'd drive the bodyguards insane, making sure every slight noise or shadow was thoroughly investigated.

I'd had a serious come-to-Jesus with her about PTSD and what she could and could not say to my daughters. She was doing her best to match her face to mine, calm and smiling. Still, her shoulders were tense, and right before the girls got home, she'd questioned me relentlessly about how the search for Lexie Pine was going.

Not well. Neither the police nor Marshall and Gabrielle had any traction. Marshall agreed with me: This boded ill. An innocent Lexie, one who had not helped her mother commit kidnappings and murders, would come forward to claim her mother's body. Best case, she was on the run, far away. If she was close, this deep in hiding—it spoke of very bad intentions.

"Ugh! Another date night?" Anna-Claire asked, giving her sister a sideways glance that spoke volumes.

I'd dressed myself so carefully, as if for a date, choosing a floral sundress that was the modern version of the dress I'd once worn to the High Museum. It had a swirly skirt that ended above the knee, and I'd thrown a light sweater on over it, peach-pale and flattering. I'd used a heavy hand with the makeup, trying for the kind of fresh and natural pretty that takes an hour and a thousand products when the starting face was as tired and haggard as my own.

"Yep," I told my daughters, cheery, cheery.

Anna-Claire had already been sucked back into her phone, but Peyton gave me a long, hard look. She sensed that something was up. Of course, with her anxiety she always sensed that something was up. It was inevitable that sometimes she would be right. I smiled, reassuring. I knew how to play the role of her mother. My body knew how to telegraph soft, reassuring lies.

"We're tired of being cooped up. This will be over soon." I was lying to my own mother as much as my children. She stood, bobbling Robert, a less convincing smile than mine plastered on her face. "You guys can order dinner, but you had pizza last night. Get noodle bowls or Thai. Something with vegetables."

"Pizza can have vegetables," Peyton said.

"You heard me, Peyton Rose," I said. God, but I was tired. I handed her my black Amex.

Except it wasn't really mine, was it? It had my name on it, but it was Trey's account. All our credit-card accounts were Trey's.

I didn't want to think about that. That was the kind of thought a woman had when she was about to leave her husband. I looked at my girls, my baby. I wasn't going to do that, was I? Not over a fraction of a fraction of a second—but this was Trey's argument. I didn't find it any more compelling when I made it to myself.

Perhaps he'd softened. After all, I'd sprung so much on him

yesterday. Perhaps with time, and thought, and my support, he would accept that his experiences and memories of that night had been quite different from Lexie's. He wanted to talk. That was good. He was reaching out. And God, he loved me. I wanted to believe he'd do the right thing in the end. I wanted to believe we'd find a way to keep each other.

I left the night-shift bodyguards at the house with Mom and the kids. Mills and Maxwell were staying with me, earning overtime so a peace talk or a negotiation or a marriage-ending silence could play out. Maxwell parked in the huge garage. It had a pretty stone façade and an elevator lobby with sparkling-clean glass doors. Here, in Trey's world, even the garages were quite lovely.

Brick walkways with covered awnings ran around the courtyard, three paths cutting across the green. Maxwell and I took the most direct route, straight from the garage's glass doors to the restaurant. Mills took the longer path to Trey's office building, going to escort him down.

The hostess seated me at the table I'd reserved, while Maxwell took a seat at the outdoor bar. From there he had a good view of the whole courtyard. A Regina Spektor song played softly through the subtly placed speakers. The other full tables were across the bocce-ball court. If Trey and I stayed calm, we would be able to talk quite privately.

I wanted no interruptions, but I set my phone faceup on the table anyway, the sound still on. If my mother or my girls texted or called, I had to see immediately.

A young waiter with a swooping 1950s hairdo came over, and I ordered an old-fashioned for Trey and for me a pale Viognier, sister to the wine Trey had bought for me all those years ago at the High Museum. *I should have coffee*, I thought. My eyes felt full of sand, and my whole body hurt. But I wanted that honeysuckle taste in my mouth, sweet and rich, reminding me of our good history.

Across the courtyard the garage's glass doors swished open, and a middle-aged couple holding hands came out. They headed toward

Haven. Behind them I caught a glimpse of yellow hair and wide eyes watching me, predatory, so cold for one so young. I closed my eyes. The doors swished closed. When I looked again, there was no one behind the glass.

Yet I could still feel her gaze, haunted and haunting, waiting for me to betray her. Waiting for me to take any olive branch Trey offered even if it meant forgetting I had ever seen that picture.

I shook my head no. I was playing a role, being the same Bree I'd shown my children today, elegant and secure. The one who now knew exactly how to pronounce the name of the wine I'd just ordered. She was a true person. She was me. Still, I knew better than anyone that the human body could hold two truths at once. Inside, the girl Coral had recognized lived on. Betsy's best friend. My mother's daughter.

Both could accept what Trey had done. Both could forgive him. But the girl I had long been at the root of me could not live with his denial of it. I made a silent vow to the ghost of Lexie's youth and promise, the one I could still feel watching. I would never ask Marshall to burn the other copies. I would not forget.

The drinks came. I took a sip of wine. Trey and Mills came out of his tall office building, splitting so Mills could go join his partner at the bar. Trey came to my table, his face unreadable. He sat down across from me.

I could still feel Lexie's gaze. I closed my eyes. Drank again, more deeply. I'd spent a lot of time on my makeup, but I wanted to scrub hard at my grainy, heated eyes. I made myself keep one hand on my napkin, the other on my wine. The last time I'd taken such care with my appearance, I'd been heading to his firm's Spring Gala to murder his old friend.

"Hi," my husband said.

"Hi."

The waiter was back. Trey told him we might order dinner later. "For now bring us a cheese plate and some of those marinated olives." The waiter whooshed away. I looked at my husband, and he looked back. He spoke first.

"I overreacted last night. I'm sorry, Bree. We're both flayed, so neither of us handled things well. But I need you to believe me. I didn't do a damn thing to Lexie Pine that she didn't start. That she didn't want. It kills me, just kills me, to think you can't believe me."

I thought he said these things because his own belief was shaken. He looked pale and as wrung out as I felt. I stared into his sincere eyes, open wide, true blue, begging me to believe that he was not a rapist. But he was. His gaze begged me to believe he was a good man. He was that as well. For the first time, it occurred to me that Trey could not be an anomaly.

I'd always thought of rapists, especially the college kind, in terms of serial criminals. Predators, with something black and broken at the heart of them. At Georgia State, Betsy and I had gone to dorm seminars where we learned how to not get raped. There we learned we must use the buddy system, open our own drinks, and never leave them unattended. They told us, *Most men are nice. But there are a few bad apples out there who will hurt you. They come to parties specifically to find that girl who is alone and drunk and vulnerable. The one they can peel away from the edge of the herd. Don't be that girl.*

They never told us about other kinds of danger. Now I met my dear, sweet husband's gaze, and I wondered how many perfectly nice men, grown up or grown old, had in their younger years lost a night, like Trey. Drunk or high or both. In packs or alone. And something happened. Once.

These days, in the high school where my nieces went, they had seminars for the boys as well, teaching them how to not be rapists. College, too, I assumed. Trey's generation hadn't. Mine either; Betsy and I had understood that not getting raped was our job. We had to behave right. To stay safe from bad men, yes. But those seminars had also made it our job to protect nice boys from raping us.

"What do you want to do?" I asked. I would not replay last night's argument again in public, and he had come out swinging. He was saying he could not admit it or live with it. He was saying if I pushed him, I would break us. I could feel the heat of Lexie's furious gaze. I would not betray her. I did not want to lose my marriage.

He said, "We should go to therapy together, is what I'm thinking. Talk all this through with a mediator."

I felt an instant brightness. I nodded, hope surging back. Marshall had two more copies of that picture. A therapist would see in it what I saw. He or she could help Trey come to terms with it. Help him see. We could work through it.

"I think that's a wonderful idea." My phone buzzed against the table. I looked, anxiety jacking, but it was not Mom, or the girls, or even the night-shift bodyguards. "It's Marshall."

"Take it," Trey said, gaze sharpening with interest. "Maybe they found Lexie Pine. Put it on speaker."

I didn't want to. Marshall calling me felt oddly private. But there might be news. I did as he asked. "Hi. I'm with Trey. Did you find her?"

"Yeah. The cops did anyway." He spoke quietly, almost solemn. "You are, I promise you, one hundred percent safe now."

I went hot and cold at once, relieved and afraid, wondering what she'd told them.

If I called her a liar, was I any better than Trey? I had given Spence those pills after all. I should own it. Owning my own bad choices was the exact thing I was asking Trey to do. A strange peace came over me then. I had decided. I wouldn't hurl myself into confessions, but I would not, under any circumstances, call Lexie Pine a liar.

"Holy shit!" Trey said. He grinned at me, instantly giddy. "God, what a weight off! Where was sh— One sec, Marshall."

The waiter was back with the olives. We all went silent until he set them down and left.

Then I asked Marshall, "Are you upstairs? We're at Haven. Come down and tell us all the details."

I didn't want to be alone with my husband right now. His eyes were bright, as if his offer and my acceptance of counseling had solved us, and then this good news came, and now this was a date. I couldn't be that girl, celebrating, toasting. He would take it as capitulation. I could not imagine allowing his lips on mine, or his hands on my body. Not yet. Not until he saw.

Marshall said, "I was out following a lead when I got the call. I'm thirty miles away. Sorry." He sounded so somber.

"How'd they find her?" Trey asked, impatient.

Marshall said, "They took cadaver dogs up to Funtime. This morning, early, but I only heard now. They went to look for Geoff Wilkerson. And they found him. He was buried in a shallow grave in the gold-mine boxes, where the soil was soft and very loose. It was probably the only place where a woman as old and sick as Coral Lee Pine could dig a grave."

That damped Trey's joy down. Mostly. "That's awful."

"Yeah," Marshall agreed. "Anyway, the dogs found Lexie, too. Same place. Pretty much right beside him."

My eyes met Trey's, blinking, and for a moment I didn't understand.

Trey got it, though. "Lexie Pine is dead?"

Over his shoulder the glass doors swished open again. A gaggle of men in suits came out and walked toward the hotel. The dark garage behind them looked like a cave mouth, black and haunted, the gold of Lexie's hair gleaming somewhere deep inside it.

Marshall said, "Yeah. No DNA confirmation yet, of course, but the body had her ID on it. ID and some heroin. The M.E.'s best guess is that she overdosed. Months ago."

"Months ago?" I echoed.

Impossible. Coral had said that Lexie was watching me, that Lexie had been at the firm's gala, secreted on a dark path or one of the shadowed bridges, making sure that Spence died. Coral had told me it was so.

I blinked. Perhaps she had been. Watching from somewhere. Watching from wherever little broken birds went when they died.

"Yeah," Marshall said. "No official time of death yet, but it was weeks before Geoff disappeared."

I was sick and dizzy hearing this. I remembered Coral telling me, *Losing a child would be the worst thing.* That's what she'd decided, when she began to seek revenge. God help her, she'd truly known. The rehab had failed. Lexie had overdosed. The death of her only child was the thing that set Coral in motion.

"Holy shit," Trey breathed. He picked up his glass and drained most of his drink.

The glass doors had not closed. That gold gleam shone. Now she was moving, emerging from the darkness into the fading sunlight.

Lexie. She was walking toward us. Marshall was wrong. He had to be wrong, because she was here. Lexie, lovely in an immaculate white dress that flowed around her slim, lithe body. Her smooth young face had no expression as she came, unhurried and business-like, down the brick walk. She held a flat white clutch in front of her hips, clasped demurely. Her pale hair, tumbling in loose waves around her pretty face, gleamed in the setting sun.

Marshall was still talking. Trey was answering. Their words devolved into a mishmash. I closed my eyes. Marshall must be right; she was dead. I stared into a million colors swirling on the backs of my lids. Real Lexie, if alive, would be close to fifty, would look more like sixty. Marshall *must* be right.

I opened my eyes, and still she came. I glanced at the bar. Mills was saying something to his partner. They were drinking Cokes, alert, watching the perimeter. They did not seem to see anything amiss. She was not the danger they were looking for. Or perhaps only I could see her.

As the ghost of Lexie Pine stepped off the path, her white shoes pressing down the grass, as Marshall's and Trey's voices swirled nonsensically around me, I fell strangely calm. This felt fair. This felt right, that I should be so haunted. I had not fought hard enough for her. I'd earned this. I wondered if Trey would see her, too. I wondered if he'd see her face and tell the truth.

"Look," I said, soft. Too soft. "It's Lexie." The buzz of male voices continued. Neither of them heard me.

She was only steps away now, coming directly to our table, not the hostess stand. Her face was set in lines both beautiful and terrible.

"Hey," Mills called. "Hey!"

He saw her, approaching. He saw her, and so she was real; it was as if a gauze were stripped from my eyes.

This was not Lexie Pine. Lexie was dead. But oh, I knew this broken girl. I knew her face.

The white rectangle that she held, it was not a clutch purse. It was a flat white envelope. Exactly like the one Coral sent me. It was even now falling to the ground as she dropped it, the gun she had hidden behind it aimed and ready.

Her shadow hit us. At the bar Mills was already in motion. Trey started to glance behind him.

"Kelly, wait!" It was all I had time to say before the boom of gunfire filled the courtyard.

Her bullets hit Trey like punches to his back—one, two, three— knocking him forward into the table. Trey looked so surprised. At almost the same moment, red bloomed between Kelly's breasts, knocking her back, and her arms jerked her gun off target. Her next bullet kicked up a tuft of grass.

There was now a steady rhythm of unendurable sound, Mills and then Maxwell firing in short, controlled bursts. Her white dress bloomed with more red poppies as she fell backward, dropping her gun as Trey grabbed the tablecloth and slid sideways out of his chair, pulling our drinks and the little dish of olives as he went.

He lay on his back on the green grass. I stared at my husband, frozen. He looked perfect, his white shirt pristine, tie still knotted. Unharmed. Her bullets must have stopped somewhere inside him.

"Kelly!" I said again. Now I was rising, but in such slow motion. I felt my legs knocking my own chair over. In my peripheral vision, I saw our fancy-haired waiter moving so much faster than I could, blanching, screaming, turning to run, dropping the cheese plate he was bringing us.

"We're security! Security!" I heard Mills yelling.

I was trying to untangle my feet from my fallen chair. I had to get to Trey. He stared up, blue eyes meeting mine. He was not afraid. He looked, if anything, surprised.

I dropped to all fours behind the table, but by the time I landed, the gunfire had already stopped. I heard people running and screaming, a cacophony of panic all around me.

Maxwell yelled, "Hold your fire, you fucking moron!"

I saw my purse beside me, a huge leather bag, its wide mouth gaping open. I had to get to Trey. And yet my purse mattered. It mattered because I had daughters. Trey had daughters. Why these two thoughts came together, I had no idea, but my wise hand understood. My hand reached out, and then Coral's white envelope was in it. I saw Kelly's name and her address in Gadsden written in Coral's crabbed, dark hand. The envelope felt thick with photos. My wise hand folded it away into my bag.

Then I crawled toward my husband.

To my left a chalk-faced citizen had pulled his own gun out of his jacket and was swiveling it from Kelly Wilkerson's body to our ex-soldiers, its wobbling black gaze passing over Trey, then me as he turned.

"Holster your goddamn gun before I put you down!" Maxwell yelled, Mills chiming in, "We're security! It's safe now!"

I crawled to Trey. Leaned over him. His eyes were wide, still meeting mine. His mouth jerked open, sucking at the air. Just past him Kelly Wilkerson lay in a twisted heap of crimson, the blood still spreading, staining more and more of her white dress. Her eyes met mine as well, no longer holding anger. No longer holding anything.

"Trey," I said.

"I'm cold," he told me. He choked, and red blood, the first of his I'd seen, came trickling out the corner of his mouth.

I grasped his shoulders, leaned down close, my hair tumbling around his face. His breath pulled in and out, raspy and desperate. Should I turn him over? I could put my hands over the holes, try to keep the wet, red life from pumping out of him. But his hands clutched feebly at my arms.

"Bree?" he said. "I'm sorry."

"I know, baby. It's okay. I'm here with you. I'm with you, do you understand?" I said, and God, I meant it. I leaned down to kiss his dear, dear face. "Hold on."

His grasp failed. His fingers fell away. He said, "I'm so, so sorry."

"We'll work it out. I love you," I said. Again I meant it. Both of these things were true. Then I told him, "You're going to be all right."

Even as I said the words, I knew. I knew I was a liar.

27

BREE ONLY TALKED about it once.

Not Trey. Marshall and Bree talked about Trey all the time, keeping his memory alive for his children, same way they both told Betsy stories for Cara.

And they talked about Coral, and Lexie, and Kelly Wilkerson, though the more honest of these conversations never happened when the children were around. Bree said to him, over and over, how much she wished she'd obeyed Coral one more time; Coral had told her to call Kelly. Bree believed she should have called Kelly right after her own envelope came. Coral had not explicitly told Bree that she was also sending Kelly a letter, but Bree felt she should have guessed that. And she'd known, they both had, how unstable and angry Kelly was.

Kelly's envelope had arrived the day after Bree's. When she saw the pictures, read the letter, she waited until her husband came home for lunch, and then she shot him five times. She put the gun inside a pillow to muffle the shots. While he bled out, she coolly showered, changed, made up her pretty face, and then reloaded.

Marshall believed that Kelly had not meant to survive long after Trey. She'd dressed herself beautifully, the way some suicides did, then looked up Trey on the Internet and driven straight to Atlanta to lie in wait for him in the parking garage outside his job.

In the spring, when she got melancholy, Bree would say, "If only I'd reached out to her. Coral said I should. Coral told me, when you get your letter . . ." A thousand times she fell silent, and then she'd sigh and tell him, "Trey should have apologized to her." He wouldn't know if she meant Kelly or Lexie or both. He thought that Kelly and Lexie sometimes became the same person in her head.

So it wasn't like she stuffed it down. She talked about all that shit: Robert's kidnapping, Spence's death, Coral, everything. She'd discussed it endlessly with both Marshall and her therapist. She still did.

But the lamb thing. That? She only said it once.

It was St. Alban's winter break, right at the end of February. In Georgia it already felt like spring. Bree hated it when the air turned warm each year. Hated the transition that reminded her the anniversary was coming. Every year it felt as if spring came a little earlier, making the warm march to the anniversary stretch out even longer. That was probably true, Marshall thought. The world cooking to death.

The third year she asked Marshall to take the week off, and he had agreed. The weather change shifted the moods of both Bree's girls as well. They were weepier, more temperamental. They missed their dad more. They had a week off called "winter break," for all the high was getting close to eighty. He decided that they all needed to opt out of the endless spring.

In Bonaire it felt like summer. Peyton was calmer and A-C was kinder, watching palm trees sway in the breezy brightness. All four of the kids loved the big iguanas who lived by the villa's private pool. One was out basking near the deep end that afternoon, sunning himself fearlessly as the girls floated nearby, his weird, floppy toes splayed and his chin up.

The girls were tired from scuba, all three drifting on bright floats. Purple, yellow, blue. Trey had been an avid diver. He'd always meant for his kids to learn. Bree was making good on that. Of all of them, Marshall probably loved scuba most, even though with four ladies and five heavy dive bags, he got stuck with most of the gear rinsing.

It was nice to have the option to take up such an expensive sport. To be able to say, *Fuck it, the weather changed and we feel sad—let's go to the Caribbean.* Bree had said yes immediately. No thinking. Just, *Yes, let's do that.* As if it were a reasonable plan to on the spur of the moment buy seven business-class tickets, rent a five-bedroom villa, pay for diving lessons and equipment.

Marshall had wondered if in another decade or so he wouldn't blink at an unplanned, unsaved-for vacation.

It was a good problem to have. He was getting used to it. He didn't really need to work, actually, but God, he loved his job. With Bree he had real backup. She and Cara were thick as thieves. She looked at his girl and she saw Betsy, same as him. There was no reason not to do the thing he loved. So detectives earned a little less money than lead investigators at tier-one law firms. Really not an issue these days.

The girls chatted lazily on their floats. Peyton in the middle, buffering. Two divas under one roof was a lot of divas, and the more Cara came into her mother's sly and sparkling beauty, the more she held her own with A-C.

He was glad the diving tired them out. The cast list for *Chicago, Junior,* the high school's spring show, had landed while they were at the airport. Cara had been cast as Roxie Hart, the part A-C had gone after, while A-C was Velma Kelly, the part Cara wanted most. The girls were juniors, and they'd won the lead roles over quite a few disgruntled seniors. They ought well be damn happy. And they were happy. Mostly. Just there was a lot of side-eye happening on this trip.

That was the downside, he thought. To the money. What they needed, they already had, pretty much on tap. Most of what they wanted, they got. They thought the world was like that. Shocking how fast Cara had come to think the world was like that. He and Bree were working on it.

He sat beside his wife, both of them dangling their feet in the bright blue water. They were holding hands, on and off, but they kept having to let go to stop Robbie from drowning himself. The little rat kept lunging off the pool steps. Whoever was closer would leap down and drag him back. He trusted his water wings too much. He trusted the whole damn world too much.

On the other hand, his trust was kind of lovely.

He went again, and Bree leaped after him. Robbie was positive, with the willful surety of three-year-olds, that he could swim all the way to the deep end and join his sisters on their colorful floats.

"Stay on the steps," Bree said again, dragging him back.

He crunched his whole face up and said his favorite word. "No! I wanna go to da floaps!"

The last word devolved into a howl. Marshall got up and lifted him out in one smooth move and carried him away from the pool. Bree's mom had come along to babysit while they dove each morning. Now she was in the shade of the villa's long porch, reading her book. Marshall toted his son, writhing and protesting, back to her.

He plunked Robbie down on the lounge chair by Shelly Ann and said, "Time out, kiddo."

Robbie hurled himself prone, weeping dramatically.

Marshall turned to Shelly Ann. "Can I top you off?"

"It's just juice!" she said.

"I know."

"It's not even one o'clock."

Vigilant as ever. No way she would drink with the kids in the pool. Even with Marshall and Bree right there.

"Five minutes," Marshall said to Robbie, who responded by savagely kicking the cushions.

Marshall left him to seethe at the terrible injustice and got a couple cans of Modelo from the patio's mini-fridge. He brought them back poolside and handed Bree one, sitting next to her, close. She popped hers open and then took his hand.

On the patio Robbie let out a heaving, dramatic sigh. They exchanged smiles.

"So this is three," Bree said.

"Oh, yeah," he agreed.

They sat watching the girls drift, holding hands and drinking their cold beers, until it got quiet. Marshall glanced back.

Robbie had forgotten he was in time-out. He was trying industriously to open A-C's water bottle. He was always like this, busy and engaged and into things, his brow furrowed with concentration. He was like his father, for all that he called laid-back Marshall "Daddy." A-C and Peyton called him Marshall, of course. He loved Bree's girls, deeply, and they loved him, but they were Trey's. It would be disrespectful to try to bust that up by asking them to call him "Dad," like Cara did.

But Marshall had saved Robbie's life. He and Bree had come through those long two days together, and in the end he'd pulled the baby from that horseshoe of explosives and set him in his mother's arms. Perhaps it had been a kind of birth.

Marshall was the only father Robbie would know; Robbie was the only son he'd have. He and Bree had decided it would be hard enough to blend the kids they had, especially since some people, Bree's in-laws, for example, thought their quiet wedding came a little soon.

Marshall had been pretty absolute and medical about it. The day of the procedure, he'd thought, *I am a man who will have one kid*. He'd been okay with it. Robbie had snuck up on him, and Cara had confided that Robbie didn't feel like a step. For as much as he looked like Trey's small clone, thick and sturdy, with that same round face and snub nose, Robbie belonged to all of them.

A-C had moved her float to the center, and now she and Cara started singing. Harmonizing. Peyton, he knew without looking, would be rolling her eyes. The song was a Roxie-Velma duet from the upcoming show, which meant they would practice it over and over until Peyton lost her mind. The two songbirds were really wailing, Cara's dusky brown leg hooked over A-C's longer, paler leg as they sang, asking each other again and again if things were good, or great, or swell. And then they sang the kicker, a repeated line about how nothing could ever stay the same.

No shit, ladies.

Cara and A-C sat up tall, wobbling on their floats, so they could hoist invisible prop Gatling guns and spray the pool with invisible bullets as they sang. All very Chicago. Peyton took advantage of their concentration to slip into the water and tip A-C's float over.

The locked legs got Cara, too. They came up sputtering and growling, and then all three were giggling and pushing and shrieking, fighting to dunk one another. They'd gone from two juniors and a sophomore to preschoolers like Robbie in a heartbeat. It made Marshall smile.

Bree watched them, smiling, too, but Peyton's crafty crocodile slide to tip A-C, that was a move straight out of Trey's playbook. And Peyton had her father's face, same as her brother. He saw the hollow sorrow in Bree's eyes.

She was happy, though, he thought. Most of the time. She loved him deeply. She liked that he was a cop. She liked that he had a nose for liars and could almost smell bad intentions. That he understood fighting and violence and guns.

He made her feel safe. That was how she'd come to be his, after everything. She always wanted him around. When he was there, she forgot, first for minutes, then hours, then whole days, and now sometimes for weeks, that her mother saw the world more clearly than she did.

He told her that she was safe and her children were protected with his presence, his actions, his words. That might be the thing she loved about him most of all.

He was lying, of course. The world was dangerous and broken.

But people had to feel safe anyway, to get on with the business of living.

She would never truly forget, though. She was changed. She was neither the girl he'd grown up with nor the woman he'd fallen for. No one could go through what she had gone through and come out the same.

But she was still Bree, and Bree, to him, was breathing. He would kill for her. He would die for any of these children. So. Here they were.

She turned back to check on Robbie. Her mother was trying to open the water bottle for him, and he was holding it away from her, saying, "I do it myseff!" That was his second-favorite thing to say, right after no. In the dappled shade of the porch, his face so set and willful, it was like they were staring at a tiny Trey.

Bree squeezed his hand, and when he turned to smile at her, he saw that the hollow sorrow had deepened.

"Sometimes I think he was a lamb," Bree said. He knew from the tone exactly who she meant.

"A lamb?" he said. It was not how he remembered Trey.

"He did it, you know," she said. "He raped her."

They talked about Trey every day. There were pictures of Trey and Betsy all over the house. So yeah. They talked about him.

They didn't talk about this. They had never talked about this. Even when he came to the hospital to sit with her while Trey was in the six-hour surgery that he would not survive. Even when she slipped him the envelope with all the other photos she'd apparently stolen from the crime scene before getting on the ambulance with her husband.

Which, damn. That was some Betsy-level boldness. Some folks might even find that cold. But Marshall? He'd admired it. She was a mother, bone deep. Her girls and her son would never stumble across the picture of their father raping Lexie Pine up on the Internet. Lexie herself had been past needing the acknowledgment. In another hour the doctor would come out and tell them Trey was past being able to give it. The whole story had not even come out. The Cabbats had a part in that, he thought, the way the news stories had all died quick and local.

"I know he raped her." Marshall kept his tone even, nonjudgmental, as he asked, "But he's a lamb?"

"Like an Old Testament lamb," she explained. "I think a million men have done the same damn thing. Most of them never paid."

He understood then. Kind of. "They should have paid, you mean."

"But they didn't," she agreed. "There are so many of them out there. Boys who had mothers and sisters and sweethearts, who grew up to have wives and daughters and careers. They act as if this one thing never happened. They tell themselves the story in another way until they believe it. Or they don't tell it at all, and they make themselves forget. But meanwhile they raped a real, live girl. She has to live with it. She sees them pop up in her Facebook feed when class reunions happen, sees their wedding and birth announcements in the paper. She has to eat it, this thing they did, and it eats at her. It's wrong. It's awful."

"Yes," he agreed.

"They should make amends," she said. "They should face her, and confess, and try to make it right. They should go to jail and do volunteer work and show their sons they must be better. They should have to live with it, too, because I think no matter what they tell themselves, it must stay in them. A canker in them. A black place."

"Yes," he agreed again.

"But they don't, do they? Most of them don't. Certainly not the rich ones. Not the ones in packs, who lie for each other. Not the ones who lie to themselves. These fine young men all go on and have their bright futures." The way she said those words, he knew she'd thought them before. She said them like they were a bad taste in her mouth that she was trying to push out. "They don't pay."

He saw it now. "Trey was the lamb."

She nodded. "It's like the world picked one, to be shot for it, to lie there bleeding in the grass, apologizing. I wish that they would all pay their own damn bills. Him included. If only . . ."

She might have said more, but Robbie came running back then, hurling himself violently into her arms. "Time-out ober! Gramma says!"

She laughed, and Marshall had to grab her to keep them both from falling into the pool. That was the end of it. She never spoke of it again. Not in that way. Instead she kissed the corn-colored hair on top of her boy's head, gathering his stocky, solid body in her arms.

"I think Grandma had enough time-out," she said to Marshall, eyes sparkling. "Maybe it's nap time."

"No!" Robbie said instantly.

"I mean Grandma's nap time," Bree told him, and he smiled his sunny smile and grabbed her face in his small, fat hands, ramming his forehead hard into her nose as he went to kiss her.

"Oof! Careful, baby," she said, laughing, touching her nose. "Ouch!"

"Gentle hands on Mommy," Marshall told his son.

Robbie stood on Bree's thighs, his sturdy legs braced, and patted softly at her cheeks. "Gemple hands on Mommy," he agreed.

All three girls were back on their own floats. Peace had been restored. They lay in a leg-locked chain, Peyton in the center, now singing loud and tunelessly along. They were asking again if the world was grand, and fun, and great. And good.

Watching Robbie pat his mother's face, so soft, Marshall thought that it was as good as the world could be. Considering the world.

"You're sweet," Bree told her son, kissing his sweaty cheek. "You are so sweet!"

He would be, Marshall thought. They would work to make it so. And yet under her fond tone, he heard something else. Not sorrow. That had faded again. Something reverent, as if the words were more than an endearment. As if they were a tiny prayer.

ACKNOWLEDGMENTS

I AM PROFOUNDLY grateful to all you readers, librarians, and book-sellers who read, buy, and stock my books and who recommend them both in person and online. You gift me a career that is an absolute joy. Thank you! These words are inadequate. But, thank you! I'll keep writing as long as you keep reading.

I share my main character's deep love for Atlanta's innovative, eclectic theatre scene; Scott and I regularly see shows at places like Alliance Theatre, Horizon, 7 Stages, Dad's Garage, and Shakespeare Tavern. I actually saw Caryl Churchill's *Traps* at our favorite local the-atre, Actor's Express, in their inaugural season. Bree did not play Syl.

My editor, Emily Krump, is smart and subtle and a mighty cham-pion of my work. I so appreciate the way she and everyone at Wil-liam Morrow have given me a publishing home where I can grow and change. Huge thanks to Liate Stehlik, Jennifer Hart, Tavia Kowal-chuk, Kelly Rudolph, Maureen Cole, Christine Edwards, Andy Le-Count, Mary Beth Thomas, Ashley Mihlebach, Carla Parker, Rachel Levenberg, Virginia Stanley, Eric Svenson, Ploy Siripant, Mary Ann Petyak, Shelby Peak, Julia Elliott, and Maureen Sugden (who spots the word I am currently overusing to a criminal degree, every book).

Thank you to my onetime editor and current agent, Caryn

Karmatz Rudy. *Mother May I* is dedicated to her, and it's about time. Her influence is shot through all my published work, which is infinitely better for it. My gratitude and deep, fond regard for my first agent, Jacques de Spoelberch, is eternal.

Lydia Netzer and Abbott Kahler, Group is like delicious medication. Sara Gruen, make me a tiny book of this! Alison Law, you are invaluable. My local writer posse helped ferment this book and I love them: Anna Schachner, Reid Jensen, Ginger Eager, and Dr. Jake Myers.

I love you, Scott. I love you, Sam and Maisy Jane. I love you, family: Betty (and Bob, always), Bobby, Julie, Daniel, Claire, Eleanor Rose (our new, tiny Jackson, already clearly a prodigy!), Erin Virginia, and Julian (also new, also a prodigy, but much larger), and Jane, and Allison.

My Jesus people keep me breathing. I love you, New Revised Standard Dinner Club (Brownings and Garbers and Myers, oh my), and First Baptist Church of Decatur, especially the Beloved Community of STK. I love you always, Slanted Sidewalk, small group, and the popular girls (looking at you, Julie and Amy) who fundamentally shaped me and my writing.

Love and gratitude to the students and board members and teachers and volunteers and employees who together make Reforming Arts. Our voices matter.